BABY, IT'S YOU

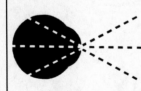

This Large Print Book carries the
Seal of Approval of N.A.V.H.

RAINBOW VALLEY

Baby, It's You

Jane Graves

THORNDIKE PRESS
A part of Gale, Cengage Learning

GALE
CENGAGE Learning·

Farmington Hills, Mich • San Francisco • New York • Waterville, Maine
Meriden, Conn • Mason, Ohio • Chicago

GALE
CENGAGE Learning®

LIBRARY OF CONGRESS CATALOGING-IN-PUBLICATION DATA

Names: Graves, Jane, 1958–
Title: Baby, it's you / Jane Graves.
Description: Large print edition. | Waterville, Maine : Thorndike Press, 2016. | ©2014 | Series: Rainbow valley | Series: Thorndike Press large print romance
Identifiers: LCCN 2015036643| ISBN 9781410486295 (hardback) | ISBN 141048629X (hardcover)
Subjects: LCSH: Single fathers—Fiction. | Family-owned business enterprises—Fiction. | Large type books. | BISAC: FICTION / Romance / Contemporary. | GSAFD: Love stories.
Classification: LCC PS3607.R386 R35 2016 | DDC 813/.6—dc23
LC record available at http://lccn.loc.gov/2015036643

Published in 2016 by arrangement with Grand Central Publishing, a division of Hachette Book Group, Inc.

Printed in Mexico
1 2 3 4 5 6 7 20 19 18 17 16

To Stephanie Rostan. Thanks a million for your excellent advice, your unwavering support, and for always giving it to me straight. You're the kind of agent every writer wishes they had.

Chapter 1

When her nausea kicked up for the umpteenth time that day, Kari Worthington left the bride's room, crossed the hall, and slipped into the bathroom. Locking the door behind her, she leaned against it for a moment to keep from throwing up. Then she stumbled across the room, kicked the train of her dress out of the way, hiked up her skirt, and sat down on the toilet lid. She buried her head in her hands as best she could with her veil in the way, wishing her stomach would quit churning and that horrible, breathless, gaspy feeling would go away.

A strand of bright auburn hair escaped the monstrous pile on her head and curled down her cheek. She tried to stuff it back, but it was hopeless. It had taken the stylist more than an hour that morning to gather her hair and incarcerate it at the crown of her head, and the woman had frowned the

7

whole time. That was nothing new. Kari had spent her whole life with everybody around her trying to stuff parts of her back into place — both parts that showed and parts that didn't.

She tried to tell herself it was just nerves, that every bride felt like this on her wedding day because marriage was such a big step. But was that really true? Did every bride really need a barf bag only half an hour before marrying the man of her dreams?

No. Assuming her groom really *was* the man of her dreams.

She thought about Greg. Handsome, intelligent, serious Greg, who had dropped by her office a year ago and asked her out. It wasn't the first time a man at work had done that, but as time went on, they tended to lose interest in spite of her family connections. Something about her unusual outlook on life tended to make them slowly drift away, and pretty soon she'd be out there on that limb by herself all over again.

As it turned out, though, Greg endured her offbeat personality like a real trouper. But sometimes she thought he seemed *too* accommodating, as if she were an applecart he didn't want to upset. After all, there were big advantages to being married to the boss's daughter. Kinda made a guy fire-proof. Not that Greg would ever get fired. He was a younger version of her father, right down to his designer suits and his iPhone tapping and his power lunches. Anytime she was around him, she felt as if she should be standing up straight even when she was lying flat on her back.

And speaking of lying flat on her back . . .

Sex with Greg had always been okay. Just . . . okay. Not that she'd ever had sex that was *better* than okay to compare it to, but she knew it had to be out there somewhere. Why else were all those odes and sonnets and love poems of yesteryear written, not to mention about a million love songs since the beginning of time? People were out there living and loving with all their hearts, and sometimes Kari lay awake at night, fervently wishing she was one of them.

She and Greg had dated for a year. Then came the ring. Then their engagement party. The minister who performed their premarital counseling pronounced them a match made in heaven. But Kari remembered thinking that the priest's blessing had less to do with her compatibility with Greg and more to do with the fact that her father was extraordinarily wealthy and believed wholeheartedly in tithing.

Through it all, Kari had just let herself get swept along. There had always been a dress to try on, a caterer to consult, the wedding planner from hell to endure. One week passed, and then the next. Then came the Big Day, and what was she doing? Sitting on a toilet lid in her wedding dress feeling as if she was going to throw up. For all that Greg was nice and accommodating and unerringly patient, she saw the looks her father exchanged with him sometimes. *I know she's a handful,* her father's eyes would say, and Greg's would say, *Don't worry, sir. I can handle her. You can count on me.*

She heard a knock at the door. "Miss Worthington!"

Oh, God. Not Hilda. She couldn't take one more moment of Hilda Baxter. Stuart Worthington had spared no expense for his only child's wedding, including hiring the wedding planner to the rich and famous. Today she looked like a gigantic prune in her multilayered indigo dress, her face all puckered with irritation, and if she didn't leave Kari alone, she was going to wrap her hands around the woman's neck and squeeze until her eyes bugged out.

"Time's running short!" Hilda shouted through the door, sounding more like a prison guard than a wedding planner. "You need to be walking down the aisle in exactly twenty-three minutes!"

Kari closed her eyes. Twenty-three minutes. In only twenty-three minutes she would be a married woman. *Twenty-three minutes . . . twenty-three minutes . . . twenty-three minutes . . .*

The words reverberated inside her head so maddeningly that she put her fingertips to her temples and rubbed hard, trying to drive them away. She'd just about succeeded when a new mantra took over.

Twenty-two minutes . . . twenty-two minutes . . . twenty-two minutes . . .

Kari jerked her head up, trying to shake that thought away. She had to do this. It wasn't just Greg and her father and Hilda and all those guests. It was Jill, too, who was waiting in the bride's room to join her on that trek up the aisle. Jill had been her best friend since they'd roomed together at Rice University, and now Jill was the only one Kari wanted standing next to her when she got married.

Kari imagined the look of disbelief that would spring to Jill's face if she told her she was having second thoughts. After all, Jill thought Greg was the catch of the century. But that was mostly because she had a thing

11

for the *GQ* type. She didn't really *know* Greg.

Most of the time, Kari felt as if she didn't, either.

Her second thoughts were nothing new. She'd been having them for some time now. She'd just thought that the happy, gushy bride thing would take over the closer the wedding got and she'd realize how silly she was being.

Now all she could think of was escaping.

She froze. Leave her own wedding? Could she *do* that?

She took a deep, shaky breath, trying to settle her nerves, but her stomach still felt as if it was tumbling around in a clothes dryer. She grabbed her tote bag she'd brought to the bathroom with her, fished out her car keys, and stared at them.

There it was. Her ticket out of there.

She dropped the keys to her lap. Good heavens — what was she thinking? She couldn't just get into her car and drive away. What kind of a crazy person *did* something like that?

She put the keys back into her tote bag and rose from the toilet lid. Looking in the mirror, she straightened her veil as best she could, then opened the bathroom door. The door to the bride's room was dead ahead. If she was going to marry Greg, it was now or never. And never wasn't an option.

But all at once Kari imagined what it would be like when she went back inside. Jill would fluff the train of her dress, telling her one more time how lucky she was. Hilda would clap her hands and herd her toward the altar, where Greg would be waiting, eager for the last block of his perfectly structured life to fall into place. For one of the few times in his life, her father would be smiling, the weight of the world lifted from his shoulders as he married off his kooky daughter to a younger, more resilient version of himself. In exactly twenty-one minutes she would become —

No, no, no! I can't do this!

The words rang so loudly inside Kari's head that for a moment she wondered if she'd screamed them out loud. Suddenly her feet felt fused to the floor, as if her dainty wedding slippers were stuck inside concrete blocks. Then, out of the corner of her eye, half a dozen steps down the hall, she saw a sign that made her breath stick in her throat.

"EXIT."

She stared at it, mesmerized by the glowing red neon. Suddenly she had the most irrational feeling that the only place where

13

there was oxygen to breathe was outside this church, and if she didn't leave right now, she'd fall over, turn purple, and die on the spot.

Maybe *never* was an option after all.

Without another thought, Kari pulled her keys out of her tote bag and hurried down the hall. She hit the bar on the security door and swept it open, running into the secluded side parking lot of the church. She clicked the remote to unlock the driver's door of her Lexus, suddenly met with the challenge of the century: cramming her dress along with herself behind the wheel. Fortunately, a whole lot of motivation kicked in, and in a matter of seconds, she was stuffed in, strapped in, and ready to go.

With a shaky hand, she stabbed at the ignition with the key. She managed to insert it on her third try, feeling like a lifer going over the fence at Huntsville. She paused for a moment and glanced back, sure she would see people pouring out of the church to try to stop her, but no. They were all still inside, blissfully ignorant of the fact that everything was in place for the wedding of the year, except maybe a bride.

But in the end, would anybody be all that surprised? For once in Kari's life, her history of rash, impulsive behavior was going

14

to pay off. *That's Kari,* they'd all say. *Running away from her own wedding. Could we really expect anything else?*

Kari knew that a more confident woman would be able to look her fiancé dead in the eye and tell him she didn't want to marry him. But she knew if she did, Greg would try to talk her out of it. Then her father would get into the mix. Then Jill would tell her again what a catch Greg was and beg her to reconsider. Then Hilda would freak out and start throwing commands around like a third world dictator, and all hell would break loose. If Kari actually had a backbone, she could have endured all that, but right now it felt like wet spaghetti. In no time, they'd be shoving her up the aisle and she'd be saying those vows, and before she knew it, she'd be a miserable married woman for the rest of her life.

She took a deep, shaky breath. This was it. Her moment of truth. She could stay and continue living as she always had, with other people pushing her around, or she could take charge of her own life.

It was time to take charge.

She started the car and drove out of the parking lot to a side street behind the church, pretty sure nobody had seen her. Once on the main road, though, she realized

15

she had no clue which direction to go. North to Dallas? Or west to Austin?

Austin. It was a weird city. Oddball people lived there. Since she'd always been one of those herself, she'd blend in better. And it was closer. She could drive there, get a room at a nice hotel like the Driskill or the InterContinental, order something large and chocolate from room service, and then sit back and figure out what to do next.

Then all at once she thought about Boo, her precious little terrier Jill was taking care of while she was on her honeymoon. Right now Kari had no plan. How long would she have to stay gone until the heat was off?

He'll be okay. Jill will take care of him. Just go!

But as Kari pulled up to the next stoplight, guilt crept in. No matter how wrong this marriage would be, she couldn't leave without saying something to somebody. She decided to text Greg, knowing he'd have his iPhone with him even as he was ready to walk up the aisle. On vibrate, of course, but with him nonetheless, because that was the kind of guy he was. And that — *that right there* — was part of the problem. Her ringtone was a frog croaking, which made her smile every time she heard it. How was she supposed to marry a man whose ring-

16

tone sounded like — of all things — a telephone ringing?

I'm so sorry, she punched in. *I can't marry you. It's not you, it's me. I'm just . . . sorry. I'll be in touch later.*

Then guilt raised its ugly head again. Greg didn't deserve this. He didn't deserve being left at the altar in front of three hundred people.

Then she thought about those looks between him and her father, the ones that said she wasn't going to be so much Greg's wife as she was a rock around his neck he was willing to endure. In a few decades, when Stuart Worthington died and went to that big boardroom in the sky, it would all be worth it to Greg. And it would be worth it to her father, too, to spend eternity knowing his flighty, flaky daughter was well in hand.

I didn't pick him, Dad. You did.

And something about that made her guilt melt away.

Kari stared at the text message, trying to think of something else to say, but there really wasn't anything, so she hit "send."

Then the light turned green, and she hit the gas.

As Marc Cordero went down the elevator

of San Jacinto Hall to get Angela's last box from the car, he wondered where along the way he'd lost his mind. He should have insisted she go to a smaller school. Or maybe to junior college for a year or two. Hell, he should have locked her in her bedroom and thrown away the key so he'd never have to deal with any of this.

The University of Texas had sounded so safe and civilized when the college counselor at her high school had talked about it, and when he and Angela visited the campus, it had seemed relatively tame. Of course, that had been during the summer session, when only a fraction of the place was occupied.

Neither of those things had prepared Marc for the chaos of move-in day.

The madness had actually begun an hour ago, twenty miles outside Austin. Marc had followed Angela's car with his truck, which he was using to help haul all her belongings to campus. They'd crept along the highway for what seemed like forever. Marc had sworn there had to be a five-car pileup ahead, but it turned out that it was just a traffic jam caused by students heading to UT.

Unbelievable.

The moment the campus came into view, Marc got a sick, sinking sensation in his stomach. Lack of control always did that to him. Dropping his daughter off at this place was making him feel more out of control than he had for the past eighteen years, and that was saying a lot. Angela, on the other hand, got out of her car, took one look at the campus, and her face lit up exactly the way it had when she was six years old and saw Magic Kingdom for the first time.

Six years old. Magic Kingdom. Where the hell had the time gone?

Marc grabbed the last box from his truck and headed back into the building, sidestepping one person after another, feeling as if he was navigating a sidewalk in Shanghai. A few minutes later, he got off the elevator and headed down the hall to the twelve-by-sixteen-foot space Angela was sharing with a girl from Lubbock who'd also taken potluck on a roommate. They seemed to get along well already, which he guessed was a good thing, except the girl had a tattoo of some Chinese symbol on her upper arm, a ring through her nose, and frizzy hair dyed death black.

Angela lifted her arms to put a framed photo onto the top shelf of her bookcase, hiking up her shirt. It was one of those midriff things she wore with jeans slung a few inches below her belly button, which was pierced with a silver ring. God in heaven — why had he given in on that?

Because she'd begged for weeks, driving him crazy until he'd finally told her she could pierce anything she could cover up later for a job interview. Then he'd read something in one of her magazines about labia piercing, and that was when he'd known for a fact that this parenthood thing had gotten totally out of control and he didn't stand a chance anymore.

"Where do you want this?" Marc asked.

"On the dresser," Angela said.

He set the box down and turned back, brushing his hands together, but before he could ask Angela if she needed any help unpacking or maybe hanging some stuff on the walls, she said, "I'll walk you back downstairs."

Marc wasn't ready for this. He was even more not ready than he imagined he'd be. "Uh . . . okay." He turned to Angela's roommate. "It was nice to meet you."

"Nice to meet you, too, Mr. Cordero," the girl said with a smile, but her eyes said, *Now go away.*

Marc and Angela walked back to the elevator lobby. The elevator doors opened, and three boys got off. As they passed by, one of them eyed Angela with too much interest, a hulking jock type who looked as if he was itching for another notch on his bedpost.

"What are you looking at?" Marc growled.

The kid stopped. Swallowed hard. "Uh . . . nothing, sir."

"That's right. You're looking at nothing. And nothing is over *there.* My daughter is over *here,* and she's *not* nothing. So if you're looking at nothing, you're not looking at her. Are we clear on that?"

The kid's eyes went big as searchlights. "Yes, sir."

"Now, beat it," Marc snapped.

As the kid hurried off with his buddies, Angela spun on Marc, looking horrified. "Dad! Why did you *do* that?"

"Nothing's changed just because you're here and I'm in Rainbow Valley," he said, striding onto the elevator. "No dumb jock just looking to get laid is going to mess with you."

"So what are you going to do?" Angela said, following him onto the elevator. "Drive an hour so you can kick his ass?"

"Don't think I won't."

She stabbed the down button on the elevator panel. "I can't believe you don't trust me."

21

"I trust you. It's guys like *him* I don't trust."

"Could you embarrass me any more, Dad?" she said, throwing her arms into the air. "Huh? Is it even *possible*?"

Didn't she get it by now? He just wanted her to be safe. That was all. But in this place . . . good God. He saw danger around every corner. Why didn't she?

Right about then, their tiny town seemed like a 1950s sitcom set in comparison. Everybody knew everybody else in Rainbow Valley, so kids knew if they got out of line, word would eventually get back to somebody who would shove them back in. Marc had always been able to intimidate Angela's boyfriends with a frown, a gruff voice, and a few subtle words of warning. In fact, there had been times when he swore he was smiling, but Angela told him he still looked pissed, which meant he scared her boyfriends to death. That was fine with him if it meant they kept their distance. But what was he supposed to do now? Could he make sure they didn't mess with his daughter when he was an hour away in Rainbow Valley?

The problem was that he knew what teenage boys were like because he'd been one. Things could happen you never expected and certainly weren't ready to deal with. It was funny how after all these years he could barely remember what Nicole looked like, only that he'd been crazy in love with her and teenage sex had seemed like a wondrous gift from God.

Then came Angela.

A month later, Nicole was gone. Couldn't handle being a mother. As if Marc had been any more prepared to be a father.

In the years that followed, he'd felt as if he didn't have a clue what he was doing. Angela's childhood seemed like nothing but a blur in his mind right now. Then came the god-awful early teenage years, with hormones running rampant and all that shouting and door slamming, making him feel as if he was doing everything wrong and she'd be rolling her eyes at him for the rest of their lives.

But the older she got, the more things leveled out, until it looked as if the sleepless nights and the constant worry and the occasional heartache were giving way to the kind of warm, comfortable relationship he'd always wanted them to have. And as he looked at his daughter now, skimpy shirt and all, he thought maybe he'd done a pretty damned good job of raising her.

"You're right," Marc said as the elevator

doors opened on the first floor. "I shouldn't have embarrassed you. You're not a kid anymore. I know you can take care of yourself."

Those words came harder to him than anything else, because he wasn't sure he believed them. He knew he'd better believe them, though, if he expected to get any sleep for the next four years.

Angela gave him a little shrug. "It's okay. That guy looked like a jerk, anyway."

That was Angela. So forgiving. Sometimes a little too forgiving. He wanted to shout at her, *If you meet a guy who behaves badly, don't you dare excuse it!* But if she hadn't learned that lesson already, was repeating it now going to make any difference?

As they walked to his truck, Marc dreaded every step he took more than the one before it. He clicked open his door with the remote, then turned back to Angela.

"Do you want me to stay for a while? Maybe take you and your new roommate to get a bite to eat?"

Angela looked back over her shoulder. "Uh . . ."

Marc held up his hand. "Never mind. You already have plans."

"It's just that Kim and I thought we'd walk around campus and check things out a little. Just to see what's going on. You know."

Silence.

"I don't like missing harvest this year," Angela said.

"You hate harvest."

"Yeah, I know," she said with a little shrug, folding her arms and staring down at her blue-frosted toenails. "But it's all hands on deck, you know?"

Marc felt a stab of remembrance. That was what he'd told her from the time she was old enough to snip grapes off of vines. *At this vineyard, everybody pulls his weight. And that goes double if your name is Cordero.*

"Uncle Daniel is coming back," Marc said. "We'll get it done."

She nodded, then smiled briefly. "Do you remember the time when I was six and I ate fifty-four Tempranillo grapes?"

That felt like a hundred years ago. Had it really been only twelve? "I was thrilled you could count that high."

"Purple puke isn't pretty, is it?"

"Not in the least."

"Why didn't you stop me?"

"Because experience is the best teacher."

Angela looked over her shoulder at the sea of students, then back at Marc. "Then maybe I'd better go experience some stuff, huh?"

25

This is it. It's time for you to go, old man. So go.

"Call me if you need anything," he told Angela.

"I will."

"Or even if you don't."

She nodded. For a few seconds, neither one of them spoke. Then Angela's face crumpled. She took a step forward and wound her arms around his neck in a desperate hug. Suddenly she was six years old again, with her little hands holding on tightly because of a bad dream or a scraped knee, or sometimes just because he'd been twice as important to her because he was Dad and Mom all rolled into one. As he held her tightly, she whispered, "I love you, Dad," into his ear, and he whispered that he loved her, too.

Finally she pulled away, sniffing a little. He opened the door to his truck and got inside. She took a few steps back from the curb and wiped tears from her eyes. As Marc started the car, he was pretty sure he was going to cry, too, and he hadn't done that since he was seven years old.

No. Get yourself together. This is a good thing. For the first time in eighteen years, your life is your own.

He put the truck in gear. Angela waved

26

good-bye, and he waved back. As he drove away, he glanced in his rearview mirror to see her turn around and walk away from him and into her new life.

It was time for him to do the same.

By the time he was heading back toward Rainbow Valley, he was ticking off all the reasons why this new chapter in his life was going to be a good thing. But before he could change his life completely, he had to get through harvest. Daniel would be there in a few weeks. That had been their agreement. As soon as Angela was in college, Daniel would come back to Cordero Vineyards to assume responsibility for the family business for the next three years, carrying on the tradition Marc had guarded all this time.

Once his brother took over, Marc intended to hop on his motorcycle and hit the open road. Where he'd go, he didn't know. That was the most amazing feeling of all. *He didn't know.* To have the next three years of his life ahead of him virtually unscripted was something he couldn't have imagined when he'd changed his first diaper eighteen years ago. And once he was motoring down the open road and happened to meet a woman who was out for a good time, he was going for it. The only women he intended to have anything to do with were ones who wanted what he wanted — great sex with no strings attached. He couldn't even imagine what that was going to be like, but he sure as hell intended to find out.

To kick things off, at eight o'clock tonight he intended to jump headfirst into the life of bachelorhood that becoming a father at seventeen had never allowed him to live. He was going to sit in his brand-new La-Z-Boy recliner in front of the sixty-inch LED TV he'd bought last weekend and watch a preseason football game. But first he was going to stop at the Pic 'N Go and buy as much junk food as he could get his hands on, crap he rarely kept in the house because parents who put sugar and trans fats in front of their kids these days were evidently going to hell. But if he chose to get a little diabetes and heart disease himself, that was his business.

It wasn't as if he hadn't watched a ball game in the past eighteen years, but tonight was different. He didn't have to worry that Angela was out with friends and she hadn't come home yet, or that he'd turn around to see an army of teenagers traipsing through his house, or that he needed to put a decent dinner on the table for his kid so the food police didn't come after him. Tonight it was just him alone in the house with no responsibility for anyone but himself, with nothing to do except cheer on the Cowboys and clog his arteries. And he was going to make the most of it.

Then he thought about Angela and felt a flicker of worry, along with an empty spot inside him that came from missing her already. He thought about calling her, then thought again. *You taught her right. Now let her live her own life, and you live yours.*

He checked his watch. It was still a few hours until kickoff. He looked at the horizon, where dark clouds churned against an iron-gray sky. Even though a heavy rainstorm was predicted, he'd be home before it hit. In his recliner. In front of his television. Living it up. He felt a moment of worry about the grapes, then brushed it off. Harvest was weeks away, with plenty of time for them to recover from a heavy rainstorm. Rain or no rain, nothing was going to screw up his good mood tonight.

Absolutely nothing.

He was only thirty-five years old. He'd paid his dues. Now it was his turn. As of tonight, he was starting a whole new life.

Three hours later, Kari drove along a dark, deserted country road somewhere in the

29

Texas Hill Country, gripping the steering wheel so tightly her fingers ached. Rain fell in such a deluge against her windshield that her wipers could barely sweep it away. The road beneath her tires was growing slicker by the minute. Worst of all, her gas gauge was in the red, which meant if she didn't find a station soon, she'd be stuck by the side of the road in the middle of nowhere.

She'd intended to get a hotel room in Austin. What she hadn't counted on was a gazillion people swarming the city for move-in day at the University of Texas. They'd sucked up every decent hotel room for miles around, so she decided to head for San Antonio.

Then came the rain.

Pretty soon the bad weather led to an accident on the freeway, and she'd gotten stuck in the snarl of traffic. Her engine had idled for over an hour until she had less than a fourth of a tank of gas left. She finally got the chance to exit the freeway to search for a gas station, only to end up on a road completely devoid of everything. No cars, no people, no buildings, no nothing. It was as if she was driving through a black hole, except there was rain and thunder and lightning. The longer she drove, the more the road wound around until she had no clue which direction she was going.

She'd yanked off her veil and tossed it into the backseat about a hundred miles ago, but she was still stuck in her wedding dress. It was compressing her ribs so much that she couldn't breathe, and if she didn't get out of it soon, she was going to keel over and die. Why hadn't she stopped at a Mc-Donald's and changed? She could have changed clothes, grabbed a Big Mac, and been back on the road in ten minutes, which meant that right now she'd be comfortable and full. Instead, she was incarcerated inside a wedding dress, starving, with no clue where on earth she was. She'd just been so hell-bent on getting to Austin that she hadn't wanted to stop.

Then she saw it. Up ahead. Or were her eyes playing tricks on her?

No. It was real. Light glimmered faintly through the falling rain.

Maybe it was a service station. Maybe one of those *deluxe* service stations where she could get a cup of coffee and a sub sandwich and a brownie for dessert and wait out the worst of the storm. Then she could ask directions, gas up, and eventually she'd get back to the freeway, then to whatever luxury hotel she could find. She would hand her keys to the valet, get a room, ditch this

31

dress, soak in the Jacuzzi tub for about an hour, and then —

All at once, something darted in front of her. Her mind barely registered *deer* before she wheeled the car hard to the right to miss it. As the startled animal scrambled away, Kari felt the bump and grind of the gravelly shoulder of the road beneath her tires. She tried to turn back, but her car slid sideways down a shallow embankment and smacked into a tree. The force of the impact slung her sideways, whipping her neck hard to one side and banging her head. The windshield shattered, and pellets of safety glass rained into the car like a shower of diamonds.

And then everything went still.

Strangely, the car was still running, but when she turned to see the tree trunk embedded into the passenger door, she realized she wasn't going anywhere. She turned off the ignition, her hand shaking so hard she could barely hold onto the key. The engine died, leaving only the sound of the rain pounding against the car and her pulse throbbing inside her skull. With the windshield gone, rain hit the dashboard, bounced off, and splatted against her face.

In a surge of frustration, she pounded the steering wheel and shouted a few curse words at the top of her lungs. When that didn't unsmash her car and put it back up on the road, she clutched the steering wheel and dragged in a deep, ragged breath.

Get a grip. Where's your cell phone?

She felt around on the dripping-wet seat, then on the floorboard beneath her feet, before she finally found it. She'd turned it off earlier to avoid the deluge of phone calls and texts she knew she'd get. When she turned it on now, she felt marginally better when it lit up and the car wasn't completely dark.

And she couldn't get a signal.

She tossed it to the seat beside her, wondering what in the world she was supposed to do now. She had yet to see anybody else on this godforsaken road. It was dark and cold and wet and her head hurt, and she was starting to get just a *tiny* bit scared. If she'd only stayed in Houston, she'd be at her reception right now. Clean and dry and eating and drinking and dancing and . . .

And married.

Then she saw it again in the distance. The light she'd seen right before going off the road. Where there was light, there was help, right? Unfortunately, it wasn't coming to her. She had to go to it. But walk in this horrible storm?

Then again, what was her alternative? She

had no windshield so she was already drenched anyway. She might as well try to find help. And if she didn't get out of this dress soon, it was going to squash the last breath right out of her.

She grabbed her tote bag and stuffed her cell phone inside it. With a deep breath, she shoved as much dress as she could out of the way, then followed it out of the car, wincing at the pain in her wrenched neck and across her shoulder where the seat belt had dug in. As she climbed the incline to the road, rain hammered her mercilessly, her dress dragging through the mud behind her.

When she reached the road, she felt a little woozy. Maybe she should have eaten something today besides half of the granola bar Jill had shoved at her, but she'd been so sick at the thought of becoming a married woman that she hadn't been able to eat anything else. And dragging layer after layer of mud-caked Duchess satin and Chantilly lace behind her was just about to wear her out.

And the rain still came down.

It's not a disaster, it's an adventure . . .

She kept saying that to herself, over and over, because they said repetition was the key to making yourself believe something.

34

She liked adventures. She lived her life looking for them. But she generally preferred being dry and alive to enjoy them.

As she drew closer to the light, a jagged bolt of lightning sizzled to earth, exploding in a loud burst of electricity and momentarily illuminating a sign just up the highway. She slogged through the mud for another few minutes until she reached it. It was a painted wooden sign with grapes and wine bottles and the words *Cordero Vineyards* in white cursive letters shadowed in bright crimson. Now she realized the light she'd seen was coming from a structure on that property. Closer now, it looked like a farmhouse. Unfortunately, it was at the end of a very long driveway, and she was about to faint from exhaustion.

Kari imagined the person she hoped would answer the door — a grandmotherly woman who would invite her in, fix her a cup of tea, then cluck sweetly over her until the storm let up and she could figure out what to do next.

Then another bolt of lightning exploded so close it made even Kari's wet arm hairs stand on end. *Get out of this rain, or you're going to be a barbecued bride.*

With a deep breath, she turned onto the property, focused on the light, and kept on walking.

Marc checked his watch. It was almost eight. He poured the jar of gooey, fake cheese crap he'd microwaved over the tortilla chips, then threw a handful of jalapeño slices on top. *Ah.* Food of the gods. For tonight and hereafter, to hell with healthy. His new motto: "Live fast, die young."

He liked the way that sounded, smooth and careless, throwing caution to the wind. Then his brain veered off on a Dad tangent: *Yes. That's an excellent plan. Just make sure your life insurance is paid up first.*

Crap. Responsibility was going to be a hard habit to kick. He needed to think bachelor thoughts.

He stuck a package of Double Stuf Oreos under one arm, then picked up the nachos and a beer and headed to his living room. He put the food on the end table and collapsed in his recliner, tipping it back to maximum comfort level with his feet up and his head on the pillowy backrest. Then he reached for the remote and turned on the game.

Outside the rain came down in buckets. Thunder boomed. Lightning crashed. And Marc couldn't have cared less, because he was inside this house where it was warm and dry, and tonight, right there in his living room, the Cowboys were going to beat the daylights out of the Steelers.

To complete the picture of total decadence, Brandy lay on the rug at his feet. He'd felt generous tonight and had given her way too many of her favorite dog treats. Now she was lying upside down, asleep and snoring, her bushy golden retriever tail flicking back and forth as she dreamed of chasing rabbits through the vineyard. Marc took a long drink of beer and let out a satisfied sigh. Life didn't get any better than this.

The Cowboys won the toss and lined up to receive the kickoff. The Steelers kicker took off toward the ball.

And there was a knock at his door.

Marc whipped around. Somebody at his door? In this storm?

Brandy leaped up and started barking. Marc grabbed the remote, hit the "pause" button, and went to the entry hall. He opened the door. He blinked. Blinked again. And he still couldn't believe what he saw.

A woman stood on his porch. Her hair was hanging in a dripping wad on one side of her head, and rain trickled off her nose. Raindrops clung to her eyelashes, shimmering in the dim porch light. Considering the

37

storm, all that made sense. But what was that monstrosity she was wearing? She looked like Glinda the Good Witch after a bout of mud wrestling.

But as he looked her up and down, light slowly dawned, and he had the feeling the first day of his new life had just gone straight to hell. She was dripping wet. She was dirty from head to toe. She looked lost and lonely and helpless.

And she was wearing a wedding dress.

CHAPTER 2

Brandy must have been equally stunned by the woman standing on the porch, because she stopped barking and stood motionless, looking up at Marc with a whimper of confusion. *But I'm ready, boss. If whatever that thing is steps out of line, I'm on it.*

But the woman wasn't stepping out of line. In fact, she wasn't saying anything. She just stood there staring up at Marc, her eyes wide. He looked past her to the driveway and didn't see a car. How the hell had she gotten there?

"Can I help you?" he asked.

A smile flickered on her face, then died. "I-I kinda had an accident down the road, and I was wondering . . ."

Marc came to attention. "Accident? What happened?"

She teetered a little. "I was driving, and there was this deer . . . I didn't want to hit him . . ."

"You swerved to miss a deer?"

She nodded. "And now my car is wrecked."

"Forget about that. Are you all right?"

"Uh . . . yeah. I think so."

All at once, lightning crashed. The woman's eyes flew wide open. She came to life, bounding across his threshold, dragging approximately two tons of wet, muddy dress behind her. She spun around, her hand at her throat and her eyes still wide with surprise, acting as if she'd just cheated death. Given how lightning was exploding all around his house, maybe she had.

"Aren't you going to shut the door?" she said, her voice shaky.

Marc closed the door, then turned to face her. There were mascara rings under her eyes. Her hair was dangling in a wet blob, and he couldn't tell what color it was. Maybe a little bit red?

Brandy walked back and forth nervously, still trying to make sense of this woman. But if Marc couldn't figure it out, what chance did his poor dog have?

"What happened to your shoes?" he asked.

She looked down. "I don't know. I think the mud sucked them off my feet about a quarter mile ago." She held her hands out helplessly, looking down at herself. "Look at me. I'm a mess. This dress . . . oh, God. Hilda would just die if she saw me now!"

"Who's Hilda?"

"My wedding planner. She freaked out when a pearl fell off the train. What would she do if she saw this?"

"What's your name?" he asked.

"Kari Worthington," she said. "You must be somebody . . . Cordero. I saw the sign."

"Marc Cordero. Now tell me why you were driving around in the country after dark in the middle of a storm wearing a wedding dress."

She opened her mouth to speak, but nothing came out. Then her eyes slowly filled with tears. Marc felt a glimmer of panic. *No! No crying!* There was no crisis on earth that couldn't be made worse if a woman started to cry.

"Why are you crying?" he asked, afraid she was going to tell him.

"I couldn't do it," she said. "I couldn't marry Greg. So I ran."

"Ran?"

"There were only twenty-two minutes left. Twenty-two minutes before I was going to be a married woman. And I just couldn't do it."

"You left your own wedding?"

Her face crumpled, but she kept the tears

41

at bay. "Yes."

"Let me get this straight. You got into a car in this weather in a wedding dress and just *drove away*?"

"No! Well, not exactly. It wasn't raining when I left Houston."

Marc drew back. "Houston? You drove all the way here from *Houston*? That's over two hundred miles!"

She held up her palm. "Now, it's not as bad as it sounds. See, I was going to drive to Austin, but then the hotels were all full because of parents taking kids back to college, so I thought I'd go to San Antonio. But when I headed that direction, the rain came and there was an accident and traffic was a mess and I was running out of gas, so I got off the freeway to find a gas station and then I got lost. And then there was the deer, and . . ." She shrugged weakly. "And here I am."

Marc had news for her. It really *was* as bad as it sounded. "You need to call somebody to come get you."

"No!" she said. "Whoever I call will talk me into getting married. And I can't do that. I'll be miserable for the rest of my life!"

All this should have kicked off Marc's usual reaction to a crisis, which was to wade in, take control, and solve the problem, but

42

he'd never encountered a problem like this. A woman who ran away from her own wedding into a driving rainstorm? In what weird universe did *that* happen?

"Okay," Marc said. "Your car. Is it drivable?"

"Well, it's kinda wrapped around a tree. No windshield. So I guess I'd say . . . probably not."

"You're two hundred miles from home. Do you know anybody in the area? Anybody at all?"

She shrugged weakly. "To tell you the truth, I don't even know where I am."

"Didn't you bring a map with you?"

"No. I didn't exactly plan to run away."

"Still, you might have stopped along the way. Regrouped. Gotten organized. Put a little thought into —"

All at once she put her hand to her stomach and started to weave, her eyes dropping closed. Marc took hold of her wrist to steady her. It felt cold from the rain and so fine boned he could wrap his entire hand around it.

"What's the matter?" he asked.

"Sorry. I'm just . . . I'm just having a hard time . . . breathing . . ."

"What's wrong? Are you sick?"

"No," she said, her face contorting. "It's

this dress. It's so tight. And my stomach feels funny. I haven't eaten much in the last couple of days."

"Why haven't you eaten?"

"Because my dress was too tight. I needed to be able to get into it on my wedding day."

"I'll get you some crackers —"

"No. The dress is too tight. If I eat something, I'll barf it right back up."

She hadn't eaten because the dress was too tight, but because the dress was too tight, she couldn't eat? One of Marc's biggest pet peeves was circular logic that led nowhere. How did anyone get off a roller coaster like that?

"And it's worse now," she said, her breath fast and shallow. "I think the dress is drying and shrinking. I need to get out of it."

"But you don't have any clothes to put on," Marc said.

"No. I have clothes. They're in my luggage."

"Where's your luggage?"

"In my car."

"And your car is in a ditch."

"Yeah."

Marc sighed. He was no psychic, but he was having no trouble predicting the near future. He was going to be wading through a muddy ditch to pull suitcases out of a wrecked car.

"Where did you have the accident? East on the highway or west?"

She looked at him blankly.

"Never mind," Marc said. "Surely you'll know which way to go once we reach the gate."

"The gate?"

"My front gate. I'll take you to your car to get your luggage. Then I'll drop you off at a hotel in town. You can check in, get cleaned up, and change clothes. Then tomorrow you can deal with your car."

"But the weather —"

"It's letting up."

Actually, Marc wasn't too sure about that, but it didn't matter. One way or another, he was taking her to town. Then he'd get back to his football game and pretend all this had never happened.

"Come with me," he said, heading for the kitchen.

She trudged along behind him, the train of her dress making a wide, muddy streak across the tile floor. It looked as if a gigantic slug had slithered through his house. As they came into the kitchen, Sasha was in her usual spot on top of the refrigerator. She was Siamese, and from the day Angela brought her home as a kitten, it was as if she knew she came from royal stock. That refrigerator was her throne, and she judged every situation that passed before her like the princess she was sure she was.

How about it, Sasha? Does Her Majesty have a solution to this problem?

Marc stopped in the mudroom and put on a raincoat and a pair of rubber boots, then grabbed a poncho for Kari.

"No sense in getting wetter than you already are," he said as he eased it over her head and pulled it down, then tugged the hood up over her blob of hair. The poncho was Day-Glo yellow. She looked like Big Bird in a wedding dress.

He still didn't know why she'd left her fiancé at the altar, but in the end it didn't matter. He only knew he wanted this woman out of his house as quickly as possible so he could get back to his new life.

A few minutes later, Kari sat in the passenger seat of the biggest pickup truck she'd ever seen, listening to the roar of hundreds of horses under the hood as Marc motored down the storm-darkened highway. He drove every bit of the speed limit even though the rain still poured. At first she thought, *Daredevil,* only to realize every move he made seemed careful and measured, as if he knew every hill and curve as well as he knew his own name.

As he was stuffing her and her dress into the passenger seat of his truck, she'd seen two rifles on a gun rack in the back window of the club cab pickup. Her heart stuttered at the sight, but she told herself to stop being silly.

Ignore the guns. This is rural Texas. Five-year-olds carry guns in rural Texas.

Left to her own devices, Kari generally associated with men who played guitars and wrote poetry because at least they understood her creative, disordered mind and didn't cringe when she dyed her hair purple. When she dated men her father approved of, they wore sport coats over their two-hundred-dollar jeans, talked about the stock market, and got exasperated when she wanted to try a vegan restaurant.

Either way, nothing had prepared her for Marc Cordero.

He was a big man with a big truck and big guns, and every indication said he wasn't the least bit happy to be taking her anywhere on a night like tonight. He hadn't cracked a smile from the moment he'd opened his front door. And as she gave him a sidelong glance now, she forgot her wrecked car, forgot the storm, forgot everything but the man sitting next to her, a man who looked as if he could pick her up and snap her in half if he chose to.

But she couldn't say she hated it.

She glanced at his hands on the steering wheel, big, strong hands that looked as if they could split firewood without an ax. Underneath that raincoat was a body to match his hands, with a chest and shoulders so broad he could have made two of any of the men she knew. She didn't know exactly what it took to run a vineyard, but it was clear he'd gotten his gorgeous body and his golden tan the hard way — by spending long hours working in the sun. She glanced back at his left hand on the steering wheel. No ring.

But why was she bothering to look?

Because he's sexy as hell, that's why.

But that didn't matter. The last thing a pushover like her needed was a man to push her over. If Greg had been able to do it, she wouldn't stand a chance with a man like this one.

"So you run a vineyard?" she asked.

"Yep."

"You have a nice house."

"It's home."

That was the one word that described it perfectly. It had a wide front porch with a wooden swing, and on the inside the oak floors, thick rugs, and country kitchen made it feel cozy and warm. For a second her brain flashed to her father's house — three times the size and cold as ice.

"Are you sure your car is this direction?" Marc asked. "We've gone a long way."

"I walked a long way."

"Wait. There it is."

Marc slowed down, then made a U-turn to pull onto the shoulder near where her car had gone off the road. He shined his headlights on it as best he could, then held out his hand. "Keys?"

She handed him the keys and he got out of the truck. The rain had let up some, but still it pelted him as he walked purposefully down the incline to where her car rested in the ditch. He unlocked the trunk and grabbed two of her biggest suitcases. She'd filled them so full she was sure she'd be charged extra at the airport, but Marc lifted them as if they were nothing. He brought them up the hill and stuffed them behind the seat in the extended portion of the club cab. He did the same with the other two. Then he climbed back into the truck and slammed the door, shoving the hood of his raincoat off his head. His boots slopped mud onto the plastic floor mat beneath his feet.

"That's a lot of luggage," he said as he put the truck in gear. "Where were you going?"

"Bali," she said. "Ten days."

"You needed four bags for ten days?"

"It was my honeymoon. I did a lot of shopping before I left."

"Hope somebody canceled the trip."

Didn't matter. It was a gift from her father. Given his money, that was the last thing he cared about. Forget the *vacation* to Bali. He could have *bought* Bali.

As they drove away, Kari glanced over her shoulder. "What do you think about the condition of my car?"

"Hard to tell until Rick hauls it out. It could be anything from a flat tire and a little body damage to a total loss."

Kari watched out the window as they sped down the highway through the shadowed trees. Minutes later they rounded a bend and she saw lights up ahead. Soon they passed a sign that read, "Rainbow Valley, Texas." And beneath that, "Home of the Rainbow Bridge."

"Rainbow Valley, Texas?" Kari said.

"Uh-huh."

"Never heard of it. What's the Rainbow

50

Bridge?"

"Long story. Ask Gus. He loves to tell it."

"Gus?"

"He and his wife run the bed-and-breakfast I'm taking you to."

They passed a few farmhouses on the side of the road. The rain had diminished to a heavy drizzle, and up ahead she saw a water tower with the cartoon faces of two dogs and a cat painted on it. Then she saw the street names. Llama Lane. Persian Place. Appaloosa Avenue.

"Why are all the streets named after animals?" she asked.

"Another long story. Gus will oblige."

Marc slowed his truck and turned onto a street called Rainbow Way. Businesses lined both sides, most of which had begun life as houses and been transformed. They were a mix of architectural styles, or maybe they'd just been added to and subtracted from so much over the years that each one was its own work of art. They were painted fun, cheerful colors. Kari was transfixed. Even through the rain, this place looked delightfully funky, like Oz without the Munchkins. She could only imagine what it looked like on a sunny summer afternoon.

They approached a town square. Vintage streetlamps illuminated the falling rain. In the center of the square was a large gazebo painted bright yellow and surrounded by flowering shrubs. The darkness and the rain should have made everything look dreary, but Kari had never seen anything so enchanting in her life. She'd felt a little depressed earlier, but how could anybody look at this place and not feel like dancing?

"This place is so cute!" she said. "Look at all the storefronts. Wait — Cordero Vineyards? You have a shop in town?"

"Yep. We move a lot of wine that way."

"It's cute, too."

Marc just shrugged. "Tourists love it, particularly the big animal lovers."

"Animal lovers? But you sell wine."

"Yeah. Top Dog Merlot. Crazy Horse Cabernet." He gave her a slight roll of the eyes. "We have a wine called Sex Kitten. My sister talked me into that one."

Kari smiled. "Really?"

"It's one of our best sellers. Unfortunately that means I'm stuck with it. Everybody loves doggies and kitties. There are big bucks in that."

"You don't sound happy about it."

"On the contrary. Making a buck makes me *very* happy."

"I noticed *you* have a doggy and a kitty."

"My *daughter* has a doggy and a kitty."

Kari came to attention. "You have a daughter?"

"Yes."

"Does she live with you?"

"Not anymore. I dropped her off at UT this afternoon for her freshman year of college."

That astonished Kari. Most men with college-age kids were well into their forties. Marc clearly wasn't.

"So you were in Austin this afternoon, too?"

"Yeah."

"You don't look old enough to have a daughter in college."

"I'm plenty old enough."

She looked at his left hand again. "I don't see a ring."

"That's because I don't have a wife."

"Are you divorced?"

"Do you always talk so much?"

"Truthfully? Yeah."

"Well, I generally don't. So if you keep it up, pretty soon you may be talking to yourself."

Kari took the hint, but it was all she could do not to ask a dozen more questions. Some folks thought she was a little nosy, but she liked to think of it as simply being interested in other people. A highly attractive man who

53

was relatively young with a college-age daughter and no wife? There had to be a story there, but judging from the inaccessible look on Marc's face, she was pretty sure she wasn't going to hear it.

Marc passed the square and turned right onto a street behind it. He pulled into a small parking lot beside yet one more house turned business. It was a three-story Victorian painted blue, with a high-peaked roof and scrollwork detail.

He parked his truck, circled around it, and unstuffed Kari from the passenger seat. As he guided her toward the big front porch, she noticed paw prints painted on the sidewalk beneath her feet and several stone cats along the way peeking out from behind the shrubbery. Marc took her up the steps and through the front door, shoving her dress unceremoniously into the foyer behind her. A little brown-and-black mutt let out a few barks and trotted over to them. He circled around Kari, sniffing her with the same interest Marc's dog had.

Kari looked around, delighted by the interior of the house. To her right was what looked like a parlor. To the left was what had probably once been a living room or library, but it had been rearranged and reworked to create an area for the front desk. Straight ahead was a gorgeous oak staircase with a stained glass window towering over the midfloor landing. It took a moment or two for Kari to realize the stained glass was a representation of Noah's ark. How cool was *that*?

Over the front desk was a sign that read: "Animal House. A Bed & Breakfast for Cats and Dogs. Feel Free to Bring Your People."

Just then a man stepped through a doorway to stand behind the desk. He had a short swirl of gray hair and wore a pair of bifocals around his neck. At one time he'd probably been at least six two, but age had taken its toll and hunched him down to about six feet. He wore a pair of khaki pants and a short-sleeved plaid shirt that barely harnessed the belly that lopped over his buckstitched belt. He took one look at Kari and froze. Then slowly he turned his gaze to Marc.

"I always assumed I'd be invited to the wedding."

"Nobody got married, Gus," Marc said.

"Not even me," Kari said.

"She needs a room for the night," Marc said.

"Or maybe several nights," Kari added.

"She had a car accident near the vineyard in the middle of the storm," Marc said.

"Wearing a wedding dress?"

"Long story."

"Not really," Kari said. "I ran away from my own wedding. I got lost on a deserted highway. I swerved to miss a deer and landed in a ditch. I walked to Marc's house. He brought me here so I'd have a place to stay."

"She's right," Gus said. "That's not long at all."

Marc checked his watch. "Gus? A room?"

Just then a small black-and-white cat leaped onto the counter and sauntered across it, arching her back and rubbing the length of her body along Gus's arm. He petted her absentmindedly.

"She's pretty," Kari said, stepping forward to pet her, too.

"Name's Fanny," Gus said. "Short for Fantasia. One of my grandkids named her after the Disney movie, but Marc still thinks it sounds like a stripper name."

"Gus?" Marc said. "Are you in the hotel business or not?"

Gus smiled a little, then pulled his keyboard across the desk and started poking at it. As he took Kari's information, Marc retrieved her luggage from his truck.

"How many days did you say you're staying?" he asked Kari.

"I don't know."

He eyed the four huge suitcases. "Sure you're not moving in?"

"You never know," she said with a smile. "I like this place."

Kari reached into her purse for her credit card, but Gus waved her away. "My machine's down," he told her. "Drop by the desk tomorrow morning. If it's working again, I'll run your card."

"What about incidentals?" she asked.

"We got no incidentals around here. This is a bed-and-breakfast. You get a bed and breakfast."

"Movies?"

"We got a bunch of DVDs in the dining room. Take your pick. Just bring them back after you watch them. We have wine and cheese and cookies and such at three o'clock every afternoon, if you're interested. Those are freebies. So you'll know, Jasper and Fanny aren't the only two critters in the place. If any of them end up in your room, be sure to shoo 'em out before you go to sleep. And watch Fanny. She'll slip into your room and creep under the bed when you're not looking, and then you'll find her on your pillow an hour later."

Kari thought about Boo, who curled up next to her every night. That had bugged the hell out of Greg, which was just one more thing that should have been a red flag.

Gus handed Kari the key to the room. "The only rooms I have open right now are on the third floor."

"I'm guessing there's no elevator."

"Sorry, no."

She looked down at her dress, then behind her at the muddy train. It had been all she could do to drag it along as she trudged down the highway after the accident. The dress wasn't even close to dry yet. With the weight of the water it had absorbed, she doubted she could even make it up the stairs.

Marc sighed. "Wait a minute."

He clearly saw the problem, because he took off his raincoat and kicked off his muddy boots. Moving around behind her, he gathered the train of her dress in his arms.

"Up the stairs," he told her.

As she walked up to the midfloor landing, Gus called out to Marc, "Estelle's in Waymark with Chloe and the new baby, so the bed hasn't been made up yet. I'll bring linens in a minute."

By the time Kari made it to the third floor, she was about to drop. She opened the door to room 302. Once inside, Marc let the train fall to the floor.

"Stay on the hardwood floor to take it off," Marc said. "It's easier to clean. I'm going down for your luggage."

Kari took off the poncho and gave it to Marc. He left the room, making two trips to bring her luggage upstairs. She gave him a smile. "Thanks for your help."

"I'll call Rick first thing in the morning and tell him where your car is. Drop by his place tomorrow and he'll let you know what it's going to cost to get it fixed. Gus will give you directions."

Without another word, he turned around and left the room, closing the door behind him.

Kari just stood there dumbly, blinking with disbelief. She didn't know what she'd expected him to do next, but after all they'd been through tonight, she thought at least he would say something to wrap up the occasion, like "Nice to meet you," or maybe "Have a nice life."

But he'd said nothing.

Never mind. Doesn't matter. You have to get out of this dress.

She reached her hands behind her back. Felt for a button. When she came up short, she stretched her arms a little more. Felt around again. Still nothing.

And then it struck her.

It had taken Hilda and Jill ten minutes to fasten this dress up the back, one minuscule button at a time. Kari realized she might be able to unhook some of the lower ones, but she didn't have a prayer with the ones in the middle of her back.

A tremor of panic seized her. She might as well have been in a straitjacket. She dropped her hands to her sides and considered her options. As it turned out, she had only one.

Hoisting as much of the muddy train as she could, she hurried to the door and yanked it open.

"Wait!"

A few seconds later, Marc came back up the stairs and peered at her from the landing. "What?"

"I have a little problem."

His brows drew together with irritation. "What problem?"

"Uh . . . this dress . . ."

"What about it?"

"The buttons are in the back. There are about a thousand of them, and they're really tiny."

"So?"

"So . . . I can't get out of it by myself."

Marc blinked. "What do you mean, you

can't get out of it by yourself?"
 "I need you to take it off me."

CHAPTER 3

Marc was stunned. Take it off her? As in *undress* her?

"I can't do that."

"You have to," Kari said.

"No. I don't believe I do."

"I told you I can't breathe. If I don't get out of this dress, I'll probably faint dead away. Is that what you want?"

Her hand went to her stomach again, her already-pale complexion turning white. He couldn't exactly hand this one off to Gus. But with Estelle gone, what was he supposed to do? Beat on doors until he found a woman who wouldn't mind unbuttoning a wedding dress?

He came to her door, dropping his voice. "You don't even know me, and you want me to unbutton your dress? Hadn't you better rethink that?"

"I don't know. Do I need to rethink it?"

He narrowed his eyes. "How do you know

I'm not a dangerous man?"

"Are you a dangerous man?"

"Of course not!"

"Then there's no problem, is there?"

"You don't take the word of a dangerous man when he tells you he's not dangerous!"

"But if you're *not* dangerous, I can take your word for it, right?"

Marc's number two pet peeve. Convoluted logic that led to the right conclusion. *God,* he hated that.

"Actually," Kari said, "it was dumber for me to get into your truck with you. God only knows where you might have taken me. At least here if I scream, somebody will hear me, right?"

Right, Marc thought, even though he didn't want to say so, particularly since she smiled when she said it. He wasn't finding a whole lot funny about any of this.

"And if you had nefarious intent," Kari added, "would you have taken the trouble to bring me here?"

Marc screwed up his face. " 'Nefarious intent'?"

"Sorry. I was a lit major. I like big words."

"Oh, for God's sake," he muttered, stepping back inside the room. He moved around behind her, nudging her dress out of the way with his foot so he could come up closer to her. She was right. There were approximately four thousand tiny buttons closed with fabric loops. He tried the first button, but his fingers were just too damned big. It was as if she was asking him to thread a needle with a rope.

"Uh . . . how's it going back there?" she asked.

"I'm working on it."

He pulled one of the little loops, and after a while he managed to shove the button through it.

"There," he said.

"There what?"

"I got one of them."

"One?"

"Do you know how tiny these buttons are?"

"You're going to have to work faster than that."

"I'm doing the best I can."

A minute later, he'd undone the second one. Had it been too long since he'd undressed a woman? Was that the problem? Use it or lose it? Or did he just need a magnifying glass for these damned buttons?

Which brought him to another not-so-nice conclusion. Maybe his eyesight was going, too.

"Please hurry," she said, a tremor of panic

in her voice. "I think it's shrinking as it dries."

"Look, you've already said you can't do this yourself. So right now I'm all you've got."

"I know. But that doesn't make breathing any easier."

He fumbled with button number three, poking and pulling. "Can you suck in a little bit?"

"If I could suck in," she said pointedly, "I could breathe. And if I could breathe, this wouldn't be a problem. How many more?"

"Do you want me to count buttons or unbutton them?"

She sighed. "Keep going."

"These buttons are just too small," he said. "Hell, the dress is, too. Why are you wearing a dress that's too small?"

"You have to order a wedding dress months in advance. How am I supposed to know exactly what size I'll be when it finally comes in?"

"Isn't that what tailors are for?"

"You can let something out only so much."

He fumbled with button number four a little longer. It was hopeless. "Do you plan on wearing this dress again?"

She looked down at herself with a sigh. "No. It's ruined."

Marc reached into his pocket, pulled out a pocketknife, and flipped it open. He tucked the tip of the knife beneath one of the fabric button loops, gave it a flick, and the button came loose. He freed another one. And another.

"How are you doing that?" she asked.

"Pocketknife."

She spun around. "You're *cutting* the button loops?"

"Do you want out of this dress or not?"

"This dress cost five thousand dollars!"

Marc drew back. "For *one dress*?"

"It's Vera Wang."

"Very what?"

"No. *Vera* — oh, never mind." She sighed. "Keep going."

He continued like that all the way down. As the sides of the dress parted, her body slowly relaxed. His gaze trailed down the indentation of her spine, which curved gently all the way to her waist, with skin that looked so soft and fragile he was sure one touch would leave a bruise. As she took a deep breath, her body shifted and the dress fell open a little more, revealing the top of her baby-pink panties. Marc's heart beat faster. Something about that little scrap of fabric peeking out just about did him in. He'd been too long without a woman. That was the problem. When just the sight of a pair of panties made him hot, he had some serious catching up to do.

Three more buttons, and the task was done. As he clicked his knife shut and returned it to his pocket, she turned around slowly, her hands clasping the bodice of the dress against her breasts to hold it up. As she stared up at him, for the first time he looked past the raccoon rings and the wet lashes and focused on her eyes. They were green. No, more than just green. He'd always prided himself on being a concrete thinker with no room in his ordered mind for metaphorical crap, but suddenly he had a mental picture of the shimmery color of dewdrops glittering on grape leaves in early autumn.

Where the hell had *that* come from?

He tried to look away, but *away* turned into *down.* From one of her shoulders to the other was an expanse of creamy skin sprinkled with raindrops that shimmered in the dim lamplight, complete with delicate collarbones overlaid with a dainty pearl necklace. He couldn't stop staring at her. He couldn't even blink. He swore he was staring so hard his eyeballs were turning to dust.

As his gaze moved lower still, he zeroed in

on the most beautiful thing he'd seen in ages — her breasts swelling above the lacy bodice of the dress she held against her. He didn't get it. Brides were supposed to at least pretend they were sweet and virginal, only to wear dresses that made men picture them naked. And that was exactly what he was doing right then. He knew he should be ashamed of himself for that. Rescue a damsel in distress, then fantasize about ravishing her? What kind of man *did* that?

One who hadn't seen a naked woman in so long he barely remembered what one looked like.

"Oh, no," she said. "Look at your shirt. It must have gotten muddy when you helped me up the stairs. I'm sorry."

She touched her fingertips to his chest, tracing the muddy blotches. Marc had been so preoccupied by having a near-naked woman standing in front of him that he hadn't even thought about his muddy shirt. And now all he could think about was her soft, soft hand *on* his muddy shirt. Then she flattened her palm against him, and when he felt the warmth of it, his nerves went haywire. Her hand against his chest was actually making him hard, so hard he was sure not an ounce of blood was getting to his brain. She flexed her fingers against his chest, and fireworks exploded inside his head.

Then it dawned on him. Good God. Was she actually coming *on* to him?

He wasn't sure. But if she was, it was wrong. So wrong. She was a marginally crazy woman who'd left her fiancé at the altar not five hours before, standing in front of him wearing a muddy dress with her hair in a wet blob on the side of her head. So why did none of that seem to matter to him? Why could he think of nothing else but tossing her down on that bed and having his way with her?

Suddenly he heard footsteps in the hall. He jerked around just in time to see Gus push the door open — the one Marc realized now that he'd left ajar.

Gus stopped short, looking back and forth between them. Kari was standing with her back to the door. That dress was unbuttoned below her waist. And those damned pink panties . . .

He had definitely gotten an eyeful.

"I was just bringing you sheets and whatnot," he told Kari, holding them up. "Tell you what. Why don't I just leave them right here on the dresser?" As he set them down, he had the nerve to smile. "You kids have a good time now."

With that, he stepped out of the room and closed the door behind him.

"Well, *crap,*" Marc muttered.

"What's wrong?" Kari asked.

"I have to go."

"Uh . . . okay," she said, and he swore she sounded disappointed. *Wishful thinking?*

It didn't matter. He had to get out of there. It didn't bother him for somebody to know he was with a woman. But it did bother him for somebody to think he was ravishing a helpless woman he didn't even know an hour after she was in an accident. He would have liked to have said he didn't care about any of that, but in a town the size of Rainbow Valley, gossip took on a life of its own.

He headed for the door, calling back over his shoulder, "Like I said before, I'll talk to Rick in the morning to tell him where to pick up your car. Gus will tell you how to get to his place."

"Okay."

He started out of the room only to turn back. "And the next time you think about doing something like leaving your wedding and driving two hundred miles, check the weather report."

"I will."

70

"And for God's sake, take the dress off first."

She nodded. He left the room, then stuck his head back inside again, pointing his finger at her. "And don't you ever — *ever* — let a man you don't know undress you again."

"Even a nondangerous one?"

"You know what I mean. You lucked out tonight. Never forget that."

Marc left her standing in the middle of the room, still clutching that dress to her breasts, and trotted down the stairs. He went straight to the bench near the front door to put his boots back on. Gus had settled into an overstuffed chair nearby, wearing a smirk that said he thought the whole thing was just a little too funny.

"That wasn't what you think," Marc said, grabbing one of his boots.

"Hey, no business of mine," Gus said.

"She couldn't get out of the damned dress," Marc snapped. "There was nobody else to help her, so I had to unbutton it. That's all that happened."

Gus waved his hand. "What my guests do is none of my concern, long as they don't tear up the place." A smile curled the corner of his mouth. "Though if you'd stayed all night, I'd have had to charge you for a

71

double."

"Gus, for God's sake. I don't even *know* that woman!"

"If I were you," Gus said, "I'd get to know her."

"She ran away from her own wedding not five hours ago. That means she's got a problem. Maybe a lot of problems. I don't need a woman with problems."

"You're pretty darned picky for a man who's got no woman at all."

"No woman beats a crazy one." Marc pulled his other boot on. "Whatever you do, don't tell Estelle."

"Are you saying my wife's a gossip?"

"Are you saying she's not?"

"Don't worry," Gus said. "Your secret is safe with me."

"There isn't any secret!"

"Yeah? Then should I go ahead and tell Estelle that thing that's not a secret?"

"Oh, never mind," Marc said, standing up. "Tell everybody you can think of. In fact, why don't you take out an ad in the *Rainbow Valley Voice* and let the whole town know?"

"Now, I like gossip as much as the next person," Gus said. "But I don't generally spend money to spread it around."

"You don't have to," Marc said, putting

on his raincoat. "You're married to Estelle. Good night, Gus."

Gus smiled. "Good night, Marc."

Marc opened the door and went back out into the dark, gloomy night, looking forward to the day when he'd be leaving this town and all its dumb gossip behind. He wanted to go to a place where nobody knew him. Where he was a face in the crowd. Where he could misbehave all he wanted to and nobody was around to care.

Wherever that place was, it sounded like heaven on earth.

As for Kari, he had no idea how long she was staying in town, but he vowed to steer clear of her until she left. But just as he was getting into his truck, something occurred to him.

No. Not your problem. You're done. Go home.

He started the truck, but instead of backing out of the parking space, he froze with his hand on the gearshift. A few seconds later he killed the engine again, blowing out a breath of irritation. Finally he got out of the truck and trotted back inside.

"Gus!"

Gus stuck his head around the doorway.

"She hasn't eaten much in the past couple of days," Marc said. "Can you feed her tonight? A sandwich or something? She might not ask you herself."

"Sure thing. Should I put a rose on the tray and tell her it's from you?"

Marc frowned. "Good *night,* Gus."

"Good night, Marc."

Marc hopped back into his truck and started for home. *There.* He was finally free of the whole situation. Kari Worthington had more baggage than a transatlantic airliner, and he wanted nothing more to do with her. He'd call Rick in the morning and get him to haul her car out of that ditch just as he'd told her he would, but that would be the end of it. After tonight, his involvement in other people's problems was going to be a thing of the past. Then once harvest was over he was leaving Rainbow Valley, and the freedom Nicole had grabbed for herself all those years ago would finally be his, too.

Kari stood in the middle of room 302, her eyes closed and her hand still clutching the bodice of that horrible dress, trying to get her racing heart to slow down. She'd seen that mud on Marc's shirt. Before she knew it, she was touching it. Then she went from touching *it* to touching *him.* And that was when her heart started beating so crazily it took her breath away.

The trouble was that she'd never been known for her restraint and circumspection when it came to anything in her life, and men were no exception. Once something caught her attention, she had a hard time letting it go. And the more ill-advised something was, the more she found herself focusing on it, imagining the possibilities. And the more possibilities she imagined, the more her heart sped up inside her chest until she was in serious danger of fainting dead away.

She'd never been attracted to big, powerful men, but as she was standing there staring at Marc after he'd gotten her out of that dress, a vision had suddenly filled her mind of a hot interlude in an out-of-the-way inn with a sexy stranger while a storm raged outside — a wild, hot, dangerous affair that made her melt from the inside out. In the entire year she'd dated Greg, not once had she felt that deep-down, all-encompassing, prehistoric, gotta-have-him-now sensation that had swept through her when she stood in front of Marc. But he clearly hadn't felt a thing. He hadn't even *blinked.* In fact, as soon as Gus showed up, he acted as if he couldn't wait to get out of there.

Oh, well. Maybe it was for the best. Should she really be lusting after one man only hours after she'd left another one at the altar?

With a heavy sigh, she stepped out of the dress and kicked it aside. Then she turned and caught her reflection in the dresser mirror. Her hand flew to her mouth, stifling a scream.

Her hair looked as if it had gotten caught in a wind tunnel, then been doused with a bucket of water. She had dirt on her face. Mascara was everywhere except on her eyelashes. The Creature from the Black Lagoon with swampy moss hanging off him would have been more appealing than she was right then.

Well, now she knew at least one reason Marc had run. What man wanted anything to do with a woman who looked like a horror movie monster?

She went into the bathroom and took a long, hot shower. Then she put on her robe and plopped down in the middle of that gorgeous king-sized bed. She grabbed her phone and looked at her text messages. Three were from Greg, telling her he loved her and was worried about her, and he was asking where she was. Four were from Jill, filled with her usual hyperbole. *Have you lost your mind???* And there were several phone messages from both of them, too.

76

There wasn't a single word from her father.

That made Kari weirdly nervous. She swore she could feel his anger radiating through two hundred miles of atmosphere to light squarely on her shoulders. Thinking about it, though, was it really so surprising he hadn't contacted her? Once when she was sixteen and stayed out past her curfew, he hadn't done what the average parent would do and just called her best friend's house to make her come home. Instead, he'd sent one of his uniformed security guards to pick her up. He understood quite well that teenage humiliation was a stronger deterrent than parental disapproval, and he never hesitated to use it. To this day she was still living off the warning he'd given her when she was only ten years old. *There are consequences, Kari. For everything you do — good and bad — there are consequences.*

She couldn't even imagine what consequences he might be considering right now.

For a moment Kari closed her eyes and imagined what this day might have been like if her mother were still alive. She remembered little else about her mother except her smiles, which she'd showered on her eight-year-old daughter even through her last days when cancer had taken its toll. If she'd been at the church today, would she have laughed and told Kari not to worry, that it was normal for a bride to have cold feet? Or would she have taken her in her arms in a loving hug and told her not to worry about the wedding, the expense, the guests, or even her fiancé, that her happiness was more important than any of those things?

Sometimes Kari tried to remember what her parents' relationship had been like before her mother's death, but the memories were so frail and wispy that they floated away every time she tried to hold them in her mind. She only remembered the pain and anguish she felt after her mother was gone. Instead of her father filling that void for her, he seemed to distance himself more with every day that passed. Soon he stopped talking about her mother altogether, almost as if she'd never existed. And now Kari wondered: Would he be the man he was today if she had lived?

There was no way to know.

Kari did know one thing, though. Somehow she knew that no matter what she'd done today, her mother would have forgiven her.

If only her father would do the same.

She decided to text Greg back, just something short so at least nobody would think she'd disappeared for good. *I'm fine,* she told him. *Don't worry. I'll be in touch.*

Please come home, he texted back. *I love you.*

Kari didn't know if that was true or not. She only knew she felt strangely nonemotional when she looked at his words. It was as if she'd already detached from him and she was talking to a stranger.

She tossed her phone aside, only to pick it up again. After a moment she decided it might be wise to tell somebody where she was. Not Greg. Not her father.

That left Jill.

She clicked on her friend's number, and after a moment, Jill came on the line.

"Kari!" she said. "I've been worried to death about you!"

"You don't have to worry. I'm fine."

"Where the hell *are* you?"

"If I tell you, you can't tell anyone else."

"But Greg —"

"No! Especially not Greg. Or my father. Please, Jill. You have to promise me."

"No way. You need to come home. You need to —"

"Jill . . . *please.*"

Jill sighed. "Okay. I promise."

"I'm in a town called Rainbow Valley. It's

not far from Austin."

"Wait a minute. I'm looking you up on Google Maps . . . oh, my God! You drove that far?"

"Yeah."

"It's late. Where are you staying?"

"At a place called Animal House."

"Huh?"

"It's a bed-and-breakfast."

"What kind of name is that for a bed-and-breakfast?"

"A strange one. But it's a really cute place. We're always looking for a fun hotel for a girls' weekend, so maybe we could —"

"Kari! Will you focus? When are you coming home?"

Kari paused. "I don't know."

"Greg is worried sick. You have to come home and get married."

"Jill. Please try to understand. Greg doesn't love me. And I don't love him, either. It was wrong from the beginning."

"No. You should see him. He's frantic."

"What did my father say?" Kari asked.

Jill was silent for a moment. "He's worried about you, too."

Kari squeezed her eyes closed as guilt crept in again. She'd embarrassed him in front of a church full of his friends, golf buddies, and business associates, and he held grudges like nobody else. Pretty soon Kari would have to face that music, but the last thing she wanted to do in the next few days was start up the band.

"I can't believe this," Jill said. "I just can't *believe* you ran away from your own wedding. No. Wait a minute. Yes, I can. You're the person who once dragged me to Cancún for the weekend with an hour's notice. So why should this surprise me?"

"I know," Kari said. "I know. It's weird. But I couldn't think of anything else to do. If I had stayed, I would have ended up married."

"You *should* be married! Greg is perfect for you!"

No. She knew she'd done the right thing. Just because Greg seemed so perfect to Jill didn't mean he was perfect for *her.* It had just taken Kari a long time to figure that out.

"Jill? Do you know he makes notes on his phone to remember to clip his toenails once a week?"

"So he's hygienic. What's wrong with that?"

"His idea of a good time is to organize the apps on his iPhone."

"Is that really a problem?"

"He reads the *Wall Street Journal* while

81

he's going to the bathroom, Jill. Are you listening to me? Does that sound like a man I'd be compatible with?"

"What can I say? Opposites attract."

No. That wasn't true. Kari was starting to realize that her relationship with Greg had been more about pleasing her father than about marrying the man of her dreams, opposite or not. But since she was only just now admitting that to herself, she didn't go there.

"There's something else," Kari said.

"What?"

"Well, I kinda had a little accident."

"Accident? Are you all right?"

"I swerved to miss a deer, and I ended up in a ditch. I don't know the condition of my car yet. I might not be able to come home even if I wanted to."

"Do you want me to come get you?"

"No! No. Please, Jill. *Please.* I don't want to go back to Houston yet."

"Kari —"

"I have to go now. Just promise me you won't tell anyone where I am."

"I won't. But —"

"I'll call you again soon."

Kari hung up the phone and took a deep, calming breath. She'd go back soon. Just not now. Probably not tomorrow, even if her car was drivable. Past that, she didn't know. She knew she shouldn't be avoiding the issue. Maybe it would take a few days to fix her car, and by that time she'd find the guts to jump into it, head back to Houston, and stand up to all of them.

She hoped so, anyway.

Just then the telephone in the room rang. She picked it up to hear Gus on the other end, who told her he could make her a quick bite to eat if she wanted it. Kari had never said yes so fast in her life. Now that she was out of that awful dress, she was hungrier than a bear coming out of hibernation.

She tossed her robe aside and put on a pair of capri pants, an off-the-shoulder summer top, and sandals. She would have preferred a pair of jeans, a T-shirt, and a pair of flip-flops, but the honeymoon wardrobe in her luggage didn't include those things.

On her way out the door, she sidestepped the dirty mound of lace and satin, resisting the urge to give it a good, swift kick. She hadn't liked it in the first place, but Jill and Hilda had talked her into it, telling her she looked like Cinderella. As always, she'd let herself be swayed by what somebody else wanted.

No more.

Tomorrow she intended to find the nearest Dumpster and hurl that thing over the edge. And she vowed the next time she got married and she picked out a dress, hers was the only opinion that was going to matter. And that applied to whatever man she married, too.

She went downstairs and found Gus in the kitchen. He was creating a sandwich piled high with meat, cheese, lettuce, tomatoes, and a whole bunch of other stuff. She climbed onto a barstool at the kitchen island, and when he finally set down the plate in front of her, it was all she could do not to stuff the whole sandwich in her mouth at once.

"This is really good," Kari said. "Thank you."

"You're welcome."

Jasper walked over and sat at her feet, looking up at her longingly.

"I think he wants a bite," Kari said.

"Up to you."

Kari pulled a small piece of sliced chicken from her sandwich and tossed it to the dog. He snapped it out of the air and looked for more.

"That'll do, Jasper," Gus said, then looked at Kari. "If he doesn't stop mooching, he's going to weigh three hundred pounds."

"So what's the deal with animals in this town?" Kari asked Gus as she ate. "The street signs. This place. Marc said you could tell me the story."

"Yup. It begins with the legend of the Rainbow Bridge. Ever heard of it?"

"No."

Gus leaned over with his elbows on the bar. "It all started back in the 1930s with a lady named Mildred Danforth. At one time, her father owned all of Danforth County. Mildred was a spinster — never got married. She lived with her father until he died. Then she inherited all his land. With no husband, it was just her and every stray animal she could take in — cats, dogs, horses, wild animals, you name it. Later she deeded most of the land for the town of Rainbow Valley to be built. But there was one thing she insisted on or there was no deal."

"What's that?"

"That the valley portion of the land stay untouched forever. Mildred died a few years back, but it's still against city ordinance to step foot on that part of the property. See, she believed there was something special about that valley."

"Special?"

Gus lowered his voice dramatically. "She believed it was a spirit world tied to earth where animals go after they pass on."

Kari smiled. "Seriously?"

"Oh, yeah. And once the animals arrive there, any disease they had is gone. They forget any abuse they might have suffered. Age is erased, too, and they're young again. And they stay in that little piece of paradise, just playing and eating to their hearts' content and sleeping in the grassy fields, until . . ."

Kari leaned forward, feeling like a preschool kid during story time.

"Until their human companions arrive," Gus said. "And when they do, they run toward each other and have a wonderful reunion."

For some reason, Kari's eyes teared up. She realized if the story was true, then someday she'd go to the valley and Boo would be there. He'd see her out of the corner of his eye. His head would pop up, and those tiny legs would carry him as fast as he could run toward her. She'd scoop him up and probably cry all over him.

"Then after they reunite," Gus said, "the most amazing thing happens."

"What?"

"A rainbow appears, stretching into the

clouds as far as the eye can see. All the animals a person has known and loved gather with him, and together they cross that Rainbow Bridge to heaven."

Kari tried to swallow the lump in her throat. No such luck. "That is *such* a cool story. So that's why there's so much animal stuff in Rainbow Valley?"

"Yup. Most people don't believe the legend, of course, but they can't argue with the money it brings into the town, particularly during the Festival of the Animals we have every fall. Tourists love the animal thing."

She smiled. "So do I."

"Got a pet?"

"A cairn terrier. He's mostly that, anyway. I think he's a few other things, too."

"Where are you from?"

"Houston."

Gus shook his head. "Houston's a hellhole. Crime. Pollution. Clogged-up freeways. Take my word for it, honey. *This* is the kind of place you need to be living."

Kari wasn't completely sure about that. She'd always been a big-city girl. But it did seem like a really nice place to visit.

"So where's the valley from here?" she asked.

"There's an overlook down Rainbow Way

a piece. That's the best place to get a good look at it. You can't go into the valley itself, of course. It's off-limits."

"How about you? Do you believe the legend?"

He shrugged. "Sure. Why not? Nobody knows what happens to us after we're gone. Or to our pets. I figure that's as good an explanation as any."

"But do you believe the Rainbow Bridge is in *this* valley?"

"I guess you're thinking, *Why there?*"

"Yeah, I guess so."

"Maybe a better question is, *Why* not *there*? Maybe Mildred knew something the rest of us didn't."

Good point.

"How about Marc?" Kari asked. "Does he believe the legend?"

"Marc doesn't believe much of anything he can't see with his own two eyes," Gus said. "But he knows tourists like it, and he likes tourists."

Kari rose from the stool. "Thanks so much for the sandwich. It was nice of you to think of me."

"It was Marc's doing. He told me you hadn't eaten much in the past few days, and he wanted to make sure I fixed you something."

For the first time Kari stopped to think about just how much Marc had done for her that night. Taken her into his house. Found her car. Retrieved her luggage. Taken her to a place to stay for the night. Helped her up the stairs. Unbuttoned her dress. Asked Gus to make sure she ate something. And he was going to make sure somebody took care of her car.

She remembered once how she'd asked Greg to pick her up at the airport, and he made the kind of face that said she was inconveniencing him. She'd wanted to shout, *I'm not asking for a ride to Montana!* But in the end, she'd just called a car service and had a nice chat with the driver all the way from Houston Intercontinental to her apartment. But now a man she didn't even know had gone out of his way to make sure she was safe and secure, and it gave her the kind of warm fuzzies she hadn't felt in a long time.

"It was no coincidence, you know," Gus said.

"What?" Kari asked.

"You could have gone off the road just about anywhere, but you ended up at Marc's place. That means the good Lord was looking out for you tonight."

Kari was so exhausted from dragging that god-awful wedding dress around for hours that the moment she crawled into that glorious king-sized bed with the pillow-top mattress and the softest linens on the planet, she went unconscious. When she woke the next morning, it was almost eleven o'clock.

She threw back the covers. *My car. I have to check on my car.*

Half an hour later, she was heading downstairs, this time wearing a tropical print dress and turquoise sandals, more clothes from the resort wear collection in her suitcases. Gus was at the front desk.

"Morning, Kari," Gus said.

"Good morning," she said with a smile. "Sorry I missed breakfast. I just couldn't drag myself out of that wonderful bed. Those linens are *amazing.*"

"Estelle would love to hear you say that. They cost more than the beds did, but she insisted."

Kari leaned over and gave Jasper a pat, and he gave her a happy pant in return. "I need to go to Rick's Automotive and check on my car. Can you tell me how to get there?"

Gus gave her directions, and she said, "After I see him, I think I'll grab some lunch at the cute little café I saw on the square." She started toward the door.

"Uh, Kari . . ."

She turned back. "Yes?"

"We've got a little problem," Gus said.

"What?"

"I ran your credit card this morning. It was declined."

Kari froze. "Declined? Why?"

"I don't know. All I know is that the bank declined the charge. Is there any reason you can think of why that might happen?"

"No. Of course not. There's no way —" She stopped short, putting her hand to her mouth. "Oh, wait a minute! Yes, there is. I charged a whole bunch of stuff for my honeymoon. I probably reached my credit limit." She walked over to the desk, pulling out her phone at the same time. "If you'll give me a minute, I can transfer some money from my checking account, pay the card off, and then you can charge my room to it."

A minute later, Kari had her account pulled up on her phone. She looked at the balance. Looked again. It couldn't be.

Her account had a zero balance?

No. That was impossible. There should

have been thousands in there, and yet there was nothing?

"Is something the matter?" Gus asked.

"No, everything's fine," Kari said, even as her stomach turned over with apprehension. "There's just a glitch of some kind. I'll give my bank a call."

But Kari had a horrible feeling that everything wasn't fine. She looked up her bank's telephone number and called them. She was shocked when the customer service rep told her what she already knew.

She had no money.

"All the funds were transferred out of that account," the man said.

"That's impossible," Kari said. "It's my account, and I didn't touch it. There must be some mistake."

"No, ma'am. There's no mistake. That account was emptied last night."

Kari felt a rush of anxiety. Identity theft?

She'd heard those commercials over and over about the dangers of somebody stealing her identity. She'd always thought maybe she should get one of those services that alerted people of any suspicious activity on their accounts, but like everything else, she'd always put it off.

Maybe that had been a big mistake.

"I'm afraid somebody's stolen my identity

and emptied my account," Kari said.

"I suppose that's possible, but in this case, I don't think so."

"Why not?"

"Because it was someone with your last name who transferred the funds."

"My name? What are you talking about?"

"His name is Stuart Worthington."

CHAPTER 4

Kari froze. Her father? Her *father* had emptied her bank account?

"Wait a minute," Kari said. "I never authorized my father to move that money."

"No authorization was necessary, ma'am. Stuart Worthington is a signer on the account."

For a moment, Kari was confused. She hadn't authorized that, either.

Then she remembered. It was an old bank account, the first one she'd opened as a teenager. At the time, her father had insisted on being a signer. She'd never taken his name off it. And now he'd cleaned it out. But *why*?

There are consequences, Kari. For everything you do — good and bad — there are consequences.

In a blinding rush, she saw what he'd done. If he made sure she was broke, she'd be forced to return to Houston, where he'd use his overbearing influence to try to get her to marry Greg. She knew her father was demanding and domineering and just a little bit underhanded, but she never imagined he'd do something like this.

She hung up the phone, her mind spinning. What was she supposed to do now?

"Kari?" Gus said. "Is something wrong?"

"Uh . . . no. It's just going to be a little while before they complete the transaction. I hope that's not a problem."

"No. No problem at all." Gus smiled. "Just let me know."

Kari sat down in the parlor and opened her wallet, at which time she discovered she had exactly $162.54 to her name. That probably didn't even come close to what she needed to get her car fixed. It would barely pay for the one night she'd stayed at Animal House that she already owed, which meant her plan to stay in Rainbow Valley until she decided what to do next had just been shot to hell.

"Well, look at that," Nina said, standing at the cash register and flipping through an Excel spreadsheet. "Two more cases of Sex Kitten out the door." She pushed a strand of her long, dark hair behind her ear and looked at Marc innocently. "Who would *ever* have thought it?"

"Damned stupid name for a wine," he muttered.

"Most of our names are damned stupid," his sister said. "But you can't argue with the bottom line." She tossed the spreadsheet aside. "So you got Angela settled in the dorm?"

"Yep."

"What's her roommate like?"

"If Ozzy Osbourne and Courtney Love had a kid . . . there you go."

Nina smiled. "So she's a little alternative? Tattoos? Piercings?"

"Yes and yes."

"Don't worry. I've met some pretty normal kids who look like that."

"Not around here, you haven't."

He went to the back room to retrieve a case of wine, while Nina rang up a customer buying an electric corkscrew. Sales had been good lately, and with the festival coming up soon after harvest, they were on track to have a record year. By the time he turned the management of this business over to Daniel, he was determined that it be in the best condition in its history.

"Oh. I almost forgot," Nina said, when Marc came back and the customer was out the door. "Tell me about the bride you undressed last night."

Marc nearly dropped the two bottles of wine he held. "Where the *hell* did you hear about that?"

"From Gus. He dropped in for a minute this morning."

Marc was going to kill Gus. One bullet. And then he was going to turn himself in, confess, and spend the rest of his life in a five-by-eight-foot cell in Huntsville knowing he'd done the world a favor.

He shoved the two bottles of wine onto a rack. "She had an accident on Highway 28 last night. She walked to the house and asked for help. I took her to Animal House to stay the night."

"Yeah. I heard that." She smiled. "And other stuff, too."

"She couldn't get out of her dress, somebody had to help her. That was all there was to it."

Nina gave him a sly smile. "I would have paid any amount of money to see the look on your face when she showed up at your door."

"She needed help. I helped her."

"Gus says she's really pretty."

"She's nuts. She ran away from her own wedding."

"He wasn't commenting on her mental

capabilities."

"Yeah? Well, being beautiful is worthless without a brain to go with it."

Nina laughed. "If any other man said that, I'd call him a liar. But not you."

"You know how I hate chaos, and that woman has it in spades."

"Oh, for God's sake, Marc. You're so damned uptight. You *need* a little chaos in your life. Angela is gone. You have that big ol' house all to yourself. Live a little, will you?"

"Daniel will be home soon."

"Like Daniel doesn't approve of having a good time?"

She was right. Unfortunately, everything that was wrong with his brother started with good times. He played things loose. Shot from the hip. That was Daniel, through and through, which was why his brother fit in really well with the dot-com crowd. They were a bunch of young, live-for-today people who never looked past the next deal. Daniel might be a millionaire right now, but it wouldn't surprise Marc if he eventually blew every penny.

He shoved more bottles onto the rack. "I intend to have plenty of good times. But not one of them is going to involve a crazy woman."

"She may have had a good reason for leaving her wedding. Did you ask her why she did it?"

"She decided she didn't want to get married."

"Besides the obvious."

"None of my business."

"Think about it, Marc. How many young, eligible women show up in this town? Might want to take notice when one does. You never know when the next one might happen along."

But Marc was leaving Rainbow Valley, which meant he had no intention of starting any kind of relationship with a woman, which meant Nina was barking up the wrong tree.

Marc's phone rang. He grabbed it, looked at the caller ID, then hit "answer."

"Hey, Rick. What's up?"

"I towed that Lexus in this morning, but the owner hasn't been by. Any idea where she might be?"

"No. She was supposed to come by your place first thing."

"Took me a while to get that thing out of the ditch. Ate most of my morning."

Marc sighed. "I'll check on her. See where she is and get her over there. What's the condition of the car?"

"Not good. There's body damage all along the right side. It'll cost thousands to fix, but I can do it. What I can't fix is the bent frame. She'll have to get an insurance adjuster out here to make it official, but trust me, that car is totaled."

Marc winced. He had no idea what Kari was going to do when she found out her car was a total loss, but that was her problem.

"I'll get her over there soon," he told Rick.

"Thanks. Appreciate it."

Marc hung up, letting out a breath of frustration. Where the hell *was* she?

He thought about just calling Animal House and talking to her, but Gus would have to put the call through, and the less he was in the middle of all this, the better. Instead, Marc decided he'd head over there just in case something was wrong. After all, he'd been the one to ask Rick to take the time and trouble to tow Kari's car in to his shop, so if there was a problem with her getting over there to get his estimate of the damage and pay him for his time, he needed to find out what it was. They would carry on a one-minute conversation. It would be business, nothing more. And then he'd be on his way.

"I have to go straighten this mess out," Marc muttered.

"So you *are* seeing her again?" Nina said.

"I owe it to Rick to make sure this gets taken care of. That's all."

Nina smiled. "Uh-huh."

Marc thought about biting back, but that only encouraged her to be even more of a pain in the ass. She was one of those believers in soul mates, one man for one woman, love everlasting. That was the kind of relationship she and her husband Curtis had. Ever since his death in an industrial accident a year ago, she hadn't so much as looked at another man. It was only now that she'd even begun to smile again. So at least if she was bugging Marc about his love life, she was back to being the sister he remembered.

Marc left the shop, walked the two blocks to Animal House, and trotted up the steps to the porch. He went inside and walked to the front desk. Gus was nowhere to be seen.

Marc turned and looked across the entryway. Glancing through the parlor door, he saw a woman sitting on the sofa. She had her head in her hands and her elbows resting on her knees. She wore a dress in a bold floral pattern that was so bright it just about blinded him, with tiny straps that went over her suntanned shoulders. His gaze traveled from the spot just above her knees where her dress stopped all the way down to her sparkly blue sandals and her toenails, which were painted an iridescent pink, admiring the most beautiful legs he'd seen in some time. But it was her hair that really caught his attention. It cascaded in wild waves over her shoulders like a copper waterfall. Nice. *Very* nice. Then she lifted her head.

Good God, it was Kari.

He couldn't have imagined her looking like *this* today when she'd looked like *that* last night. When she'd been muddy and wet, he would have had a hard time guessing her age. Looking at her now, though, he could see she was probably in her late twenties. *Too young for you,* he told himself, but he just couldn't seem to stop staring. So this was the woman who'd been hiding under dirt and rain and that ridiculous wedding dress?

Stop gawking. You're here for a reason.

But before he could go into the parlor to talk to her, he heard the door to the inn open behind him. He turned to see a man and a woman come inside. The woman was tall with blond hair pulled into a ponytail. She wore a pair of jeans and a tank top, and in her arms was a small dog that looked like a cross between some kind of terrier and a rag mop. The man wore slacks and a polo shirt, looking as if he'd been heading to a country club and lost his way.

Kari stood up. "Jill!"

The woman turned at the sound of Kari's voice. She let the dog down, and he ran to Kari. She scooped him up, and he licked every inch of her face, squirming like a worm on the end of a hook.

"Boo! Sweetie! I missed you so much!"

Then Jill came into the parlor, and Kari hugged them both at once. Marc had no idea who these people were, but her friends showing up could only be a good thing.

"I'm *so* glad to see you," Kari said. "But what are you doing here? I told you I'm not going back to Houston. Not yet."

"I know, but . . ."

"But what?"

"Well . . ."

"What?"

"Greg came with me."

The man walked into the parlor, and Kari's mouth fell open. "Jill! I told you not to tell him where I was!"

"I'm sorry," Jill said. "But I thought you two needed to talk."

"I don't *want* to talk!"

"No," Greg said as he walked toward Kari. "We definitely need to talk."

Kari hugged her dog closer and refused to

look at him. He stopped in front of her.

"Kari, I love you," he said. "Don't you know that?"

Kari was silent.

"Do you know how I felt when I realized you were gone?"

"I'm sorry about that," she said. "I know it wasn't the best way to deal with it, but —"

"Never mind. Forget it. All I want is for us to be married."

"I don't think that's a good idea."

"You thought it was a good idea when I gave you the ring," Greg said, his voice edging into impatience. "And when we had our engagement party. And during our rehearsal dinner. So where along the way did it stop being a good idea?"

"I'm sorry. I really am. But . . ." She exhaled. "Think about it, Greg. Are we really right for each other?"

"Yes. Of course. We're very compatible. The minister who married us said so, didn't he?"

Marc could tell Kari wasn't convinced, and Greg clearly wasn't happy that she didn't share his point of view.

"If you're worried about being embarrassed when you come back," Greg said, "it won't be a problem. Your father and I covered for you."

"Covered for me?"

"We told everybody you were sick."

Kari drew back. "You lied?"

"Would you rather we'd have told the truth?"

"The truth? Do you even know what the truth is?"

"You got cold feet. A lot of brides do."

"But *why* did I get cold feet? Did you stop to think about that?"

"It doesn't matter," Greg said. "We're getting married, and that's the end of it."

Even at the distance Marc was away from them, he sensed the guy's undercurrent of anger. Patient on the surface, pissed underneath. A tiny shiver skated between Marc's shoulders, telling him trouble was brewing. He stood up tall, watching intently as the guy inched closer to Kari.

"So here's what's going to happen," Greg went on. "You and I are getting in my car, and we're driving back to Houston. Then we're going to the justice of the peace. He's a friend of your father's and very discreet. We're getting married. Then we're going to send out announcements to everyone who showed up to the wedding that day, letting them know we're man and wife. And then we're going to pray your father overlooks the humiliation you've put him through."

Kari swallowed so hard Marc could see her throat move at twenty paces. "I don't care how my father feels about it."

"Really?" Greg snapped. "You don't care? Well, you'd *better* care. See how far you get when you don't have your daddy to give you a job!"

"I don't need that job," Kari said, her voice quivering. "I'll get another one."

"Right. This economy stinks. If people with actual skills can't get a job, what hope do you have?"

Kari looked away, stroking her dog nervously.

"He pays you about twice what you're worth at a job that could be cut from that company tomorrow. Try to find another employer who'll do that."

Kari was silent. Then Greg got a calculating look on his face. "Tell me, Kari. Have you checked your bank account lately?"

She drew back. "You *know* about that?"

"Yes," he said smugly. "I know about it. Still think you're staying here?"

"I can't talk to you anymore right now."

Kari started to walk away. Greg grabbed her arm and pulled her back around. "You're not going anywhere."

She tried to pull her arm away. "Greg,

please! Let me *go!*"

He tightened his grip and gave her arm a hard jerk. "Stop all this nonsense and get in the damned car!"

An alarm bell went off inside Marc's head. Words were one thing. A physical threat was another. He didn't tolerate that kind of behavior from a man toward a woman. *Ever.*

He strode into the parlor. "Hey! What do you think you're doing?"

Greg froze at the sound of Marc's voice, and Kari's eyes went huge with surprise. Greg gradually let go of her arm. "Who the hell are you?"

"Forget the introductions. Just keep your hands off her."

"This is none of your business."

"You grab her arm like that again, and I'm *making* it my business." He turned to Kari. "Do you want to go with this guy?"

She looked at Greg, then at Jill, swallowing hard once again. "No. I don't."

Marc turned to Greg. "Beat it."

Shock spilled over Greg's face. "*Excuse* me?"

"You heard me. Get out of here."

Greg turned to Kari. "Who the hell *is* this guy?"

"He's a friend of mine," Kari said.

"You have friends in this dinky town?"

"Yes," Marc snapped. "She has friends in this dinky town. And if you touch her again, this *friend* is going to be all over you."

"Yeah? What are you going to do?"

"You know the easiest way to find out?"

"How?"

"Grab her arm one more time."

Greg turned to Kari. "Are you going to let him talk to me like that?"

Kari flicked her gaze to Marc. "Yeah," she told Greg. "I think maybe I am."

Greg's expression turned ugly. "Gimme the ring."

"What?"

"The ring! Give it to me!"

With an expression of disgust, Kari yanked the ring off her finger and slapped it into his palm.

"Sooner or later you're going to be sorry about this," Greg said. "But then it's going to be too damned late!"

He spun around and stormed out of the parlor. Jill watched him leave, then turned to Kari. "What the *hell* do you think you're doing?"

Kari drew back with surprise. "What am *I* doing?"

"How can you turn your back on Greg? *How?* He's smart, he's handsome —"

"Didn't you hear the things he said to me?"

"Of course he said those things! He's angry! You would be, too, if he'd humiliated you in front of three hundred people!"

"I'm sorry about that," Kari said. "I really am. But I just didn't see another way out. If I had stayed, everybody would have talked me into getting married. But I can't marry Greg. He doesn't love me."

"Doesn't love you? He gave you that big, beautiful diamond ring, didn't he?"

Kari was silent.

"And you gave it back to him. I can't *believe* you gave it back to him! And he bought that gorgeous condo for you, too. What does that tell you?"

"He didn't ask me how I felt about it. He just bought it."

"Well, I sure wouldn't mind if a guy surprised me with an incredible place like that."

Kari winced. "I'm not really all that crazy about it."

"Not crazy about it?" Jill threw her hands up. "Have you completely lost your *mind*?"

"All that stuff . . ." Kari exhaled. "It just doesn't matter to me."

"I know you think it doesn't," Jill said, her voice low and angry, "but that's because

109

you've always had money. You grew up in that huge house. You have a father who's a gazillionaire. The whole time we were in college, I had to scrimp and work two jobs, while you had so much money to throw around you could barely carry it all!"

Kari looked stunned. "Is that what you've thought all this time?"

"I didn't care so much back then, because that was just where you came from, you know? But now . . . God, Kari! I'd *kill* to have a man like Greg, and you just walked away from him!"

"I know it seems crazy," Kari said. "I know that. But I was sitting there in that wedding dress, thinking about marrying him, and it just seemed so . . . so *wrong.*"

"But it's *not* wrong. You were just nervous. A lot of brides get nervous!"

Kari closed her eyes, shaking her head slowly.

"You're going to regret this," Jill said. "If you don't make up with him and go back to Houston —"

"I can't!"

Jill's expression hardened. "You can and you should."

Tears filled Kari's eyes. "I can't believe you're talking to me like this. Haven't we always stuck up for each other?"

"Yes! But you've never done anything this stupid before!"

Kari looked positively stricken by Jill's words. "Do you really think it's stupid for me to refuse to marry a man I don't love?"

"For God's sake, Kari! *Learn* to love him!"

"Should I have to do that? *Learn* to love the man I'm going to marry?"

"Fine! Stay here. Ruin your whole life. I hope you *never* come back to Houston!"

With that, Jill spun around and left the inn, her footsteps echoing against the hardwood floor of the entryway. Marc heard the door open, then slam behind her. Kari visibly shuddered at the noise, hugging that hairy beast even closer to her chest and looking distressed. A tear coursed down her cheek, and she swept it away with the back of her hand.

"Don't cry," Marc said. "That asshole's not worth it."

"It's not Greg," Kari said, sniffing. "It's Jill. I thought we were friends."

"Friends don't betray you like that."

"I know. I just thought she would understand."

"Why did you get engaged to that guy in the first place?"

She shrugged weakly. "Everybody thought it was such a good idea. Particularly my

111

father. Greg works at his company, and my father thinks he's wonderful. Mostly because they're just alike."

"He seems hell-bent on marrying you, but he doesn't seem to give a damn about how you feel about it."

Kari was silent.

"I'm just stabbing in the dark here, but does your father happen to have money?"

She paused. "Yeah."

"A lot of it?"

"More than you can possibly imagine."

Marc was beginning to get the picture here, and it wasn't pretty. The asshole wanted to marry her for her money. Maybe he even saw himself at the helm of the old man's company someday, so he gave her a ring and conned her into an engagement. Her father seemed to think it was an excellent match, so the pressure was coming from two sides. And her friend Jill wasn't a friend at all if she thought marrying that guy was a good idea. It appeared everybody in Kari's life pushed her around like a chess piece, right up to the day the pawn finally revolted.

"Thank you for sticking up for me," Kari said. "That was nice."

"It wasn't nice. Nice had nothing to do with it. It was just a logical reaction to bad behavior. You have to call a halt to that kind of crap the instant it begins, or you'll have more trouble than you know what to do with."

"Okay, then," she said. "How about if I thank you for being logical?"

Marc didn't know what to say to that. He only knew it was time for Kari to do whatever she had to do to get out of Rainbow Valley and on the road back to Houston. Surely she had other friends who could help her. She could return to her old life minus a certain asshole, and Marc would finally be free of the drama he hadn't asked for in the first place.

"Rick called me this morning," he said. "He said he pulled your car out of the ditch, but that you hadn't come by yet. I thought you were going over there first thing."

"I was," Kari said. "But I slept late. And then when I came down here . . ." Her voice faded away.

"Look, I just came to tell you that you need to go see Rick. I asked him to haul your car in, so he needs to be paid for his time."

"Yes," she said on a sigh. "I know."

"Just so you know, he thinks the car is a total loss."

"What?"

113

"He said the frame is bent, which means it would cost more to fix the car than it's worth."

"Oh, no." Kari sat down, her body going limp, then dropped her head to her hands. The rag mop scurried in a circle on the sofa, then jumped down to sniff a potted plant.

"Your insurance should reimburse you for the current value of the car," Marc said. "Just call your insurance company, and it'll all be taken care of."

"I can't do that."

"Why not?"

"Because I don't own the car. Not exactly."

"What do you mean?"

Kari sighed. "It's in my father's name."

Marc was confused. "Why?"

"Because he gave it to me as a gift a few years ago."

"And he never put it in your name?"

"That's right."

"So call your father and get him to talk to the insurance company. One way or another, you'll get a check."

Kari looked away. "I'm afraid there's a *teensy* little problem with that."

Marc felt a glimmer of apprehension. The last time he heard the word *problem,* he got stuck unbuttoning a wedding dress. Unfor-

114

tunately, she was looking up at him with those amazing green eyes, so he couldn't stop himself from asking, "What problem?"

And then she told him, and Marc knew for sure that the chaos had only begun.

"Are you *serious*?" he said. "Your own father cleaned out your bank account?"

"It looks that way. He's a signer on the account. He can do that."

"Why is he a signer on your account?"

"It's an old account from when I was in high school."

"And you never took him off it?"

"It was never a problem before. And if he emptied my bank account, you can bet there's no way he'll turn in a claim for the damage on the car and then hand the check over to me. He's trying to force me to come back to Houston. He thinks if I'm broke, that's what I'll do."

"My God," Marc said. "Is there a part of your life your father *doesn't* control?"

Kari was silent.

"You said your only credit card is charged to the hilt. Is that right?"

"Uh-huh."

"Do you have any cash?"

"Not much."

"Can you pay your hotel bill?"

"Barely."

"You can't even feed yourself, can you?"

She sighed. "Not for long."

"And now I've chased away the only person who could get you back to Houston?" he said, his voice escalating. "Why didn't you *stop* me?"

"You told me I shouldn't go with him!"

She was right. That was exactly what he'd said. And it was because nothing made him angrier than to see a man treat a woman that way. *Nothing.* So what else could he have done?

Kari stood there looking lost. The goofy little rag mop whimpered, then licked her chin. "Do you really think I should have gone with him?" she said quietly.

Marc twisted his mouth with irritation. "No," he muttered. "No! Of course not. That guy's an asshole. You shouldn't get within ten miles of him. But that means you have a big problem."

"I know."

"So what's your plan now?"

"Well, I was thinking about that before Greg and Jill showed up."

"And?"

"Nothing came to me."

Then she was silent. At least her mouth was silent. Those gorgeous green eyes wouldn't shut up. And he couldn't turn her

116

away any more than he could ignore a kitten in a snowstorm. Or, more accurately, a dirty bride in a rainstorm.

"Did Gus give you something to eat last night?" he asked her.

"Yeah."

"You said you slept in. Did you miss breakfast?"

She sighed. "Yeah."

"Come with me."

"Where are we going?" she said.

"To Rosie's for lunch. I'll buy. But by the time we finish eating, you're going to have a plan. And then you're going to put it into action."

CHAPTER 5

When Marc stepped into that parlor and told Greg to take a hike, he'd seemed like a superhero to Kari. Showing up out of nowhere, standing there with those powerful arms folded over that big, broad chest, skewering Greg with that intense warning expression — yep. Superhero. *Her* superhero. And his self-assurance had oozed over and filled her with the kind of confidence she couldn't have imagined feeling only seconds before.

But now reality was setting in. Her superhero sat across from her in a booth at Rosie's Café, looking at her as if there were only certain things he used his superpowers for. Solving her problems in a way *she* liked didn't appear to be one of them.

"No way," she said as she swallowed yet one more french fry from heaven. "I'm *not* taking a bus back to Houston."

"What else are you going to do? You have

no money, no job, no car, and no place to stay. Tell your father to give you your money back. Then get a real job instead of a throwaway one at his company so he doesn't control you anymore. Tell him you're making your own decisions from now on. And if the asshole comes within ten yards of you again, get a restraining order. There. You have a plan."

"You make it sound so easy."

"It is. If that's what you want, just say it. People will get on board."

"Sure. They'll get on board with *you.*" She shrugged weakly. "Greg may have been right about me getting another job."

"But you have a degree, right?"

"In English literature."

Marc sighed. "Yeah, there's not a big market for people who quote Shakespeare. What was your job at your father's company?"

"I was a marketing specialist."

"What exactly did you do?"

"I assembled consumer opinion data by compiling, formatting, and summarizing graphs and presentations."

"So you made copies and stapled them together?"

Kari glared at him.

"You still have expenses back in Houston.

What about your rent?"

"I'm living with my father right now."

Marc screwed up his face. "Seriously?"

"My apartment lease was up. I moved into my father's house for a few weeks until the wedding so I wouldn't have to sign a new lease. The house is so big he barely even knew I was there. Then after I got married, I was going to move into Greg's condo with him."

"So you have no apartment rent to pay right now."

"That's right."

"Good. That means you can get something cheaper than you had before. That'll go with your new job that I'm guessing won't pay as much."

Kari squeezed her eyes closed. "This is a lot to think about."

"Yeah, but the faster you deal with it, the faster you can get on with your life."

"They're still going to try to get me to marry Greg."

"Where's your backbone? Are you telling me you might actually marry the asshole after all?"

"No!"

"Are you sure about that?"

"Yes. Of course I'm sure!"

"Because if you're that easily swayed,

maybe you never should have left. Maybe you need to be married to a man who'll tell you what to do."

"I do not!"

"I'm not seeing much evidence of that."

"Hey! I left my own wedding, didn't I?"

"Leaving was easy. Going back and taking care of yourself. *That's* what's hard."

Kari pursed her lips, hating the way that sounded, mostly because he was right. But she knew in her heart it was a mistake to return to Houston. No matter what Marc said about people getting on board with what she wanted if only she spoke up, she was still afraid she'd fall back into her same patterns all over again where she let everybody else's opinion matter except hers.

"And do you know how you make sure you succeed?" Marc went on. "You burn your boats. What that means is —"

"I know what it means. Alexander the Great. The Persian War. After they landed on the enemy's shore, he burned their own boats so they couldn't fall back. They *had* to win the battle."

"I thought you were a lit major."

"Like nobody ever wrote a book about that?"

"As I was saying," Marc said, "if you burn your boats, you have no choice but to fight to the death."

"Oh, that's uplifting."

"Go home. Get face-to-face with your father. Quit your job if he hasn't fired you already. *Burn your boats.* That way you have no choice but to succeed on your own."

Rosie swept back by their table again. She was a forty-something woman with short brown hair and a pot of coffee in her hand. According to Marc, she wasn't a waitress. She owned the place. And she looked even more frazzled than she had the last time she stopped by their table.

"Can I get you guys anything else?" Rosie said.

Marc looked at Kari. She shook her head. The double cheeseburger she'd just inhaled would probably hold her for a week.

"We're good," Marc said.

Rosie turned to Boo. "How about you, sweetie?"

When Boo's ears perked up, she reached into the pocket of her apron and pulled out a dog biscuit. She laid it on the vinyl seat beside him, and he snapped it up. That was the third one she'd given him from what she called Rosie's Bottomless Basket of Doggy Biscuits.

"You're getting slammed today," Marc said.

"Two tourist buses," Rosie said. "Good for business, but Jolene quit to stay home with her baby."

"Hard to find good help?"

"First I have to get a few applicants. All I've had was one woman who wanted to bring her three children to work with her. Three dogs I'd consider. Three kids — no."

"I hear you. Harvest is coming up soon. I never can get enough good help."

"If I hear of somebody who wants to pick grapes, I'll send them your way."

As Rosie hurried away, Kari said, "I couldn't take the bus even if I wanted to. After I pay Gus for the room, I probably won't even have enough money left for bus fare."

Marc reached into his wallet, pulled out two twenties, and tossed them on the table. "That'll cover it."

She flashed him a tiny smile. "Gee, you must really want to get rid of me."

"It's just what needs to happen. You'll be glad you went back." He paused. "Assuming you stand up for yourself."

That hit Kari harder than she would have imagined. Marc clearly had no faith in her ability to stand up to anyone. In fact, she'd been nothing but a gigantic pain in the ass to him since the moment she arrived, and she was pretty sure the only thing he wanted to see of her was her face in the window of that bus as she headed out of town. Just thinking about that made her miserable, and tears burned behind her eyes.

No. Don't cry. Damn it, don't you cry!

"I'm going to the ladies' room," she said. "Will you please watch Boo?"

Before he could say anything, she scooted out of the booth and hurried toward the ladies' room, where she grabbed a paper towel and dabbed her eyes. All her life her father had treated her as if she was at best a helpless relative he had to support, and at worst a rock around his neck he wished he could rid himself of forever. But right now something made her feel even worse. She sensed that Marc felt exactly the same way about her that her father did. And for some reason she didn't fully understand, his respect was something she wanted to have.

Kari heard the door open. She turned to see Rosie come into the ladies' room. She saw Kari's face and stopped short. "What's wrong?"

"Nothing," Kari said.

"Yeah? In my experience, nobody cries for nothing."

Kari almost said, *My whole life sucks,* but she swallowed the words before they could pop out. She'd just listened to Marc tell her it was time to take control of her own life. Whining didn't seem to fit into that new paradigm he was trying to acquaint her with.

"I'm just having a little setback," Kari said.

"Sorry to hear that, sweetie. I take it you're a friend of Marc's?"

"Yes," she said, because what was a friend, anyway? Somebody you went to when you were having a problem and needed help? He'd given her plenty of help last night, hadn't he?

"Don't worry, then," Rosie said. "He'll help you out, whatever your problem is. He's good like that."

But he wants me to go back to Houston, and I'm scared to!

As Rosie headed to one of the stalls, Kari stood helplessly by the sink, knowing she should go back out to the restaurant. But the moment she did, Marc would pay the bill, shove the money for bus fare at her again, and tell her to hit the road.

A minute later, the toilet flushed, and Rosie came out of the stall. She went to the sink to wash her hands. Kari washed her hands, too, so she wouldn't look as if she was loitering in the bathroom, even though she was. After they both dried their hands, Rosie headed for the door, and Kari wanted to cry all over again. She obviously couldn't stay in Rainbow Valley with no place to live, no job . . .

Wait a minute. *Job?*

"Rosie?"

Rosie turned back. "Yeah?"

Kari's mind was spinning in a direction she wasn't sure was the right one, but she followed it, anyway.

"Didn't you say you have a job opening for a waitress?"

"Yes."

"That's part of my setback," she said. "I need a job."

Rosie walked a few steps back toward her. "Yeah? Have you ever waited tables?"

"Well . . . no."

"Kids?"

"Just the four-legged kind."

"Do you live in Rainbow Valley?"

"I'm relocating. That's why I need a job. Would you consider hiring somebody with no experience?"

"Most of the time I have to. Experienced waitresses are tough to find. But it's hard work." Rosie looked her up and down. "Sure you don't mind getting your hands dirty?"

She started to tell Rosie she'd been way dirtier than this as recently as last night.

Instead she said, "Nope. I don't mind at all."

"The hours suck. Morning shift starts at six a.m., and the evening shift goes until eight at night."

"That's fine."

Rosie looked unsure for a moment, then nodded. "Okay. If you're a friend of Marc's, you're hired. But only on a trial basis. That's the way I do it with everybody who goes to work for me. Most people don't realize just how hard waiting tables is, and most of them wash out."

"I won't."

"Don't hold your breath on that, sweetie. Let's see how it goes first. Once you and Marc are through with lunch, come see me and you can fill out the paperwork. What's your name?"

"Kari Worthington. Can you tell me what the job pays?"

Rosie quoted an impossibly small hourly rate, and Kari's heart sank.

"But I have waitresses who make decent livings from tips alone," Rosie said. "It's all about the hustle."

With that, she left the bathroom, and Kari turned and looked at herself in the mirror. Okay. How hard could it be to wait tables? All you had to do was ask people what they wanted and then go get it for them. No, it didn't pay much, but right now she needed just enough to keep body and soul together until she could figure out what to do next.

Marc sat at the table glaring at the rag mop, and the rag mop stared back. Then slowly the dog turned to look at Kari's plate. He'd already grabbed one french fry when Marc wasn't looking. No way was *that* happening again.

"Don't you even *think* about it," Marc said.

He inched closer.

"Hey."

Closer still.

"Hey!"

The dog recoiled, retreating to the corner of the booth, where he turned to look back at Marc. Marc sighed. Of course Kari would have a dog as undisciplined as she was.

"Hey, Marc. I didn't know you were coming here for lunch."

He turned around to see Nina approaching the table. *Oh, crap.*

She slid into the booth across from Marc, only to stop short when she saw the rag mop. "Oops . . . what's this?"

"A dog."

"I wasn't asking for species identification.

Whose dog is it?"

Marc didn't want to go there. He just didn't. "Kari's."

"Kari? Who's Kari?"

"I'm Kari."

Marc winced at the sound of her voice. He gave her a quick glance, then turned back to Nina, who already had a calculating look on her face. Oh, this was going to be just *great*.

"Ah," Nina said. "You wouldn't happen to be the woman who had an accident last night while you were wearing a bridal gown, would you?"

Kari smiled. "Yeah. That's me."

Nina held out her hand. "Hi. I'm Nina. Marc's sister."

Kari shook her hand. "Kari Worthington."

"And who's this?" Nina said, scratching Boo behind the ears.

"His name's Boo."

"Well, hello there, Boo. Aren't you a sweet puppy?" Then Nina turned to Marc. "Hey!"

"What?"

"Will you shove over and let Kari sit down?"

"She was sitting over there."

"I can sit over here now," Kari said. "I'm finished with lunch."

Marc let out a breath and moved over.

Kari squeezed into the booth beside him. Even in a place filled with the scents of Texas home cooking, he could smell her. He didn't know if it was soap or shampoo or perfume, but it was as if somebody had stuck a bouquet of flowers in the seat next to him. He wasn't a flowery kind of guy, but that girlie smell got his attention every time, especially when it was radiating from a body like Kari's.

And she's nothing but drama, drama, drama, he reminded himself. *You don't need that.*

"Nina? Who's at the shop?"

"Rupert got there early. He scheduled a special wine tasting with one of the tour groups coming through today. Did you see the buses?"

"Yeah. I saw the buses."

"So . . . ," Nina said, "you two are having lunch?"

She put a great big question mark on the end of her sentence, asking for more information, but no information was ever enough for his sister, so why even go there?

"We were just leaving," Marc said. "Kari has a bus to catch."

"No bus," Kari said, smiling brightly. "Change of plan."

"What change of plan?" Marc asked.

"I'm not going back to Houston. I have a

130

job now."

Marc stared at her dumbly. "You what?"

"I have a job. I'm working here. Rosie hired me."

"When did that happen?"

"In the ladies' room."

"Let me get this straight. You went into the ladies' room and came out with a *job?*"

"That's right."

"Have you ever waited tables before?"

"No, but I've eaten in a lot of restaurants."

"Rosie!" Marc called out.

Rosie turned at the sound of his voice, then came to their booth.

"Did you just give her a job?" Marc asked.

"Yeah."

"Just like that?"

"I need a waitress, and nobody else is beating down my door for the job."

"Did you check her references?"

"References don't mean squat. People fake them. And even if they're real, all an employer will give you are the dates of employment, and that's about it. I'd rather just try somebody out on the job. Besides, I figured if she was with you, then she's okay."

Great. Just for once, Marc wished he had a crappy reputation.

Rosie turned to Nina. "What can I get you?"

"A BLT and sweet tea."

"Coming up."

As Rosie walked away, Marc said, "The job can't pay anything."

"Rosie said I could do pretty well with tips if I hustle," Kari said.

"Do you have any idea how hard it is to be a waitress? Particularly on the weekends when the tourists pack this place out?"

"Hey! You gave me a big lecture about how I have no backbone and I can't take care of myself. So now that I'm trying to take care of myself, you're giving me a hard time. So which is it?"

"You gave her a lecture?" Nina said.

"Advice," Marc snapped. "*Good* advice." He turned back to Kari. "Okay, so you've got a job. Now what?"

"What do you mean?"

"Where are you going to live?"

"I'll rent an apartment."

"With what? You have no money."

"You have no money?" Nina said.

"Long story," Kari said.

Actually, it wasn't long at all. Her father was as big an asshole as her ex-fiancé, but the last thing Marc wanted to do was launch into *that*.

Kari's smile faded. "Do you suppose there are any landlords in town who might be willing to postpone a deposit?"

"What kind of businesspeople would they be if they did?" Marc said. "Then there's your first and last month's rent. And everybody might love animals around here, but that doesn't stop them from collecting a pet deposit."

Her smile disappeared altogether. "Oh. Yeah. I guess you're right."

Silence.

Boo put his paws on the table and whimpered. Nina handed him over to Kari, who snuggled him against her chest and looked forlorn.

"Well, there *is* another option," Nina said.

"What?" Marc said.

"Let her stay in the cottage at the vineyard."

Marc came to attention, shaking his head. "No. We don't rent the cottage."

"I didn't say you should rent it to her. Just let her stay there until she gets a deposit together for an apartment." She looked at Kari. "It's not much. Just a tiny studio. There's not even a bedroom. Just a pull-out sofa. A microwave, a sink, and a small fridge. Bathroom with a shower."

"Sounds perfect," Kari said, then turned to look at Marc with a hopeful expression. He could have shot Nina.

"No," Marc said. "You're not staying there."

"Just until she gets on her feet," Nina said.

"I don't want anyone staying in the cottage right now."

"Oh, come on, Marc," Nina said. "You've let other people stay there over the years."

"I said no." Marc turned to Kari, nodding at his phone. "I checked the schedule. The bus leaves in less than an hour. If you'll let Gus know you're heading to the bus station, he'll arrange for somebody to pick up your luggage." He grabbed up the two twenties and held them out to her.

Kari glanced at Nina, who looked at Marc with an irritated frown, then turned away. Finally Kari took the money, her face falling into misery all over again. "Thank you for everything you've done for me," she said to Marc. "I don't blame you for not being able to do more."

He should have been happy about that. So why did it make him feel like crap?

"Will you give me your address so I can return the money to you later?" she asked.

"No need."

"No. I insist."

"Cordero Vineyards, Rainbow Valley, Texas. It'll get there."

Kari nodded, looking even more forlorn

134

than before, and her sad, defeated expression almost made him change his mind. But he couldn't give in. How was she supposed to stand up to her father if she didn't return to Houston? He had to hold his ground. No matter what Nina thought, it was best for all concerned. It *was*.

Wasn't it?

"Well, then," Kari said. "I guess I'd better be going." She turned to Nina. "It was nice to meet you."

"Nice to meet you, too," Nina said. "You be careful now."

Kari rose from the booth, put her purse over her shoulder, and she and her disorderly little dog went up to speak to Rosie. Then Marc watched out of the corner of his eye as she left the café and disappeared down the street.

Nina sat back and eyed Marc carefully. "That wasn't like you."

"What do you mean?"

"You've let all kinds of people stay in that cottage over the years. Last fall after the wildfire, you let that man and his wife who lost their house stay there for a whole month. So why not let Kari stay? Is it really that big a deal?"

"I don't even know her."

"You didn't know that man and his wife,

either, yet you stepped right up to help them."

"They had a problem through no fault of their own. Kari left her fiancé at the altar and ran. If she'd confronted her problem instead of running, she wouldn't have ended up here."

"Not everybody is like you, Marc. Confrontation is hard for some people. Kari's as sweet as she can be. Why won't you help her?"

"You offered her the cottage without even asking me," Marc said.

"I had no idea it would be a problem."

"And then I was the one who had to say no."

"So say yes instead."

"Not this time."

"Marc —"

"Will you knock it *off*?"

Nina clamped her mouth shut, but he could tell she still had plenty to say.

Marc hated being the bad guy. He hated Nina insisting on something he *did not want*. And he hated feeling as if he was doing something wrong when, at this point in his life, nothing was more right.

So why did he feel like the biggest jerk alive?

"I know what this is about," Nina said.

"Oh, you do?"

"You think your life is going to be just rosy the day you get to hop on that motorcycle and head down the highway, and you're already resenting anybody you think might get in the way of that."

Yes, by God, that was exactly right. It was nice that Nina was aware of how he felt. What wasn't nice was her tone that said he had no right to feel that way.

"But here's what you don't know," Nina said. "When the time comes, you won't be able to do it."

"That's where you're wrong. I *am* getting on that motorcycle. I *am* heading down the highway. And everybody else can take care of themselves for a switch."

Without another word, Marc slid out of the booth, paid the check, then left the café. He went to where his truck was parked in front of the wineshop and got in, telling himself he'd done the right thing. Kari was doing what she needed to do. She was going back to face the music. Then maybe she'd finally get her life in order. Yes, it was a very good thing.

He started his truck and headed back down Rainbow Way toward the highway. He'd already spent too much time in town today when there were a hundred things he needed to do back at the vineyard. But as he drove, his mind began to wander.

Who would pick Kari up at the bus station in Houston? Her friend, Jill, who thought she and the asshole were just *perfect* for each other? Her father who ran her life like a prison guard? The asshole himself who wanted her name on a marriage license so he could enjoy that nice big inheritance coming Kari's way when her father finally kicked the bucket?

Marc shook away those thoughts. It didn't matter. She needed to face up to the challenge. Sometimes people needed to have their backs shoved against the wall until they came out fighting.

But would Kari come out fighting? Or would she give in and be stuck in a marriage with a man who saw her only as a means to a very lucrative end?

She needs your help.

No. Go home. She's not your problem.

But if she goes to Houston, she may be miserable for the rest of her life.

Butt out. She has to learn to stand on her own two feet.

He slowed his truck and pulled to the side of the road. He put it in park and gripped the steering wheel, listening to the voices parry inside his head until he was so confused he didn't know which way to turn, and confusion was a state he didn't like dealing with.

Shake it off. You don't even know her. And you're certainly not responsible for her.

Finally he put his truck in gear, hit the gas, and headed for home.

CHAPTER 6

An hour later, Marc was trimming the bushes that surrounded his back deck when his phone rang. He pulled it from his pocket and was happy to see Angela's name on the caller ID.

"Angela! Hey! How are things going?"

"Great! I'm having a blast."

Oh, thank God. He loved hearing that happy lilt in her voice. "No! School is serious business. Why am I paying all that tuition if you're not miserable? I want my money's worth."

Angela laughed. "Too late. I love this place. How are things at home?"

Marc thought about Kari. No need to bring *that* up. "It's only been a day, so . . . just about the same as when you left."

"Yeah, I guess nothing much has had time to happen, huh?"

If only she knew. "How are you and your roommate getting along?"

140

"Great. We've got the room all set up. And we found out we have two of the big freshmen lecture classes together."

Then Marc heard something in the background he didn't like. "Is that a boy's voice I hear?"

"Yeah. It's a friend of Kim's. He brought his roommate along. We're going to a movie this afternoon. Classes don't start for a few days, so we thought we'd play around a little."

Marc cringed. He remembered Kim and her tattoos and piercings and that hair that looked as if she'd dyed it jet-black and then stuck her finger in an electrical socket. What were the chances that she hung out with guys who were drug-free virgins heading for the dean's list?

"Sorry, Dad. I just called to say hi, but I gotta go now. Everybody's waiting for me."

No. He wanted to keep talking. To what end, he didn't know. He hated this. As soon as the connection was gone, she could be anywhere. He wouldn't know if bad things happened, and the worry would begin all over again.

"Dad? Are you there?"

"Okay," he said. "I'll talk to you soon."

Marc hit the button to disconnect the call and stuck his phone back into his pocket.

So this was what it was going to be like for the next four years? Short little phone calls that made him worry until she called again for another two-minute conversation that made him worry about something else?

Then all at once he heard a loud noise coming from the front of the house. An engine? If so, it was a very *large* engine. Brandy leaped up and began to bark. Marc tossed the hedge clippers aside and came around the side of the house, and he couldn't believe what he saw.

A bus had pulled into the circle drive in front of his house. The driver was closing the luggage compartment and climbing back onto the bus. A woman stood beside the bus next to a crapload of massive suitcases wearing a dress that looked like a tropical explosion.

The bus began to pull away. Marc took off running, shouting at the driver, but the bus never slowed down. As it disappeared up his driveway, he stopped and stood there helplessly, then slowly turned to look at Kari.

She looked small in the midst of those huge suitcases, holding that french-fry-stealing rag mop. The dog yapped once, then looked at him quizzically. Brandy tilted her head, clearly unsure what to think about a dog that looked like one of her fuzzy chew toys.

He walked back and stopped in front of Kari. He rubbed his hand across his face, then let out a long, weary breath. "Okay. How did you get that bus driver to bring you here?"

"The route passes right by the vineyard. I just asked him if he'd mind dropping me off."

"Are you nuts?"

"Not completely. You told me to do it."

"What are you talking about? I didn't tell you —"

"Yes, you did. You told me to burn my boats."

"What?"

"Now that the bus is gone, I have to convince you to let me stay in your cottage, or I have no place to sleep tonight. It's not exactly a fight to the death, but if I have to drag all that luggage back to town, it'll probably kill me. So I guess it's pretty much the same thing."

Marc couldn't believe it. How had she managed to use his own words so thoroughly and completely against him?

"I meant for you to do all that boat burning in Houston," he said.

"I picked a different battle."

"What if I put you in my truck and take you back to town?"

"You could do that," Kari said. "But I'll be knocking on your door again within the hour. I know that staying here is a lot to ask, but according to your sister, it's not unprecedented. So what's it going to be? Are you going to let me stay in your cottage, or do I sleep on your front lawn?"

Good God. This woman was stuck to him like a barnacle on the side of a ship.

"I don't get you," Marc said. "You want to stay in a town you know nothing about. Work in a place you know nothing about. At a job you have no experience for."

She smiled. "It's an adventure. I like adventures."

"Yeah," Marc said wearily. "I gathered that. And you want to stay here when you don't know a damned thing about *me*."

"Actually, I know a lot about you."

"You met me last night. How could you possibly —"

"Trust me. I know. The important stuff, anyway. Everybody I talk to says you're a good guy. Gus. Rosie. And you didn't let Greg push me around." A light breeze picked up a strand of her hair and swept it across her face. She brushed it away with her fingertips and peered up at him with

144

those beautiful green eyes. "As long as I'm with you, I don't have to worry. Nothing bad will happen to me."

Ah, *crap.* He did *not* need to hear that.

The problem was that he couldn't forget how that guy had grabbed her arm. If he'd do that in a public place with other people looking on, what would he do in private? Marc knew that kind of guy. It wasn't a matter of *if.* It was a matter of *when,* and just the thought of it made anger slither up his spine. Thinking about it, if she went home to Houston now, anything might happen. She just wasn't strong enough yet to haul off and kick the guy where it would hurt the most. Marc was glad he'd chased that asshole out of town, and if he had the opportunity, he'd do it all over again.

But that wasn't all. Even now in the midst of this crazy situation, he couldn't keep his gaze from wandering places it shouldn't. To her red hair spilling over her shoulders in long, loose waves. To the outline of her breasts against the thin fabric of the dress she wore. To those gorgeous green eyes that were turning him into a spineless moron. Even though the word *no* formed inside his head, he just couldn't get it to come out of his mouth.

It was official. He was a sap. A gutless,

pathetic sap who couldn't even utter a simple two-letter word.

"Okay," he said on a sigh of resignation. "You can stay."

Her eyebrows flew up. "I can?" Then she smiled. "Wow. That was easier than I thought it would be."

"Don't get cocky. It's only until you get a deposit together to rent an apartment. Or wash out of your job. Whichever comes first."

"The deposit will come first. I already called Rosie to tell her I was taking the job after all."

Marc grabbed her two biggest suitcases. "We'll see how it goes."

He started down the path toward the cottage. Kari put her dog down, pulled up the handles on her two smaller suitcases, and hurried after him.

"I'm going to pay you back," she said. "I don't know how exactly, but I'm going to. Maybe I can help you with your harvest. You said you needed somebody to help pick grapes. That sounds like fun."

Fun? Good God, she had no idea what she was saying. Picking grapes was hard, dirty, sticky, sweaty work that even strong, healthy men had a hard time with, and she was about as substantial as dandelion fluff.

"We'll talk about that when the time comes," he said.

But the truth was that the time wasn't going to come. He hadn't been joking when he told her he expected her to wash out of her job at Rosie's. If she lasted past the first day it would be a miracle. But that would mean she'd no longer have a job, and when that happened, what in the world was he going to do with her then?

He's letting you stay.

Those words echoed over and over in Kari's mind, but she could still scarcely believe them. There was definitely something to be said for the boat-burning thing.

They circled the house, and when the cottage came into view, Kari was sure she'd ended up in Disney World by mistake. It looked like a miniature prairie-style house with wooden steps leading to a wide front porch. The clapboard siding was painted a cheery peach color that made her happy just to look at it.

"What a cute place!" Kari said.

"It's orange," Marc said. "I hate orange."

"No," Kari said. "It's peach."

"That's what Nina said, too, but you're both wrong. It's orange."

"So why'd you paint it this color if you

hate it?"

"Nina insisted. She says I have no color sense. I have color sense. Every time I see orange, I sense that it's an ugly color."

"What color did you want to paint it?"

"White."

"Oh. White is nice."

No, it wasn't. White was boring. Ugly. Utilitarian. Only people with zero imagination painted anything white. But telling Marc his sister was right and he was wrong probably wouldn't be well received.

They climbed the porch steps, and Marc pulled his keys from his pocket and opened the door. He set the luggage down inside, then grabbed the two suitcases Kari was struggling with and put them beside the others. She looked around and couldn't help smiling. It was as if she'd stepped back in time twenty years. Along one wall sat a flowered sofa that was paired with a rattan coffee table, with a bean pot lamp sitting on an end table next to it. A kitchenette lined one wall, with Formica counters and white appliances. The place was definitely dated, and there was a layer of dust on everything, but it was cute nonetheless. And definitely better than sleeping in the street.

Boo ran in circles, sniffing and yapping in a dizzying dance of sheer delight. Marc's dog tried galloping after him.

"Brandy!"

The dog made an about-face and hurried back to Marc's side, her head ducked, looking properly chastised even though she still quivered with excitement. Finally Kari intercepted Boo and scooped him up.

"What *is* that thing, anyway?" Marc asked, nodding at Boo.

"What do you mean, what is it? It's a *dog.*"

"No," he said, pointing to Brandy. "*That's* a dog." He pointed to Boo. "*That* looks like a bad toupee."

"He's a cairn terrier. Well, most of him is, anyway."

"Exactly how destructive is he?"

Uh-oh. "Destructive?"

"Does he tear things up?"

She lifted her chin. "I'll have you know Boo went to Canine Cotillion, the finest obedience school in Houston. He was a standout student. The instructor said he'd never had a pupil like him."

"When we were at Rosie's and you were in the ladies' room, he grabbed a french fry right off your plate. I guess he missed the class on table manners."

"Once he settles in, he'll be fine."

From the look on Marc's face, he clearly

149

didn't believe that. Frankly, Kari didn't believe it, either. What she hadn't told Marc was that Boo was a standout student at Canine Cotillion because he was deaf to every command the instructor tried to teach him. Kari held out hope that Boo might eventually graduate, right up to the moment he peed on the guy's shoe. After that, she just accepted the fact that Boo was going to be a sweet, loving, door-pawing, shoe-destroying, inappropriately barking dog for the rest of his life.

"There are some canned goods and other nonperishables in the pantry," Marc said. "Help yourself to them. They should tide you over for several days."

"Okay. Thanks."

"There are a few cans of dog food, too."

She nodded.

"Well," Marc said, crossing his arms. "I guess you did it. You talked me into letting you stay in the cottage."

"Yes." And it felt *so* good.

"And you have a job."

"That's right."

"Question," Marc said.

"Yes?"

"How are you going to get to work?"

Her brain froze. "What?"

"When it's time to go to work in the

morning, what are you going to do?"

Kari blinked, stunned at the question. Oh, *crap*. The vineyard was miles from town. *Miles.* She'd already determined that walking there would likely kill her. Even a bicycle was out of the question. There was a reason they called this the Texas Hill Country, and she wasn't exactly in tip-top physical condition. As full of herself as she'd felt before, that was how deflated she felt now.

"Well . . . I'm not sure," she said.

"That wasn't part of your plan?"

She shrugged weakly. "Well, I guess I thought maybe . . ."

"Maybe what?"

"Well, okay. Actually, I didn't think. But you go to town every day, right?"

"Nope."

"But you were in town this morning. At your shop?"

"Yes. But I just make deliveries now and then with no particular schedule. Nina runs it."

"Oh." She stared at Marc, dropping her chin and peering up at him like a puppy who'd peed in the corner, thinking maybe if she looked pathetic enough he'd take pity on her. Unfortunately, she was looking for pity from a man who, by all indications, had very little of it to give.

"Any ideas?" Marc said.

Damn it. One glitch. One stupid, stinking glitch and her whole plan was coming unraveled.

"Don't worry," Marc said. "I have a solution."

Kari brightened. "You do?"

"Yes. I have a car you can drive. But you won't like it. In fact, the moment you see it, you may decide to get back on that bus after all."

"No! I will! I'll drive anything that'll get me there. Anything!"

"Okay, then. Come with me."

They left the cottage, and Kari followed Marc toward the barn. They went around to the side of it, where a tractor was parked, along with something that had the appearance of a car. If not for the four tires, though, identification might have been impossible.

"This," Marc said, "is the Bomb."

Kari winced. "The Bomb?"

"It's a 1989 Vista Cruiser nine-passenger station wagon."

Kari thought about her cute little Lexus that was dead on arrival and felt a stab of longing. This had to be a test. Marc was offering her the most noxious vehicle on the planet just to see if she'd turn tail and run.

152

She walked closer, feeling as if she was approaching a pile of toxic waste.

"What's that stuff peeling off the sides?" she asked.

"Fake wood grain. It's like contact paper only crappier."

"What color did it used to be before the rust ate it up?"

"As I remember, it was blue."

"That's the biggest car I've ever seen."

"Yeah. When it was new, *Car and Driver* named it the safest car on the road. A train could hit it and the only thing damaged would be the train. For sheer safety, nothing beats this baby." He gave it a hearty pat on the fender. "Which is why it was the only car I ever let my daughter drive."

Kari looked horrified. "You inflicted this disgusting thing on her? What did the other kids say?"

"They laughed their asses off."

"My God. Your poor daughter."

"There's no use giving a teenager a decent car. They'll just back it into something and tear it up." He paused. "Or swerve to miss a deer and wrap it around a tree."

"Funny."

"Angela bought a new used one when she went to college. I told her I'd match whatever she saved. She saved, I matched."

"Thank God. If she'd had to drive this one to college, she'd have probably stayed home."

"Going against the crowd builds character."

"Why do you call it the Bomb? That makes me a little nervous."

"Angela called it that. She swore it was such a mess it was going to explode."

"So that's possible? It might actually explode?"

"Nah," Marc said. "It's way more likely that the engine will overheat or the starter will go out."

"What do I do if it does?"

"Call me. That way when you have to walk home, I won't wonder where you are."

"How sweet." She looked back at the car. "You're serious about this, aren't you?"

"Deadly."

"You're sure it runs?"

"Like a top. Too bad it doesn't run like a car."

With that, Marc tossed her the keys. She caught them midair.

"It has a full tank of gas," Marc said. "That should hold you until you can afford to put gas in it yourself." He nodded over his shoulder. "Come with me. I want you to meet the guys who work here. They need to know who you are so they don't wonder why a strange woman is wandering around."

He took her down a path to a big metal warehouse-like structure he referred to as "the barn." Inside she saw barrel after barrel stacked almost to the ceiling, along with shiny stainless steel equipment with all kinds of hoses sticking out of it. Two men stopped what they were doing and walked over. One was a Mexican man who looked to be in his late fifties who Marc introduced as Ramon, and the other was a tall, gangly, thirty-something guy named Michael who wore a Rangers baseball cap and iPod earbuds.

"This is Kari," Marc said. "She's going to be staying in the cottage for a few weeks."

Kari reached out to shake their hands, only to have them smile and hold up their dirty palms.

"Michael and Ramon are the only employees on site right now," Marc said. "The three of us handle the work for part of the year, and then I have contract guys who come in for pruning and harvest and some of the spring prep. About all we're doing now is staying ahead of insect infestation and getting the equipment ready for crush and fermentation."

"Crush?"

"After the grapes are picked and destemmed, a machine splits the skins to let the juice escape."

Kari smiled. "Like Lucy Ricardo stomping the grapes?"

"That's how it used to be done. We have a machine for that now, thank God."

"Darn. I was looking forward to hiking up my skirt and getting purple feet."

Ramon smiled. "Ah. A traditional woman. I like that."

"Anything for the cause," Kari said, appreciating Ramon's smile since Marc didn't seem to have any of his own to offer.

Ramon and Michael went back to work, and Marc led Kari out of the building. "Feel free to walk around the vineyard," he told her. "But don't distract the guys. They have work to do. And keep the rag mop close. There are coyotes and bobcats out here."

Okay, she'd never thought about the wildlife. Poor Boo wouldn't stand a chance against a house cat, much less a bobcat.

Marc pulled his phone from his pocket, poked around on it for a moment, then put it away again. "I have work to do," he told her. "Let me know if you have any problems at the cottage. Keep the place clean, and turn the lights off when you're not there. No sense wasting electricity."

With that, he turned and walked away. She'd hoped maybe he wasn't going to act totally like a landlord, that he might even invite her to dinner at the Big House. Unfortunately, no invitation seemed to be forthcoming.

A little disappointed, Kari went back to the cottage. She tossed the keys to the Bomb on the dresser, then looked in the pantry. She saw five cans of pork and beans, three cans of corn, six boxes of macaroni and cheese, and a box of granola bars. That was what she had to eat between now and the time she could get a discounted lunch at Rosie's or buy a few groceries for herself. She sighed. It beat nothing. Barely.

Next she opened her suitcases and put her clothes away. She had enough basic personal-care stuff with her to hold her for a while, and she had plenty of clothes and shoes since she always overpacked. Unfortunately, none of them were terribly practical for work, but they'd have to do until she could afford to buy more.

She looked at her phone. She had only a few weeks left before she'd be getting a bill for next month's service. Since she couldn't imagine being without her phone, she'd have to find a way to pay the bill even if she didn't eat.

A short time later, she was settled in, feeling pretty good about things. But as it grew later, she got just a little bit scared.

Yeah, she'd managed to tell Greg she didn't want to go back to Houston with him, but that was because she'd had a very large, very intimidating man backing her up. And she'd also succeeded at getting a job, but probably the only reason Rosie had hired her was because she said she was a friend of Marc's. She had a place to live and food to eat, but again . . . Marc. And he'd told her pointblank he expected her to fail.

She scooped Boo up and cuddled him against her. She had to make this work. If she didn't, she'd be back in Houston.

Without Marc.

Later, as evening fell over the cottage, she glanced out the window and saw Marc on his deck, holding a glass of wine, staring out over the vineyard. Something about the way he stood there, strong and tall, made her breath catch in her throat. Then he sat down in one of the Adirondack chairs on the deck. Brandy came and lay beside him. He pulled out his phone, poked around on it, looked up at the sky, poked a little more, then put it away. Then he picked up his wineglass again and watched as the sun slipped below the horizon.

When Kari finally closed the blinds, she realized her heart was racing. What was it about Marc that made her insides melt? She could watch him twenty-four hours a day and still it wouldn't be enough.

Then her gaze wandered to a photograph on the top of the dresser. It was of Marc and a teenage girl who had to be his daughter. Marc was sitting down, and his daughter stood behind him, leaning over with her arms wrapped around his neck. She was smiling.

So was Marc.

So there it was. Proof positive he'd smiled at least once in the past, and it elevated his handsome face into another realm entirely. Just the sight of it touched something inside Kari, something she tried not to think about.

Since her own mother's death when she was eight years old, she'd felt so alone. No hugs, no smiles, nothing. Her father had filled her life with nothing but rules and regimentation, and just about the only time he spoke to her was to tell her she was doing something wrong. Christmases came and went with opulent gifts, elaborate dinners prepared by staff, and then her father retiring to his study as soon as it was all over because work couldn't wait, even on holidays. Any attention she received came from nannies, but bonding with any of them had been a lost cause. She remembered one in particular she'd loved, a twenty-something woman who'd worked for families who'd traveled overseas and had endless stories about museums in Paris and skiing in Switzerland and camera safaris in Africa. But she'd been a little too cheerful and flamboyant for her father's taste, and he'd sent her packing, replacing her with a woman who smiled even less than her father and kept schedules like a train conductor.

Kari quickly learned not to show off any accomplishments, because they were never enough. Unfortunately, big accomplishments had never been her forte. After all, she hadn't had the lead in the school play in the seventh grade, she hadn't graduated valedictorian, and she hadn't gotten into an Ivy League school.

Then Greg came along, a younger version of her father, another man in her life who didn't love her as much as he tolerated her. And now Jill had turned on her, telling her how dumb she was not to marry Greg, when it should have been obvious to anyone close to her that it would only make her miserable. Sometimes Kari had the feeling that the only deep, abiding love she was destined to feel in this life had died the day her mother had.

She looked back at the photo, at Marc's beautiful daughter and his warm, genuine smile, and she felt a shot of envy so powerful she had to close her eyes to block out the feeling. There was no doubt in Kari's mind that *this* girl knew what it was like to be loved.

Kari set the photo back onto the dresser, clicked the lamp off, and lay down. She closed her eyes. Soon she was on the edge of sleep, and weird, dreamy, nonsensical images swirled through her mind. She saw a lost, barefoot damsel in distress, wandering through a vineyard wearing a poufy white dress, desperate for a glimpse of her hero. Then she heard hoof beats in the distance. After a moment her white knight appeared, big and strong and powerful. As he galloped toward her, she felt his all-encompassing, everlasting love wash over her with a certainty that left her breathless.

And as he swept her onto his trusty steed, he was smiling.

CHAPTER 7

Dragging out of bed at 6:00 a.m. the next morning was a killer, but Kari was determined to be on time for her first day of work. She showered, dressed, ate another granola bar, and begged Boo not to pee all over the cottage while she was gone.

Kari had underestimated exactly how bad driving the Bomb was going to be. The headliner had come loose over the driver's seat. It sat on top of her head, getting little pieces of whatever a headliner was made of in her hair. The radio didn't work. The car smelled like a hundred-year-old coffin that had been pried open. About once every quarter mile, the car gave a little lurch that made it seem as if the engine was going to die, but it never did.

She arrived at Rosie's with three minutes to spare. Parking the Bomb was like docking the *Queen Mary,* but she wedged it into a space behind the café and went inside.

Rosie greeted her with a W-9 form, an application to fill out, and a pink bib apron that read, "Pets Welcome, People Tolerated."

After Kari filled out the paperwork, Rosie introduced her to one of the other waitresses. Gloria was a dark-haired woman who looked to be about Kari's age, whose engaging smile and easy manner made Kari's apprehension start to melt away.

"Ever wait tables before?" Gloria asked.

"No," Kari said.

"Doesn't matter. I'm sure you'll pick things up fast."

Then another woman came through the kitchen door into the restaurant wearing skintight jeans, an equally skintight baby tee, and a Rosie's Café apron. She was tall and solid with a pouf of Texas big hair, and she wore so much mascara Kari was surprised she could keep her eyes open.

"Morning girls," the woman said, circling around the counter to pour herself a Diet Coke. "How was your weekend? Wait — never mind. Let me tell you about mine. I went out with Hank Waddell. Only we didn't go out. We stayed in. And *whew!* That man will wear a woman out." She stopped short and looked at Kari, her face falling into a frown. "Who are you?"

"Kari Worthington," she said with a smile

and stuck her hand out. "This is my first day."

The woman ignored Kari's hand. "So have you ever waited tables before?"

"No," Kari said, letting her hand fall self-consciously back to her side. "This is my first job as a waitress."

"It's harder than you think. You're wearing sandals. What's with that?"

"It's all I have right now."

"By the end of your shift, your feet are going to be killing you. You'll have blisters on top of your blisters. But hey, it's your funeral."

As the woman sauntered off, all of Kari's prior apprehension returned with even more heaped on top. She turned to Gloria. "Who was that?"

"Bobbie Arnette." Gloria sighed and lowered her voice. "She can be kinda mean. But she's a good waitress, so Rosie keeps her around. Flirts with every guy who walks into the place. Most people don't know what she's really like, so she makes more tips than the rest of us put together. You probably ought to just try to stay out of her way."

"Okay, girls," Rosie said. "Sheila called in sick. That means each of you is going to have to take a couple of extra tables. More work, but more money." She turned to Kari. "I want you to follow Gloria around for the morning shift. If you're picking things up, I want you to take a couple of your own tables at lunch."

Kari felt a shot of apprehension. "Uh . . . okay. Yeah. I can do that."

Gloria showed Kari the order pads, took her to meet the kitchen staff, and gave her the lowdown on as many procedures as she could. Gloria also introduced her to Marla, a gnarled little woman who was approximately 120 years old. She'd been the hostess at the café long before Rosie had bought it, and she'd probably die behind that faux walnut hostess stand. Gloria told Kari that when Marla finally passed, they'd probably put her ashes on a shelf behind the counter so she could spend eternity there, even though it seemed as if she already had.

Then came the customers.

As they streamed through the door, Gloria stopped her tutorial and said, "Follow me, and keep your eyes and ears open."

Kari couldn't believe what happened over the next two hours. Shadowing Gloria was like trying to follow a herding dog as he was rounding up a flock of sheep. She shot left and right, from one table to another, then to the cash register, then to the kitchen and back again. Dog biscuits here, high chairs there, more coffee, endless plates and baskets of food, and directions to the bathroom. Before long, Kari's back hurt, her feet were on fire, and she was sweating right through her shirt. She wasn't sure she could remember a single bit of the advice Gloria shared with her along the way.

"How long does it usually stay busy at breakfast?" Kari asked, shoving a stray lock of hair out of her eyes.

"Right on into lunch," Gloria said.

Kari groaned inwardly. As the lunch rush geared up, Rosie told her to take one of the smaller stations in the restaurant with only three tables. But to Kari, it seemed like three hundred.

She waited on a family of four. She got three of their orders right. One of the kids ended up with a grilled chicken sandwich instead of chicken nuggets, and she had to put the order in again. She wanted to tell the parents that fried stuff wasn't good for the kid anyway and she was doing him a favor by bringing something grilled, but she didn't think that would go over too well.

Then one of her customers called her over. "How about that chicken fried steak? It's been twenty minutes."

Chicken fried steak? *Oh, God.* Had she

even put that order in?

Soon everything was a blur. The orders, the plates of food, the cooks slinging hamburger patties and sandwich fixings and french fries, and the whole time she felt either Bobbie watching her, waiting for her to screw up, or Rosie watching her when she *did* screw up.

Later in the shift, Marla led two men to one of Kari's tables. They were young, attractive, and wore no wedding rings. Bobbie instantly came to attention.

"Whoa, *mama,*" she said, eyeing the two men. "That table's mine."

Kari blinked with surprise. "I thought . . . isn't that my station?"

"Hmm. I'm afraid you're mistaken about that. But you're new, so that's probably why you're confused."

As Bobbie sashayed off to sidle up next to the men, Kari and Gloria went into the kitchen.

"What's she doing taking a table in your station?" Gloria asked.

"It's okay. It would have overloaded me."

"But it's your table. She shouldn't hijack you like that."

A few moments later, Bobbie came into the kitchen.

"Bobbie," Gloria said. "You just took one

of Kari's tables."

"She was moving too slow. It would have been next week before they got their food."

"She's new. Those guys would have cut her some slack."

"Nobody should have to cut anybody any slack around here." She looked at Kari. "You got two choices. Get moving or get lost."

She grabbed two burger baskets from under the warming lights and flounced out of the kitchen.

"I can't believe she just said that," Kari said. "She acts as if she owns the place."

"I know. She's awful."

"If she's so awful, why doesn't Rosie do something about her?"

"Rosie likes her people to fight their own battles, as long as they don't do it in front of customers. She says that's the only way problems stay fixed for good."

It sounded to Kari as if Rosie could use a good human resources director, but it wasn't her place to say so.

Next, Kari waited on a man with glasses and dirty-blond hair who looked to be in his late thirties. A camera sat in the seat beside him. He said he was an amateur photographer, and he'd heard Rainbow Valley was very picturesque. Like every other tourist who came in there, he seemed particularly interested in the apron Kari wore. He asked to take her picture, which meant she had to fake a smile, and it just about broke her face. Unfortunately, he also wanted to talk. *How long have you lived in Rainbow Valley? Where are you from originally? How long have you worked here? Do you like it?* She couldn't be rude, but every moment she spent making small talk was a moment she wasn't getting her work done.

Kari had two orders come up at once. Because she couldn't remember which order she'd put in first, she decided to take both. She grabbed two of the plates and balanced them on her forearms the way she'd seen the other waitresses do, and held two more in her hands. If she could carry twice as much food at once, she'd get things to tables faster and keep her customers happy. Then maybe she'd get more than pocket change for tips.

She headed for the kitchen door, feeling perfectly balanced and right on top of things. She turned ninety degrees to edge the door open, only to have it open the other way and smack her in the hip. The baskets slipped out of her hands and went flying. They hit the ground, bouncing their contents into the air about the time she twirled around and landed facedown on top of them, her forehead smacking against the floor.

Her first thought was that somebody had come in the Out door. But when she turned over and sat up, she realized she'd tried to go out the In. And it was Bobbie who'd been coming in.

"Jesus," Bobbie said. "You broke my fingernail! I paid thirty bucks for that manicure!"

"I'm sorry," Kari said from the floor, hoping she didn't have brain damage.

"Always go to the *right,*" Bobbie said in the snottiest voice imaginable. "Good God. Were you raised in one of those wimpy countries where they drive on the left side of the road?"

Gloria came through the door, saw Kari on the floor, and hurried over to help her up. "Kari! Oh, honey, are you okay?"

"Yeah," Kari said, even though she wasn't. Her hip hurt and her head throbbed. She had ketchup and mustard on her apron, mingling with a smear of gravy.

Gloria helped her to her feet. Kari swapped aprons and kept on working, but the whole time she felt as if she was going to cry. Finally when her shift was over, she sat down on one of the stools at the counter, every muscle in her body screeching with pain. She'd never been so tired in her life. Never. What had she been thinking when she took this job?

Rosie sat down next to her. "Remember how I said you'd get the hang of the job?"

"Yeah?"

"I think maybe I spoke too soon."

Kari felt a rush of apprehension. "Look, I know I had some problems. But it was so busy today. Busier than usual, from what the other girls said."

"We have a lot of those days."

"And Bobbie —"

"Bobbie can be a pain in the ass, but she gets the job done. Part of working here is learning how to deal with her, because I can't spend my whole day breaking up squabbles. I'm your boss, not your mother."

Kari looked down at her lap, feeling miserable, and Rosie's face softened. "Maybe Marc was right, sweetie. Maybe this wasn't such a good idea after all."

"I need this job."

Rosie sighed. "Why don't you think about it and give me a call later? But I gotta tell you. If you keep working here, it's going to be an uphill battle. For both of us. Sometimes it's just best to call it quits."

With that, Rosie got up off the stool and

circled around the counter to take a customer's order. Kari stood up to take off her apron. Just the act of moving from the stool to her feet made her back muscles feel as if somebody had stabbed them with a red-hot poker. What had she been thinking when she'd taken this job?

All the way back to the vineyard, she felt miserable. What was she supposed to do now? Rosie was right, of course. She wasn't cut out to wait tables. Now she was going to have to tell Marc she couldn't handle the job. He'd probably be happy about that. After all, hadn't he wanted her to get on that bus and leave town?

Of course, the Bomb's air conditioner didn't work, so by the time she got back to the vineyard, sweat was pouring down her temples and the back of her neck, plastering her hair against her skin. She pulled the car to a halt and killed the engine. Marc was down by the barn. She was going to have to go down there and tell him what had happened, but the thought of it made her sick to her stomach. If only she could have stuck it out. If only Bobbie hadn't been such a horrible bitch. If only every muscle in her body wasn't screaming with pain.

She folded her arms on the steering wheel, rested her head there, and closed her eyes.

How had she gotten herself into this mess?

"Taking a nap?"

Kari jerked her head up to find Marc standing by the driver's window. Had she actually fallen asleep?

He opened the door. *Damn it.* That meant she had to get out.

She swung her legs around and made an attempt to stand, but it took her three stabs at it before she finally came to her feet. A moan of pain started to come out of her mouth, but she gritted her teeth and kept it to herself. It wasn't remotely fair that he was hot and sweaty but looked gorgeous, while she was hot and sweaty and looked like roadkill.

"So how did your first day go?"

She glared at him.

"You seem to be a little sore."

"I'm *a lot* sore."

"Don't worry. It'll get easier."

"No, it won't."

"Sure it will. You're just not used to spending that much time on your feet."

Kari said nothing.

"You'll be fine," he said. "Trust me. You're tougher than you think you are."

Clearly he thought that just by speaking those words he could make them happen. Well, there was a whole lot more to this situation than just a little positive thinking.

"I made a mess of things," Kari said. "Maybe . . . maybe it's best if I don't go back."

Her words hung in the air for several seconds. Then Marc turned away and shook his head.

"What?" she asked.

"So you're giving up right off the bat?"

"I'm not giving up. I just found out I'm not cut out for waiting tables."

"Is there anything you *are* cut out for?"

"Just because I haven't found my niche yet doesn't mean —"

"Your *niche*? Seriously? You're not trying out a hobby, Kari. You're working to support yourself."

"I know, but —"

"So you quit?"

Kari hated this. "Not yet."

"But you're going to."

She was silent again.

"Well, I can't say I'm surprised."

"Hey! You were the one who said how stupid it was that I was going to wait tables!"

"No. I believe I told Rosie how wrong I thought it was for her to hire you. Looks as if I was right." He glanced at her feet. "Why are you wearing shoes like that to wait tables?"

"It's all I have."

"There's most of your problem. You need sneakers."

"No kidding."

"So find a way to get some."

"Yeah. I'll reach into my magical suitcase. They're right next to the baby unicorns."

"Take this seriously and you might find a solution."

"Marc! I'm *dying* here!"

"So quit. I'll buy you another bus ticket, take you to the station, and you can go back to Houston and marry the asshole. There you go. Problem solved."

With that, he turned around dismissively and strode back to the barn, leaving Kari feeling like the biggest loser alive.

Damn you! You have no idea how I feel!

She folded her arms and leaned against the car, feeling miserable. She hurt in places she didn't even know she had. She had no decent work shoes and no money to buy them with. The work was impossibly hard, and all she wanted to do was quit.

But then what?

All at once she realized she'd done this all her life. She'd always told herself it was just because she saw something better on the horizon and didn't want to waste her time, but the truth was that when the going got tough, she quit. She quit the swim team in tenth grade because practice clashed with an afternoon TV show she wanted to watch. In college, as soon as a class got hard, she dropped it, which was why it took her five years to get a liberal arts degree. She'd run away from her own wedding because she hadn't had the backbone to call it off before she was sitting at the church in a wedding dress. Now she was running away from Rainbow Valley because she refused to stick it out in a job that was harder than she'd anticipated.

She hated the way Marc had looked at her. He thought she was as useless as Greg did. As her father did. As Rosie did. Was there anyone in this life who respected her? Even a little bit?

She had the most gut-wrenching feeling that the answer to that question was no. And that was the worst blow of all. The trouble was, if she quit this job, it meant she really was at rock bottom. What was she going to do then? Crawl back to her father and beg him to give her job back? That job that wasn't really a job at all, but simply a means her father used to allow him to call the shots? If she couldn't even handle this job, how was she supposed to get another one that didn't involve working for her father?

They're right. All of them. You are useless.

She'd known Marc all of two days, yet the fact that he was a good, dependable, honorable man was so crystal clear to her that she'd have stated it under oath. And when he'd turned his back on her and walked away, his disappointment still lingered in the very air she breathed. Oddly enough, of all the people in her life right now, he was the one whose respect she craved more than anything. With every minute that passed, that feeling ate away at her a little more, and pretty soon it hurt worse than her strained muscles and her pounding head, which meant there was only one thing she could do.

She got into the Bomb and drove back to Rainbow Valley, ignoring the pain, ignoring the odds stacked against her, ignoring the fact that Rosie had essentially fired her but had been kind enough not to actually say the words. She parked in the lot behind the restaurant and came through the back door, trying not to look as if she could barely walk. Rosie was sitting at the counter poking at a laptop. Kari slid onto the stool beside her.

Rosie sighed. "Honey, what are you doing back here? You look like you're about to drop."

177

Kari lifted her chin. *Oh, God. My neck muscles!* "I need to talk to you."

"I thought things were settled."

"No. Things aren't settled. I have something else I need to say."

"Talk fast," Rosie said. "I have a lot of work to do before the dinner hour gears up."

Kari swallowed hard and started in. "I know you think I'm a lousy waitress and that there's no hope I'll ever be a good one. I know Bobbie hates me, so there's that problem, too. But I'm not quitting."

Rosie raised an eyebrow. "Is that right?"

"That's right. I'm going to come into this place every single shift I'm scheduled and try my damnedest to do a good job. And you can bet I'm going to screw up. I'm going to drop things. My tickets will be out of balance. Some of the customers will probably yell at me, and I'll earn zero tips. But I'm not going to make it easy for you to get rid of me, because I'm not going to quit. *I am not going to quit.* If you want me out of here, you're going to have to fire me."

Rosie sighed and shook her head. "Why are you doing this to me?"

"Because I need this job."

"Part of life is knowing when to quit."

"Yeah, sometimes it is. But since I already know how to do that, now I need to learn how to keep going."

Rosie stared at her a long time with a deadpan expression. Then she looked away, shaking her head. "I can't afford to lose any more dishes."

"I know."

"The hourly wage sucks. If you don't make any tips, you'd be better off rummaging through sofa cushions for loose change."

"I know that, too."

"No telling what Bobbie's liable to do if you show up here tomorrow. Remember, I can only call the sheriff *after* she's committed assault and battery."

"I hear you."

Rosie twisted her mouth with irritation. "You're not cut out for this, you know."

"I know."

Rosie tapped her fingertips on the Formica counter, and Kari could almost feel her brain working. Then, with a heavy sigh, Rosie slid off her barstool. "You got the six a.m. to three p.m. shift tomorrow. Don't be late."

As Rosie strode into the kitchen, Kari felt as if she'd voluntarily signed up for life in prison. But she still had a job. As she slid off the stool, the backs of her calves felt as if they were on fire.

Ow. Ow. *Ow. Ow! OW!*

She walked as delicately as she could to the back door and got into the Bomb. Coming back there tomorrow morning would likely be hell on earth all over again, but she was going to do it no matter what. If she dropped dead, so be it. At least she'd die trying.

She drove back to the vineyard, where she parked the Bomb. Then she walked resolutely up the steps to Marc's deck and knocked on his back door. Several seconds later, he answered. Before he could even open his mouth, she started in.

"Just so you'll know, I went back to town. I talked to Rosie, and I'm keeping my job."

Marc's eyebrows rose. "Is that right?"

"That's right. It's the worst job I've ever had. I hurt in places I didn't even know existed. But even if it kills me, I'm going back. So don't you *ever* again suggest that I should go back to Houston and marry Greg. No matter what I have to do, that is *never* going to happen. Do you understand?"

"Yes, ma'am. I understand completely."

"Good. Now I'm going to stumble back to the cottage, take a shower, and fall into a coma. If you'll excuse me?"

She turned around and walked back down the steps, then headed down the path to the cottage. She let Boo out to run around the yard and pee, then went inside to sit down before she fell down. Then she saw tiny teeth marks in the legs of two of the wooden chairs at the dinette table. Great. That was just what she needed. Boo eating the cottage, one bite at a time.

She rested for a minute, then went in to take a shower. It felt good, but not good enough. She put on a robe and collapsed on the sofa again. For the next hour, she watched a little TV, avoiding her ex-favorite shows like *Hell's Kitchen* or *Restaurant: Impossible.* People yelling at other people in restaurant kitchens just didn't hold the same entertainment value for her it had the day before.

She still hadn't heard a word from her father. Not one. More than once since she'd left Houston, she'd imagined him telling her he understood why she'd run and that he supported her decision not to marry Greg.

When would she ever learn?

When she was ten, she'd fantasized that he would surprise her with a trip to Disney World, and he'd ride Splash Mountain with her and not care if he got wet. When she was twelve, she imagined him sitting through her ballet recital, then telling her she was the next Anna Pavlova. When she was sixteen, she envisioned him coming to her soccer game and cheering when she made a goal. But if all those things had never happened, what made her think anything would change now?

Then she heard a knock at her door.

With a deep breath, she hoisted herself off the sofa and walked gingerly to the door. She opened it to find Marc on the porch. He brushed past her and came inside. He carried a big box, which he set down on the dinette table.

"What are you doing here?" she asked.

"You're going to have a hard time keeping that promise."

"What?"

"To never quit your job. You can't expect to be successful at something if you don't have the proper tools."

"What are you talking about?"

He reached into the box. "First — ibuprofen. It's an anti-inflammatory, so it'll take away the muscle pain." He grabbed a glass from a kitchen cabinet, filled it with water, and handed her two of the tablets. She stared at them dumbly.

"Kari. Take the pills."

"Marc —"

"Take them."

She took the pills and downed them as he reached into the box again.

"Your biggest problem is shoes," Marc said. "What size do you wear?"

"Six."

"Then these will be too big." He pulled a pair of raggedy sneakers out of the box and put them on the floor. "But here are two pairs of socks. Wear both of them and the shoes will probably be okay."

"Whose shoes are they?" she asked.

"Angela's."

"Your daughter? You're giving me her shoes?"

"Do you need them?"

She didn't know how to answer that without appearing helpless. But maybe it was just as bad to appear ungrateful.

"Yes."

"Then wear them." He pulled a heating pad from the box, which he plugged in and laid across the pillow at the end of the sofa.

"Your back's bound to hurt. Sit down and lean against that."

She sat down, feeling like a Raggedy Ann that had gotten hit by a train. She turned and pulled her feet up on the sofa, resting her back against the pad. As it heated up, she couldn't believe what Marc pulled out of the box next. If her muscles weren't ripped to shreds, she'd have leapt off the sofa and grabbed it right out of his hand.

"Wine?" she said.

"Yep. Nature's anesthesia."

He grabbed a wineglass from a kitchen cabinet, uncorked the bottle with a practiced twist and pull, and filled the glass. He handed it to her.

"Drink this."

She sipped the wine. *Oh, God.* It filled her mouth with the most amazing flavor, and as she swallowed, she felt the soft burn all the way down her throat. Her body slumped as the wine went south, bringing on a sense of relaxation she certainly hadn't expected to feel tonight.

"Good wine," she said, sipping it again. "*Really* good."

"It's our 2010 Cabernet. Our best vintage yet. Just the right amount of rain and sun that season. Most years we're not that lucky."

"So luck plays a part?"

"It's about the only thing you can count on. Not having any."

"Tough business?"

"You don't know the half of it."

Marc pulled out two more things — Band-Aids and triple antibiotic ointment — and put them on the coffee table. Then he sat down on the other end of the sofa.

"Give me your foot."

Kari blinked. "What?"

"A few of your blisters must have already popped, and you don't want them getting infected. Your foot."

With a Herculean effort, she lifted one leg and held out her foot. He took it in those big hands and rested it on his thigh. He opened a Band-Aid, squirted antibiotic ointment onto it, and stuck it over one of her blisters, working slowly and diligently.

And Kari just sat there, staring at him with disbelief.

She remembered how she'd once asked Greg to rub her sore neck, and he gave it a halfhearted effort with one hand while he checked stock prices on his iPhone with the other. This was different. So incredibly different. Just the feel of her foot resting on Marc's rock-hard thigh was sigh worthy, not to mention the care he took over every one of her blisters. They'd hurt like hell before, but now she didn't even feel the pain.

"You've done this before," she said.

"What?" he said, never looking up from his task.

"Fixed boo-boos."

"Yeah. Once or twice."

Big understatement there. Parenthood

meant dealing with scraped knees and elbows all over the place. And as Kari thought about this big, tough man with his young daughter in his lap, drying her tears and putting on Band-Aids . . .

It seemed so out of character. Maybe that was why it gave Kari such a warm, squishy feeling inside.

With Marc so tuned in to his task, she could stare at him all she wanted to. And she really wanted to. She let her gaze wander from the short, dark brush of beard along his jaw, to the smooth bronze skin of his cheeks, to the tiny lines radiating out from the corners of his eyes, saying that he actually did smile once in a while. As she took another sip of wine, she started to think about other things, mostly those hands of his somewhere on her body besides her feet.

"What was so bad about the job?" he asked her. "Aside from the obvious."

"Well, there wasn't much I didn't screw up. I messed up orders. I brought the wrong stuff to people. And the menu. There must be a thousand things on it."

"Memorize it."

"There's no time for that."

"Bring a menu home tomorrow night and study it. Being a waitress is no different from any other job. You just have to learn the basics. How are you getting along with Bobbie?"

Kari froze. "You know about her?"

"Everybody who eats at Rosie's regularly knows about her. Tourists not so much, which is why she's still there."

"You might have warned me."

"Just don't take any crap from her, and you'll be fine." He stuck on another Band-Aid. "Speaking of burning those boats, have you had your mail forwarded here?"

That hadn't even crossed her mind. "Uh . . . no."

"If you're living here now, you need to do that. USPS.gov. There should be a form out there to fill out."

"I will."

"So how are you feeling now?"

The ibuprofen, the wine, the heating pad, a sexy man putting Band-Aids on her blisters . . . what *didn't* make her feel good?

"Much better," she said.

Marc applied the last Band-Aid and removed her foot from his thigh, and she settled back with a sigh of pure contentment. Nobody in her adult life had ever done anything like this for her. On the surface, Marc was big and gruff and demanding, but beneath it all was a kindness and compassion she never would have imagined, and it drew her to him like nothing else. Now she hoped he would pour himself a glass of wine and stay for a while. After that, who knew what might happen?

"Okay," he said. "It's time for me to go."

Kari's eyes flew open. "Go? Why?"

"I'm finished here. I'll leave everything. You'll probably need all of it again tomorrow."

No! She didn't want him to go. She wanted him to stay there forever so this feeling would *never* go away.

"You don't have to go," she said.

"I have work to do."

"After dark?"

"Accounting stuff."

"Why don't you forget that for tonight? Stick around? Have a glass of wine?"

"Can't," he said. "Things pile up."

"Don't you ever relax?"

"Not when there are things to do."

As he rose to leave, Kari felt a rush of disappointment. But what was she supposed to do? Grab him by the arm and forbid him to leave?

"Wait," she said. "I'll lock the door behind you. Assuming you lock things all the way out here."

"*Always* lock doors," Marc said. "You

188

never know."

Of course he would say that. Mr. Practicality. And of course Mr. Practicality couldn't stick around and have a glass of wine if there was an iota of work to be done. To say she was attracted to him was an understatement. To say he was frustrating the hell out of her was a bigger one.

Suppressing a groan of pain, she rose from the sofa and followed him. When he reached the door, she called out to him.

"Marc?"

He stepped back into the room. "What?"

She stopped in front of him. "Thank you for all this."

"It was no big deal."

"No. It was a big deal. Believe me. A really big deal."

"A pair of shoes, a heating pad, a couple of Band-Aids —"

"No. You don't understand. Nobody's ever done stuff like this for me before."

The words were out of her mouth before she really thought about them. Now she was stuck feeling just a little bit pitiful, particularly when a look of disbelief came over Marc's face.

"Ever?"

"Yeah. Ever."

"But when you were a kid, surely —"

"When my mother was alive, I guess."

"How old were you when she died?"

"Eight. After that, my father's staff was nice to me. But it wasn't the same." She shrugged. "You can pay people to do all kinds of things. Doesn't mean they care."

Marc just stared at her as if her words didn't compute, and suddenly she wished she'd kept her mouth shut. She'd looked pitiful enough when she'd almost quit her job. The last thing she wanted to do was look even more pathetic now.

"What made you change your mind about the job?" Marc asked.

"I don't know. It doesn't matter. Thanks again for helping me," she said, having a hard time looking at him. She nodded toward the door. "Go ahead. I'll close it behind you."

But he didn't move. Instead, he continued to stare at her. It was just like at Animal House that night, when he hadn't even blinked. He just stared at her stoically, as if he was feeling absolutely nothing. Zero. Nada. Zilch.

So why wasn't he leaving?

He flicked his gaze to her almost-empty wineglass. "Now that I think about it," he said, "they say people who drink alone have a drinking problem. You're new in town. We

190

wouldn't want people jumping to the wrong conclusion."

Kari's heart bumped hard against her chest, her stomach quivering with anticipation. "Exactly. It's like you said when we were at the inn. This is a small town. Word gets around."

But he made no move to grab another wineglass and fill it. She held her breath, wondering what he was thinking. His gaze played across her face, then moved downward to her chest, then lower to the V of her robe where it dipped down between her breasts. It had fallen open slightly when she rose from the sofa, but the last thing she wanted to do right then was pull it shut. As far as she was concerned, he could look at anything he wanted to as long as he wanted to.

They both stood motionless, the air between them growing hot and heavy. Evening was turning to dusk, and the dim light from the single lamp gave the room a dreamy, otherworldly feeling. Or maybe it was the wine. Maybe she didn't know. She only knew she loved the feeling and didn't want to lose it.

Then his attention turned to a spot above her eyes, and his brows drew together with concern.

"What's the matter?" she asked.

"Is that a bruise on your forehead?"

"Yeah."

"What happened?"

"I came out the kitchen door. Unfortunately, it was the door you're supposed to use to come *in.* I've learned that's a felony when you're working in a restaurant."

He lifted the hair on her forehead to examine it more closely.

"It's okay," she said. "It doesn't hurt."

"If I'd known about it, I'd have brought an ice pack."

"No need. I'm fine."

He moved his fingertips downward, letting her hair fall back against her forehead. But to her surprise, instead of pulling his hand away, he traced those two fingertips all the way along her cheek to her jaw, then wrapped his callused hand around the side of her neck and stepped closer.

Oh, my God.

She couldn't meet his eyes. Didn't dare. She just stared straight ahead at that big, rock-hard chest and prayed he didn't stop. She leaned into him, closing her eyes at the heavenly feeling of her body pressed against all that bone and muscle. All the sexy thoughts she'd been having about him since she came to his door two nights ago melted into a red-hot jumble in her mind until thinking wasn't an option. She couldn't have mustered up a single coherent thought if her life depended on it. Whatever pain she'd felt earlier had vanished. She only knew she wanted Marc. She wanted him here. And she wanted him *now.*

"This is a bad idea," he whispered.

Kari felt a shot of desperation. "No. It's a good idea. An *excellent* idea. In fact, it's the best idea I've come across all day."

He moved his other hand around to the small of her back to pull her closer, and her heart went crazy. But he still did nothing else. Good *God.* Did he have to have so damned much self-control?

"What's wrong?" she said, barely able to breathe for the anticipation she felt. "Do you have a girlfriend I don't know about?"

"No. No girlfriend."

"And I no longer have a fiancé."

"But you just left him at the altar two days ago."

"Which was better than marrying the wrong man."

"Okay, that's logical," he said.

And then he kissed her.

CHAPTER 8

Logical? Marc couldn't believe he'd said that. There was nothing logical about this — not one damned thing — which was probably why he couldn't keep his hands off Kari. If he'd been following *logic,* he'd have been out the door already.

That was where he'd intended to be. Out the door. But then she'd mentioned how nobody had ever done nice things for her, and then he'd seen that bruise on her forehead and realized what a tough day she'd just had, and now . . .

And now he was kissing her and loving every minute of it. She returned his kiss with a fierceness that astonished him. He loved the way she tasted — sweet and hot and silky smooth — everything he'd imagined she would be. It was as if he'd fallen into an alternate universe, one where a beautiful woman had appeared in front of him and all the restrictions he'd put on his love life for the past eighteen years had been blasted away.

Then her hands were on his shirt buttons, flicking them open with the enthusiasm of a prospector who'd spotted gold and was going after it. If he'd been in his right mind he might have called a halt to this. But not only had he lost his train of thought, it had veered off the track and plunged over a cliff.

It's just you, this woman, and nobody else. What do you need? An engraved invitation? Go for it!

He ripped off his shirt and tossed it aside, then went for her robe. He loosened the tie and pushed it off her shoulders, and she gave a little shimmy and it dropped to the floor behind her. He saw what she had on underneath it and froze. Leopard print panties. And that was all.

Holy shit.

He felt like some kind of Pavlov's dog where this woman's panties were concerned. What could she possibly wear that *didn't* turn him on?

His gaze rose to her breasts. It was just as he'd suspected. They were the Eighth Wonder of the World, clearly the ones God gave her, so he felt justified in deciding they were just about perfect. He spread his hands wide over them and rubbed them in circles, squeezing, releasing, kissing her deeply at the same time.

Just touching her made his jeans grow tighter by the second. He shifted, trying to take away the exquisite pain, but only one thing was going to cure that problem. He couldn't remember ever wanting a woman this much. He was dying to make love to her, willing to walk through fire for it.

He pulled away and sat down on the sofa to yank off his boots. When he stood again, she pressed her hands against his chest and dragged them down to his belt buckle. In no time she had his belt off and then he was kicking both his jeans and underwear aside. She fell back on the sofa, and he stopped for a hard-breathing moment to stare down at her.

"My God," he whispered.

"Don't stop now."

He sprang into action again, sliding those leopard panties down her hot, silky thighs. He pulled them all the way off and tossed them aside.

"Damn," he muttered. "Sofa bed. Gotta pull it out."

"Forget that," she said. "Don't need it. Right here. Just like this."

Her eyes were alight with excitement, those green eyes that had messed up his mind in ways he'd never felt before. All he wanted to do was fall on top of her, slide inside, and make love to her until his nerves exploded.

Then he remembered.

Condom. Christ, he didn't have a condom! What the hell was he supposed to do now? *Think. Think!*

Okay. Daniel stayed at the cottage whenever he was in town. And he never hesitated to entertain women. Lots of women. And that meant he needed lots of condoms. Marc only hoped he'd left a few behind.

"Wait," he told Kari, pointing at her. "Don't move. *Do not move!*"

He jerked open the dresser drawer and plowed through it. He shoved pens, notepads, paper clips, and other assorted junk aside. *Come on, Daniel. Don't let me down now!*

Then he saw it. A whole freaking *box* of condoms. He opened the box and snagged one of the plastic packets. It was the most beautiful thing he'd ever seen. Would she think it was weird if he kissed it?

He ripped it open. Rolled it on. Then he turned, fell between her legs, and slid inside her, groaning out loud with the sheer pleasure of it. She was so hot and tight that he damned near came on the spot. He wanted to go slow. Knew he should. But it had been too long. Too damned *long*, and now he couldn't get enough. He had to move hard and fast. Had to. His brain was telling him to go slow, but his body was telling him to hit the gas. His body was winning. Kari's fingertips dug into his back, and no matter how hard he thrust, she lifted her hips to meet him, urging him on, and that shoved him even closer to the brink. Her breath was fiery hot against his neck, coming faster and faster with every stroke.

Then she gasped, a single sharp intake of air. Then the gasp became a groan of pleasure. Her thighs tightened around him. She whispered his name between hot, heavy breaths. He whispered hers.

And then he was coming.

He plunged deep inside her, gritting his teeth against the indescribable sensations. Oh, God . . . this was it. What he'd wanted for so long, what he'd lain awake nights thinking about. Maybe any woman would have made him feel this way. Or maybe she had to have wild auburn hair. Electric green eyes. Breasts to die for. Long, tanned legs he could slide his hands up until they reached the promised land.

He lifted himself away from her, then sat down on the end of the sofa, his breath still labored, his body still a boneless mass of pure ecstasy. Kari sat up next to him, leaning in to kiss his neck.

"Hang around for a while," she whispered. "You never know what might pop up again later."

That sounded damned good to him. If there was more of this in store for him, he'd move in permanently, and the two of them could have sex for the rest of eternity.

Then all at once he had a terrible thought. He froze, turning it over in his mind, trying to dismiss it, but he couldn't. It had been a long time since Daniel had stayed in the cottage. Too long?

He grabbed the condom box. Blinked to focus. And there it was. The date. He groaned out loud.

The condoms were *expired*?

"What's the matter?" Kari asked.

He had condoms in his bedroom back at the house. Nonexpired ones, because he was a man who was always prepared even though the chances of him needing them were nil. Why hadn't he taken Kari up there? If he was going to do this, why hadn't he done it *right*?

He tossed the condoms back into the drawer, went to the bathroom to clean up, then came back to the living room.

"Marc?" Kari said. "What's the matter?"

"I was right before," he said. "This was a bad idea."

Kari blinked. "Huh?"

"I have to go."

"Go? Why?"

He yanked his jeans on. Then his boots.

"Marc, tell me what's wrong."

"The condoms," he said finally.

"What about them?"

"They're expired."

"Uh . . . okay . . . just how expired are they?"

"Two months."

She let out a breath of relief. "Just two months? That's okay. Those things are good for years. The manufacturers wouldn't have cut it that close. It's not like the clock hits midnight on the expiration date and suddenly they're worthless."

"We don't know that." He headed for the door, putting his shirt on as he went.

"Marc, wait." Kari scrambled off the sofa and caught up with him. "You're overreacting."

Overreacting? He had news for her. When it came to defective condoms, there was no such thing as overreacting.

But he didn't want to go into it. He didn't want to talk about his pregnant teenage girlfriend who had their baby and then deserted them. About the crushing responsibility of a newborn baby. About the feeling of claustrophobia that had crept up on him in the past few years until it threatened to smother him. About how he'd seen that expiration date on those condoms and it had brought it all back to him, making him wonder if he wasn't repeating the mistakes of his past like a horny teenage kid without a lick of common sense.

He opened the door and left the cottage without looking back. He knew if he didn't, he'd be sunk. It wasn't fair to walk out on Kari like this without another word. In fact, he was being the jerk of the century for doing it. But nothing — absolutely *nothing* — was going to keep him in this town now that he finally had the opportunity to leave.

Kari could stay in his cottage until they were both old and gray, but what had just happened between them was never going to happen again.

A few days later, Kari was leaning against the wall in the kitchen at Rosie's for five breath-catching seconds when Gloria came through the door.

"Bad morning?" she asked.

"No. I'm okay."

"You're such a liar," Gloria said with a smile. "But don't worry. It'll get easier."

But so far, that hadn't been true. It wasn't getting easier. The morning rush had been unholy. Marla had triple seated her because people hated to wait at the front of the restaurant when they could see empty tables. *Sit them down and bring them coffee,* Rosie said, but even that was a challenge for Kari to do in a decent amount of time, much less take their orders. She wore Angela's old sneakers, which helped, but even two pairs of socks and Band-Aids didn't keep her blisters from hurting. Bobbie took one look at the shoes, made a face, and asked her if she'd been cleaning out horse stalls.

And Marc. She couldn't stop thinking about Marc.

She'd had rugs pulled out from under her a time or two, but this time she'd been dumped squarely on her ass, and it had hurt ten times worse than her back pain and blisters. Ever since he'd walked out the door a few nights ago, the only time she saw him was at dusk every evening when he sat out on his deck with Brandy, drinking a glass of wine and staring at the setting sun. She understood the expired condom thing, even though she didn't think it was as big a deal as Marc did. What were the odds of that being a problem?

"Come on, Kari," Rosie said. "Get moving. The place is packed."

Kari sighed and pushed away from the wall, telling herself she had to concentrate on her job. She knew part of the equation that added up to success was smiling at everybody all the time. She tried that. She really tried. She'd go to a table and look all happy, but the moment she returned to the kitchen and realized she hadn't written down what kind of dressing somebody wanted on their salad, she'd worry that maybe there was something else she'd forgotten, and she could feel that smile wilting like a daisy in the desert.

She watched Bobbie flirt with a couple of guys in a booth by the window. If she leaned over any farther to take their order, her breasts were going to fall right out of her shirt and tumble onto the table. Kari had never been particularly good at flirting. It always came off sounding stilted and stupid, so if she had to practically disrobe to make a few tips, she was screwed.

As the morning rush edged into the lunch rush, Kari ran to the kitchen to pick up two orders of chicken fried steak. Bobbie was standing beside the warming lights, her fists on her hips, shouting at one of Rosie's newer cooks who had started working there only a few days before Kari had, a fifty-something Mexican man who just stared back at Bobbie blankly.

"Come on, Carlos!" she said. *"Ándale! Ándale!"*

But Carlos was acting as if his hands weighed three thousand pounds each. Finally he put the sandwich under the warming lights.

"That's wheat bread!" Bobbie said. "The order was for white! Will you get it *right?*"

When Carlos gave her a helpless shrug, Bobbie narrowed her eyes. "You understand every bit of what I'm saying."

"No hablo inglés."

"Wrong. Rosie wouldn't have hired you if you couldn't speak halfway decent English. You *hablo* all the *inglés* you feel like *habloing!*"

Carlos gave her a wide-eyed look and another shrug.

"Blanco bread!" Bobbie said. "*Blanco!* And you'd better have it ready the next time I come in here!"

Bobbie headed for the cooler to grab a couple of premade house salads. Carlos frowned at her, then turned to Kari and gave her a smile and a wink. He dipped his ladle into a big pot on the stove.

"Extra gravy," Carlos said, plopping an extra-huge serving onto the top of the chicken fried steaks. "Your customers — they like."

Carlos put the plates on the warming ledge.

"Gracias," Kari said as she grabbed them, giving Carlos a grateful smile at the same time. It wasn't the first time he'd given her customers a little extra, and she really appreciated it. In fact, all the other people there tried to help her every way they could, even though sometimes it seemed like a lost cause.

Everybody except Bobbie.

Bobbie knew Carlos liked Kari and didn't like her. All the cooks in the kitchen felt the same, mostly because Kari was polite to them rather than demanding. But since most of them were half scared of Bobbie, they didn't generally cross her.

Kari started toward the kitchen door, chicken fried steaks in hand, telling herself she was okay. She could do this. She could fill her brain with all kinds of things and still remember all of it and in the right order. All it took was a little practice.

Then Bobbie stuck her head back into the kitchen. "Table six wants you."

Kari stopped short, slumping with frustration. "What for?"

"They're asking about their food. And they've decided they need a high chair for the kid after all. And crackers. And extra napkins. And more water."

Kari closed her eyes with frustration.

Bobbie sighed, and for maybe the first time, a look of sympathy came over her face. "Which table are those chicken fried steaks going to?"

"Nine," Kari said. "Why?"

She held out her hands. "Give them to me."

Kari narrowed her eyes suspiciously. "Why?"

"Will you just give them to me? I'll deliver them, and you take care of table six."

Kari didn't like this. Not one little bit.

"Hey, I'm offering to help you," Bobbie said. "It'd be pretty ungrateful if you didn't take me up on it."

Kari still didn't like it, but she was in a bind. Finally she handed her the plates.

"Now, get out there," Bobbie said. "Or you can kiss your tip good-bye."

Kari left the kitchen, swinging by to grab a high chair, only to go to table six and be told they'd never asked for one.

Then she heard the crash.

She set the high chair down and hurried back to the kitchen. Bobbie stood over two broken plates on the floor, their shards mingling with lumps of chicken fried steak and gravy. She put her hands to her face. "Oh, my! I'm sorry, Kari. I can't believe I was so clumsy. They slipped right out of my hands."

Kari looked down in horror. *No, no, no!* This meant the order had to be put in again, and it was going to be ages before those people got their food. And her tip would go right out the window.

As she stood there staring at the carnage, Bobbie said, "I have an idea. Why don't you ask your friend Carlos to fix you two new chicken fried steaks? Oh, wait. Silly me. He doesn't *hablo inglés.*"

As she flounced out of the kitchen, Kari wanted to cry. Just start boohooing at the top of her lungs. But then she pictured herself crawling back to her father and asking for her money back. He'd give it to her. She knew he would. The question was, what would she have to do to make that happen?

And Marc. No matter how frustrated she was with him right then, his words of encouragement still rang inside her head. *Trust me. You're tougher than you think you are.*

And that meant she had to keep going.

She put in an order for two more chicken fried steaks, and Carlos said he'd move them to the front of the queue. Then she went back out to the dining room to deal with demanding customers and her own aching feet.

That afternoon, Marc walked the sloping landscape of the vineyard, where row after row of grapes hung heavily on their vines. The green of their ragged leaves was edging into gold, signaling the last few weeks of ripening. This morning he'd felt a breath of cool air in spite of the heat, like a gentle tap on his shoulder, a whisper in his ear: *Autumn is coming. Then harvest. Pay attention. Read the signs. Be ready.* He could almost feel life bursting from the grape clusters as they ripened on the vine, tiny globes of potential energy that would become a kinetic explosion at harvest.

He stopped beside Ramon, who was examining one of the vines and the clusters of grapes it held. His face was deeply tanned and fissured, a product of long summers working in the Texas sun. His hands were growing gnarled, with enlarged joints that were the first indication of the arthritis he tried so hard to hide. It wouldn't be long before pruning vines and picking grapes would be out of the question for him, but Marc knew he'd crawl out to the vines before he finally admitted he couldn't do it any longer.

"Looking good," Ramon said. "But I did see half a dozen wasps this morning."

Marc's heart skipped with apprehension. "Any nests?"

"One."

This wasn't good. Wasps were generally almost nonexistent through most of the growing season, but when the sugar content increased in the last days of ripening, the pests could descend on a vineyard and destroy the fruit.

"Set the traps and keep watch for damaged fruit. If you see it, get it out of the field. And be on the lookout for more nests. And pray we don't get another hard rain in the next few weeks."

"I think we're in the clear from this last one," Ramon said. "There's still plenty of time for the grapes to settle and the sugar to stabilize."

Soon that magical moment would come when the acidity decreased, the sugar content rose, and a perfect equilibrium was reached. Then it was time for harvest. Determining that moment began with lab tests, but it ended with much more objective things. Taste, weather conditions, plus something that couldn't be quantified — the intuition of an experienced vintner.

Marc's grandfather had begun this vineyard in 1948, and his father had grown it to the size and quality it was today. The outbreak of Pierce's disease in 1996 had damned near wiped them out, but they'd come back, planting new vines and rejuvenating the ones they'd been able to salvage.

Marc remembered his father taking him out into the vineyard when he was a boy, showing him the vines, pointing out mold or pests and telling him what to do about them. As the grapes ripened, he demonstrated how they should look and feel and taste. Then came harvest, which was some of the hardest, dirtiest work a man could possibly do. But the harvest party made it all worth it, when they opened a bottle from a prior year's vintage and his father toasted their success. Those times were written across Marc's memory in indelible ink, memories that would stay with him for the rest of his life.

His father had tried to instill those same feelings for the family business in Daniel, but he was always immersed in computers and video games and anything else that didn't involve the day-to-day operations. Working in the vineyard was Daniel's definition of hell on earth.

"It looks as if we'll be harvesting a little sooner than last year," Marc said. "They're moving fast."

"When will Daniel be here?"

"He said sometime next week, but with Daniel you can never be too sure."

Ramon just nodded.

"I know how you feel about him running the place."

Ramon held up his palm. "None of my business."

"No, it *is* your business. You've been part of this vineyard for the past twenty years. You know your opinion is important to me."

"Daniel . . ." Ramon shook his head. "I'm just not sure about him. That's all."

"He knows what it takes. He grew up at this vineyard."

"You know it's nothing personal. I couldn't love him more if he was my own kid. But he's just not cut out for this. Not like you are."

It didn't matter whether Daniel was cut out for it or not. Three years. That was their deal. He could certainly keep the place going that long, particularly if Ramon was there with his steadying hand. But Daniel

211

was also impulsive. Prone to coming up with ideas he was dying to implement whether they made sense or not. More distractible than a kitten who'd spied a string. Focused on cars and women and the next big deal. But they had a bargain, and Marc intended to hold him to it.

"I have to get out of here for a while," Marc said. "Just for a few years. I'll be back."

"So you're keeping the vineyard after that?"

For a long time, Marc didn't respond. Couldn't respond. He didn't know what the next three years would bring. What would he see out there in the world that was more enticing than running a vineyard for the rest of his life? He, Nina, and Daniel would all have a say in the decision, but when it got right down to it, the vineyard was Marc's to keep.

Or his to sell.

"I'm not sure what I'll be doing with it," he said. "But it'll be a few years before we make a decision."

"A lot can happen in a few years."

Marc knew just how true that was. A poorly timed harvest. A too-cold summer. Birds and bugs and rabbits and mold. Any one of those things could turn a potential banner year into a subpar vintage that would screw up the reputation Marc had tried so hard to maintain.

"What happens happens," Marc said.

"I wonder what your dad might say about that," Ramon said.

Marc turned away, hating the sound of those words.

Ramon sighed. "I'm sorry. That was out of line."

"No. It's okay. It's not as if I haven't done a little thinking about that myself." He looked at Ramon. "You'll stay, won't you?"

"I've been here a long time. Seen this place through the good times and the bad. I can't imagine being anywhere else." He paused. "I can't imagine *you* being anywhere else."

Sometimes Marc couldn't, either. But he knew that was only because he'd never lived anywhere else. The moment he got the chance to see what was out there for him, Rainbow Valley wouldn't seem so important anymore.

It was the perfect time to leave. Curtis had been gone almost a year now. Nina was getting over the shock of his death, and she had plenty of money from the settlement the company had provided after the accident to live comfortably even if she didn't work. Angela intended to become a veterinarian, and since there was room in Rainbow Valley for only one vet and that post was occupied, she'd probably never live there again. And Daniel had enough money to last him for the rest of his life, so taking three years out to run the vineyard wasn't interfering with his livelihood.

But until then . . .

Marc thought about Kari, her stunning green eyes, her beautiful breasts, her gorgeous naked body lying on that sofa. It had been as if dormant cells inside him had suddenly come to life, making him want her with an intensity that bordered on insanity. Being with her was like getting a head start on the life he'd envisioned all these years, a chance to get a little crazy, have a little fun. What could possibly be wrong with that?

Maybe she was right. Maybe he had overreacted. Manufacturers didn't cut it that close on the quality of their products versus expiration dates. He needed to ease up. Relax. Take precautions, of course, but let logic and reason rule. In spite of everything, he needed to stop worrying about it. He was a logical man, and it just wasn't logical to get uptight about those kinds of odds.

He wanted her again, no matter how out-of-bounds it seemed for the man he'd been

all these years. But after the way he'd acted,
what were the chances that she'd want him?

CHAPTER 9

When the waitresses at Rosie's got to the end of their shift that afternoon, Bobbie did what she always did. She asked the rest of them how their day had gone, then proceeded to tell them how much she'd made in tips. Most of the time she blew everybody else out of the water. But if somebody happened to make more than she did, there was always an excuse. She'd had six tables with nothing but women, and women were terrible tippers. The air conditioner was acting up, and the customers in her section complained about being hot. The cooks couldn't get a steak right to save their lives. But when she outperformed the rest of them, it was because she was next in line for induction to the Waitress Hall of Fame.

For Kari, that day had gone pretty much like the past ones had. She'd made so little in the way of tips that if things didn't change, she was never going to be able to support herself. She was just about ready to take her meager earnings and call it quits for the day when Nina came through the door.

"I'm meeting a friend," she said to Kari. "Why don't you keep me company until she gets here?"

Kari sat down at a table across from Nina, relishing the chance to rest for the first time that day.

"So how's the job?" Nina asked.

"It's okay. I mean, it's a little hard because I've never waited tables before. But I'll get the hang of it."

Nina leaned in and spoke softly. "So how are you getting along with Bobbie?"

Uh-oh. In spite of what Marc had said about her, it made Kari nervous to say what she really thought. That could be dangerous in a small town like this. "Oh. Just fine."

"Well, that must mean hell finally froze over," Nina said quietly. "Bobbie Arnette doesn't get along with anybody. You wouldn't be telling me a fib now, would you?"

Kari sighed. "Well, sometimes she is a little hard to deal with."

"There you go. Now, *that's* the Bobbie I know."

"I don't think she likes me."

"Bobbie doesn't like anybody."

"But I didn't do anything to her. All I did was show up."

"Oh, no," Nina said. "You did way more than that."

Kari was horrified. "What?"

"You had the nerve to be gorgeous. Bobbie doesn't like anyone prettier than she is."

"She's pretty."

"Honey, she looks like a mud fence compared to you."

"So what do I do about it?"

"Gain fifty pounds, chop off all that gorgeous red hair, and stop wearing deodorant."

"Is that all?"

"No. Throw in a breast reduction, and you two can be best buddies."

Kari sighed. She knew the job would be a challenge, but she hadn't expected any of the other waitresses to be.

"How are the tips?" Nina asked.

"Not great."

"Hmm. Are you having fun with it?"

Kari was aghast. "Fun?"

"Waiting tables is hard work, but you can't let anyone see that. This is a tourist town. A lot of people come here on vacation, and they want to relax. If you look like you're always out of breath, that makes the whole situation tense. People don't like that."

No tension? That was like asking a person being chased by a bear to pretend they were out for a Sunday stroll.

"Just try to have a good time," Nina said. "People having fun always look like they know what they're doing."

Kari did like to find the fun in anything she did, but pasting on a big smile when she had to be on her feet for hours each day with half a dozen people wanting something from her all at once while she was sweating like mad and wearing ugly shoes . . . well, that was a real challenge.

"So how are things going at the vineyard?" Nina asked. "Is the cottage working out for you?"

"It's great." *And if Marc came back, it would be even better.*

"I wasn't surprised to hear that Marc let you stay there."

"Yeah? I was."

Nina laughed. "That's because you don't know Marc. Sometimes I want to shoot him dead for being so bossy. But he always does the right thing in the end. When the going gets tough, he's the guy you want in your corner. And don't you dare tell him I said that, or he'll become so insufferable the rest of us will *all* pick up a gun."

Kari told Nina about Marc showing up at her door with a boxful of things to help her feel better.

"That doesn't surprise me, either," Nina said. "Remember, this is the man who acted as if it was such an imposition for you to stay there."

"How long has he been divorced?" Kari asked.

Nina looked surprised. "Divorced?"

"Uh . . . yeah. I assumed —"

"Marc was never married."

"What?"

"Angela's mother was his high school girlfriend. She got pregnant, then ran off after Angela was born. Marc would have married her, but she didn't want anything to do with a baby or a husband."

"You mean he raised Angela alone? And he was only in *high school*?"

"Yeah. And Daniel and I were just kids ourselves when Angela was born. I was fifteen, and Daniel was thirteen. Our father was dead, and our mother was in bad health. She's gone now, too. Marc was already calling the shots at the vineyard by that time, even with going to school."

"Then he had a baby on top of everything?"

"Yeah. But if there's anybody who can

220

handle the hard stuff, it's Marc."

Kari was stunned. She'd assumed he'd been divorced somewhat recently, but he'd never been married at all? His high school girlfriend had gotten pregnant and then left him with a newborn baby? Then it struck her. Maybe that was why he took his condoms so seriously. Suddenly what had happened between them a few nights ago was making a lot more sense.

Just then a woman came into the café wearing jeans and a T-shirt, a tote bag slung over her shoulder. She was tall and thin with dark, silky hair pulled into a ponytail. When she walked up to their table, Kari realized she was the friend Nina was meeting.

She pulled out a chair and sat down. "Sorry I'm late," she said breathlessly. "Had a family who was adopting a cat. Had to finish that up."

"Kari, this is Shannon North," Nina said. "She's the director of the Rainbow Valley Animal Shelter."

Kari shook her hand. "That's a pretty cool job. I bet it keeps you busy."

"You have no idea."

"Kari's new to Rainbow Valley," Nina said. "She started working for Rosie, but she's a little tight on money so she's staying in the cottage at the vineyard." Then she turned to Kari. "Shannon's meeting me to work on her wedding plans."

"Wedding?" Kari said. "You're getting married?"

"Yeah," Shannon said with a smile. "At the vineyard next month."

"So where's Luke?" Nina said. "I thought he was coming, too."

Shannon frowned. "Funny thing. He said he had to meet the contractor who's building a barn for the rodeo school at exactly the same time we were meeting to talk about the wedding."

"Wish I'd known," Nina said. "We could have met at another — *oh.*"

"If we met at two in the morning, suddenly that would be the time he was meeting the contractor. What is it with men and wedding planning? He just keeps smiling and saying, 'Whatever you want.' "

Greg had done something similar with their wedding. Only with him, it had been *Whatever your father will pay for.*

"So how are plans going for the rodeo school?" Nina asked.

"Great. Marc was out last week to help Luke repair some of the fence around the property, so now he can start looking for livestock." Shannon smiled. "It's his dream, and now it's coming true. I've never seen him so happy."

In spite of her words about Luke and his aversion to wedding planning, Kari could tell just how much Shannon loved him. She was practically glowing with it, and Kari would bet her last dollar that Luke felt the same. *That's it,* she thought. *That's how it's supposed to be.* All she could remember about the days before her own wedding was Hilda screeching, her father writing checks, and her own conviction about getting married slowly slipping away.

"Marc has given Luke a lot of business advice, too." Shannon sighed. "We're sure going to miss him when he's gone."

Kari came to attention. "Gone?"

"After harvest is over, Marc is leaving Rainbow Valley," Nina said.

Kari was stunned. "Why?"

"Well, if he weren't so young I'd call it a midlife crisis. But since he's only thirty-five . . ." She exhaled. "Hell, I don't know. He's got it in his head that he just wants to be by himself for a while. So he's turning the vineyard over to our brother and heading out."

"For how long?"

"Three years. Then we're all coming together again to decide what to do with the vineyard. If Marc wants to come back, we'll keep it. If he decides to live somewhere else, we'll sell it and split the proceeds. To be fair, after taking care of other people all this time, he's earned the right to do just about anything he wants to. I just wish leaving wasn't one of those things."

Kari couldn't believe it. Here she was trying to integrate herself into this town at the same time Marc was looking ahead to leaving it? A terrible sinking sensation came over her, a sense that something she wanted desperately was destined to slip right out of her grasp.

As if she'd ever had it in the first place.

"So . . . how are things going between you two?" Nina asked.

Kari's heart jolted. "What do you mean?"

Nina shrugged offhandedly. "I just hoped you were getting to know each other."

"Well, he did come by a few nights ago with that stuff, but . . ." She wondered what else to say. It didn't seem right to tell the *whole* story.

"Okay," Nina said. "Here's the truth. I want my brother to stay in Rainbow Valley. I was hoping you'd give him a reason to."

"You actually think he'd stay on account of *me*?"

"I don't know," Nina said. "If you were seeing each other . . ."

"We're not."

"Would you like to be?"

Yes! But he doesn't want me!

Or maybe he really did, and it was just the condom issue. He was just thinking too hard about all of it. The trouble was that she could speculate all day long, but she had no idea what was really going on inside his head.

Nina waved her hand. "No. Forget I said that. It's crazy. You barely know each other. And it's none of my business, anyway." Then she turned to Shannon and stage-whispered, "What do you think? Is there a chance?"

Shannon smiled. "Well, last I checked, Marc's not blind. And Kari isn't, either."

Okay. Enough was enough. Kari decided it was time to talk to Marc. The conversation might go nowhere, but they were going to have one whether he liked it or not.

Later that evening, Marc grabbed a glass of wine and went out to the deck. Brandy followed him there and lay at his feet, letting out a doggy sigh before closing her eyes for a nap.

He hadn't been able to get Kari out of his mind. He'd seen paradise. Lived it for a few blessed minutes. Now he wanted to go back there. He wanted to make up for all the time he'd lost in the past eighteen years. He wanted to crawl into bed with Kari and make love to her for hours on end, leaving only long enough to consume the necessary food and water to stay alive. He wanted to make rabbits cry with envy. He wanted to have so much sex that Ripley himself wouldn't believe it. But what had he done?

He'd run away from the very thing he was dying to have.

Brandy suddenly leaped up, wagging her tail. Marc looked down the path and saw Kari walking toward the house, wearing a pair of shorts and a tight little T-shirt. Having a beautiful woman on his property was unsettling. Having a beautiful woman on his property he'd seen naked was downright unnerving. He had no idea what she wanted, but she probably hadn't shown up to heap forgiveness on him for what he'd done a few nights ago.

She climbed the steps to the deck and sat in the chair next to him. "Nice night, isn't it?"

It was. But he didn't think that was what she had on her mind. He certainly didn't have it on his.

"Yeah," he said. "Nice. Wine?"

"No, thanks."

Silence.

"At least the heat seems to have broken," Kari said. "It wasn't even ninety degrees today."

"Uh-huh."

"Is there any rain in the forecast? Surely after the storm a couple of nights ago —"

"I don't think you're here about the weather."

"No. I'm not." She paused. "I talked to Nina today."

"Oh."

"She told me a few things."

"Such as?"

"She said Angela's mother was your high school girlfriend. And that she left right after Angela was born. But maybe you'd rather she hadn't told me that."

Marc shrugged. "It's no secret. The whole town knows it."

"If you'd told me, I might have understood the other night just a little bit more."

Marc looked away, feeling guilty. But it was a hard thing for him to talk about. Always had been. To this day it still brought back memories of that moment he realized Nicole was gone, leaving him with a newborn baby and no clue how to take care of one. Those had been the most difficult days of his life, ones he didn't like to think about no matter how much he loved his daughter.

For a long time they sat in silence, the chirp of crickets grating against the stillness of the night. The evening breeze kicked up a few fallen leaves on the deck until they rustled softly.

"Shannon was with Nina today," Kari said. "They were planning her wedding. It's cool that you guys do weddings here."

"Uh-huh."

"She said you're leaving Rainbow Valley."

So she'd found that out, too. "That's no secret, either."

"Where are you going?"

"Don't know yet."

"Seriously?"

"Seriously. I'm just getting on my bike and hitting the road."

"Bike?"

"Motorcycle."

Her face lit up. "Motorcycle? You have a *motorcycle*?"

"Yes."

"Oh, my God! I *love* motorcycles! Can I see it?"

He couldn't believe the rapturous expression on her face. It was as if she was a five-year-old kid talking about a paint pony with a silver-trimmed saddle. This was a new experience for him. Angela didn't like the engine noise. Nina told him a motorcycle was a death trap whether he wore a helmet or not. Daniel's fondness for motor vehicles extended only to those with four tires and a 350-horsepower engine. But this little wisp of a woman actually *liked* motorcycles?

"Sure," he said, liking the thought of showing it off to somebody who actually appreciated it. "Come on."

He rose from his chair. Kari followed him down the deck stairs, and they walked to the garage, where he lifted the overhead door. And there it was. A big, gleaming monster of a motorcycle with a black leather seat and chrome so polished she could have used it as a mirror.

"Oh, my God," Kari said reverently, walking toward it as if she were approaching the gates of heaven. "It's beautiful!"

"It's a touring bike. Made for comfort. I intend to put a lot of miles on it."

"When I was in college, I dated a biker for a couple of months," Kari said. "Rode all over the place with him. When my father found out, he came completely unglued. The biker didn't work out, but I've loved motorcycles ever since." She glanced at Marc. "Mind if I sit on it?"

He nodded toward it. "Go ahead."

She slung a leg over it and sat down, holding onto the handlebars. There was something about this beautiful, delicate woman with that powerful engine between her legs, smiling with ecstasy, that made him hot. Hell, was there anything about her that *didn't* make him hot?

"There's nothing like riding on one of these," she said. "It feels as if your life is on fast-forward. I love that feeling of the landscape whooshing by. It's like you're driving headlong into life rather than sitting around and just letting it happen to you. It makes you feel so . . . I don't know. Free?"

That was it exactly. That was how Marc felt when he was on the back of a motorcycle. When he was in his truck, it was all about work. When Angela was younger and he'd owned an SUV, it had been all about getting her back and forth to school and being a shuttle service for her and her friends. But when he was on his motorcycle, it was all about him and nobody else.

"I've always ridden behind somebody," Kari said. "I don't know how to ride one alone." She faced him, her eyes alight with excitement. "Can you take me for a ride?"

All at once Marc had a flash of Kari behind him on that bike, her arms wrapped around him, those gorgeous thighs pressed up against his. He only wished he could make that happen right *now*.

"Can't," Marc said. "I don't have another helmet."

Kari's face fell into a disappointed frown.

"Maybe I can borrow one for you."

She smiled again. "I'm going to hold you to that."

She stood up and hiked her leg back over the seat, and when she did, she stumbled a little. Marc caught her arm to keep her from falling. As he steadied her, he softened his grip until it was more like a caress, because the last thing he wanted to do was let her go. Since the moment he'd met her and found out she'd run away from her own wedding, he thought her crazy impulsiveness was something he needed to run from. But now — tonight, *this moment* — he had the feeling maybe it was exactly what he'd been so desperate to run *to*.

"I shouldn't have left like that the other night," he said quietly. "It was a rotten thing to do, and I'm sorry."

"I understand why you did it," she said, her gaze never leaving his. "But I don't think there's anything to worry about. And if we just take a trip to a drugstore, we won't have anything to worry about next time, either."

Next time?

Marc's heart jolted hard when she said that, and within seconds his brain was

231

already conjuring up images of what *next time* might be like.

But that wasn't the only thing they needed to consider.

"You know I'm leaving Rainbow Valley," he said.

"I know. But are you leaving right now?"

"No."

"Then what does that have to do with having sex?"

"I'm just not looking for any kind of commitment."

"What makes you think I am?"

"You're not?"

"I just got out of a bad engagement," she said. "I'm not going there again anytime soon."

"Oh."

"So we're on the same page?"

"Same page?"

"No commitment. No strings. Just sex. How do you feel about that?"

Holy crap. *What* did she say?

Wait. Nothing on earth was that simple. He knew he should stop and think about this. But as she stared up at him, he couldn't seem to make the logical side of his brain engage. Her carefree attitude was intoxicating. Her talk of motorcycles and freedom and life whooshing by was like crack to him right now. He'd told himself if a willing woman crossed his radar, he'd go for it. This one was giving him carte blanche to have the kind of sex he'd been dreaming about with the freedom to walk away when it was over. She'd handed him the keys to heaven. Wasn't it about time he took them?

"Uh . . . okay," Marc said, still a little stunned. "I guess we are on the same page."

"Good." She put her hands on his chest and pushed. Off-balance, he took two steps backward and hit the wall. Then she stepped forward, took his face in her hands, and kissed him.

He was so startled that for a moment all he could do was let it happen. A tiny part of his brain told him just how crazy this was, but something had changed. Something was different. Crazy was what he wanted, and that was exactly what this woman gave him. She was kissing him hard and deep with a kind of abandon he'd never experienced before, as if there was nothing on this earth but the two of them desperate for each other. That was what he wanted. More of her. *All* of her.

Marc reached beneath her shirt and flicked open the front clasp of her bra, shoving the cups aside. He squeezed one of her breasts, then strummed her nipple with his thumb. She moaned against his mouth, then ripped her lips away and jerked her shirt off. Her bra came off along with it, and he yanked them both from her hand and hurled them aside. She trailed her fingers down the front of his shirt, flicking the buttons open. Then she flattened her palms against his chest, dragging them down to his belt buckle. He grabbed her hands.

"Inside."

"Not yet," Kari said.

She shoved his hands away and had his belt unbuckled in record time. She whipped it out of the belt loops and threw it aside, the buckle clinking against the concrete floor. Seconds later, she had his jeans unbuttoned. She shoved them down along with his underwear just enough to free him. Then she dropped to her knees in front of him.

Marc froze with anticipation. No. No way. Was she actually going to do *that*? Right here? Right now? Right in the middle of —

Holy *shit*.

She wrapped her hand around him. He took in a sharp, silent breath, his raging erection turning to solid rock. She slid her hand down its length all the way to the base, and then he felt her hot breath against the tip. Slowly she closed her lips around him.

He dropped his head back against the wall with a harsh groan, gritting his teeth, his eyes squeezed closed. She licked and teased, then took him deeper into her mouth. He reached down to thread his fingers through that beautiful auburn hair, tightening them almost involuntarily against her scalp.

He'd never felt anything like it in his life. Never. *Never.* He knew they should be inside. Behind closed doors. Only crazy people did things like this. But the truth was that he didn't care where they were. At that moment, all he knew was that her mouth was on him, moving in a way that was so hot, so carnal, so unbelievably *perfect* that he couldn't think about anything else. All he wanted was *more.*

Then all at once he heard something. An engine. Soft at first, then louder. What the hell . . . ?

A car. It was a car. And it was coming down the road from the front gate to the house. He froze, listening, waiting for the car to stop in front of the house and the engine to die. But it wasn't stopping. The engine noise grew louder. The car was coming all the way around the house to the garage.

"Kari," he said, barely able to speak. "Kari!"

She looked up at him. He took her by the upper arms and pulled her to her feet. "Somebody's here!"

"Who?"

He yanked his pants up. "I don't know. Your shirt! Grab it!"

"My bra. I need to —"

"Forget the bra," he said, buttoning his own shirt. "Just put on your shirt!"

As Kari grabbed her T-shirt and pulled it over her head, Marc fastened his jeans and buttoned his shirt. He ran a hand through his hair and scooted her bra around the back tire of his motorcycle with the toe of his boot just as the car wheeled around and parked in front of the garage. They stood there nonchalantly as a man got out of the car. In the darkness outside the barn, Marc couldn't make out who it was. Then he stepped into the light, and Marc almost groaned out loud.

He was dressed in jeans, beat-up sneakers, and a T-shirt that read "Professional Beta Tester. Give Me the Free Stuff." He looked back and forth between Marc and Kari, and the look of surprise on his face morphed into a broad, brilliant smile.

"Holy crap, Marc," he said. "Angela's been at college only a week. You're not wasting any time, are you?"

236

"Daniel?" Marc said. "What the hell are you doing here?"

CHAPTER 10

Kari was confused. Who was Daniel, and why was he smiling at the same time Marc looked slightly homicidal?

"What do you mean, what am I doing here?" Daniel said. "You knew I was coming."

"You're a week early," Marc snapped.

"And here I thought you'd be thrilled to see me."

"You should be at the house. What are you doing down here?"

"The house was dark. I saw the light in the barn."

"Go away."

"Marc? Where are your manners? Shouldn't you introduce me?" He strode over to Kari, holding out his hand. "Hi. I'm Daniel. Marc's brother."

Now she remembered Nina mentioning his name, but she still had a hard time believing it. This congenial, gregarious man was Marc's *brother?* The family resemblance was there. They were both big men with the same build, but the intensity Marc exuded with every breath was totally absent in Daniel. He had dark, shaggy hair that brushed his collar in the back, a mouth that was clearly used to smiling, and eyes that sparkled with mischief.

Kari shook his hand. "Nice to meet you."

"Kari is staying in the cottage," Marc said. "Just for a few weeks."

"Ah," Daniel said.

"She had some bad luck."

"Uh-huh."

"So she's a little short on money."

"I see."

"We were just . . . looking at my motorcycle."

That grin again. "Oh, you were, were you?"

"What are you doing here already?" Marc said.

Daniel shrugged. "Missed you, dude. Couldn't wait to see you."

"That's a load of crap."

"I'm running from the law and need to hide out?"

"Another load of crap."

"I'm terminally ill and came home to die?"

Marc glared at him. Daniel leaned toward

Kari and whispered, "He didn't buy it. What do I do now?"

"I don't know." She turned to Marc. "What does he do now?"

"He goes in the house," Marc said. *"Now."*

"No problem, bro. Oh, by the way . . . did you know your shirt's buttoned wrong?"

Marc looked down at himself, closing his eyes with frustration, then turned his gaze back up to glare at Daniel.

"I'd point out a few other things wrong with this picture, such as your belt on the ground over there, but I don't think they'd be well received. But y'all don't stop on my account, you hear?"

"Go!" Marc said.

Daniel gave Marc one last grin and left the garage, heading up the path to the house.

"I'm sorry," Marc said, once his brother was out of earshot. "Daniel has a way of showing up unannounced."

Kari inched closer, sliding her hand up Marc's chest. "Well, he *did* say not to stop on his account . . ."

Marc closed his eyes, drooping with frustration.

"Okay," Kari said, dropping her hand to her side. "I hear you. I guess the mood *is* kinda screwed up."

"Thanks to Daniel."

"How long has it been since you've seen him?"

"A year and a half."

"You'd better go catch up."

Marc let out a breath. "I hate this, Kari. After the other night —"

"It's okay. Tomorrow's another day, right?"

But Kari wasn't completely sure of that. As soon as Marc left there, he might start being Marc again and thinking too logically about what was going on between them. He might go back to thinking it wasn't a good idea, and having his brother in the house would probably only compound the problem. But what else could she do but bow out for now?

As Marc headed for the house, rebuttoning his shirt as he went, he was having a hell of a time walking. That was what happened when he was rock hard but was forced to fasten a pair of jeans. He was lucky he'd even been able to button the damned things.

Damn you, Daniel. Your timing sucks!

As he walked to the house, he got a good look at the car Daniel had driven up in, and he felt an entirely different kind of frustration.

It was a sports car. On closer inspection, a

Porsche. Fire-engine red, of course, because his brother didn't know cars came in any other color. Evidently he'd gotten tired of the Corvette he'd bought last year and decided to trade up.

Marc came through the back door to find Daniel sitting at the kitchen table, leaning over to scratch Brandy as she writhed in ecstasy on the floor. Daniel was her hands-down favorite family member, and no wonder. He sneaked her table scraps, let her jump all over him, and thought it was funny when she chewed on his shoes, which turned into her chewing on everybody else's shoes. After a visit from Daniel, it took Marc a week to get his well-behaved dog back again.

"What a surprise," Marc said. "You have a new car."

"Yep," Daniel said. "A Porsche 911 Carrera. Sweet as can be. Zero to sixty in four-point-three seconds."

"When did you buy it?"

"A week ago. Saw it in a dealership window and had to have it."

"How many tickets so far?"

"Only two. Would have been three, but the third cop was a woman. She took one look at my handsome face and just couldn't do it." Daniel gave Brandy one last pat and sat up. "Okay. My turn. When did you start stocking the cottage with beautiful women?"

Marc figured he could either tell the story now or have Daniel bug him about it for the next hour. Finally he just sat down and related the events of the past few days as matter-of-factly as he could, but that didn't stop his brother from acting as if the story was entertainment at its finest.

"Are you telling me a beautiful woman just showed up on your front porch out of the blue?" Daniel said. "Like a gift from God?"

"No. If God was going to send me a woman, he would have sent a clean, dry one who didn't just leave her fiancé at the altar."

"Who cares? She's gorgeous."

Marc hadn't missed how Daniel had flashed his too-charming smile at Kari, then paid entirely too much attention to the clear outline of her braless breasts beneath her T-shirt, and it grated on his nerves like nothing else.

"Hey, I'm proud of you," Daniel went on. "You've had a 'No Admittance' sign up for years. It's about time you unlocked the door. And look what was standing on the other side when you did."

"Will you stop talking about Kari? What goes on between us is our business."

"No problem. I have another woman on my mind, anyway."

Marc slumped with dismay. "Tell me you're not talking about Terri Vaughn."

"So you don't think she'll be glad to see me?"

"Glad to see you? You'll be lucky if she doesn't grab a shotgun and blow you away. After what happened last time you were at City Limits, you deserve it."

"Come on, Marc," Daniel said, rubbing his hands together. "Let's go grab a beer. I love living dangerously."

It had been a year and a half since Daniel had come back to the vineyard, giving Marc enough time to forget what his brother was like. A year and a half to forget, five minutes to remember.

"Fine," Marc said. "But I'm driving. And don't expect me to help you out. If bullets start flying, you're on your own."

City Limits was a blue-collar bar and grill located at the intersection of Highway 28 and the middle of nowhere, opened by Les Parker in the 1960s in response to Rainbow Valley liquor laws. The fact that it was inches outside the city limits gave the establishment its name and brought the wrath of the upstanding citizens of Rainbow

Valley right down on Les's head. Evidently back then, an evening of drinking and dancing condemned a person to hell for eternity.

Decades later, Terri Vaughn bought the place and ran it in Les's tradition, offering cold beer, hot barbecue, and an easygoing atmosphere that welcomed locals and tourists alike. Only a few citizens remained who believed a trip to City Limits excluded a person from walking through the Pearly Gates, but Marc was afraid the moment Daniel showed his face there again, Terri was going to personally send him up there to see if that rumor was true or not.

The crowd was light as Marc and Daniel slid onto barstools. Terri was behind the bar, drawing a couple of frozen margaritas for customers. Her long blond hair was tied in a loose ponytail. She wore tight boot-cut jeans slung low on her hips and a T-shirt that hugged her breasts in a way that left nothing to the imagination. She moved with the authority of a woman who took no crap from anyone, but at the same time she wore the smile of a businesswoman who knew how to keep her customers happy.

"My God," Daniel said on a breath. "Is it possible for her to be a year older and even hotter than the last time I saw her?"

Terri laughed at something one of her

customers said, then turned around. The moment she laid eyes on Daniel, her smile vanished.

She sauntered over with a stone-faced, narrow-eyed stare. Placing her palms on the bar, she leaned in and looked at Daniel as if he was dirt on the bottom of her boot. "Daniel Cordero. I do believe I threw you out of here. I expected that to stick."

Daniel assumed a properly chastised expression. "Now, you know I'm real sorry about what happened that night. And I did pay for the damages."

Terri flicked her gaze to Marc, then looked back at Daniel. "Here's the deal. I'll let you drink in my bar, but only because you're with Marc. But if you get out of line again, not even your brother will be able to save you."

"Enough about Marc," Daniel said. "Let's talk about us."

Terri's glare sharpened. "I'm running a bar. Unless you're placing an order, you and I got nothing to talk about."

"Coors," Daniel said with a smile. "And make sure it's ice-cold. It'd be a shame to warm up this frigid relationship we've got going."

Terri turned to Marc. "The usual?"

"Yep."

"Coming up."

A minute later, she set the drinks down, giving Daniel a stare that was even frostier than the beer. As she walked away, he tilted his head and followed every shift of her hips. Marc was surprised his tongue wasn't dragging on the ground.

"If she sees you looking at her like that, she'll bust your balls," Marc said. "Then she'll bust the rest of you."

Daniel sighed. "Yeah, but what a way to go."

"What are you doing here a week early?"

"Besides throwing a wet blanket over my brother's love life?"

"Yeah," Marc deadpanned. "Besides that."

Daniel shrugged. "Bad breakup. Figured I'd move on before she put a contract out on me."

"What is it with you and women? Do you have to drive all of them to the brink of homicide?"

"Any day I'm still breathing I consider a good day. Hey, speaking of women, when is Angela coming home for a visit? I'm sure she's dying to see her favorite uncle."

Speaking of *women*? At age eighteen, Angela qualified. But would there ever come a day when Marc looked at her and didn't see a seven-year-old girl with a ragged, self-inflicted pixie haircut and a missing front tooth?

"With luck, it'll be a long time," Marc said. "The longer she stays at school without coming home for a visit, the more comfortable I'll know she is." He paused. "I'm a little worried about her. UT is a big place. She's not used to that."

"She'll be fine, particularly with the boys. She's gorgeous. They're gonna love her."

"You said that just to piss me off, didn't you?"

"Angela can take care of herself. You worry too much." Daniel took a sip of his beer. "If you'd let me pay for her college, at least you could stop worrying about that."

"I don't worry about that."

"Then it would be the only thing you don't worry about."

"We've been through this. It's my responsibility, not yours."

"Well, I'm getting ready to take all kinds of responsibility off your shoulders. Might as well throw that into the mix."

"It's handled."

"It's a drop in the bucket to me," Daniel said. "Let me pay it. Then you never have to think about it again."

"Keep your money. It's easy to spend too much and then wish you hadn't. Are you saving? Might want to think about the future."

Daniel frowned. "Great. Here it comes again. Your rainy-day speech. Christ, Marc. I'm your brother, not your kid. I don't need your advice about every fucking thing."

Marc wholeheartedly disagreed with that. He wanted to ask Daniel who he thought had raised him from the time he was thirteen years old. Who made sure that there was enough money put away for his college after their parents were gone, because he had a genius-level IQ and it would have been a waste if he hadn't had the chance to go to college. Was it really so unreasonable for Marc to worry that even the incredible amount of money his brother had been able to make he would fritter away? If that happened, one more person would end up on Marc's list of people to worry about all over again. But since he'd hoped for a whole evening to go by before he and Daniel got into it over something, he decided it was best to drop it.

Daniel eyed Terri again, zeroing in on her ass as she bent over to pick up a stray straw off the ground. Then he looked back at Marc. "Did I tell you I spent some time in Napa recently?"

"No. You didn't mention that."

"Being a part owner of a vineyard is surprisingly good date bait."

"Right up there with being a millionaire?"

"Nah. Money only gets you so far. But wine — *that's* romantic. I spouted all kinds of crap about vintages and appellations and color and clarity. Pour a woman a glass of wine and talk about *mouth feel,* and she's yours."

"Dad would be so proud. He taught you all about wine making so you could pick up women."

Daniel looked heavenward. "Thanks, Dad. Appreciate it."

"I don't suppose you've finally developed a taste for the stuff, have you?"

"Oh, hell no," Daniel said. "If I never see another glass of wine again, it'll be too soon."

"You've actually got a better palate than the rest of us. Like it or not, you know what you're tasting, and that's all that matters."

"I'd probably know every nuance of Drano if I tasted it, too. I'd just rather not."

The irony was a little too much for Marc to handle. He'd never been able to discern the more subtle notes of a really good bottle of wine, while Daniel could describe every mouthful in excruciating detail. *But it's still bullshit,* Daniel always said. *Say anything with enough authority, and people will believe it.*

"What were you doing in Napa?" Marc asked.

Daniel shrugged. "Just poking around. Talking to a few guys. I have a couple of ideas about how we might be able to tweak the aging process."

Marc felt a twinge of foreboding. "Napa's not the Hill Country."

"I know. But a lot of stuff still applies."

Marc didn't know why he was surprised. This was nothing new. Daniel always thought he had a better way of doing things, because his brain was moving constantly. He always had the best of intentions, but the outcome was always in question. When you were working with intangibles like bits and bytes and something wasn't coming together, what did it hurt to throw out a million or so and start over? But grapevines were a real, physical product that couldn't withstand one bad decision after another without doing the kind of irreparable damage that would affect a vineyard for years to come.

Daniel waved his hand. "Forget about it for now. We'll talk about it later. Let's have another beer."

When he signaled Terri, she looked at

Marc. He nodded, and she brought them another drink. Then Daniel glanced up at the baseball game playing on the TV over the bar, and they turned their conversation to the Rangers and their chances of heading to the World Series.

Later Terri picked up their empty glasses and laid down the check. Marc grabbed it, only to have Daniel pluck it out of his hand and pay it with a credit card. Then as they were getting up to leave, he reached into his wallet, pulled out a hundred, and tossed it on the bar. Terri flicked her gaze to the extravagant tip, then reached over and picked it up.

"Hmm," she said, flipping it over and back with her fingertips. "Looks like what they say is true. A fool and his money are soon parted." She slid it back across the bar. "There's your money back. But you're still a fool."

As Terri walked away, Daniel shook his head with admiration. "A woman who can't be bought. You don't see that every day."

"Then you've been hanging out with the wrong women."

"It's official. I'm in love."

"You are *so* out of your league."

"Nah. We're both playing in the majors. She's hot, I'm hot. Where's the problem?"

"That's it," Marc said. "We're out of here."

Kari sat on the sofa in the cottage watching some dumb TV sitcom, but her mind was on Marc.

She was dying for him. *Dying.*

A few minutes ago, she'd looked out the window to see his truck parked near the garage, so she knew he and Daniel were home again. But when half an hour passed, then an hour, it was clear she wasn't going to see Marc again that night. She told herself it was because he hadn't seen Daniel in such a long time, that it had nothing to do with his logical brain kicking in again and telling him maybe they shouldn't be together.

That was what she told herself, anyway, or she was going to go crazy.

All at once, Boo jerked to attention and let out a flurry of barks. He leaped off the sofa and ran to the kitchen window. Curious, Kari followed him to the kitchen and looked out the window. Darkness had fallen, and a single mercury vapor light cast a weak glow over the area. At first she saw nothing and started to turn away, only to see a strange shadow several yards from the cottage.

Then the shadow moved.

Shocked, she stumbled backward several steps and stood there, breathing hard. A man was walking through the trees. A man she was sure wasn't supposed to be there.

She hurried forward again and closed the blinds. After a few more seconds, she flipped one of the blinds up and looked out. The man had moved to a bank of trees closer to the cottage, and she had the distinct feeling she was being watched.

She dropped the blind as if it was on fire. It couldn't be one of Marc's employees. It was late, and the trees surrounding the cottage were nowhere near the vines. And it looked as if this guy was trying to stay hidden.

Every horror movie she'd ever seen flashed through her mind. They always took place in out-of-the-way locations just like this vineyard, which was miles from civilization — slasher movies with knives and scythes and chain saws. Boo barked again, but any evil person worth his salt knew that bark wasn't coming from a German shepherd or a pit bull. Just from one tiny dog who looked as if he should be trotting up the Yellow Brick Road.

She ran to the front door and made sure it was locked. But what about the windows?

She needed to make sure those were secured, too, but that meant she had to go near them, and she sure as hell didn't want to do that.

Her phone. Where was her phone?

There.

She grabbed it off the end table in the living room. Calling 911 would do her no good out there. Thank God, Marc had given her his number. She punched the button, her heart beating madly. Waited through three rings.

"Kari?"

"Marc," she whispered. "There's a man outside the cottage."

"What do you mean? At the door?"

"No. He's lurking in the trees, and he's moving closer. I think . . . I think he's watching me."

"Any idea who it is?"

"No. None."

"Is the door locked?"

"Yes."

"Stay put. I'm on my way."

Kari laid down her phone, only to pick it up again as if it was a life preserver on the end of a rope. She waited in the living room, wondering if she should turn out the lights. Then wouldn't it be harder for her rapist/murderer to find her if he should happen to burst through the door?

No. She couldn't sit in the dark. That would freak her out completely. Instead, she gathered up Boo and held him close to her chest, feeling his little heart beating like mad, hating the way he kept looking at that kitchen window. Then she heard what sounded like a car engine in the distance, and Boo let loose with another burst of barking.

Then all at once she heard three loud raps. "Kari! Answer the door. *Kari!*"

Oh, thank *God.* It was Marc.

She put Boo down and leaped off the sofa. She hurried to the door, unlocked it, and flung it open. Marc and Daniel strode into the cottage, and they were both carrying rifles. *Yes.* Men with guns. She liked that. She liked that a *lot.*

"Are you all right?" Marc asked her.

"Yeah. I'm fine."

"You were right. There was definitely somebody out there. But by the time we got there, he was taking off through the trees."

"I thought I heard a car engine."

"You did," Daniel said. "There's a dirt road that runs along the western edge of the vineyard. That's how he got away."

Kari closed her eyes and took a deep breath. "Scared the hell out of me. Who could it have been?"

"I don't know," Marc said. "We've had our share of itinerant people wandering across our property, but they don't make getaways in cars."

Kari swallowed hard. "Why would somebody be poking around the cottage?"

"A few houses and businesses in Rainbow Valley have been broken into in the past week, but I can't see burglars coming way out here. How about that fiancé of yours?"

"*Ex*-fiancé. And he wouldn't be walking through woods for any reason. The closest he gets to nature is when he hits a golf ball into the trees. So who do you think it was?"

"I don't know. But until we find out, pack your things. You're moving up to the house."

Fifteen minutes later, Marc and Daniel had moved the last of Kari's suitcases to the house. It felt odd being there, particularly with Daniel knowing what was going on between her and Marc. But her alternative was to stay in the cottage, never knowing when the scary man would come lumbering back through the forest, this time with his trusty chain saw. Much better to be in the big house with big locks and big men with firearms.

With Daniel in the guest room, Marc said the only other room available was Angela's, so he put Kari in there. As he gathered her suitcases in one corner, she circled her gaze around the room. As weird as it felt being in the house, it felt even weirder being in a teenage girl's room, even though Angela's was different than she imagined most would be. The furniture looked antique, with a vintage handmade quilt on the bed. Where rock star posters should have been were posters of horses and other animals.

"I take it your daughter is an animal lover?" Kari asked.

"She wants to be a vet. She used to work at the Rainbow Valley Animal Shelter in the summer and on weekends during the school year."

"Yeah, I met Shannon North the other day. Nina introduced us at Rosie's."

"Shannon was good to Angela," Marc said. "Wrote one of her college recommendation letters."

Boo walked over to Marc and barked.

"What does he want?" Marc asked.

"Nothing."

"Then why is he barking?"

"I don't know. Doesn't Brandy ever bark for no reason?"

"Nope."

Marc had a dog with as much self-control as he did. What a surprise.

"Try to keep him from chewing something up while he's here, will you?" Marc said.

Kari put her fists on her hips. "What makes you think he'll chew something up?"

"The teeth marks on the dining room chair in the cottage."

She dropped her hands to her side. "Oh."

"Bathroom's in there. The bed should still be made up. Anything else you need?"

"No."

"Are you sure?"

"I'm sure."

"Good."

In one smooth move, Marc kicked the door shut with the heel of his boot, grabbed Kari around the waist, and pulled her up next to him, giving her a look so hot it practically melted her panties.

"I believe we have some unfinished business."

CHAPTER 11

When Marc slid his hand along Kari's neck, pulled her to him, and kissed her, she thought she must have fallen into some kind of dreamworld where fondest wishes come true. She loved how he slipped his tongue into her mouth and stroked it against hers. She loved the way his hand tightened against his neck as he kissed her. She loved the way he smelled, clean and masculine, like a big, brawny man who lived life outdoors. When she started to get a little light-headed, she ripped her mouth away for a quick intake of air, as if she was a drowning woman who'd lifted her head above the surface, only to lock lips with him again and succumb to the delicious drowning sensation one more time.

He backed off, grabbed the tail of her T-shirt, and yanked it over her head. They both went after his shirt buttons, and once his shirt was off, he pulled her up next to him again, crushing her bare breasts against his chest, kissing his way along her neck as he stroked her thigh. She slid her hand down to his crotch, where she felt his hard-on bulging beneath his jeans.

"When you didn't come down to the cottage," she said, breathing hard, "I thought maybe you'd decided we shouldn't do this."

"Oh, *hell* no."

"Does the door have a lock?"

"Don't need one."

"Daniel —"

"If he comes in here, he's a dead man. Then I'll kick his body into the hall and keep on going."

She smiled. "I don't think I've ever had a man offer to commit fratricide for me."

"Another one of those big words?"

"It means —"

"I know what it means. It means nothing is stopping us this time."

He turned around, gave the gorgeous handmade quilt on the bed a hard yank, and slung it to the floor. Then he reached into his pocket, pulled out three condoms, and tossed them on the bed.

She looked at them with surprise. "When did you grab those?"

"Earlier. I wasn't going to get caught without one again."

"I take it they're not expired."

"Like I said. Nothing's stopping us this time."

Marc laid her down on the bed and yanked off her jeans, leaving her wearing nothing but her purple satin panties with the pink hearts on them she'd gotten on sale at Victoria's Secret.

"As much as I love these, they gotta go," he said, pulling them off.

"You love my panties?"

"You have no idea. But right now they look better on the floor." He tossed those aside, too, then he turned back to look at her. "My God, you're gorgeous."

"I am?"

"Believe it."

Every word he spoke seemed to be drenched in lust, and it turned her on like nothing else. He was out of his jeans in no time, barely kicking them aside before he was stretched out beside her on the bed. He teased his fingertip across her nipple, and then his mouth was on her, and she arched her back and maybe even whimpered a little because she wanted more. More, more, *more.* She closed her hand around his cock and stroked him. She was hot and swollen and dying to feel him inside her, and when he finally moved between her legs, she thought she'd die from the anticipation she felt. He slid his hand beneath her ass and plunged inside her with a harsh groan. She arched up against him because it felt so good. He moved harder and faster, and she had the most glorious sensation of him filling her completely, moving in and out, the friction causing red-hot sensations to streak through her, every new one building on the last, every stroke pushing her higher and higher.

Then she felt it. A tiny spark that became a blazing inferno in five seconds flat. And then she was coming . . . a hot, indescribable sensation that rolled over her like surf crashing against a shoreline. He moved like a man possessed, and she loved it. *Loved it.* Seconds later, Marc buried his face in her neck, his hot breath scorching her skin. "Oh, God . . . Kari . . . *yes . . .*"

A raspy sound of pleasure radiated from deep in his throat, and he quivered beneath her hands. He craved discipline and self-control more than any man she'd ever met, so when he lost control like this, she felt like the most powerful woman in the world.

A minute later they lay together, their breathing slowly returning to normal. When she thought about how she'd almost married a man who didn't make her feel one-tenth as good as she felt right now, she almost cried. She told herself that when the inevitable happened and Marc got on that motorcycle and drove away, at least she'd know what sex was supposed to feel like.

He lay on his back, his eyes closed, a sheen of sweat along his forehead. When he finally turned to look at her, his dark eyes were filled with satisfaction.

"Our bargain is working out pretty well," Marc said.

Bargain? Kari thought. *What bargain?*

And then she remembered. Their bargain. Just sex. No commitment. Fun and games. And when it was over . . .

"Yep," Kari said, suddenly feeling not so great about that. "So far, so good."

"We decided on just sex," Marc said. "The question is, how much sex?"

"I don't know," she said with a teasing smile. "How much do you want?"

He pulled her into his arms again, and by the look in his eyes, he actually meant to see how much they could accomplish in a single night. A warning flashed inside her head. *He's leaving soon. Stop now, or you'll be sorry.*

Uh-huh. Right. That was going to happen. She'd been hot for Marc almost from the first moment she met him. Now he wanted to have as much sex with her as they both could stand, and she was going to say no?

When Kari rose the next morning, it was after ten. She lay in bed for a moment, thinking about the night before, and took a deep breath of pure delight. Then she took another one to welcome her first whole day off since she'd started working at Rosie's.

Hallelujah.

Marc was up and gone already, so she took a shower, got dressed, and headed downstairs. She found Daniel in the kitchen wearing a pair of plaid boxer shorts and a T-shirt that said "I Haven't Lost My Mind. It's Backed Up Somewhere." His smushed-up hair and day-old beard told her he probably hadn't hauled himself out of the sack much before she had. He was sitting at the table with a cup of coffee and a two-pack of cold Pop-Tarts, poking away at his phone.

"Hey, Kari. Coffee's over there."

She turned to see Sasha sitting on the kitchen countertop next to the coffeemaker, her tail curled around her legs, gazing around as if she owned the place. Kari gave her a few strokes along her back. The cat arched up into her hand, then sat back down again.

"I'm surprised Marc lets Sasha on the countertop," Kari said.

"He doesn't. She knows what she can get away with."

"So she doesn't sit up there when Marc's around?"

"Nope. But Uncle Daniel makes it a point to spoil all living things in the Cordero household." A tiny smile curled his mouth. "Drives Marc nuts."

Kari poured a cup of coffee and sat down at the table. Daniel shoved the last of one of the Pop-Tarts into his mouth and slid the other one toward her. "Go ahead. One's my limit on cardboard and rubber fruit."

Kari grabbed the Pop-Tart and nibbled on it. "Where's Marc?"

"Where he always is this time of morning. Giving each grape a little kiss. Takes him a while, but he swears they grow better." He tossed his phone to the table. "Shit. Wi-Fi sucks in this house. I gotta do something about that."

"I couldn't help but notice that you drive an extremely cool car," Kari said. "What do you do to afford a Porsche like that one? If you don't mind my asking."

"Now, why would I mind a woman asking that? Gives me a chance to tell her I'm filthy rich."

"How filthy?"

"That Porsche was a hundred grand, and I didn't even bother to talk the guy down. If you ever want to get behind the wheel and take it for a spin, let me know."

"Seriously? Didn't you hear the story of how I ended up here in the first place?"

"Honey, that's what insurance is for."

"I've been driving one of Marc's cars."

"One of his cars?"

"The Bomb."

Daniel looked horrified. "He's got you driving that piece of shit?"

"Beats walking. So where did you make your money?"

"Developed a little website creation app for small businesses. Google wants to rule the world, so they bought me out. They didn't want to do anything with it. They just wanted to make sure I'd never end up being competition. To them, I was peanuts, but I'll never have to work another day as long as I live. And now here I am, Mr. Cosmopolitan, coming back to Rainbow Valley, Texas, to run an estate vineyard. Now, tell me, Kari. Where along the way did I lose my mind?"

"I don't know. I kind of like it here. It's peaceful."

"You don't strike me as a peaceful kind of

girl. You had Marc half-naked in the garage. I couldn't imagine any woman on earth who would have been able to pull that off."

"Maybe he's crazier than you think."

"Nope. Not my brother. The devil clearly made him do it."

Kari smiled. "So I'm the devil?"

"God, I hope so. Somebody needs to get Marc to loosen up."

"That's his plan, isn't it? Once he leaves the vineyard and you take over?"

"Yep. That was the deal we made when Angela was about fourteen. Three years. Then either he comes back to run the place again, or we sell it and split the profits. I'm paroled either way, so I don't care."

"Which do you figure it's going to be?"

"Guess it all depends on whether he finds a better deal out there somewhere."

Kari had a flash of that "better deal" being a woman, and she didn't like it.

"So what's your take on why he's leaving?" Kari asked.

"Freedom, baby. The open road. No strings, no commitments. He wants to dump responsibility and head out." Then Daniel shrugged. "Actually, I'd hoped it was just Angela's teenage girl crap that made him want to leave, and he'd get over it once she grew up and became a human being again. No such luck. So here I am, holding up my end of the bargain."

"So how do you feel about running the vineyard?"

Daniel picked up his phone again. "That was the deal we made."

So he didn't exactly feel great about it. Truth be told, Kari could see why. Daniel seemed about as suited to running a vineyard as Marc did to becoming a dot-com millionaire. She didn't think she'd ever seen two brothers more different from each other in her life.

"Thanks for the yummy breakfast," she said, tossing the Pop-Tart wrapper in the trash. "I think I'll go watch Marc kiss a few grapes."

Kari went outside and was met by a warm morning sun and a bright, cloudless sky. She saw Marc with Ramon and wandered over. Oddly, they weren't looking at any of the vines. Instead they were examining a rosebush. Closer now, Kari could see there was one planted at the end of every row of vines.

"Good morning," she said.

When Marc looked up, she was pleased to see his eyes flick to her breasts, her legs, and back up again. Then a tiny smile crossed his lips. "Good morning."

Ramon nodded a greeting, then clipped a branch off the rosebush the two men were looking at. "I'll check it out," he said as he walked away.

"What's with the rosebushes?" Kari asked.

"Have you heard about canaries in coal mines?"

"Sure. The canaries are way more sensitive than the miners, so if the canary faints, it means there's less oxygen in the mine and the miners need to watch out."

"Exactly. The rosebushes are more delicate than the vines. If they show mold or pest infestation or signs of drought, it means we'd better pay close attention to the vines, because sooner or later those things will be a problem for them, too. Ramon took a clipping that looked a little suspicious back to the lab."

Marc pulled his phone from his pocket and poked at it for a moment. He looked up at the sky, then poked again.

"You can't seem to keep your hands off your phone," Kari said. "So what are you hooked on? Facebook? Cat videos? Porn?"

"Weather."

"Weather?" She looked over at his phone and was stunned. "Good Lord. How many weather apps do you have?"

"I don't know. Six?"

"That's an obsession I've never heard of."

"Our business depends on the weather. You know that rainstorm we had the night you ran off the road? We're just lucky there's time before harvest for the grapes to recover from that."

"Recover? I thought rain was good for growing things."

"Some rain. But not too much."

"But you have all these sloping hills. Doesn't the water just run off?"

"With grapes, water isn't taken in just through the roots. It goes through the grape skins, too. Too much water, and the grapes split. If the skins have already been compromised by bugs or birds or mold, it makes it that much easier for the water to damage them. If they're not ready to be harvested, they rot on the vine."

"I didn't know grapes were that delicate."

"Believe me, grapes can be a real pain in the ass. If you don't pick them at exactly the right time, the acidity can be off. They need a certain amount of sugar to ferment properly. We picked the grapes just in time last year, right before a huge rainstorm that went from late one afternoon until before dawn the next day. If those grapes had still been on the vine, the water would have bloated them and thrown their chemical composition off. A whole crop can be ruined that way. Fortunately, we had the crew booked and they got the job done in time."

"I always figured you just pulled the grapes off the vines, squeezed out the juice, and that was that."

"I wish it were that simple."

"I didn't realize you were at the mercy of the weather like that." She shook her head. "Wine making is a tough business, isn't it?"

"Why do you think I'm ready to leave it all to Daniel for a while?"

Kari could see why. What she couldn't see was Daniel actually running the place.

"Daniel said you kiss all the grapes every morning to make them grow better."

"Daniel's a smart-ass."

"So when's he taking the helm?"

"I'm scheduling the crew, but I want him to call the shots during harvest this year."

"So you can make sure he's doing it right before you go?"

"Exactly."

Kari could see why Marc would want out from under all that work and worry. But she'd also seen the way he stood on his back deck and looked out over the vineyard as the sun was setting. It was a look of pride unlike anything she'd seen before. How could he want to leave something he'd spent so much of his life perfecting?

Kari left Marc working in the vineyard and went back to the house, where she spent most of the day in the den with her Kindle. She read one of the fifty or so books she'd already downloaded at the same time she provided her lap as a place for Boo to take a nap.

Later she made dinner for Marc and Daniel because she figured she should do something to pull her own weight. She found the ingredients for spaghetti and salad in the kitchen, which wasn't all that great a meal, but Marc said anything he didn't have to cook himself tasted like five-star cuisine.

After dinner they all went into the den and watched some intensely masculine spy movie that Daniel and Marc seemed tremendously interested in but Kari couldn't have cared less about. What she did care about was how Marc's hand wandered over to her thigh, where it stayed for the majority of the movie. He moved his thumb back and forth in a slow, mesmerizing motion that made her think of sex with him all over again.

At one point, Daniel paused the movie and went to get beer for all of them. Kari asked Marc if he'd talked to the sheriff about the prowler the other night. Marc said the sheriff had no idea who it might have been, and that had been the end of it. She let out a silent sigh of relief. Yeah, she wanted to know who was hanging around who shouldn't have been, but she was also glad that Marc seemed to be in no real hurry to get to the bottom of things so he could send her back to the cottage.

When the movie was over, he led her to his bedroom, which was oozing with the same masculinity he was, complete with a huge, rough-hewn four-poster bed, a massive dresser, heavy linens, western prints on the walls, and a black iron chandelier in the center of the high ceiling. Just sweeping her gaze from one side of the room to the other made her heart beat faster. Then he introduced her to that king-sized bed, and her heart rate went through the roof.

Later, when they finally settled down to sleep, Marc pulled her into his arms with her head resting on his shoulder. As she listened to his rhythmic breathing and felt the warmth of his body radiating to hers, Kari could honestly say she'd never felt so content in her life.

The next morning when Kari parked the

Bomb and went into the café, she greeted the other waitresses with a smile on her face and a song in her heart. She felt as if one of those Disney bluebirds had flown through the window and landed on her shoulder. Even Bobbie couldn't screw up her good mood today. She remembered what Nina had said. *Just have fun with it.* And that was exactly what she intended to do.

During the breakfast rush, Kari made a concerted effort to keep that smile on her face, and by the time lunch rolled around, she was starting to feel as if she truly was getting into the swing of things. Marla seated a family of four in her section — Mom, Dad, and a pair of towheaded twins about six years old, and she decided to put Nina's suggestion into action.

Mom ordered a fried chicken salad, and Dad went for the brisket sandwich. The boys ordered hamburgers. Kari wrote it down, then leaned in to talk to the kids.

"If I tell you something," she said in a stage whisper, "will you promise not to tell your parents?"

Both the boys' eyes grew wide.

"I'm new here, so I mess up a lot. If you order a hamburger, there's no telling what I might bring you instead." She leaned in closer. "What if I *really* messed up and brought you something awful?"

"Like what?" one of the boys said.

"Like . . . a *zombie.*"

Both boys' eyebrows flew up. "A zombie?"

"If I brought you one of those, would you eat it?"

One of them grinned. "I'd eat it!"

"So would I!" the other one said.

"Even if it tried to eat you first?" Kari said.

The boys giggled. "We'd eat it before it could eat us!"

"I'm just warning you," Kari said dramatically, looking over her shoulder with trepidation. "That kitchen is a scary place. No telling *what* might end up on your plate!"

One of the boys turned to his mother. "We get to eat zombies!"

The mother smiled at Kari. She winked furtively and headed to the kitchen to put in the order.

"Carlos?" she said. "Will you do me a favor?"

"Anything for you, *señorita,*" he said.

"I need a couple of naked burgers. Buns and meat only."

Carlos complied, and she stepped to the grill side of the kitchen beside him. She grabbed pickles and put them on the open-faced burgers for eyeballs. Shredded lettuce became hair, and she created the rest of the face with a mustard squirter, adding ketchup blood to make it look as disgusting as possible.

Bobbie walked over and looked over her shoulder. "What the hell is *that*?"

Kari smiled. "Just flirting with the male customers."

"You're *so* weird," Bobbie said and flounced off with a couple of orders of nachos.

"Anything else for burgers?" Carlos asked.

"Nope. This'll do." She smiled. "You know, you speak amazingly good English."

"Sometimes good," he said with a smile, then glanced at Bobbie leaving the kitchen and frowned. "Sometimes not so good."

Kari returned to the table with lunch for Mom and Dad, and then she set the baskets down in front of the boys.

"Zombies!" they said.

"What?" Kari said, fluttering her hand against her chest and looking horrified. "Oh, no! I just *knew* I was going to mess up the order! I'm so *sorry*!"

One of the boys took the top bun and squashed it down on the rest of the burger. "There. I killed it!" The other boy did the same, and then they both picked up their burgers and gnawed into them, giggling the whole time. And Mom and Dad couldn't stop smiling.

When Kari brought the check, she drew an oozing zombie on it with frightful hair. Dad showed the boys, who laughed all over again. The parents thanked her on their way out the door. She took the credit slip from Marla, looked at the tip, and just about fell over backward. She did some quick math in her head. *Twenty-five percent?*

For the rest of her shift, Kari felt as if she'd found the key to the mint. Bobbie hated kids, she loved them. This was *perfect.* She found out little boys liked zombies. Little girls liked puppies and kittens. It was amazing the creatures she could create with just about anything on the kids' menu. And parents liked anything that kept their kids happy, smiling, and still in their seats. Nina had been right. Once she started having fun with it, everything seemed to change, and the day flew by.

"So how'd it go today, girls?" Bobbie said at the end of their shift.

Kari usually hated the sound of those words. But when she added up her tips, she almost gasped out loud.

She'd made a buck more than Bobbie.

It was only a single dollar, but it seemed like a million. When Kari reported the amount, Bobbie's face went stark white.

"Well," Bobbie said, suddenly sounding a little shaky. "It's because you waited on a party of eight this morning."

"You're right," Kari said. "It was probably just a fluke."

"Of course it was a fluke."

"I know," Kari agreed. "It couldn't possibly happen again."

Bobbie got a calculating look on her face. "I guess we'll find out tomorrow, won't we?"

Kari felt a rush of total exhilaration, and for the first time she was actually looking forward to her next shift.

As she was leaving the café a few minutes later, Rosie called out to her.

"Kari. I forgot to give this to you earlier. Nina dropped it by this morning."

Rosie handed her a paper gift bag. Kari peeked inside, surprised to find a bottle of vanilla-scented lotion, a nail file and a couple of bottles of polish, facial moisturizer, shower gel, and several other personal-care items Kari hadn't packed for her trip to Bali and was dying to have.

Then she saw a note card. "Thought you might need some girlie stuff," it said. And it was signed "Nina." A whole herd of warm fuzzies gathered in Kari's stomach. She barely knew Nina, yet she'd done this for her?

Instead of heading back to the cottage, Kari made her way down the square to the Cordero wineshop. She opened the door, and bells clinked against the glass. It was a beautiful shop, with rough-sawn wooden racks full of wine from floor to ceiling. The walls were painted a dark, rich burgundy with hand-painted grapevines meandering along them. High on one wall was a sign encouraging people to adopt pets from the Rainbow Valley Animal Shelter. A pair of tabby cats lay on a corner bookshelf in a sleepy tangle of paws and heads and tails. A young couple with a little brown mutt on a leash were picking out a bottle of wine.

A woman came out of the back room with a name tag that read "Bonnie." She was a short, stout, forty-something woman whose instantaneous smile made it impossible for Kari not to smile back.

"Hi," Kari said. "I'm looking for Nina."

"You just missed her. Business has been slow this afternoon, so she and Manfred took a walk down to the Overlook." The woman stuck out her hand. "Hi, I'm Bonnie. You must be Kari."

Kari was surprised. "How did you know who I was?"

"You fit Nina's description. Hard to miss that gorgeous red hair."

"I've never been to the Overlook. Maybe I'll just go down there and talk to her. It's down the street on Rainbow Way, right?"

"Two blocks," Bonnie said. "When you reach the sign, hang a left down the brick path."

Kari left the shop, put the bag Nina had given her into the Bomb, then made her way across the square toward Rainbow Way. She walked past the Book Tree, where she stopped for a moment to look at a window display of Texas-themed coffee-table books. A few doors down, she walked past Tasha's Hair Boutique. When Kari was in college, she'd had a very cool pink streak in her hair, which had replaced the purple, which had replaced the blue. When she'd graduated and gone to work for her father at his company, of course that kind of personal expression hadn't been acceptable. She'd been keeping her hair under wraps ever since.

Well, now that she no longer worked for her father, maybe a little personal expression would be in order. She smiled at the very thought of it. A few of Rosie's waitresses had obvious piercings and a few tattoos, so Kari doubted she'd object to a couple strands of hair in an unusual color. Later. When she could finally afford something other than necessities.

As she turned onto Rainbow Way, she passed a thirty-something man with a camera taking photos in the direction of the gazebo. A second later, she realized he was the guy who'd wanted her to pose for pictures at Rosie's. After she walked by, she looked back over her shoulder to see him taking one more photo, this time of her. Then he gave her a friendly smile.

Normally she didn't object to a man's admiring gaze, but now she felt self-conscious. After all, what was there to appreciate when she was wearing a pair of turquoise capris, which were cute, and Angela's beat-up sneakers, which weren't? It was like wearing a cocktail dress with flip-flops. Most men had no fashion sense whatsoever, but she was sure this one was appalled at her lack of it.

Doesn't matter. Beats blisters. Keep walking.

When she reached the sign Bonnie had talked about, she made a left onto a brick path that wound through the trees. When the trees finally parted, Kari stepped onto a deck that was cantilevered over a precipitous drop-off. Beyond it, tree-covered hills rolled and crisscrossed, lit by the golden glow of the afternoon sun. It looked almost too beautiful to be real.

Nina sat on a park bench on the cantilevered deck, staring out across the valley. A bulldog lay at her feet, relaxing in the warm stillness of the afternoon.

"Hi," Kari said.

Nina turned around, and a smile came to her face. "Kari! Hi."

"Mind if I sit down?"

"Not at all."

Kari sat next to Nina. "Bonnie told me you were here. I just wanted to thank you for the stuff you sent over. You didn't have to do that."

"I just thought you might be able to use a few things you might not buy for yourself right now."

"It was really nice. Thank you." Kari looked across the valley. "It's pretty here. I had no idea Rainbow Valley even existed."

"It's a nice place to live. I'm glad you'll be staying for a while."

"So am I." She leaned over and petted the bulldog, who panted his approval. "And this must be Manfred. Bonnie said he came on this walk with you."

"Yeah."

"He's such a sweet dog."

Nina smiled. "Curtis and I adopted him from the animal shelter when he was just a puppy. That's been . . . let's see. Eleven years ago."

Kari glanced down at the ring Nina wore. "Curtis? Your husband?"

"Yeah." She paused, a melancholy expression passing over her face. "He died last year."

Kari felt a stab of sympathy. "I didn't know. I'm so sorry."

"He worked at the power plant near Waymark. There was an accident. He lived for a few days, but he just couldn't hang on." Nina's eyes grew misty. "He tried so hard, but he just couldn't."

"That must have been so difficult for you."

"It was. I don't know what I'd have done without Marc. He told me to stay home from the shop as long as I needed to, that he'd take care of everything. And he did. I still don't know how he ran the shop and the vineyard at the same time."

Kari smiled. It was just as Nina had said. When the going got tough, Marc was the guy you wanted in your corner.

"He's offered to do some work around my house," Nina went on. "Help me get it on the market. I hate going home to all that empty space by myself every night, so I really should move. But there are just too many memories." She wiped her fingertips beneath her eyes. "I'm sorry. I'm just feeling a little emotional. Today is our anniversary."

"Your anniversary?" Kari said. "Oh, I'm sorry! I wish I'd known. I shouldn't have come down here. You probably wanted to be alone."

"Actually, I'm glad you showed up. Keeps me from crying so much I screw up my mascara."

"You must really miss Curtis," Kari said.

"Yeah. And now Manfred is getting on in years. The vet says he has liver disease. There's nothing he can do, so it probably won't be very long before he . . ." She stopped for a moment, swallowing hard. "I don't know what I'm going to do when he leaves me, too." She reached down to stroke Manfred's head. "He's such a good dog. Some people say animals have no soul, but they're dead wrong. *This* dog has a soul."

Manfred looked up at Nina, his eyes adoring and perceptive at the same time. Kari had never really thought about whether animals had souls before, but looking at Manfred now, she had a feeling Nina was right.

Nina glanced at her watch and wiped her eyes again. "Oh, shoot. Look at the time. I told Bonnie I'd be back in half an hour. And here I've talked your ear off." She smiled at Kari. "Thanks for listening. It was nice to be able to talk about Curtis. Particularly today."

"It was nice to hear about him."

"It's hard talking to Marc and Daniel about him. Men. They never know what to say. Especially Marc. I know he cares, but . . ." Nina smiled and shook her head. "Sometimes he is *so* clueless." Then she glanced at the valley one last time, that melancholy expression coming over her face again. "Curtis is out there, you know."

"What do you mean?"

"In his last hours, he talked about Manfred. He said he was going to wait for him at the Rainbow Bridge. And then he said the two of them would wait for me."

"Is that the way it works?" Kari said. "Can people wait there, too?"

"I don't know. I think maybe the Rainbow Bridge works any way you need it to. I like thinking about Curtis being down there with the animals, healthy again, waiting for us." She let out a shaky sigh, and tears filled her eyes again. "Or maybe it was just his way of telling me he'll love me forever."

Kari couldn't imagine loving a man that much and then losing him. But still she knew that kind of love had to be worth every bit of the anguish somebody would have to face when they lost it.

Chapter 12

"Just think about the cost savings if we didn't have to store and replace barrels," Daniel said. "Damned things are expensive. Micro-oxygenation will solve that problem."

As Daniel looked up at the stacks of oak barrels he deemed to be archaic and useless, Marc fought to hold his temper, but it wasn't a battle he was sure he could win. When they were at City Limits and Daniel talked about tweaking the aging process, Marc had no idea he was talking about *this*.

"Have you priced those barrels lately?" Daniel asked.

"Doesn't matter," Marc said. "We have to have them."

"From France? Seriously?"

The morning sunlight angled through the door, casting a warm glow across the weathered wood. Yes, the barrels came from France, but only because that was where a vintner went if he wanted the best money could buy. If the best barrels came from the bottom of the ocean, Marc would find a way to excavate them.

"They're not necessary," Daniel said. "We could use tanks instead. Stick a few oak chips in them, and *bam!* Instant oak flavoring."

"So you want our wine to have fake oak flavoring?"

"If the consumer can't tell the difference, why not?"

"*I'll* know the difference."

"A lot of vineyards are using the process," Daniel said. "Good ones. It's not that out of the mainstream."

"Our goal isn't to be mainstream. Mainstream is average. Our wine is *not* average."

"But it'll speed up the process. We can get the wine out the door a whole lot faster."

"This isn't about speed."

"It could be. And think of the control we'll have over the process. All the tanks will be linked together. Their lines will be thermostatically monitored during fermentation, and the whole thing will be computer controlled."

"So you figure as long as you hook something up to a computer, it's automatically faster *and* better?"

"Generally, yeah. Only makes sense."

"Wine making isn't about fast and cheap and fake, so get this micro-oxygenation thing out of your head."

"If you understood it better, then maybe —"

"Understood it better? Are you serious? I understand it completely. It's a half-ass way of making wine, and I'm not interested. I can't even imagine what Dad would have to say about it."

Daniel shook his head slowly, as if he couldn't believe his brother was being such an idiot. "Here's a news flash, Marc. Sometimes our father was a real asshole."

With that, he strode away, waving his hand dismissively. Marc gritted his teeth, wishing he could deck his brother for saying that, then toss in a few extra whacks to knock some sense into him.

Their father had been strict. No argument there. Sometimes a little intolerant. But Marc had respected him in a way that Daniel never had. And it was because Marc had always seen Cordero Vineyards as a living, breathing entity that required a firm hand and fierce determination to keep it alive. This place had history. Every vine, every furrow of dirt, every grape they cultivated was because of something their grandfather had started decades ago and their father had carried on.

Marc wasn't sure his brother understood any of that. When Daniel spent a day working in the vineyard and then looked at the dirt beneath his fingernails, what did he feel? An age-old sense of purpose that carried him through from one exhausting day to the next or the need to take a shower so he could head to town and pick up women? When the grapes ripened to the point of bursting, did he feel a sense of pride in nurturing the vines to produce another stellar crop or cringe at the backbreaking labor required to harvest them?

Marc was starting to face the truth. If he handed the management of Cordero Vineyards over to Daniel and left Rainbow Valley, when he returned he might not even recognize the place his father had entrusted to him all those years ago.

When she got back to the vineyard that afternoon, Kari looked out the kitchen window and saw a big black truck parked on the driveway near the barn. She went out the door for a better look, and Boo followed her. He ran to the edge of the deck and looked down the hill to the grape arbor. Two women and a man stood near it. After a moment Kari realized it was Shannon and

Nina, along with a man she didn't know. On a leash beside them was a big black-and-white dog.

Boo barked, then ran down the stairs and galloped toward the other dog. The big dog spun around and came to attention. He was four times the size of Boo, with jaws like a T. rex's. Pit bull? If so, he'd be able to gobble Boo up in a single bite.

A little worried, Kari ran down the stairs toward the grape arbor, but fortunately all the dogs were doing was circling and sniffing the way dogs did when they were interested in each other, not what they did when one was considering having the other one for lunch.

"Hi, Kari!" Shannon said.

"I'm sorry," Kari said. "Boo got away from me."

"No problem. He and Fluffy are getting along just fine."

Kari looked at the dog's sleek black-and-white coat. "His name is Fluffy?"

"What's the matter?" the man said. "You don't think he looks like a Fluffy?"

"Uh . . ."

"Luke named him that just to annoy me," Shannon said with a smile. "Kari, this is Luke Dawson. My fiancé."

Kari shook his hand. "Nice to meet you."

"Boo's a little doll," Shannon said, smiling down at him. "Is he a cairn terrier?"

"Mostly, I think," Kari said. "Marc thinks he looks like a rag mop."

Nina rolled her eyes. "Marc thinks a dog isn't a dog unless it's the size of the *Titanic* and keeps rabbits out of a vineyard." She turned to Shannon and Luke. "So what's it going to be on the arbor, guys? Tulle or ribbons?" She held up a sample of both.

"I like the fluffy stuff," Luke said.

"But the ribbons add color," Shannon said.

"Then get colored fluffy stuff."

"That would look like cotton candy."

"You love cotton candy," Luke said.

"Sure I do. Just not draped over a grape arbor."

"Fluffy likes the fluffy stuff," Luke said.

"The only thing Fluffy likes right now is Boo," Shannon said, watching the dogs play together. "We'll have to check with him later about the tulle." She turned to Kari. "What do you think? Ribbons or tulle?"

Kari smiled. "Now, whatever I say, I'm going to ruffle somebody's feathers. Maybe I'd better just go."

"Can I go with you?" Luke asked.

Shannon smacked him on the arm. He gave her a grin and hauled her up next to him for a kiss. "Sweetheart, if you want burlap bags hanging off that thing, we'll have burlap bags."

Shannon looked over her shoulder at Nina. "How about both?"

"Look at that," Nina said. "Already you have marital harmony, and you're not even married."

"Good," Luke said. "It's settled. Gotta go now. We have a million things to do at the shelter."

"Since when are you dying to scoop poop?" Shannon asked.

"Since you made me come here to talk about crap like tulle and ribbons."

Shannon rolled her eyes, then turned to Nina. "Thanks. We'll be in touch about the menu."

Kari grabbed Boo so he wouldn't follow them. Luke took Shannon's hand, and they walked back up the hill, Fluffy trotting along beside them. When they reached the truck, Luke opened the passenger door for Shannon. But before he let her into the truck, he pressed her up against it and kissed her, and it wasn't just a peck on the cheek. Fluffy watched as if he was crazy about both of them.

"They're really in love," Nina said quietly. "You don't see that every day."

"No," Kari said, feeling a tug of envy. "You don't."

"They knew each other in high school. Met again when Luke came back to Rainbow Valley last year." Nina smiled. "I like that. It supports my theory about love."

"Which is?"

"That for every woman, there's one man she's destined to be with. Shannon and Luke never forgot about each other because they were destined to be together."

Kari liked the sound of that. She was pretty sure she'd run away from her own wedding because she was destined *not* to be with Greg. So that left the gate open for her own soul mate to walk through. She had a passing thought about Marc maybe being that man, then brushed it away. What had their agreement been? Hot sex with no strings attached?

No forevers there.

"Curtis and I were married here," Nina said. "Right there under the arbor."

Kari heard the same melancholy tone in Nina's voice that had been there when they were at the Overlook. "I can see why. It's a perfect place for a wedding."

"Our father was gone by then, so Marc gave me away. Walked me up the aisle. Put my hand in Curtis's." For several moments, she stared at the arbor, as if she was reliving everything in her mind. Then a smile crossed her lips. "It rained that day. Can you believe it?"

"Oh, no! On your wedding day?"

"Right in the middle of the ceremony. The storm blew up out of nowhere. Father Andrews kept talking faster and faster. He'd just made it to 'you may kiss the bride' when the heavens opened up. It only lasted a few minutes, but everybody was drenched." Nina smiled wistfully. "I didn't care. I was a married woman. Since the day I met Curtis, that was all I wanted to be."

Kari couldn't help thinking that if she'd gone through with her own wedding and something like that had happened, Hilda the wedding planner would have shot herself right in front of three hundred waterlogged guests.

"Sometimes I wonder what will happen to this place if we end up selling it," Nina said. "I can walk out here now and remember all of it like it was yesterday. But what will I do if it's gone?"

"You have photos, right?"

"It's not the same thing. Out here I can hear Curtis's voice. It's as if the breeze is carrying it right to me." Then Nina laughed a little, waving her hand. "Don't listen to me. I sound crazy as a loon."

No. She didn't sound crazy. She sounded like a woman in love. But how heartbreaking was it that she had to wait until the next world to finally be with the man she was in love with?

Over the next week, Marc and Kari fell into a routine of work and play that Marc decided he really liked. If Kari had the early shift and was home in the afternoon, she'd make dinner for him and Daniel. If she had the late shift and didn't get home until eight thirty or nine, she grabbed something to eat at Rosie's. Then when she got home, either they watched TV together for a while or they went straight to bed. On the nights she left town after dark to come home, if she was more than a few minutes late, he found himself looking at his watch and worrying until he finally heard her at the door.

On Friday afternoon, Marc made a run to the shop to deliver a dozen cases of wine and got stuck in town longer than he planned. When he finally got home and came into the kitchen, Kari was standing at the stove with her back to him, stirring a big potful of something he couldn't identify, but it smelled great. She had her iPod plugged into a set of small external speakers she'd intended to take on her honeymoon with her. The music she played wasn't music at all, just a big blur of incomprehensible noise that usually annoyed the crap out of him. But the moment he saw her long legs protruding from a pair of very short shorts, all the blood in his head went south and he just didn't give a damn.

"Sorry I wasn't home sooner," he told her. "The idiot Lola hired to put some new shelves up in her shop skipped out without finishing the job."

"Lola?"

"Of Lola's Pet Emporium."

Kari laid the spoon down and faced him. "So you finished it?"

"It didn't take long. All I had to do was —"

And that was when he saw it. A two-inch strip of bright pink running the length of Kari's hair, from her part to the curly tips. He stopped short and stared at it. What the *hell*?

Just then Daniel came into the kitchen. "Whoa," he said with a smile. "Good choice. Love the pink."

"Why, thank you," Kari said, returning his smile. Then she looked at Marc. "What do you think?"

Daniel grinned. "This should be good."

He turned to Marc. "So. Tell Kari what you think of her hair."

"The pink's nice," he said.

"That's all?" Daniel said, looking disappointed. "Angela put on a temporary tattoo once, and you launched into a ten-minute lecture before you realized it wasn't permanent."

"This isn't permanent, either," Kari said. "I borrowed a box of Jell-O from the pantry."

"Jell-O?" Marc said.

"It dyes hair temporarily. I decided to do something a little crazy."

Actually, when Marc looked at that pink streak, he saw Kari through and through. Yeah, it was a little wild, but so what? He'd learned to go along with whatever Kari's whim of the moment was, because it eventually resulted in the kind of cataclysmic sex that knocked him senseless, and that was worth every crazy idea she had. The shower. The floor. Her on top. Up against the wall. He didn't care. So if she wanted to put a pink streak in her hair because she liked doing crazy things, why in the world would he object?

Marc headed to the pantry and grabbed some snack crackers, then sat down at the table and opened the box.

"Hey!" Kari said. "What are you doing? Dinner's almost ready."

"I'm hungry."

"Put away the crackers. It's an insult to the chef to eat five minutes before dinner is served."

"It's an appetizer." Marc held out the box to Daniel. "Cracker?"

"Nope," Daniel said. "I'm on my way out. I have a date."

"Already?" Marc said.

"I've been here two weeks," Daniel said.

"I guess it's not surprising," Marc said. "Quasimodo could drive down Rainbow Way in a Porsche 911 and get a date."

"So think how fast I can do it with this handsome face," Daniel said, heading for the door. "Later, guys."

As the door closed behind him, Kari said, "Are you *sure* you two are brothers?"

"That's what I've been told, but I've never believed it." Marc ate another cracker, then closed the box. "Our father used to wonder the same thing. Daniel drove him nuts."

"How so?"

"All Daniel wanted to do was play video games and poke around on his computer. And he hated working in the vineyard. That crawled all over our father like nothing else."

"But he's going to run it for the next three years?"

"That was our deal," Marc said, sticking the cracker box back into the pantry. "But I'm going to have to set him straight about a few things first."

"Like what?"

"He has this crazy idea about aging the wine with micro-oxygenation."

"What's that?"

"It's a half-ass way of making wine. I should have known he was going to go off on some weird tangent."

"Hmm. The app he created must have been pretty amazing for him to make so much money from it."

Marc's brow crinkled. "What has that got to do with anything?"

"He's an idea guy. He's telling you his ideas."

"His ideas are nuts."

"Uh-huh. So were the Wright brothers'. And Einstein's. And Steve Jobs's."

"He's hardly in that company."

"It's the way he's wired, though. To come up with better ways of doing things."

"Wine making isn't as much about innovation as it is about tradition."

"Tradition is important. But change is

good, too, isn't it? As long as it's for the better?"

"Micro-oxygenation is not for the better."

"Daniel has a hard time turning his brain off. He wants to tell you every time he has a new idea. Just talk to him about it. Make him feel as if you're listening."

"He's wrong."

"Just *listen.*"

"Fine. *Then* I'll tell him he's wrong."

"It's official. You're the most stubborn man I've ever met."

But he was also right. He'd spent his entire adult life keeping alive the tradition his grandfather had begun and his father had guarded and passed on to him. And now Daniel was going to screw it up?

"Invitations came today for Luke and Shannon's wedding," Kari said, still stirring. "They sent me one, too."

"Yeah? That's nice."

"Isn't it? I love weddings. You know. Unless it's me getting married to Greg. Oh! You know what I was thinking?"

"What?"

"Since Nina, Daniel, and Angela will all be here for the wedding, maybe we could have dinner here afterward."

"Nina and Daniel would love it," Marc said. "I'm not too sure about Angela. I haven't told her we're seeing each other yet."

"I know. You won't hurt my feelings if you don't want to include me."

"No. Actually, I think it's a great idea. It would be a good opportunity for you to meet each other."

"Great! And since Nina will be busy with the wedding, I'd be happy to cook something. Oh!" Kari hurried over to her iPod. "I *love* this song!" She jacked up the volume, and some god-awful rap song reverberated through the kitchen, but he didn't care. All he cared about was watching Kari. She went back to the pot on the stove, where she continued to stir it as she rocked her head back and forth to the music, singing along in a voice that was never going to make her a star, that gorgeous head of curly auburn hair and its pink streak bouncing along with it. She was so full of life, making Marc feel as if he was bursting beyond the straight and narrow path he'd been trudging along for the past eighteen years, showing him things along the way he'd never seen before.

He slipped up behind her, put his arm around her waist, and pulled her back against him. *God,* she felt good. Smelled even better. He gave her a kiss on the neck.

She stopped stirring, laid the spoon on the counter, and turned in his arms.

"So with Daniel gone, we have the house to ourselves, right?"

"Right."

"Ever do it on a kitchen table?" she asked.

"Can't say that I have."

She went to the table and boosted herself up on it. Then she grabbed him by the collar and pulled him between her thighs. He spread his hands on her waist and leaned in to kiss her as she looped her arms around his neck.

"We only have about five minutes," she said against his lips, "or the water's going to boil out of that pot."

"Maybe we should turn the burner off."

"Maybe we should take off our clothes and get on with it."

"Yes, ma'am."

Marc unbuttoned her shirt as she unfastened his belt. Buttons weren't quite the challenge for him that they used to be, but the bottom one on this shirt was giving him problems.

"Ticktock," Kari said. "Or dinner will be ruined. You don't want dinner to be ruined, do you?"

With a growl of frustration, he finally unfastened it and shoved her shirt open, pleased to see she wasn't wearing a bra. He took her breasts in his hands, marveling one more time at their sheer perfection. As he dove in for another kiss, she pulled his belt out of its loops, flung it aside, and started on the buttons of his jeans. The beat of the music pounded inside his head, and he had to admit that sex and rap actually went together pretty well, particularly since this time it was all about speed. He had a condom in his pocket and a hard-on for the record books, so if she wanted it fast, that was exactly what she was going to get.

Then all at once, Marc heard something behind him. The back door? His sex-fogged brain told him it must be Daniel coming back. But before he could dislodge his lips from Kari's, he heard a gasp. Then came a voice that clearly wasn't his brother's.

"Dad? What are you *doing*?"

CHAPTER 13

Marc whipped around to find Angela standing at the back door. Angela? *Angela?*

At first he was so dumbfounded he couldn't move. But then he sprang into action, yanking the sides of Kari's shirt back together. As she buttoned it, he reached over and killed the music. Big mistake. The dead silence was worse.

Angela just stood there with her mouth hanging open. Finally she swept past them, walking through the kitchen to the entryway. Then Marc heard her footsteps as she ran up the stairs.

"Where's she going?" Kari asked.

"I imagine she's going to her bedroom."

"But my stuff is still . . . uh-oh. What do we do now?"

Marc didn't answer. He couldn't answer, because he had no idea what to say. Kari had just buttoned her shirt about the time Angela marched back down the stairs.

Instead of coming back to the kitchen, though, she made a beeline to the front door. Marc heard it open, then slam closed.

"Crap," he muttered. "I guess I need to go talk to her."

"What do you want me to do?"

"Just stay here."

"I'll get my stuff. Go back down to the cottage."

"No! Not yet. I don't want you down there until we find out what was going on the other night. Stay right here until I talk to her."

Marc strode out of the kitchen to the front door. He stood with his hand on the doorknob and took a deep, calming breath that didn't calm him in the least. Then he opened the door and stepped out onto the porch.

Angela sat on the porch swing, rocking it with her toe, her arms folded, staring straight ahead.

"I wish you'd called first," he said.

"So that's the way it is now? I have to call before I come back to my own house?"

Marc sat down beside her.

"I've never seen her before," Angela said. "Who is she?"

"Her name is Kari Worthington. She's new in town."

"You're my *father.*"

"That's right."

"That was really creepy."

He blew out a breath. "Okay. I can understand why you'd feel that way."

"Stop being all understanding. That's not like you."

"I'm not understanding?"

"Not like that. You sound like one of those TV shrinks. Validating my feelings, and all that. This is weird enough already."

Well, hell. The truth was that he didn't know how to behave in a situation like this. But hadn't her whole childhood and adolescence been filled with situations where he didn't know how to behave? Why was this any different?

Because his daughter had seen him on the verge of having sex on the kitchen table. Yeah, that was pretty different.

"Why did you come home?" he asked her.

"Is it so wrong for me to want to see my family?"

"Well, no, but classes have barely started."

"You said Uncle Daniel is here. I wanted to see him."

"He's out tonight."

Her lips tightened, and he could tell she was trying not to cry. *Great.* He thought about apologizing, only to stop himself.

There really wasn't anything to apologize for. He hadn't done anything wrong. Of course, he would have preferred that she hadn't seen that particular thing he'd been doing that wasn't wrong, but now he was just going to have to deal with it.

"Kim and I had a fight," she said finally.

"Your roommate? I thought you were getting along."

"We were. For a while. But then she started staying up late. Like, till one o'clock in the morning. And she brings her weird friends over all the time. They don't like me. She told me I'm too uptight. And then I come home, and I don't even fit in here anymore."

"Don't fit in here? Of *course* you fit in here."

"Where? *She's* in my bedroom!"

Oh, hell. What was he supposed to say to that?

"I hate college," Angela muttered.

Marc's heart skipped with apprehension. "You have to give it time."

"I've given it time."

"A couple of weeks isn't enough."

She sighed, her eyes glistening with tears. "Don't worry. It's not like I'm going to drop out or anything."

He started to say, *Well, I sure as hell hope*

309

not! Fortunately, he managed to keep that comment to himself.

"I needed a break," Angela went on. "I thought if I just came home for the weekend . . ."

Her voice trailed off, and Marc felt like shit.

"It's always been just you and me, you know?" she said. "And then I came through the door and there was this other person . . ." She nodded toward the house. "Is it serious?"

He started to say of course it wasn't serious. He didn't know Kari well enough for it to be serious. But what kind of example was that to set? He was having sex with a woman, but it wasn't serious?

"We haven't been seeing each other very long," he said finally.

"Are you going to keep seeing her?"

Marc felt as if he was treading through a minefield. "Yeah. I think I am."

Angela turned away, and he could tell that wasn't the answer she wanted.

"Why is she in my room?"

He told her about the guy who'd been trespassing outside the cottage and that was what had led him to move Kari to the house. But it didn't seem to make her any happier. She let out a shaky sigh.

"What?" he said.

She shrugged weakly. "When I was at school, I got to thinking about harvest, and that afterward . . ." Tears filled her eyes again. "When I come home, you won't be here anymore."

"I won't be gone forever," he told her. "I'll be back home to visit. We can just make sure we're home at the same time."

"Not if I come home every weekend. You might be in another state or something."

"You said you thought it was cool that I was going to travel."

"I know," she said. "But now that I'm thinking about you actually doing it . . ."

No! Whether he was in Rainbow Valley or halfway across the country, it wasn't supposed to matter. She was supposed to be thrilled with college. Meeting other kids. Finding a boyfriend. Enjoying the experience. It made him miserable to think that *she* was miserable, but he had no idea what to do about it.

"If you don't want me in the cottage," Angela said, "then I guess there's nowhere for me to stay."

"I can move Kari's stuff to my room," Marc said.

"Oh, *God.*" Angela squeezed her eyes closed and dropped her head to her hands.

"No. Please, no. That's *so* weird."

Marc thought about putting Kari up for a couple of nights at Animal House, but that really wasn't a solution to the problem. Maybe this time there just wasn't one.

Angela looked up again, sniffing a little. "It's okay. I'll just go back to school."

"Angela —"

"No, really. It's all right. I'll go back. I need to face my problems, right? Isn't that what you've always said? I'm just going to go back. I'll talk to Kim. It'll be fine."

She grabbed her purse and stood up. Marc hated this. *Hated* it.

"Are you okay?" he asked.

"Of course I am. I have to go."

Without another word, she turned and trotted down the porch steps to circle the house rather than going back through the kitchen.

"Will you call me when you get back to Austin?" he called out.

"I'll text."

And then she was gone.

He went back inside to find Kari sitting at the kitchen table.

"Where's Angela?" she asked.

"She went back to school." Marc collapsed in a chair beside Kari.

"God, Marc. I'm so sorry."

"It wasn't your fault."

"Yeah, it kinda was. You're not a sex-on-the-kitchen-table kind of guy."

Marc sighed. "First Daniel, now Angela. From now on, when we get naked, maybe we'd better keep it behind closed doors."

Kari nodded. "I guess Angela doesn't like the idea of her father having a sex life. Then again, I can't imagine any kid who wants to spend much time thinking about that."

Marc exhaled, his eyes drifting closed.

"You're having a really hard time with this, aren't you?" she asked.

He was silent.

"It makes you feel guilty," she said.

"Yeah. I guess it does."

"So how did she feel about the relationships you had with women when she was growing up?"

"There weren't any."

Kari drew back. "Are you telling me it's been *eighteen years* since you had sex?"

"No! Good God, no. It's not as if there haven't been women. But every time I dated a woman in Rainbow Valley, the gossip went wild. I hated that. Everybody knows everybody else's business around here. And then Angela got older, to an age where whatever women I saw affected her, too. And then I got so busy with the vineyard, and years

313

passed, and suddenly . . . here I am."

"So you haven't had any real relation-ships?"

Marc realized just how pathetic that sounded. "No. I was always afraid of it caus-ing a problem."

"And now it has?"

Marc didn't know what to say to that. Yeah, it was a problem, but at what point was he supposed to stop worrying about how his daughter might feel about his personal life and start *living* that personal life?

"Marc, I want you to listen to me," Kari said. "If I'm causing a problem between you and your daughter, I'm out of here. All you have to do is say the word. I'm serious. What we have is just fun and games, right? That was our deal. But you and your daughter — that's forever."

Yes. Fun and games. Wasn't that what they'd agreed on? But when he thought about Kari leaving, he had the oddest sensa-tion that it would open up a hole inside him he'd never be able to fill again. Being with her was like having a window into the life he'd put on hold all these years, and the last thing he wanted to do was let her go.

"I want you to stay," he told her. "Angela is just going to have to deal with it."

When he dropped his head with a sigh, she squeezed his hand. "You're still having a problem with this."

"I'm just worried about her. She says she doesn't like school. That's why she came home."

"Don't a lot of freshmen get homesick?"

"So I hear. I just never imagined she'd be one of those kids. She says she had a fight with her roommate."

"She'll work it out."

"Maybe. But if she can't concentrate on her classes —"

"Did she do well in high school?"

"Valedictorian."

"Did you raise her right?"

"Of course I did."

"Then you have nothing to worry about. A smart girl who was raised right is going to be just fine in the end no matter what happens in the middle. So you don't need to worry."

"She told me she's not going to drop out."

"Well, that's good, right?"

"I don't like it that she even said the words."

"At her age, kids can change from day to day," Kari said. "Hour to hour sometimes. I know it's pointless to tell you not to worry because that's what you do, but things really are going to work themselves out."

She leaned in and gave him a kiss. Just the touch of her lips and the feel of her palm against his cheek calmed his nerves and cleared his mind. When she pulled away and smiled at him, he ducked his head and kissed her again, losing himself in the feeling, and soon he found himself believing every word she said. Maybe everything really was going to be all right.

The next day at Rosie's, Kari went out of her way to keep her momentum going, to let loose on the job, have fun, be charming, and play with the kids. Bobbie sidled up to the men, practically doing pole dances without the pole. As they compared tips at the end of the day, Kari just about jumped for joy.

She came out five bucks ahead of Bobbie.

Bobbie looked horrified. "That's impossible!"

"Oh, no," Kari said. "Do you think I counted wrong?"

"What I think is that you told Marla to give you all the kids. Of course you get all the tips. That's not fair."

"You've never wanted the kids," Gloria said.

"I do if that's where the money is!"

316

"You've never made much money on tables with kids before. What's going to change now?"

Bobbie looked a little bewildered at that, her brows drawing together angrily. "You're right. The last thing I want is all the snot-nosed brats." She glared at Kari. "Game *on.*"

The day after that Kari hit the ground running, smiling at everyone and making certain all her customers had a good time. She made a fuss over the babies, which wasn't hard to do because she loved babies. She ran to take photos if tourists wanted them. Even during the busiest shift, she found she had plenty of time once she got into a rhythm. If she goofed and it delayed somebody getting their lunch, she gave the customer a good-natured apology and moved her tail to correct the error. And through it all, she kept a smile on her face.

Unfortunately, camera guy showed up again and started asking her a ton of questions. Since he wasn't movie star hot, Bobbie didn't horn in, even though this time Kari wished she would. *I think he likes you,* Gloria said, and when his questions got increasingly personal, Kari was starting to think she was right. She excused herself as quickly as she could in case he was working up the nerve to ask her out. She breathed a sigh of relief when he finally asked for his check and left.

As the lunch rush wound down but there were still plenty of customers in the restaurant, Kari had a crazy thought and ran with it. She asked a couple of kids if they could balance a spoon on their noses, then proceeded to do it herself. She held her head very still, rested the bowl of the spoon against her nose, and when it looked as if it was going to stay, she held her arms out with a flourish.

The kids clapped, which led everybody else in the place to turn around and look. Kari turned slowly, showing off the spoon as it dangled from her nose, and pretty soon people were asking for spoons so they could try it. As they did, Kari took a few orders and delivered a few lunches. Bobbie rolled her eyes and told her how stupid it was, but there was nothing stupid about the attention Kari got from the customers.

At the end of their shift, when Kari innocently reported seven dollars more in tips than Bobbie, Gloria said, "Gee, Bobbie. Maybe the last few days weren't flukes after all."

Bobbie opened her mouth, ready to object, but Kari jumped in. "No! Of course they

318

were flukes! I got one really big tip today from a guy who drove his family here in a Mercedes SUV. I mean, how often do we see one of those around here?"

"Exactly," Bobbie said.

"It didn't have anything to do with the spoon thing," Kari said. "That was kind of silly."

"Of course it was silly. I mean, *really.*"

"After all, Bobbie's been at this much longer than I have. I can only hope someday I'll be as good as she is."

Bobbie's mouth moved, but no sound came out. Her face turned a funny shade of red, as if she was burning on the inside and the flames were trying to make their way out. Finally she just gathered up her money and walked away.

"Oh, my God!" Gloria said, her eyes wide. "That was the most beautiful thing I've ever seen. I thought the top of her head was going to blow off!"

Over the next several days, Kari still had fun with the families, and Bobbie continued to all but disrobe in front of the men. But for some reason, Bobbie didn't seem inclined to compare tips at the end of the day, and the snide remarks seemed to fall by the wayside. Kari didn't care if Bobbie liked her or not, because she'd learned that liking was one thing, but respecting was another.

This meant Kari could make money. Never much money at a job like this, but enough to keep body and soul together without somebody else telling her what to do with her life. She never could have imagined a job like this one in a tiny little town could make her feel so *free.*

One evening she had the late shift, and she and Rosie were the last ones out the door. As Rosie drove away, Kari got into the Bomb. She stuck the key into the ignition. Turned it. Pumped the gas pedal. It made the same horrible grinding noise it always did, but this time it didn't start.

She stopped. Backed off. Waited a few seconds and tried again. Still a lot of grinding, but the engine wouldn't turn over.

She looked back at the café, but Rosie was already gone, and the place was dark. Unfortunately, all the other shops on the square were probably closed, too.

Nina. If she hurried, she might be able to go to the wineshop and catch her before she left. With luck, she'd have jumper cables.

Kari started to get out of the car, only to see a man standing along a brick wall near an alley between two of the shops. It was dark, and at first she didn't recognize him. Then she realized it was camera guy. He just stood nonchalantly by the wall smoking a cigarette, paying no attention to her.

Then slowly he turned and looked over his shoulder.

At this distance, she couldn't tell if he was looking at her or not, but she still felt a quiver of apprehension. Now that she thought about it, how many amateur photographers his age hung around a small town like this one for weeks on end? Whenever he came into Rosie's, he was full of questions for her. Personal questions. She'd written him off as a guy who was probably interested in asking her out but didn't have the guts to do it.

Now she wasn't so sure.

Instead of getting out of the car, she locked the door, grabbed her phone, and called Marc. After three rings, he picked up.

"I have a problem," she said.

"Problem? What problem?"

"The Bomb won't start."

"Crap. Are you sure there's gas in it?"

"Yes."

"Then it needs a jump. Hope it's just the battery and not the alternator. I'll be there in a few minutes."

"Marc, there's something else."

"What?"

"There's a guy who's been in the café a

few times. He always asks to sit in my section. He asks a lot of personal questions. Now that I think about it, I've seen him quite a few times over the past few weeks. He told me he's just an amateur photographer, but I'm getting a bad feeling about him."

"What kind of bad feeling?"

"Like he's watching me."

"Then we need to talk to the sheriff."

"The guy is here right now."

"What?"

"He's standing in that alley between the bookstore and the art gallery. I think he's watching me. It's probably nothing, but —"

"No. It's not nothing. Go back inside the café."

"It's closed. Locked up."

"Who else is still in the parking lot?"

"Nobody. It's just me."

"Are you inside the car?"

"Yes."

"Lock the doors."

"I did. But Nina might still be at the shop. Maybe I could —"

"No! Don't get out of the car! I'll be there as soon as I can, but I'm also calling the sheriff."

"The guy's not doing anything wrong. What can the sheriff do?"

"Just stay put until you see either me or the sheriff. Do you hear me?"

"I hear you."

Just then the guy looked over his shoulder again, and Kari's apprehension turned into full-blown anxiety.

"Marc?"

"Yeah?"

"Hurry."

CHAPTER 14

Marc leaped into his truck and hit the highway, trying to call the sheriff along the way. When he finally got in touch with him, he was working a traffic accident five miles out of town and couldn't respond.

As Marc entered the city limits, he called Kari back to tell her he was almost there. She said the guy was still in the alley and he was still watching her.

Instead of pulling into the parking lot where Kari was, Marc parked his truck on the street behind the square three doors down from Rosie's and got out, walking quietly to where Kari said the man was standing. When Marc came around the corner of the alley, the guy jumped with surprise. Marc grabbed him by the collar, spun him around, and shoved him against the wall. The guy's eyes flew wide open with surprise, and then his expression settled into an angry snarl.

"Who are you?" Marc said. "And why are you following Kari?"

"Get your fucking hands off me!"

Marc had four inches in height and fifty pounds on the guy, so he saw no reason to comply with that particular request. "I asked you a question. You've been following Kari. Why?"

"It's not a crime to watch a woman."

"But trespassing on my property *is* a crime."

When the guy swallowed hard and didn't respond, Marc knew he'd found his trespasser.

"Let's see some ID," Marc said.

"I don't have to show you shit."

"Would you rather show the sheriff?"

"I'm not doing anything wrong."

"There are stalker laws."

"I'm not a stalker!"

"Prove it."

Marc released the guy, and he took out his wallet and produced a business card. Marc blinked with surprise. "You're a private investigator?"

"That's right."

"Who are you working for?"

Once again, the guy refused to answer.

"I asked you who you're working for," Marc said, with a heaping dose of malice in his voice.

"I don't have to tell you a damned thing."

Then all at once it came together for Marc, and he knew what the guy wasn't telling him. And the very thought of it made his blood boil.

"Her father?" Marc said. "Is that who sent you here?"

When the guy lifted his chin a scant inch and narrowed his eyes, Marc had his answer. He couldn't believe it. But after Kari's father had tried to get her to marry a complete asshole and then cleaned out her bank account when she wouldn't return to Houston, should Marc really be surprised?

"What did he hire you to do?" Marc asked.

The guy paused, clearly trying to decide how much to say. Finally he shrugged nonchalantly. "Nothing much. Just keep watch on his crazy daughter and report back."

That son of a *bitch.* "What did you tell him?"

"That his daughter is keeping company with a certain vineyard owner who can't seem to keep his hands off her. She graduated pretty fast from that cottage right up to the big house, didn't she?"

If Marc had been angry before, he was livid now. Clearly that one night outside the cottage wasn't the only time this guy had been at the vineyard. The very idea of this bastard spying on the two of them was more than Marc could take.

"Your assignment just came to an end," Marc said. "I want you out of this town tonight, or you and I are going to have a talk with the sheriff."

"Fine with me. I was getting tired of this shitty little town anyway. Though I gotta say I wasn't getting tired of watching her." He nodded toward Kari. "From what I could tell, you've been watching her plenty yourself."

"You heard me," Marc said. "Leave town. *Now.*"

"Sure. I'm out of here. But just between you and me, I know Stuart Worthington. And he's not going to stop until his darling daughter is back in Houston and under his thumb again."

The guy gave him one last go-to-hell look and sauntered off. Marc was glad Stuart Worthington wasn't standing in front of him right now. If he was, he might just have to put his hands around his throat and never let go.

Marc watched the guy walk away, then turned and strode toward the Bomb. Kari got out and met him halfway. "I saw you talking to him. Who is he?"

"He's a PI."

She looked stunned. "A private investigator? Why would he be following me?"

"Because your father hired him to."

"Oh, no."

"Oh, yeah."

"Was he the guy outside the cottage that night?"

"Looks that way. He's probably been your father's eyes and ears in this town ever since the asshole got back to Houston and told him you refused to come back with him."

"You mean he's been watching me the whole time?"

"He's been watching *us* the whole time."

Kari closed her eyes. "I'm sorry, Marc. God — I'm so *sorry.*"

"It's not your fault."

"No. It is. Ever since I showed up on your porch that night, I've been nothing but a problem for you. You had to give me a place to live. A car to drive. Then there was that mess with Angela. And now all this with my father. I wouldn't blame you if you put me on that bus to Houston, and this time you made sure I stayed on it."

"No. I don't want you on any damned bus to Houston."

For some reason, tears filled her eyes.

"What's the matter?" he asked.

"Nothing. I just —"

"Just what?"

"Thank you," she said.

"For what?"

"For wanting me here. I don't know where I'd be right now if it weren't for you." A tear trickled down her cheek, and she wiped it away. "I've never had a job that my father didn't give me or didn't help me get. I'm not proud of that, but it's the truth. The job at Rosie's — I know it's not much, but I did it myself, and that means something to me. I know you're still helping me with everything else. But eventually I'll stand on my own two feet. I promise you I will."

"I know you will," Marc said, leaning in to give her a kiss. But what he didn't tell her was that if something else happened, something insurmountable, something so hard to handle that she needed his help, he intended to be right there for her. No matter how hell-bent Stuart Worthington was on getting his daughter back to Houston, Marc had news for him. He'd do everything in his power to ensure Kari stayed right where she was.

The next Sunday morning, Kari sat on the deck with Marc, feeling the cool September breeze swirl around them. Kari flipped through her Kindle while Marc scrolled through one weather app after another, and it occurred to her that she'd never felt so happy to be anywhere in her life. The dogs were in the yard, doing what dogs did — running, sniffing, fake growling, and rolling in the grass together.

"You know Brandy's in love with Boo," Kari said. "What do you think? Are they too young for a real relationship?"

"I just want to know why good girls always fall for bad boys."

"Boo is *not* bad!"

"He barfs on the floor. Knocks over trash cans. Gnaws on chair legs. Shall I go on?"

"But he's good at heart." Kari leaned in and gave Marc a kiss. "So what's the weather report?"

"Clear skies for the next five days. There's a storm front brewing in the west, but it's supposed to swing north."

"Isn't it about time for harvest?" Kari said, hating to ask the question. Harvest meant everything was going to change for all of them, so she wasn't looking forward to it.

"Yep. I have the crew scheduled for the first of next week."

And right after that, Marc would be leaving. That meant their time together could be measured in days now rather than weeks.

If only he would stay . . .

That thought came into Kari's mind, and just as quickly she sent it packing. No sense hoping for something that was never going to happen. Instead, she needed to be enjoying every moment they did have together.

"Do you realize in all the time I've been working at Rosie's, you haven't been there during one of my shifts?" she said.

"Is that right?"

"That's right. Why don't you come over for lunch tomorrow? I'll have Marla seat you in my section. I'll show you how I can sling hash."

"Rosie doesn't serve hash."

"Must you be so literal? And I promise not to dump coffee in your lap."

"Now, there's a selling point. 'Come to Rosie's. We won't give you second-degree burns.' "

"Bring Brandy," Kari said with a smile. "I have a dog biscuit with her name on it."

Marc nodded toward the dogs, who were lying together in the sun, panting happily. "I'll have to check her schedule. She may already have a date."

Kari couldn't wait for Marc to come to Rosie's. She felt so good these days about

331

her job. Yeah, it was still hard, and she was still exhausted at the end of every shift. But she found out that when she stuck with it, it got easier, and she had actually started to enjoy going to work.

But she enjoyed going home to Marc even more.

At noon the next day, Marc parked his truck in a space on the square so he and Brandy could head to Rosie's. As he started to get out of the truck, his phone rang. When he saw Angela's caller ID, his heart skipped a few beats. He hadn't heard from her since the disaster the other night, and he wasn't completely sure what to say to her now. He took a deep, calming breath and punched the button to answer the call.

"So how are things going?" he said.

"Okay."

"Did you have that talk with Kim?"

"Yeah. I talked to her."

"And?"

"And she told me she doesn't care if I don't like her staying up late and bringing friends over. She says I'm too uptight, so it's my fault there's a problem."

Well, shit. "Can you change rooms?"

"It's too late for that. If you want to

change now, you have to get a letter from God."

"Well, it's your room, too. Have you talked to your resident advisor? Maybe she can talk to Kim."

"Oh, right. Like that's going to solve anything? It'll only piss Kim off. And then she really will be awful to me."

Marc started to say, *Come on, Angela! That's bullshit! Didn't I teach you to stand up for yourself?* But he could hear that shaky, on-the-verge-of-crying tone in her voice, so he knew he'd better shut up.

"You'll be here Sunday for Shannon and Luke's wedding, right?" he asked her.

"Yeah. I'll be there. I'd never miss Shannon's wedding."

"Kari offered to fix dinner for the family after the wedding."

Silence. And it dragged on so long Marc wondered if he'd lost the connection.

"Oh," Angela said finally. "So she's still there?"

"Yes. Will you stay for dinner?"

"I don't know. I probably need to get back to school. I have a sociology test on Monday."

"Come on, Angela. I'd like to see you for a little while."

Yet another long silence. Then a heavy

sigh. "Okay. I'll come to dinner."

Marc felt a surge of relief. "Good. That's good. I know Uncle Daniel wants to see you, too. And Aunt Nina. We'll have a nice time."

"Whatever."

That word frustrated the hell out of Marc, because she acted as if she didn't care about any of this when he knew she felt exactly the opposite. He couldn't even imagine what Sunday was going to bring.

After he said good-bye, Marc stuck his phone back into his pocket, and he and Brandy got out of the truck. As he was walking inside, he happened to see Luke coming out of the hardware store down the street. He had Fluffy on a leash.

Marc waved, and Luke approached. "Plumbing parts," he said, holding up the bag in his hand. "I *hate* plumbing."

"What's the problem?"

"Leaky faucet. Shannon tried to fix it. She's good at a lot of things. Plumbing isn't one of them."

"And now you get to fix her fix?"

"Exactly."

"Let me know if you need some help."

"Thanks," Luke said. "Here for lunch?"

"Yeah. Want to join me?"

"Shannon's expecting me back at the

shelter, but what's thirty minutes? A man's gotta eat, right?"

A few minutes later, Marla seated them in a booth by the front window. The dogs circled and sniffed, then lay down beside each other.

Marc looked over to see the kitchen door swing open. Kari came out, carrying a plate in each hand and baskets on her arms. She saw Marc and gave him a smile as she delivered the food to the family in the next booth. Then she swept by their booth and gave each dog a pat on the head and a dog biscuit.

"Hi, Luke!" Kari said, standing back up. "I didn't know you were going to be here, too." She took out her order pad. "So what's it going to be, guys?"

"Chicken fried steak," Luke said.

Kari wrote down the order, then turned to Marc.

"Double cheeseburger," he said.

"Got it. Do you want that zombiefied?"

As Marc was trying to figure out what she could possibly mean by that, Gloria breezed by. "Definitely get the zombie version," she told Marc with a wink. "It's *so* worth it."

"Then by all means," Marc said, feeling totally lost but loving the smile on Kari's face.

"Coming right up," Kari said with a gleam in her eye. Then she hurried off to give another diner his check. Marc watched her walk away, thinking how goofy she looked wearing blue capri pants with her pink apron and Angela's beat-up sneakers. But even looking goofy, he swore she was still the most beautiful woman he'd ever seen.

He finally dragged his gaze away and looked back at Luke. "So how are things going? Pretty soon you'll be a married man."

Luke smiled. "It's about time. Shannon's obsessing over the wedding. Her mother's obsessing even more. But to tell you the truth, it's the honeymoon I'm interested in."

"Where are you going?"

"San Antonio. We're just getting a suite at a nice hotel for several days. Shannon doesn't want to stay away from the shelter any longer than that. But I'm going to make sure that at least while she's on her honeymoon, she forgets all about it."

"Smart man."

"Your harvest is coming up soon. Are you really leaving after that?"

"Yep."

Luke shook his head. "We're sure gonna miss you."

"I've been planning this trip for years. Never thought the day would come."

"That's a hell of a business you're leaving behind."

"Hell is right. A vineyard is nothing but blood and sweat for the things you can control, and a lot of hope and prayers for those you can't. I need a break. Daniel will handle things."

Daniel will handle things.

Marc had said those words to himself so many times he thought he actually believed them, but saying them out loud turned out to be a very hard thing to do.

"What about Angela?" Luke asked.

"I doubt she'll come back here after college. She wants to be a vet. This town already has one and probably can't support another one."

Luke nodded.

"What was it like?" Marc asked. "Traveling the country on the rodeo circuit?"

Luke shrugged. "Pretty good for a while. Drinking. Partying. What's not to like about that when you're twenty years old?"

"A woman in every city?"

"Just about." Then Luke's smile faded. "After a while, though, I think I was pushing so hard for the championship that I didn't notice when it stopped being exciting and started being a hard, lonely life."

Marc couldn't imagine loneliness like that.

All he could see was peace and quiet and the freedom to do whatever he wanted, whenever he wanted.

"Sometimes responsibility is like a noose around your neck," he said. "I love my daughter. She's just amazing. But raising a kid is hard. Raising a kid by yourself is even harder. Over the years I've wondered what I've missed by doing that."

"Sometimes freedom isn't all it's cracked up to be."

"Yeah, but I'm sure going to give it a shot, anyway."

"If you want to leave that bad, you should do it. But I gotta tell you, Marc. I've been both places. And now all I want to do is stay."

"That's because you have Shannon."

"So find yourself a good woman." He nodded toward Kari. "I see a certain little redhead you can't seem to keep your eyes off of."

Suddenly Marc heard applause. When he turned around, he saw Kari standing on a chair. What was she doing? Balancing a *spoon* on her nose?

He wasn't sure how, but that spoon stayed there as if she'd superglued it. She held her arms out in a *ta-da!* pose. After several seconds of showing the trick to everybody in the place, she grabbed the spoon off her nose and bowed deeply, and the crowd erupted with more applause.

"She's something else, isn't she?" Luke said.

Marc couldn't have agreed more.

As she handed out spoons for everybody in the place to try the same trick, she glanced over at Marc and gave him a wink. She was crazy. He'd known that from the first time she knocked on his door. But when he looked at her now, he didn't see anything wrong with that. He saw a woman who loved life, who enjoyed people, who made friends easily, who had injected the kind of light in his life he'd totally over-looked all these years.

Then she turned toward the front of the café, and all at once her broad, beautiful smile fell into a look of dismay. Marc spun around to see a tall, stout man standing at the door. He looked to be about sixty years old, wearing a pair of sharply creased slacks, a buttoned-down shirt, and dress shoes. His salt-and-pepper hair was set into a rigidly conservative style, and judging from the heavy downward creases at the corners of his mouth, he looked as if he hadn't smiled a day in his life. And when Marc looked out the window and saw a black Mercedes sedan parked at the curb, he knew who the man must be.

Every muscle in his body tightened with anger. What was that bastard doing there?

CHAPTER 15

When Kari saw her father at the door of the café, the incongruity was so overwhelming that for a moment she thought it couldn't possibly be him. She wondered how long he'd been there, but judging from his expression, he'd seen her spoon-on-the-nose trick. She was instantly filled with the same humiliation she'd felt so many times in her life — the kind of humiliation only her father could heap on her with a single frigid expression.

She took a deep breath and walked across the restaurant. "Dad? What are you doing here?"

"May I have a word with you?" he said.

Before she could respond, he turned and walked out of the café. Kari paused for a moment and looked at Marc. His eyebrows were pulled together and his eyes narrowed in anger. That told her he knew who'd been standing at the door, and she read his thoughts as clearly as if he'd shouted them.

It's your father. Something's up. Do you need me?

It's okay, she said, moving just her lips, even though she wasn't sure it was going to be okay at all.

She left the café and followed her father to his car. His driver opened the back door. She got in, and her father followed. The interior of the car was so quiet Kari could hear the blood rushing through her ears. And in that moment she realized how much she associated the smell of the rich leather upholstery with negative feelings, and a single whiff nearly made her sick.

She couldn't believe this. Her father had driven all the way from Houston to see her. That had to mean something. Maybe it meant he would acknowledge her self-sufficiency, give her money back to her, and maybe tell her he was sorry.

Oh, right. Had her own wishful thinking ever gone her way where her father was concerned? *Ever?*

He looked her up and down, focusing on her pink bib apron. "So this is what you've been doing for a living?"

His face was all hard planes, with a bull-ish nose and eyes so impenetrable that Kari felt as if she were talking to a stranger. "Yes."

342

"Your job is waiting for you in Houston."

"I have a job."

"No. This isn't a job. This is what uneducated, uncultured people do in order to feed themselves. Is that what you want to be associated with?"

"I like it here."

He sighed — that bone-weary, long-suffering sigh intended as a wordless reprimand. There had been times in her life when that alone had intimidated her enough that she'd stopped being herself and started being whatever her father wanted her to be.

"I'd hoped the older you got, the more you'd get this kind of nonsense out of your system," he said. "Apparently that hasn't been the case."

"I don't want to go back to Houston. And I don't want to marry Greg."

"Forget him. If he couldn't hold on to you, he doesn't deserve my money."

So that was all this was to her father. A game played for money. He dangled millions in front of a man to see if he could be the one to control his wayward daughter, and when he failed, he was out the door. The very thought of that made Kari dizzy with despair. But was she really surprised? Didn't she know it already?

"I thought it was possible . . ." Kari's voice

trailed off.

"You thought what was possible?"

She nearly choked on the words, but she had to say them. "That you might be proud of me."

Her father raised a single eyebrow, tilting his head with disbelief. "*Proud* of you? For being paid a pittance to entertain the masses by balancing a spoon on your nose? I fail to see the accomplishment."

"I'm taking care of myself."

"By waiting tables and living with a man? Again — I fail to see the accomplishment."

Kari felt as if she were ten years old again, looking for any chink in her father's wall of disapproval. But now, like then, she saw nothing. She wasn't looking for total approval. She wasn't looking for a pat on the head. She just wanted some acknowledgment that maybe she was doing something at least marginally admirable by sticking it out and running her own life.

"And just so you'll know," her father went on, "Marc Cordero is hardly a wealthy man. That vineyard barely affords him a decent living."

"How do you know that?"

"Kari, please. Is there anything on this earth I can't find out if I want to?"

"I don't care whether he has money or not."

Her father shook his head with disgust. "After your upbringing, how can you stand living like a pauper?"

"I'd have an easier time if you gave me my money back."

"As I've always told you, there are consequences to everything you do. That money will remain with me until you come to your senses. Then I'd be happy to return it."

Consequences. God, how she hated that word.

"I'm still in the middle of my shift," she said, clasping her hands together to keep them from shaking. "I need to get back to work."

"I could buy that place, Kari. With a single swipe of my pen, I could own it."

Kari's heart skipped with apprehension, because she knew her father wasn't just blowing smoke. "Rosie would never sell."

"Everybody has his price."

"If you buy this restaurant," she said, her voice trembling, "I'll quit."

Her father's expression slowly turned ugly, and his voice took on an undercurrent of fury. "I gave you everything a person could want or need in this life. A decent upbringing. A college education. A position at my company. A wedding not one in ten thousand women will ever have. And this is how you repay me?"

"That's the point, Dad! You gave those things to me. You never asked me what *I* wanted!"

"And there was a reason for that. If you're given the opportunity to have what *you* want, this is where you end up."

With that, every last bit of the pride she'd felt at finally getting near the point of self-sufficiency evaporated. She knew he was angry. But if they could just talk a little when the anger subsided, maybe he'd see her point of view. Maybe that awful expression on his face would finally melt into a smile, and he'd tell her that after thinking about it, maybe he did feel just a little bit proud of her.

"Like I said," Kari told him, "I have to go back to work. But maybe we can talk again later. There are a few inns in town. Maybe you could —"

"Enough!"

Kari's heart slammed against her chest.

"I don't allow anyone to disrespect me," her father said. "No one. Not friends, not business associates, and certainly not my own daughter." He sat back and took a deep, silent breath, letting it out slowly, regaining his composure. But still the anger was there, laced around the edges of his voice. "If you forget this nonsense and come back to Houston," he said, "I'll overlook all this. But if you stay . . ." His face turned to stone. "You're not my daughter any longer."

Kari was stunned. Those words . . . those horrible, dismissive words . . . she couldn't stand the sound of them. For all her father's criticism, his manipulation, his disapproval, she'd always thought deep down that he loved her. He had to love her, didn't he? Didn't all fathers love their daughters?

Now she knew it wasn't true. It couldn't be true, or he wouldn't be talking to her like this. He was the one person on this earth who should have loved her and protected her and stood up for her. Instead, he did everything he could to tear her down into a meek, helpless waif of a woman without a shred of self-respect. She was hovering in that terrible realization that he intended to hold a hard line no matter what. That nothing she did was ever good enough, and it never would be, making her feel more lost and alone than she ever had in her life.

Then she looked through the side window of the car into the café and saw Marc staring back at her. He was so strong, so sure of himself. It radiated from him even at this distance, and just looking at him made her feel a burst of courage and resilience. She knew it was only a matter of time before he left Rainbow Valley, before she couldn't count on him being there every day for her, making her feel strong and self-sufficient. But it was because of him that maybe she could do what needed to be done right now.

She looked at her father, and this time her words came out with strength and conviction even though her hands were shaking and her stomach was in turmoil.

"Then I guess I'm not your daughter any longer."

Her father's hard, expressionless face never changed. "Well, then. You've left me no choice." He nodded toward the car door. "Get out."

In spite of everything she knew about her father, she still couldn't have imagined those words coming out of his mouth, and her heart crumbled to dust.

In a daze, she turned and opened the car door. Stepped out. Closed it behind her. Her stomach felt like shattered glass, but she kept walking. Even when she heard the car pull away, she didn't look back. She just kept walking toward the door of the café, but now tears clouded her eyes so much she wasn't even sure she was walking in the right direction. She had the sense of Marc jumping up from the booth with Brandy at his heels and hurrying out the door. He caught Kari as she reached it, and she collapsed in his arms and her tears spilled out.

"Kari? What happened? What did he say to you?"

Kari opened her mouth, but she couldn't speak. Didn't want to speak. Didn't want to verbalize just how awful her father had been to her. All she could do was cry. It was as if every lost, lonely moment of her childhood had built up inside of her, and now every one of them was being released in a torrent of tears.

"Get in my truck," Marc said.

"The Bomb —"

"Leave it. I'll bring you back in the morning."

"I can't. I have to close out. My checks. I have to —"

"Stay here."

He sat her down on one of the outdoor chairs, handed her Brandy's leash, and went back into the café. Looking through the window, she saw a tear-clouded image of him talking to Rosie. Rosie nodded, and Marc came back outside.

"Let's go," he said.

Marc helped her to her feet. He put his

arm around her shoulders and led her to his truck. All the way there, the terrible words her father had spoken to her circled around and around in her mind until she thought she'd go insane with misery.

When they got into Marc's truck and Kari told him what her father had said, Marc decided Stuart Worthington was one lucky son of a bitch not to be within his reach right now. If he had been, Marc would have ripped him to shreds.

"It's been this way all my life," Kari said. "Once — just *once* — I wanted to see something from him. Something that said he gave a damn."

Now Marc knew. Now he knew the full extent of why she'd let herself get caught up in an engagement she didn't want with a man who would have only made her life miserable. She was dying for love from a father there was no way to please.

"I miss my mother," she went on. "God, I'm twenty-eight years old, and I'm telling you I miss my mother. She died when I was eight. I'm supposed to be over that by now. I'm supposed to be *over* it."

But how do you get over that? Marc thought. *When in anyone's life do they stop looking for love?*

"Tell me about her," he said.

"I barely remember her, really. When I think about her, all I see in my mind is green eyes like mine and a soft smile. I was eight when she died. It's hard to remember stuff from when you're eight." She paused. "No, I do remember something. I remember how that smile went away any time my father came into the room."

"Why did she marry him?"

"She came from a broken home. Parents divorced. Her mother sweated blood just to keep their heads above water. It must have felt like such a relief for her to marry a man with money. But she traded a lot in return for that. My father likes controlling people, and my mother was no exception. But I think she would have done anything to keep from having such a hard life." She let out a heavy sigh. "Maybe I'm a lot like my mother. I've always settled for somebody else running my life."

"No," Marc said. "Not anymore. You're doing the right thing, Kari. No matter what your father says, there's honor in good, honest work, and what you're doing is just that. Don't listen to him. What kind of father tells his daughter she's a fool for trying to stand on her own two feet?"

"I know. But he's still my father. The only

family I have. Yeah, a few distant relatives, but essentially, he's it. Do you know what it feels like to have no one?"

Marc wanted to say, *You don't have no one! You have me!* But did she really? He was leaving soon. Was he supposed to tell her she could count on him when he might be hundreds of miles away?

"Do you like living in Rainbow Valley?" he asked her.

"Yes."

"Are you going to stay?"

"Yeah," she said. "I think I am."

"This is a good town. Good people. You're going to be just fine."

Kari nodded, but he could tell she didn't quite believe it. Suddenly that day he was going to ride off into the sunset seemed more like a curse than a blessing.

Wait a minute. *Ride?*

He didn't have a clue how to help Kari forget all this crap with her father, but he did know something that would make her feel better.

"Let's go to Rick's Automotive," he said.

Kari blinked. "What?"

He started his truck. "I promised you a ride on my motorcycle. He'll have a spare helmet you can borrow. How about it? When is your next day off?"

"Friday."

"Have you covered shifts for anybody who could return the favor on Saturday so you could be off then, too?"

"I can ask. Why?"

"Because then we can go to Fredericksburg. We can leave Friday. Stay over until Sunday. Visit some vineyards there. I have a few friends who'd be happy to see us. How does that sound?"

"What about the vineyard?"

"Daniel is there. He's supposed to be handling things, so I'm going to let him do it."

"Wait. Luke and Shannon's wedding is Sunday."

"We'll be back in plenty of time. Their wedding isn't until four o'clock."

"I have to be back early enough to cook. Nina, Daniel, and Angela are coming to dinner after the wedding, remember?"

"Don't worry. We'll come back as early as you need to."

A tiny smile came to Kari's lips. "Then let's go."

Kari had forgotten how much fun it was to feel the landscape whizzing by and the roar of the engine, and all her thoughts about her altercation with her father seemed to melt away. But the best thing of all was being able to circle her arms around Marc's waist and just hang on for the ride.

Then about thirty minutes away from their destination, the strangest thing happened. Her stomach began to swirl with nausea, and her head felt light and dizzy. At first she thought maybe she'd eaten something that hadn't agreed with her, but she couldn't imagine what that might be.

Unfortunately, it felt like motion sickness.

This couldn't be happening. She'd never had that problem when she'd ridden a motorcycle before, but there was no doubt it was happening now. As long as she looked at the horizon it wasn't bad, but if she closed her eyes the dizziness overtook her again. By the time they got to Fredericksburg and pulled into the parking lot of the motel, it was all she could do to get off the bike and stand up straight. She put her hand to her stomach.

"You okay?" Marc asked.

"Yeah. Just a little motion sickness, I think. It's been a while since I've been on a motorcycle. I'm fine."

She forced a smile and followed him into the motel office, where a grandmotherly woman greeted them and gave them keys to their room. The moment Marc closed the door behind them, he took her in his arms and kissed her. Then he swept her up in his arms and laid her on the bed, his eyes blazing with the kind of sexual desire that made her feel like the most beautiful woman on earth. He made love to her slowly and leisurely, as if they had the rest of their lives to do it.

Before they left Rainbow Valley, Marc had called two vineyard owners he knew to tell them they were going to be in Fredericksburg, and they set aside time for private tastings. Marc and Kari spent the afternoon sipping the different wines in beautiful surroundings, and she loved it. But mostly she loved hearing Marc talk about the industry with the other vintners. Mold and pests and bottling processes and harvest timing were fairly mundane things, but their conversation was filled with enthusiasm and passion and laughter. She could see the respect other vintners had for Marc, and watching the light in his eyes when he talked about Cordero Vineyards absolutely mesmerized her. She was glad she'd learned as much as she had about wine making in the past several weeks, and a few times she actually asked well-informed questions the other vintners were happy to answer.

And as Marc talked, his hand would stray

over and rest on her thigh, and then he'd turn and look at her with that smile that said he was in his element and having a good time, but also that he was glad she was there with him. Kari's mind grew a little fuzzy from the few glasses of wine she had, but all her sickness earlier had passed, and it made her feel warm and wonderful. And by the time they headed back to the motel, she knew for a fact it had been one of the best days of her life.

The next morning when Marc woke, morning light filtered through the blinds, casting stripes of warm sunshine across the bed. Kari lay on her side, her fist curled beneath her chin. Soon she stirred and shifted to her back. The covers fell away, exposing her soft, heavy breasts. Marc watched them rise and fall with every breath she took. Had he ever seen anything more beautiful?

After a moment, he reached up to stroke one fingertip softly across her nipple. Back and forth, back and forth. She was still asleep, but as her nipple rose and puckered, she began to stir beneath his touch. He rose on one elbow, closed his hand around the base of her breast, and squeezed gently. Her nipple rose enticingly. He dipped his head and flicked his tongue across it. She squirmed left and right, a soft whimper rising in the back of her throat, a tiny, plaintive cry that made his cock leap and harden.

Half-awake now, she threaded her fingers through his hair and flexed her fingertips against his scalp. He closed his mouth around her nipple, applying suction at the same time he flicked his tongue. She squirmed beneath him as if it was too much, but at the same time she held him in place and arched her back, asking for more. She kicked off the covers, pulled one knee up and let it fall to the side, her breath coming faster. He stroked his hand along her inner thigh, and her escalating breaths became hot and heavy, her moans beginning to sound like pleas.

"Now," she said.

"Now what?"

"Inside me," she murmured. *"Now."*

Impossible. He'd woken her from a sound sleep less than two minutes ago, and she was already ready for him? Just like *that*?

Finding that hard to believe, he slid his fingers between her open thighs. She was hot, swollen, and wet. If he'd been hard before, he was granite now. He'd never been the kind of man who needed frequent ego boosts, but he had to say he was enjoying this one.

"Marc. *Now!*"

Yes, ma'am.

He fumbled across the nightstand, snagged a condom, ripped it open, put it in place. Seconds later he plunged inside her. Her groan of satisfaction almost made him come right there.

Easing in and out of her, slowly, deliberately, then plunging in again. She lifted her hips with every stroke, pushing against him, taking him as deeply as she could, begging for all he could give her and then some. He pushed her right to the edge, and as she fell, he fell along with her.

Afterward, they lay together in satisfied silence. Marc thought back to the years when he was so overworked and stretched so thin he nearly snapped, and he wondered what it would have been like if he'd had somebody to share things with the way he did with Kari. Just somebody he could talk to at the end of the day to share the good and the bad. He didn't need anybody to fix anything. But if he'd just been able to talk, to open a valve and let off a little of the pressure, things wouldn't have felt so insurmountable. And if that somebody had been a woman like Kari, whose ever-present smile and gentle touch soothed him in other ways, how different might his life have been?

He told himself it could have been any woman who'd wandered along at this point in his life and he'd have felt the same, but it wasn't true. It was Kari. She was the one he couldn't wait to be with.

He traced his fingertip along her cheek, then pushed a lock of hair behind her ear. "Crazy idea," he said.

"You can't have a crazy idea," she said. "You're not a crazy person."

"You made me a crazy person. So come with me."

"Not a problem," she said with a smile. "I'll follow you anywhere. To the sofa, to the shower —"

"How about from Los Angeles to Chicago?"

Kari froze. "What?"

"You like to ride," Marc said. "How about coming with me when I leave Rainbow Valley?"

"That's crazy."

"Didn't I just say that?"

Kari was stunned. "I thought this was just a casual thing. You know. No strings."

"What could be more strings-free than a road trip on a motorcycle?"

Her first thought was, *Oh, thank God. I'm not going to have to say good-bye to him.* But that didn't mean any of this was forever. It was precisely because she was asking nothing of him that he wanted her around. If she asked for more, she had the terrible feeling she'd end up with nothing at all, because the last thing he wanted was to be tied down. But how many times in the past several days had she looked at him with longing, wishing for that moment he'd suddenly turn around, realize he belonged at Cordero Vineyards, and want to stay there forever with her?

"I grabbed this from the lobby," Marc said. "Look here."

He opened the nightstand drawer and pulled out a map of the United States. He opened it and pointed out the highway from Los Angeles to Chicago.

"This is old Route 66. That's how you see the country. Not on the interstates. On the back roads. So here's what I'm thinking. First we head to Los Angeles. Maybe hang out at the beach for a week or so. Then we hit Route 66. We can ride the whole distance to Chicago. We can do it as fast or as slow as we feel like it, and stop anywhere along the way we want to."

"But that'll take weeks."

"I have three years. What's a few weeks?"

"What about my job? I don't have any money unless I work."

t's barely more expensive for two to travel instead of one. I'll pay for everything. Believe me — Rosie has a hard time finding good help. You'll always have a job there later if you want it. Let me do this, Kari. I'd love it if you came along."

"What about Boo?" she asked.

"Daniel will take care of him. What's one more animal around there? Of course, the house will be chewed to pieces when we get back, but what the hell?"

Kari smiled, even though she didn't feel happy. He wanted her to be with him, which was a dream come true. But in that dream, they weren't on his motorcycle. They were living at Cordero Vineyards. That was the scenario she played in her head when she was in the shower, driving to work, falling asleep in his arms at night. In the end, though, it didn't matter.

Wherever Marc was, that was where she wanted to be.

Then she had a terrible thought. She'd gotten so sick when she'd been on his bike yesterday. What if she couldn't ride long distances without that sickness coming back again?

No. She wasn't going to worry about that. There were remedies for motion sickness. She simply wasn't going to accept the thought of not being able to leave Rainbow Valley with Marc. She was *not* going to accept it.

"Or maybe you want to stay in Rainbow Valley," Marc asked. "I know you've gotten to know people, and you do have your job. You've worked hard for that. So if you don't want to go —"

"Come on, Marc. Like you don't know I'm half-crazy? I don't want to be tied down any more than you do. Trust me. If it's between staying in Rainbow Valley and hitting the road on a motorcycle, which do you think I'm going to pick?"

"That's exactly what I wanted to hear." His brilliant smile made the entire room glow, but Kari could barely contain the desperation she felt. Marc wanted freedom, and she knew if she told him she wanted anything else, the last thing she'd see of him was his back as he drove out of town.

An hour later, they got back on his motorcycle to go home. As they headed down the road, at first Kari felt fine. Then nausea crept in, and she had to focus on the horizon to keep from feeling really sick. The panic she felt about that didn't help. What if this happened every time she sat behind him on this motorcycle? If she couldn't ride from Fredericksburg to Rainbow Valley without getting dizzy, how was she supposed to go across the country with him?

By the time they crossed the city limits into Rainbow Valley, she felt so dizzy that if she hadn't had a death grip on Marc, she might have gone tumbling right off the back of the bike. As they came around the last bend and she saw the "Cordero Vineyards" sign in the distance, she was filled with relief.

Deep breath. It'll be over in a minute.

As they approached the driveway leading to the house, Marc pulled his motorcycle to a halt to allow a party rental truck to pull from the driveway onto the highway. Luke and Shannon's wedding was only a few hours from now. Undoubtedly Nina was putting the finishing touches on the arbor for the ceremony and the decorations for the reception.

Marc brought his bike to a halt and let the truck pass. Then Kari was surprised to see another car coming down the drive.

"Who's that?" Kari asked.

"Don't know."

Marc waited on that one, too. As it turned onto the highway, she saw a magnetic sign on the side of the car that read, "Morgan Tank and Equipment."

Marc muttered a curse. "I can't believe this."

"What's wrong?" Kari asked.

"I need to have a word with my brother."

CHAPTER 16

A minute later, Marc stormed into the kitchen, where Daniel sat at the table poking at his phone.

"Marc. You're back."

"Yeah. I'm back. Tell me what a rep from Morgan Tank and Equipment was doing here."

Daniel froze. Then he looked back down at his phone with a careless shrug. "Just talking."

"Talking? What about?"

Daniel tossed his phone aside. "You know what about, so why are you asking me?"

"Weren't you listening when I told you how I feel about micro-oxygenation?"

"Oh, come on, Marc! Will you get with the program? Technology is the future of wine making."

"It's not this vineyard's future. We're a boutique winery. Our selling point is the care we give to every grape we pull off a vine. You start applying *technology* to what we do, and we lose our competitive edge."

"Old school," Daniel said. "You need to keep up."

"Keep up?" Marc said, his voice escalating. "You haven't lived here for ten years, and *I'm* the one who needs to keep up?"

"There's a big world out there," Daniel said. "Hard to keep up with when you've never stepped foot out of Rainbow Valley."

"I haven't stepped foot out of Rainbow Valley," Marc said, his voice quivering, "because I was operating this vineyard while you were running all over this country doing whatever the hell you pleased."

"Whatever I pleased? Whatever I *pleased* made me a fucking millionaire! Why do you always act as if that's nothing?"

"I'm not going to let you run this place into the ground."

"That's not going to happen."

"I'll be the judge of that."

"Yeah? Well, you can't do a lot of judging when you're on the back of a motorcycle heading out of town."

Now as Marc envisioned that, he saw it more as a trap than freedom. He'd be in another state while Daniel was here screwing up the business their father had entrusted to him, and that was absolutely intolerable.

"If you're so damned worried about this place," Daniel said, "why are you leaving?"

"Just because I'm leaving it doesn't mean I don't care what happens to it!"

"I don't know, Marc. I think you give up that right the minute you put it in my hands and hit the road."

So that was what it came down to? If he handed this place over to Daniel everything went to shit, and if he didn't, he was destined to be here forever?

"Right now we're stuck with oak barrel aging," Daniel said. "But as soon as I'm in charge, there may be a few new procedures at Cordero Vineyards."

"Damn it, Daniel, I've sweated *blood* over this place!"

"Right. Because you've always been desperate to live up to the old man's expectations. Well, he's dead and gone. It's your life now. Why don't you live it?"

"We had a deal," Marc said hotly. "Don't you *dare* try to back out now!"

"I'm not backing out. Just because I decide to do things a little differently —"

"You're going to destroy this place!"

"Oh, come on, Marc! A vineyard is always one bad season away from closing its doors. It could happen whether you're running it or I am."

"You really don't give a damn about this place, do you? If I sell it, no big deal. If a mold infestation takes out our crop, who cares? If you put micro-oxygenation tanks in and destroy a whole year's work, so what? If we lose this crop, we'll miss an entire vintage. It'll take us years to recover from that!"

"Assuming you decide not to sell."

"Either way it's a disaster. If we lose a crop, do you know what that does to the market value of this place? I depend on it for a living, or at least I need to be able to cash out the equity. Have you even stopped to think about that?"

"Do you actually think I'd let you swing from the end of that rope?" Daniel said. "Seriously?"

"What are you talking about?"

"If I make the wrong decision, if things go south, I'll pay you for the crop. I'll write you a check. And you know I can do it. You won't be out a dime."

"It's not about the fucking *money*! When are you going to get that through your head?"

"Then what the hell *is* it about? You say it's your livelihood. How is that not about money?"

And that was when Marc knew. His brother was never going to be able to do this. It just wasn't in him. He could learn how to operate machinery. How to prune grapevines for maximum production. But that didn't give him the heart for the business, the drive, that feeling of pride when he looked out across the vineyard and imagined the final product, bottled and ready to drink.

"Never mind," Marc said. "Let's just get the grapes in on Thursday, and then —"

"No. They need to stay on the vine at least another week."

"Another *week*? You leave them on the vine that long and the sugar level will go through the roof."

"I don't think so. And the tannins will also be softer."

"The alcohol content will be too high. Did you test the pH?"

"You told me I have the best palate of anybody in the family. So why don't you just let me taste the damned grapes and decide when to harvest?"

"No. Let's get it done. The crew is booked —"

"I rescheduled for next week."

"You *what*?"

"You want me to run this place? So let me run it."

Marc was dumbfounded. He couldn't do this anymore. He couldn't listen to his brother ignore every procedure they'd ever established at this vineyard and simply shoot from the hip. He just couldn't do it.

"You know what?" Marc said. "Fine. Do whatever you want with the place. Harvest when there's so much sugar in the grapes they taste like candy. Use fake oak flavoring. Hell, burn the place to the ground. I don't give a shit. It's all yours, buddy. We're harvesting in a week? Fine. I'll bring my shears. The minute those grapes are in, I'm out of here. Then you can deal with the aftermath."

Kari truly believed Luke and Shannon's wedding was the most beautiful one she'd ever seen. The late afternoon sun eased through the tree branches, dappling the whole area with clusters of sunshine. Friends and family gathered in front of the grape arbor to watch two people they all loved promising to love each other for the rest of their lives.

This is it, Kari thought. *This is the way it's supposed to be.*

After Marc and Daniel fought World War

III earlier, Daniel moved out of the main house into the cottage. Angela showed up with only minutes to spare and avoided talking to Kari, coming to sit next to Marc only when the ceremony was about to begin.

Marc didn't touch Kari through the entire ceremony, and she knew it was because Angela was sitting right next to him. Angela stared straight ahead the whole time, her face tight and unsmiling. Even when Shannon and Luke exchanged rings and became man and wife, her expression never changed. Kari could only imagine what was going on inside her head.

Nina and Daniel sat to Kari's left. Daniel checked his phone at least three times during the ceremony, and Nina seemed to be in another world. Her gaze never strayed from that arbor, and as fond as she was of Shannon and Luke, Kari knew she was thinking about Curtis. When Luke kissed his bride, Nina began to cry, and she had to pull a tissue from her purse to dab beneath her eyes.

The reception took place in the barn next to the oak barrels, where Nina had set up tables with linen tablecloths and wine-themed centerpieces. Candles on the tables lit the room with a warm glow. And Shannon looked positively radiant. Kari had been to a lot of weddings before, but there was something about the way she and Luke looked at each other that made Kari feel a sense of envy well up inside her. That was the wrong thing to feel, she knew, because she was truly happy for them. But she couldn't stop wondering if there would ever come a day when a man would look at her the way Luke looked at Shannon.

Then she glanced up at Marc, and the most frustrating sense of longing swirled through her. Yes, she was leaving town with him. But if he knew what she really wanted, she was sure he'd run far and fast.

"Angela's still pissed," Marc said.

"Yeah. I can tell. But she's coming to dinner, right?"

"She said she was."

"She's avoiding me," Kari said.

"She'll get over it. Daniel is avoiding *me.*"

"He'll get over it, too."

"He may. I'm not sure I will."

"I'm sorry everything's such a mess right now," Kari said. "Is there anything I can do to help?"

Marc took her hand. After a moment, he leaned in and gave her a gentle kiss.

"Angela may be watching," Kari said.

"She knows how I feel about you."

For a split second, Kari imagined him saying it. *I love you. I love Cordero Vineyards. To hell with riding across the country. I want to stay in Rainbow Valley forever.*

"I'm really glad you're coming away with me," he said. "We're going to have such a good time."

Such a good time. Didn't he know how much she wanted them to be more than just traveling friends with benefits?

After Shannon and Luke left on their honeymoon and the caterer had cleaned up, Marc made his way back up to the house with Nina. Daniel and Angela walked behind them, talking to each other but acting as if Marc didn't exist. Marc opened the back door to find Kari already in the kitchen, putting the finishing touches on dinner. Nina helped Kari set the table and bring the food to the dining room, and they all sat down to eat. The tension in the room felt as heavy as sludge in the bottom of a fermentation tank, and Marc wished he was anywhere else.

"It was a nice wedding, wasn't it?" Nina said as she passed the green beans around the table.

"Beautiful," Kari said.

Nina turned to Angela. "What did you think?"

She shrugged. "It was okay."

"I'd love to see you get married under that arbor someday."

"Assuming we still have a vineyard for me to get married in." She stabbed her fork into a chunk of chicken. Marc felt stress working its way between his shoulders, and he had to bite his tongue bloody to keep from snapping back.

"Chicken's good," Daniel said as he ate, because nothing on earth got in the way of his appetite.

"Thanks," Kari said. "I found a recipe in that old Betty Crocker cookbook in the pantry."

Angela flicked her gaze to Kari. "That cookbook was Grandma's. She didn't let anybody touch it."

"Grandma is dead, so there's no reason not to use it now," Marc said. "Otherwise, it just collects dust."

Angela pursed her lips and stabbed another bite of chicken.

"So, Angela," Nina said. "How's school?"

Oh, crap, Marc thought. Did she *have* to go there?

"Fine," Angela said.

Daniel looked up. "That's not what you told Marc."

"If she says it's fine, it's fine," Marc

snapped.

More silence, so much that the clinking of silverware sounded like Big Ben chiming the hour. Then all at once, Angela tossed her fork down with a clatter.

"It's not fine," she said.

Oh, God, Marc thought. *Here it comes.*

"I'm not crazy enough for Kim and her friends, and I'm not cool enough to pledge a sorority. So where does that leave me? *Nowhere.*"

"Who the hell cares?" Marc said. "Didn't I teach you not to follow the crowd?"

"That gives me no one to hang out with. And everybody laughs at me."

"Why would they laugh at you?" Marc said.

"Because I'm from some dinky little town most of them have never heard of. And they say I talk funny."

"Aren't they Texans, too?" Nina asked.

"Most of them are. But it turns out big-city Texans talk different than small-town Texans. I try not to talk like I talk, but I've been talking this way for eighteen years, so I don't know how else to do it."

"All that will change," Nina said.

"No, it won't. That place is so big, and I just don't fit in."

"Well, you'll just have to learn to fit in,"

Marc said.

"I don't want to fit in. I don't even want to go back."

Silence fell over the table. "No," he said carefully, trying like hell not to blow up. "You're going back to school."

Angela was silent.

"I've paid for this semester, and you're going to finish it."

"No, I'm not. I hate that place!"

"What are you talking about? You're not dropping out!"

"What do you care? You're not even going to *be* here!"

With that, Angela pushed her chair back and leaped up from the table, heading for the stairs. Then all at once she came back to the kitchen. "I don't suppose I could actually go to my own room, could I?"

"Yeah," Marc said. "It's all yours again."

Angela looked at Kari. "But that means that *she's* . . ." She looked heavenward. "Oh, *God.*"

As she stomped up the stairs, Marc flung his napkin down and stood up, scraping his chair across the floor. Enough of this. He was going to go have a word with her *right now.*

"Marc," Nina said.

He kept moving.

"Marc!"

He turned back.

"Don't you get it?" Nina said.

"What?"

"She's having a hard time at school. She could probably get through that, except she's not going to have a father to come home to when things get tough. *That's* what she's trying to tell you."

"She knew I was leaving. She thought it was fine."

"It's one thing to talk about it. It's another thing when she sees you on the verge of doing it."

Marc swallowed hard, the truth slowly coming to him. Was this what his leaving was going to do to his daughter? Suddenly he felt sick. The plans he'd been making for years, the ones he thought were set in concrete, were suddenly shifting like sand beneath his feet.

"She's just a kid," he said. "Everything seems tough to handle when you're a kid, right? She'll get over it."

"Yeah? How about me? Will I have to get over it, too?"

"What are you talking about?"

For some reason he didn't understand, tears filled Nina's eyes. What was going on *now*?

"You can't just *leave* like this," she said.

"Nina," Marc said carefully. "We've talked about this. Everything is going to be fine. Daniel will be here."

But he didn't believe things were going to be fine. Not for one second. So why was he saying it?

Because he couldn't leave unless it was true.

"I know he'll be here, but —" Nina waved her hand, a single tear coursing down her cheek. "You won't be."

Marc couldn't believe this. Nina was about as self-sufficient as any woman he'd ever known, and now she was falling apart on him, too?

"Nina," he said. "It's okay. It's not as if I'll be gone forever."

"Is that really true? You've told me — told all of us — that there's a chance you'll decide not to come back to Rainbow Valley. What are we supposed to do then? Have you even stopped to think about what your leaving means to everyone else? Or are you just going to get onto that motorcycle and drive away as if you don't give a damn about anybody?"

Marc drew back, anger surging through him. "Don't give a damn about anybody? Are you *serious*? Almost everything I've

378

done for the past eighteen years has been for somebody else. For once in my life, I'm doing something for *me*. And don't you dare make me feel like shit for doing it!"

"I have to go," Nina said.

She rose from the table, spun around, and left the room. The front door opened, then closed.

"Oh, boy," Daniel said.

"Oh, boy is right," Marc said. "I can't believe she went off on me like that!"

"Well, there *is* kind of a reason why," Daniel said.

"What reason?"

"I can't say. She swore me to silence for today."

"Hey! If there's something that explains *that*, you'd better start talking!"

Daniel sighed. "Manfred died this morning."

Silence fell over the table, and Marc felt as if somebody had punched him in the stomach. "My God. Why didn't you *tell* me?"

"She didn't want anybody to know."

"Why not?"

"Luke and Shannon's wedding. She wanted their day to be perfect, and if they knew, she thought they'd be all worried about her."

Marc dropped his head to his hands. *"Shit."* Then he jerked his head up. He took off toward the front door, trying to catch Nina, but she was already gone. He pulled his phone from his pocket and dialed her number. She didn't answer.

Kari came to the entryway.

"She should have said something," Marc said. "She should have told me. Luke and Shannon didn't have to know."

"I know. But I think she knew how Shannon in particular would feel if she found out. Manfred came from the shelter. I guess she just didn't want to chance it."

"And what about Angela? If she drops out of college . . ." Marc exhaled. "God, Kari. Do you have any idea how smart she is?"

"I can only imagine."

"Well, imagine times ten. That's what she's throwing away."

"I know you think the worst thing in the world is for her not to go to college. It's not. The worst thing in the world is for her to think you don't approve of her."

"Hey! I've never made her think that. *Never!*"

"You didn't have to. Unless I miss my guess, she's always done what you wanted her to. What was there for you to disapprove of?" Kari put her hand on his sleeve. "Have

380

you thought about sending her to another school?"

"Yes. Of course I have. But she'd need to go to another state school, or I wouldn't be able to afford it. The others might not be as big as the University of Texas, but they're still big schools. I'm not sure that would solve the problem. If she sticks it out where she is, she could still adjust and everything will be fine."

"She could. But if time passes and she's still miserable —"

"I know," Marc said, blowing out a breath. "I know."

"Just talk to her. It'll be okay."

He turned and looked up the stairs. "I will. But Nina first. I have to fix this. I'm going to her house."

He started out the door, only to realize he didn't want to deal with this by himself. Maybe this time he didn't have to. He looked back at Kari.

"Will you come with me?"

She nodded. "Let me get my purse."

Marc hated this. He never said the right things at the right time, but he had to try to say something. At least with Kari along, there was a chance he wouldn't make a monumental mistake. But when they drove to Nina's house, she wasn't there, and his frustration hit an all-time high.

"Where the hell could she have gone?" he said.

Kari looked as lost as he felt. Then all at once her face brightened. "I think I know where she is."

A few minutes later, Marc and Kari stood on the edge of Rainbow Way near the path leading down to the Overlook. Through the trees, Kari could just make out Nina sitting on the bench, staring out into the valley.

"God, I hate this," Marc said, putting his hand to his forehead. "She's going to cry, and then I'm going to say the wrong stupid-ass thing and make everything worse."

"No, you won't."

"Oh, believe me. I will. I know this is going to come as a shock to you, but I'm not the most sensitive guy in the world."

"Why don't I go down there and talk to her?" Kari said.

Marc exhaled. "No. It's my responsibility. I need to —"

"You can in a minute. Let me talk to her first."

Marc still looked unsure.

"I promise you it'll be okay."

Finally he nodded. Kari turned and walked down the brick path. She'd almost reached the park bench before Nina turned around. She had a tissue clutched in her hand. Her eyes were red, and her lashes were wet with tears. Kari sat down beside her.

"Daniel told us about Manfred. I'm so sorry."

Nina wiped beneath her eyes with her fingertips. "I didn't want to tell anyone. I was so afraid of ruining Shannon and Luke's wedding. But Daniel caught me crying, so I had to tell him." She let out a shaky sigh. "It wasn't as if it was a shock. I knew it was coming. But still . . ."

Kari nodded. "How are you doing now?"

"Not great." She caught a trickle of a tear with a tissue. "As long as I had Manfred, it was like Curtis was still here. But now that he's gone, too . . ."

"Curtis is waiting for him, remember? That was what he promised you. That he'd wait for both of you."

"But I have to wait so long," Nina said, her voice a hushed whisper. "So *long.* And I miss Manfred so much. It's only been a few hours, and already I don't know what to do without him."

Kari didn't really know what to say to that, so she didn't say anything.

"I'll be fine," Nina said finally. "Life goes

on, you know? I just have to feel sorry for myself for a little while."

Kari slipped her arm around Nina's shoulders. Together they looked into the valley, watching as the sun slipped below the horizon. Then Nina's voice broke the silence.

"Marc is crazy about you, you know."

Hearing those words made Kari want to cry herself. She was desperate to say, *Do you really think so? Do you think there's any way on this earth he'll ever love me?* But she couldn't. The more she wished for it, the more painful it was going to be when it never happened.

"We have a good time together," she told Nina. "But that's all."

"I've been hoping you might be able to get him to stay."

"Actually, he thinks I ought to go with him when he leaves."

Nina blinked with surprise. "Are you going to?"

"I don't want to leave Rainbow Valley. I really love it here. But . . ." Kari sighed, feeling that impossible push-pull all over again. "I'll follow him anywhere, Nina. Anywhere he wants to go."

"You're in love with him."

Kari closed her eyes. "Please don't tell

384

him that."

"But it's true?"

"He has Angela to think about, and she's not happy about him seeing me. He says that doesn't bother him, but I know it does. And I know he doesn't want anything that even looks like commitment."

"I wouldn't be so sure."

"He wants freedom."

"I know," Nina said. "But what we want and what we need — sometimes they're not the same thing."

But Kari knew how strong-minded Marc was. If he was convinced he was right about something, getting him to change his mind was damned near impossible.

"I'll probably get another puppy soon," Nina said.

"Yeah?" Kari said.

"I don't feel like it now, but I know eventually I will. Shannon never has a shortage at the shelter. It'd be a shame not to adopt one."

Kari nodded.

"But I'll never get married again."

"Are you sure about that?"

"I believe in soul mates. That there's one man a woman is destined to be with. For me, Curtis was that man. I already gave my heart away to him, and I don't ever want it back. So how could I give it away to another man?"

Kari couldn't imagine what it would be like to love a man with all her heart and soul the way Nina loved Curtis. And all at once an image popped into Kari's mind of her own heart slowly slipping away from her, but when she turned around, Marc was holding it in the palm of his hand.

If only that could happen someday. She and Marc. Together. If only . . .

Stop wishing for what you can't have!

Nina looked past Kari to the head of the path, where Marc sat on a bench looking uncomfortable. "Poor Marc. He has no idea what to say, does he?"

"Not a clue," Kari said. "But I don't have to tell you how much he cares about you."

"I know he does. And I'm sorry I went off on him like that, because he has a right to leave, you know? I just don't know what we're all going to do without him."

"Would you like us to walk with you back to your car?" Kari asked.

Nina nodded. She rose and walked with Kari back up the path. Marc stood up when he saw them coming. Kari could tell he still didn't know what to say. But when Nina drew closer, he simply stepped forward, pulled her into his arms, and gave her a heartfelt hug.

"I'm sorry for what I said," Nina told him.

"Forget it," Marc said.

Nina began to cry again. Tears streamed down her face and soaked into Marc's shirt, but he just kept holding her like that, rubbing his hand up and down her back. Marc might not always say the right thing, but he always *did* the right thing.

By the time they got back to the vineyard, Angela had returned to college. Daniel's car was gone, which meant he'd left the house. If history was any indication, he'd probably spend the night in some woman's bed and wouldn't be back until morning. They went to Marc's bedroom, and by the time Kari came out of the bathroom, he was in bed, the light switched off, his arm resting across his forehead as he stared at the ceiling. She crawled in beside him, pulling her pillow over to lie on her side next to him.

"What's wrong?" she asked.

"Well, let's see. Nina is lost without Curtis and hates the thought of me leaving. Angela doesn't like college, so she's probably going to drop out. And Daniel wants to wait a week to harvest. I think that's too late, but we're stuck with that decision now, because he went behind my back and rescheduled the crew. This is harvest season

387

in the Hill Country, and now I can't get one out here sooner. This whole vintage could go to hell." He exhaled. "And it's all because I'm leaving."

Kari could feel the tension radiating from Marc, the frustration, the sense that things were going wrong and he just didn't know how to make them right.

"I have a right to go," Marc said.

"I know you do," Kari said.

"Do you have any idea how hard it was to raise a baby with everything else I had to do?"

She couldn't even imagine.

"I used to take Angela into the vineyard with me in a carry cradle and hope she didn't cry because I was too damned dirty to pick her up. And then I'd go to the house at night and collapse, praying she would sleep through the night because I was so bone tired I could barely get out of bed. But the next morning I shook it off and got up again, and somehow I made it through another day. I loved her, Kari. I always have, more than anything in my life. But when Nicole left, I couldn't help feeling as if I'd gotten the short end of the stick. Sometimes I just wanted to scream, *But what about* me? I know. That sounds so selfish."

"No! No, it doesn't sound selfish. You're

not selfish. God, Marc, you're the least self-ish person I know."

"My father would have told me just to knock off the whining, gut it up, and do it. So that was what I did."

"So he was pretty tough?"

"He was a hard man. Blunt. Demanding. But he had a work ethic second to no one, and when he gave his word, it was law. Not everybody liked my father, but there wasn't anybody anywhere who didn't respect him."

In the near darkness of the bedroom, Kari saw Marc's throat convulse in a heavy swallow.

"I'll never forget the night I told him Nicole was pregnant. He got really quiet. Really still. His eyes went cold as ice. And then he said, *I counted on you to be smarter than that.*"

Marc's eyes drifted closed at the memory. Kari couldn't have imagined a man like Marc not meeting *any* parent's expectations, but she could tell by the look on his face that even if he lived to be a thousand, that feeling of inadequacy would always be there.

"A month before Angela was born," Marc said, "he dropped dead right out there among the vines. A heart attack. He was here one second, gone the next. That fast.

Gone before I could show him that even though I'd made a mistake, he could still believe in me."

And Marc had been trying to live up to his father's expectations ever since. Keeping this place running. Holding his family together no matter what. Raising his daughter. Being everything to everyone because there was nobody else to do it.

"I was scared to death," Marc said. "I was just a kid, trying to make everything work. Sometimes I wanted to hide my head and pretend none of it was happening. I wanted to go off to college the way Angela did. Maybe that's why it makes me so crazy that she's not even sure she likes it there. She has the opportunity I never had, and she doesn't even realize how special it is."

He turned and put his arm around Kari, pulling her against him. He kissed her hair, then held her tightly. "You're the only one who doesn't ask anything of me. Whenever I'm with you, it's because I want to be, not because I have to be. It seems as if my whole life has been *have to.* I didn't even know what *want to* felt like until you came along."

A wave of despair came over Kari, making her desperate to tell him how she felt about him. She loved him so much she ached with it. The words were on the tip of her tongue, fighting to get out, but she swallowed them at the last second. He loved this place. And he loved his family. But he'd never given her any indication that he loved *her*. That would lead to a relationship, which would involve the kind of responsibility he was telling her he wanted nothing to do with. Hadn't he said it? She was his *want to*. The moment she put any restrictions on him, demanded anything from him, became one more of his *have tos* . . .

She'd lose him.

Later after Marc was asleep, Kari lay awake in the dark, worry eating away at her. He wanted so desperately to leave, but she had to agree with Nina. She wasn't sure it would truly make him happy. But Kari hadn't been lying. If Marc wanted to fly to the moon, she'd find a way to crawl into that space capsule with him.

But there was a problem with that. Maybe a big problem.

How could she cross this country on a motorcycle with Marc if she got sick every time she got on one? If it was all she could have of him, that was what she wanted. But if going with him wasn't going to be an option, she'd have to say good-bye. And the thought of that was absolutely intolerable.

But speaking of sick . . .

Ever since dinner, she'd felt a little woozy. Maybe it was leftover motion sickness from the ride home. But how could that be? As the minutes passed, the feeling grew more intense until she felt as if she was going to throw up.

A shadow of a thought worked its way into her mind. It faded, then came back even stronger. She shook it away again, but finally she couldn't ignore it. She put her hand to her stomach, and for a moment she couldn't breathe. Was it possible . . . ?

Oh, God. Maybe it wasn't the motorcycle after all.

The next afternoon, Daniel avoided Marc, walking the other way when he saw him coming, and Marc knew it was going to take every bit of self-control he had not to grab his brother by the collar and tell him what a fool he was. Marc felt as if he wasn't in control of anything anymore. He usually loved this time of year, when the vineyard was the most beautiful. But looking at it now, all he saw was a disaster waiting to happen.

It was only two in the afternoon, but he decided he'd go inside, take a shower, and wait for Kari to get home. She was off today, but she'd been gone all morning.

Where, he didn't know, but as soon as she came back he wanted to talk to her. He felt as if his life was crashing in on him from all sides, as if his dream was slipping away, and he didn't know what to do to make it stop. He only knew if he could talk to her, things wouldn't seem so insurmountable.

He took a shower, which didn't make him feel remotely better. Then he went to his bedroom and got dressed. He sat down on the bed for a moment, dropping his head to his hands with a heavy sigh. Then he heard footsteps, and Kari appeared at the door. She paused there for a moment, then came into the bedroom, tossed her purse aside, and sat down next to him on the bed.

"I'm glad you're home," he said.

"I had some errands," she said quietly. "What's wrong?"

"Daniel is still avoiding me. If this vintage is anything but total crap, it'll be a miracle of God."

"He won't listen to you?"

"He never has before. Why would I think this time would be any different?"

Kari nodded solemnly. "So are you thinking about staying?"

He wasn't sure what he heard in her voice. Disappointment? Probably. After all, he'd promised her they were leaving there. Getting on the road, just the two of them. Feeling crazy and free without a care in the world. To her, life was one big adventure, and that was what he'd promised her. Now it sounded as if he was returning to the man he used to be, the one who took life so damned seriously to the exclusion of everything else.

Then all at once, he had a moment of clarity he hadn't anticipated. In the past several weeks, he'd learned what it felt like to color outside the lines, and it was because of Kari. She'd taught him to be spontaneous. To look forward to tomorrow and all the fun they were going to have. She'd given herself to him in ways a woman never had before, with total and complete abandon. She'd made him realize there was another side of life he'd never experienced, one he craved now with everything he had in him. Not only was it what he'd promised her, it was what he'd promised himself. Wasn't breaking out of that mold exactly what he'd always wanted? What he deserved after being Mr. Responsibility all these years?

"No," he said. "No matter what happens here, we're going anyway."

Her face fell. "Are you sure?"

He frowned. "You sound like my family. I thought you wanted to do this."

"I do. It's just that . . . well, are you sure *you* want to?"

"Yes. Of course I'm sure. As soon as harvest is over, we're getting on my motorcycle and leaving. It's what I've dreamed of all these years, and now that it's almost here, I'm not giving it up. I know I said I'm worried about the vineyard. But Daniel already rescheduled the crew, and I couldn't get one here any earlier if I wanted to. I can't change it, so why fight it?"

"What about Nina and Angela?"

"They'll have to learn to stand on their own two feet."

"I just don't want you to regret leaving."

"I'm not going to regret anything."

"Maybe you should wait," she said. "Get through harvest this year. Let things with Angela settle down. And Nina —"

"No! It has to be now. Now or never. Nothing is going to stand in our way. Once harvest is over, we're leaving."

"Marc —"

"Isn't that what you want? What we both want?"

"I-I don't know."

"Kari? Are you backing out on me?"

"No! It's not that. It's —"

"Good. Because it's going to be great. Just the two of us together on the open road. We

395

can do whatever we want, whenever we want. Nobody needing us, nobody depending on us —"

"Marc! Will you stop talking? Please. Just *stop*!"

Her face crumpled, as if she was on the verge of crying. He looked at her with confusion. "What's wrong?"

"I can't say it. I just —" She dropped her head to one hand.

"Kari?"

When she looked up again, tears filled her eyes. "I'm pregnant."

CHAPTER 17

The moment Kari spoke the words, Marc felt as if a frigid wind had swept across the room and knocked him flat on his back. He stared at Kari, unable to speak, unable to breathe, praying time would stop and he wouldn't have to hear another word. Wishing he could go back in time five minutes — just *five minutes* — and play this all again, only this time she wouldn't say *those words* and his life wouldn't be crashing down on him.

"How do you know?" he finally managed to say. "If you're just late —"

"I went to the doctor this morning."

"Is there any chance she's wrong?"

"No," Kari said. "There's no doubt."

Oh, God. This could *not* be happening. "The baby," he said by rote, not looking at her. "Is everything okay?"

"Yes. The doctor says everything is fine."

"You?"

"Just a little morning sickness."

He dropped his head to his hands. A few seconds later, he felt a surge of frustration and jerked it back up again. "How the *hell* did this happen?"

"The usual way."

"We used protection."

"It's not a hundred percent."

"It's damned close if you use it right!"

"We did. You know we did. Sometimes things just . . . happen."

"No, Kari. This doesn't just happen. No man on *earth* has this kind of shitty luck!"

Then he thought about the condom that first time they'd been together in the cottage. Expired. Only two months, though. Two months. They were good for years. *Years.* Could that little time have possibly made a difference? In spite of his history, he hadn't continued to worry about it because he was a logical man and it just wasn't logical to get uptight about those kinds of odds. He didn't think there had been an obvious problem with it, but he was so damned distracted, so caught up in having sex for the first time in forever . . .

So damned irresponsible.

Marc couldn't stand it. He couldn't stand that feeling of history repeating itself, that stomach-churning feeling of his life coming to a screeching halt.

"I knew you'd be upset," Kari said carefully. "And you have a right to be."

"Hell *yes*, I have a right to be!"

She shrank away as if he'd slapped her, but he couldn't say anything to mitigate his words. This was it. The one thing he'd feared the most. Being tied down for the next two decades.

"I know how you feel about this, but —"

"No, Kari, you don't. You don't have a clue how I feel about this."

"Yes. I do. I've listened to you. I've heard you say it over and over. I know how important it is for you to finally be able to live your own life. But if we just talk about it —"

"Not now. I can't right now."

"But —"

"I said I can't talk about it."

"You blame me for this, don't you?"

Maybe he did. Maybe he blamed her for being a crazy woman who left her own wedding and ended up on his doorstep that rainy night. If she hadn't done that, none of this would be happening. The irony overwhelmed him. The woman who'd made him feel free for the first time in years was the one tying him down all over again.

But she wasn't the only one at fault.

Hadn't he known what might happen? Hadn't he *known*? His father's voice echoed inside his head all over again. *I counted on you to be smarter than that.*

"No. I blame myself. Could I have been a bigger fool?"

He couldn't sit there any longer. Not with Kari looking at him like that, needing him to say things he couldn't, to tell her things were going to be all right, because right then he wasn't sure they were.

He rose from the bed, grabbed a bag from his closet, and tossed it on the bed.

"What are you doing?" Kari asked.

He threw a change of clothes in it.

"Marc?"

"I have to get out of here."

"Get out of here?"

"Ride."

"You're leaving?"

"Just for a while." He went into the bathroom and grabbed a few items.

"What about the vineyard?" Kari said when he came back in the room.

He dumped the toiletries into his bag. "Daniel is here."

That was all he could say. He couldn't think any more about that, because his mind was filled to bursting with visions of a future he never thought he'd have. He needed to clear his head. Make sense of this. Approach it logically. He needed to *think,* damn it, and get a plan. Only idiots faced challenges without a plan.

But he had no plan this time. None at all. But all he could think about was getting on his motorcycle and putting as much distance between himself and this disaster as he possibly could.

He zipped his bag, knowing he was being a bastard for acting this way. But he couldn't even look at Kari. He couldn't face what was going on. He just needed some time. With his life falling apart all around him, his plans destroyed, didn't he at least deserve that?

He brushed past her and headed for the bedroom door.

"Where are you going?" she asked.

"I don't know."

"When will you be back?"

"Don't ask me that."

"Marc —"

He wheeled back around. "Don't ask me when I'm going to be *back!*"

He squeezed his eyes closed, gritting his teeth. He didn't want to be this way. He didn't. But wasn't this how it always was? Answering to everyone? Being pulled ten different directions? Everybody *wanting* something from him?

"I went through hell back then," he said, his voice low and intense. "Nicole leaving. My parents dying. Raising two teenagers and a baby when I was just a teenager myself. Working in the vineyard until I was ready to drop. I managed only one way. By seeing light at the end of the tunnel. I don't see that light anymore."

"No," Kari said, shaking her head. "Don't you see? It's not going to be like that this time. This is my baby, too. I wouldn't even think about walking away. Do you understand that? I'm going to take care of him. Be a mother in every way there is."

"Yeah? How do you expect to do that?"

"What do you mean?"

"A few weeks ago, you couldn't even put food in your own mouth."

She swallowed hard. "I've come a long way since then."

"And you have a long way to go."

"I know. And I know it's going to be hard, but —"

"Hard? You're a waitress in a small-town café. You make next to nothing. You work odd hours, and you're exhausted at the end of every shift. Until you've tried to take care of a baby in addition to all that, you don't have a clue what hard is. I'm sorry, Kari.

But that's the truth."

"I won't be his only parent."

"But I can't be sure that I won't."

"Yes, you can! Didn't I just tell you —"

"Don't you think Nicole told me the same thing?" Marc said hotly, his voice escalating. "When she told me she was pregnant, she couldn't stop crying. I told her everything was going to be okay. She said she believed me, that she could do it as long as I was with her. But she left anyway. I woke up one morning, and she was gone. She got her freedom. I stayed and took responsibility, because I was raised to believe that no man was a man unless he did. But now *this*? When in the name of God is it going to be *my* turn?"

"I would never leave you," she said.

"Sorry, but you don't have a great track record where not leaving is concerned. Christ, Kari. You walked away from your own wedding!"

She recoiled as if he'd struck her. "Should I have stayed and married him?"

"Hell no! But you didn't exactly face the problem head-on, did you?"

Tears filled her eyes. "I mean it, Marc. I would *never* leave you."

He knew she meant that right now. But let her deal with one sleepless night after another with a screaming baby, and just how long would she last? How long would it be before he woke up one morning to find himself alone all over again?

Looking at her now, he tried to see the woman who'd brought him so much pleasure for the past several weeks, but wasn't that what had caused this problem in the first place? If only he'd held the hard line he'd laid down for himself and kept his hands off her, he wouldn't be in this situation right now.

"You don't have to worry," he said. "I'll be back. And I'll stay, because I don't have any other choice. And twenty years from now, you can bet your last dollar I'll still be here. Is that what you want to hear?"

She looked at him with a forlorn expression, her eyes glistening with tears. "I just want you to be happy."

Happy? What chance did he have of that now? "I have to go."

With that, he threw his bag over his shoulder and walked out the door.

Kari was still in Marc's bedroom when she heard the sound of his motorcycle coming up the drive, passing by the house, and then heading for the front gate. She listened, tears bubbling up inside her, until the sound disappeared in the distance and there was nothing but silence.

She loved him. God, she loved him so much. She'd almost blurted it out. She'd almost told him she loved him, that she'd loved him almost from the beginning, that there was no other man on this earth she could imagine loving more.

But he didn't love her.

That thought made her even sicker to her stomach than she already felt. If he loved her, he would have swept her into his arms and told her that nothing mattered but the life they'd created and the two of them being together. Instead, he'd done just the opposite.

He'd run.

She'd had a fantasy all the way home from the doctor that she'd tell him the news and he'd take her in his arms and tell her he loved her and he wanted to raise their baby together. How stupid could she possibly have been? That had been a silly delusion that only a fool would have. And he was right. As long as she was a waitress at Rosie's, she'd have a hell of a time raising a baby without a tremendous amount of help, and he was going to be the one providing that help. Because of that, he would resent her for the rest of their lives.

She thought about the ultrasound photo she'd held in her hand as she came into his bedroom to tell him the news. When she saw the look on his face, she was too scared to give it to him, so when he grabbed some things from the bathroom, she'd slipped it inside his bag. Now she was regretting that. Would it make things worse than they already were?

In the end, he'd be back. And she knew he'd stay in Rainbow Valley. Be a father to their baby. Even though he was angry right now, she knew he'd love their child with everything he had in him. But what would she be to him?

Nothing but the mother of his child. The woman who'd been fun for a while, then tied him down in exactly the way he feared the most.

Feeling miserable, she got dressed to go to work, so preoccupied she barely realized she was doing it. When she went to the kitchen to grab her purse and keys, Daniel was coming through the back door.

"Where did Marc go? I saw him leave on his motorcycle earlier."

She gave him a smile that she hoped looked genuine. "He decided to take it for another spin. He might be gone overnight. Wish I could have gone with him, but I have to work."

"Getting a head start on that new lifestyle, huh?" Daniel said as he grabbed a beer from the fridge.

"Yeah. I guess so." She headed for the back door. "Gotta get to work."

"Kari?"

She turned back. "Yeah?"

"Marc. Just how pissed is he?"

Daniel didn't look at her as he said it, and suddenly Kari knew that for all his bravado, he hated the fact that they weren't getting along.

"You guys are just having a difference of opinion," she said.

"He thinks there's only one way. *His* way. I have a new method of aging the wine that'll pay off big time for this vineyard, and he won't even consider it. He refuses to listen to anyone else. And not just about the vineyard. I want to pay Angela's tuition just to make things easier for him, but he refuses to let me do it even when I'll never miss the money. How stupid is that?"

"Does that really surprise you?"

"No. I just wish he'd *listen* to me once in a while." He popped the cap on the beer and tossed it into the trash. "I postponed our harvest crew until next week. I think it was the right decision. But if it's not, I'm never going to hear the end of it from Marc."

She wished she could tell Daniel that in the end, he wasn't going to have to worry about making the right decisions at the vineyard. That he was going to get a reprieve. That Marc would be staying and running the place because he had a baby now and hitting the road on his motorcycle wasn't going to be an option after all. But until she worked this out with Marc, until they came to some kind of understanding that didn't involve him looking at her as if his life had just fallen apart, she couldn't say a word to anyone.

The drone of the engine did nothing to drown out Marc's thoughts as he headed down the highway. Where he was going, he didn't know. But as the hours passed, the open road he'd dreamed of all these years seemed bleak and empty, and the longer he rode, the more unsettled he felt. He shouldn't have left. He knew that. Not with Kari looking at him like that, needing him to reassure her. But how the hell could he do that when he couldn't even reassure himself? He knew now there was no end to it. His life was never going to be his own.

Never.

For hours, Marc drove blindly down Highway 28, and as the afternoon became evening, he wasn't even completely sure where he was. Soon he came to a more populated area, where hundreds of acres of farmland became smaller acreages dotted with houses. The speed limit dropped to thirty-five, evidence that a town was up ahead. He rounded a bend and came upon a small cinder block motel with a diner attached. A weathered sign out front said, "Sunnyside Inn."

He slowed his motorcycle and pulled into the parking lot, but it wasn't until he brought it to a halt and stepped off of it that he realized how tired he was. Glancing at his watch, he was surprised to see he'd been driving for almost six hours.

He went into the office, where a grandmotherly woman ran his credit card and gave him the key to room number 6. He unlocked the door and found a small room that was trying too hard to be cheerful, with blue walls, a flowered bedspread, and cheap art nailed to the walls. He tossed down his bag, then glanced out the window to see a bar and grill a block down the street called Buck's Roadhouse, its red neon sign shining through the dusky evening light. He could stay in this room with nothing but cable TV and his own thoughts for company, or he could go get a bite to eat and a couple of drinks and forget about everything.

Five minutes later, Marc walked inside the bar to find a big, dark room lit mostly by neon beer signs and a couple of TVs behind the bar. One wall was filled with nothing but fishing trophies and cow skulls. Country music assaulted his ears, and the smell of deep-fried food filled the air. He took a seat at the bar and ordered a burger and a beer from a balding, middle-aged guy who just happened to be Buck himself. A couple of young guys with long, shaggy hair and baseball caps sat at the other end of the bar, their hands around beer bottles and their eyes glued to a monster truck rally on the nearby TV.

I'm pregnant.

Those words circled inside Marc's mind until he thought he'd go crazy. As soon as Kari told him the news, it was as if he was looking through a different lens, one that refused to let him see all the joy she'd brought him for the past several weeks.

And Daniel. He'd lucked out the way he always did, and now he was going to get to leave the place he hated and get on with his free and easy life. The unfairness of that settled over Marc like a giant black cloud.

He finished the first beer, and when his burger came, he ordered another one. But he still couldn't get his mind off what had happened with Kari, so he drank that one and asked for one more. Soon the place started to fill up. No wonder. It was probably the only entertainment within twenty miles.

The bartender switched one of the TVs to a baseball game, and Marc tried to concentrate on that, but he couldn't keep his mind from wandering again. He thought about City Limits, a place where he sat down at the bar and Terri was there to bring him his usual drink and chat a little. He could look across the room and see his friends and neighbors, and he knew every song on the vintage jukebox. It was an unsettling feeling to look around this place and see not one familiar face. And not a single person there recognized him. He remembered how much he'd craved that sense of being lost in a crowd, but now it unnerved him, as if he'd been dropped into an alternate universe where everybody was a stranger.

Then the door opened and a woman walked in, late twenties, dark hair, wearing jeans, boots, and a tank top. She slid onto a stool two down from Marc. Buck immediately drew a Bud and set it down in front of her. She pulled a cigarette and lighter from her purse, lit the cigarette with a flick of her thumb, then blew out the smoke.

She'd taken only a few sips of her beer when she turned to Marc. "I'd ask you if you're new in town, but honey, believe me. I know the men in this town, and you're definitely not one of them."

"I'm just passing through."

"Where are you from?"

"Rainbow Valley."

"Never heard of it."

"I'm not surprised."

She told him she worked at the hardware store down the street. Divorced. No kids. But her ex was a pain in the ass because he wanted to get back together and she wasn't interested. Not that he was abusive or anything like that, she said, but he had no ambition. She was going to beauty school as soon as she saved the money, and all he wanted to do was smoke pot and go fishing with his buddies.

Fifteen minutes into their conversation, she moved to the barstool next to him. Marc ordered both of them another beer and told Buck to keep them coming. But as much as Marc tried to pay attention to the woman, her voice was nothing but white noise to him. He spoke often enough to keep the conversation going, but if somebody held a gun to his head and told him to repeat anything she'd said, he'd be a dead man.

"You seem a little down tonight," the woman said. "Wanna talk about it?"

"Nope."

"Okay. Far as I'm concerned, we can stop talking altogether."

She accompanied those words with a provocative smile, sliding her hand over to rest it on top of his. She was nice. Reasonably attractive. And available. He'd told this woman he was just passing through, so he had no doubt a one-night stand was all she was looking for. All these years, he'd thought that was exactly what he would be looking for, too.

So why did the thought of it leave him cold?

Somewhere in the depths of his alcohol-soaked mind, he remembered a time when riding the back roads, seeing the sights, staying at tiny motels, and drinking at local bars had seemed like a great thing to do. And if a willing woman presented herself, he'd planned on going for it. But now as it was happening, it seemed odd and surreal, like a dream that started out pleasant enough, only to morph into a nightmare.

He pulled out his wallet and tossed money

on the bar.

"Don't leave now, sweetie," the woman said. "The party's just getting started."

"Thanks for the offer, but not tonight."

"Then stick around town for a while. Lots of sights to see."

"Right," Buck said as he passed by carrying a couple of beers. "Grandma Braddock's got herself a new lawn gnome. Sure wouldn't want to miss *that.*"

Marc said good night and headed for the door, his head so fuzzy all he wanted to do was lie down. He stepped out of the bar and started back toward the motel, feeling relieved to no longer be listening to the blaring TVs and inhaling secondhand smoke. A few minutes later, he went into his motel room and locked the door behind him. He sat on the bed and reached for his phone, intending to check the weather. Even though the vineyard was Daniel's responsibility, it was a habit so ingrained after all these years that he could be six feet under and he'd still be pulling up those apps.

His phone was dead.

He grabbed his bag to retrieve his charging cord, only to realize he hadn't brought it with him. He'd been in such a hurry to get away that he'd left it behind.

In a hurry to get away? To go where?

Here?

Were you out of your fucking mind?

He tossed his phone aside, closed his eyes, and thought of home, of the evenings he'd spent on the deck with Kari at sunset, staring at the rolling hills and the leafy vines full of grapes. In his mind, he heard their quiet conversation, felt the night breeze, saw the fireflies twinkling in the distance, and tasted the best wine ever produced in the state of Texas. Sometimes on evenings like that, he had the sense that the vineyard had wrapped itself around him, crept inside, and become part of the very blood in his veins. If that were true, how could he separate himself from it without it killing him in the process?

No. That was crazy. How many years had he dreamed of seeing Rainbow Valley in his rearview mirror? He always told himself that the moment he rode past the city limits sign and faced that new life ahead of him, any reservations he felt would vanish.

Now he wasn't so sure.

He didn't even bother to take off his clothes or pull down the covers. He just collapsed on the bed and closed his eyes, thinking about the beautiful green-eyed woman who had lit up his life like the Fourth of July. She was pregnant with their baby. He

415

was going to be a father again. And his last hazy thought as he drifted off to sleep was that maybe it wasn't a nightmare after all, but a dream come true.

As Kari drove home from work that evening, she prayed she'd go into the house and Marc would be there. He would have realized where his heart really was, his despair would be gone, and he'd greet her with a smile and a hug. But when she got back to the vineyard, he wasn't there. Neither was Daniel. It was just her alone, sitting in that big house, a house that wasn't hers, never had been hers, a house she'd have to move away from very soon because she didn't belong there.

She had no idea what Marc would say when he finally did return, but if he still had that look on his face, the one that said everything they'd done for the past several weeks had been a mistake, she'd be forced to move out even if he didn't ask her to because she wouldn't be able to stand it.

She filled a glass with water and grabbed a box of crackers from the pantry, feeling so nauseated that all she could do was collapse in a kitchen chair and try to get something — anything — down.

When she finally felt as if she might not

416

throw up, she poured a glass of wine and went out to the deck. She couldn't drink alcohol now, but just having the glass in her hand and smelling the wine made her think of Marc before all this had happened. The dogs were there with her, stretched out beside her chair, both of them particularly sedate tonight. They said dogs knew the mental state of the people they loved and behaved accordingly. In this place, where pets outnumbered people, she thought it was especially true.

Eventually she went inside and tucked herself into Marc's king-sized bed, missing him so much tears came to her eyes. As she was falling asleep, she put her hand on her belly, imagining what it would be like to have Marc do the same, then look at her with love in his eyes.

She slept fitfully that night, only to fall into a deep sleep near dawn. She didn't wake again until almost noon, feeling groggy and disoriented and sick to her stomach all over again. She threw on a robe and went into the kitchen.

Daniel sat at the kitchen table, which meant she was going to have to keep up the facade, to act as if everything was just fine when nothing was going to be fine ever again. He didn't say a word as she came

417

into the room. He just stared at his phone, and when Kari poured a cup of coffee and sat down next to him, he didn't even look up.

"Daniel?" she said. "Is something wrong?"

He slid his phone over. She recognized one of the weather apps Marc looked at a dozen times a day, and the screen showed something that made uneasiness creep through her.

"A storm?" she said.

"I saw it last night, but it was going to miss us. Look at the trajectory now."

She hit the button for live radar with a storm-tracking projection, and as she watched the bright red center of a huge thunderstorm creeping eastward, her uneasiness turned into cold, clammy fear.

It was heading straight for Rainbow Valley.

CHAPTER 18

"The storm is moving slowly," Daniel said, "but that means once it starts dumping rain, it's not going to stop for a long time. We have maybe six or seven hours before it hits."

Kari went to the window and looked to the west. The late September sun cast a stunning glow across the vineyard, where the grapes were so ripe they nearly burst out of their skins. But in the far distance, she saw pale gray clouds, ones that could become dark thunderheads within a few hours. Then she looked at the vine-covered hills and imagined the grapes soaking up all that water.

A whole vintage can be ruined that way.

The memory of Marc's words sent an icy feeling right down Kari's spine. She glanced back at Daniel. He looked angry. Frustrated. So why wasn't he *doing* something?

"Won't the rain damage the grapes?" she asked.

"Hell yes, it will."

"Then they have to be harvested."

"With what?" Daniel said. "I don't have a crew scheduled until next week!"

"Can't you find another one?"

"I already tried," Daniel said, desperation flooding his voice. "There's nobody. And Marc's not answering his phone. He's probably avoiding me. But it doesn't matter, anyway. He couldn't do anything even if he were here." He closed his eyes. "He's going to fucking *kill* me."

"Did you call Nina?" she asked him. "Angela? Can they help?"

"What's the point?" Daniel said, throwing his hands in the air. "Even if they come, we'll never get it done in time."

"Ramon and Michael are here."

"Two more people isn't going to cut it. It wouldn't even be close. Not if we have to harvest in a hurry."

"At least we can get started."

"No. It's a lost cause."

"We have to try. Can you go down to the vineyard? Do whatever you have to do to get things under way?"

"Kari," Daniel said with a look of desperation, "you don't understand. It'll take two

420

people just to get the grapes that are picked into the destemmer/crusher and then into the fermentation tanks. Those are two people who can't be picking grapes."

"Then the rest of us will just have to pick faster."

"Us?"

"I'll help."

"Are you kidding? You'll barely be able to lift one of the empty five-gallon bins, much less one full of grapes."

"But I can pick them. It can't be that hard."

"The hell it's not. It's the shittiest work imaginable."

"But do you have to have any special skills?"

"Nope. Clip the bunches with shears and throw them in the bins. But do that about a thousand times and you'll want to shoot yourself in the head."

"I don't care. I'm helping."

"Will you stop being so damned *naïve*? There are only four of us. Six if you count Nina and Angela. We won't even be able to come close to getting those grapes in. We need four times that many people!"

"Daniel, is that storm going to hit?"

"No doubt about it."

"Okay. I know you and Marc aren't getting along. But do you really want him knowing a storm was coming that was going to ruin the crop, but you didn't even try to do anything about it?"

Daniel looked away, his jaw tightening with frustration. Finally he let out a breath. "No. I don't."

"Then go down and get things started. I'll call Nina and Angela and see if they can come. Then I'll change clothes and come down there."

"Kari —"

"Daniel. *Go!*"

Daniel shoved away from the table and left the kitchen. Kari grabbed her phone and called Nina. The second Kari mentioned the extent of the thunderstorm, Nina knew the vineyard was in trouble. She said she'd shut down the shop and head over with Rupert and Bonnie. She also said she'd call Angela on the way, as well as a few other people who might be able to help. Kari felt a tiny glimmer of hope. More people. That could only be a good thing.

Then Nina asked where Marc was.

Oh, *God.* Kari didn't want to talk about that, and she didn't want to lie. But what choice did she have? "He took another trip to try out his motorcycle," she told Nina. "Daniel tried to get in touch with him, but he's not answering."

"Well, somebody needs to find him, or we really are screwed. Try him again, will you?"

"Uh . . . yeah. I will."

As soon as Kari hung up, she took a deep breath and tried Marc's number. The phone rang three times. Four. Five. And then it flipped to voice mail. She left a message, telling him the situation and asking him to call back. Surely he'd pick it up.

She went to Marc's bedroom to put on the crappiest clothes she had, and by the time she'd changed, he hadn't called back. No matter how much he thought he wanted to get away from this place, she couldn't imagine him turning his back on this kind of problem by ignoring her call.

Then she had a terrible thought.

She turned slowly to look at his dresser. The power cord for his phone was still plugged in and resting on it where it always was. He'd been in such a hurry to get out of there that he'd forgotten it.

If his phone was out of power, he'd have no way of knowing she'd called.

So there it was. If he happened to see a weather report somewhere else, he might call. If not . . .

Her only hope was that he was on his way back home already.

She knew she had every right to be upset with Marc for leaving the way he had. But as strong as he'd been for everybody else, maybe he had a right to fall apart a little when he realized the plans he'd been making for years had exploded right before his eyes. But whether he knew it or not, his love for this place went soul deep, and she'd be damned if she was going to let anything bad happen to it as long as there was breath left in her body.

Marc woke to sunlight angling through the partially open motel blinds and stabbing him in the eyes. He turned over to get away from it, only to have his head pound as if a little man was inside it, beating it with a hammer. He put his hand to his forehead with a groan, finally rolling to his back and letting out a heavy sigh. Then he turned painfully to look at the clock.

It was two o'clock in the afternoon. Good God, how much had he had to drink?

The events of the night before came back to him bit by bit, but everything seemed jumbled, like puzzle pieces rattling around in a box. He remembered walking to the bar. Having dinner and a beer. Having several beers. Then there had been a woman . . .

He whipped around to look at the bed beside him, breathing a sigh of relief when he realized he was alone.

He rose from the bed and fumbled with the coffeepot on top of the dresser. When the little red light wouldn't come on in spite of the fact that it was plugged in, he realized the damned thing was broken. He threw the coffee packet aside and put his palms on the counter, bowing his head. Then he slowly looked up again and stared at himself in the mirror. His hair was crunched to one side, and he had a day-old growth of beard that made his creased face look even more pathetic.

And his head was on the verge of exploding.

He was pretty sure he hadn't grabbed a bottle of aspirin as he was blindly tossing stuff from his medicine cabinet into his bag, but he sat on the bed and went through it anyway, hoping to find one. Then he saw something in the side pocket he didn't recognize.

He slid it out and stared at it. It was a black-and-white photo. He looked at the tiny identifying words along the bottom. *Worthington, Kari.* Then yesterday's date. Recognition came slowly, but when he finally realized what it was, his heart stood still. It was nothing but black-and-white blobs all running together, but still he knew what he was looking at.

An ultrasound photo of their baby.

The instant Kari told him he was going to be a father, every restrictive image in the book had filled his mind: Handcuffs. A straitjacket. A noose around his neck. But as he looked at this photo now, he wasn't thinking about those things. Instead his mind overflowed with memories he hadn't thought about in a very long time.

He remembered Angela walking for the first time. She'd toddled along for three shaky steps, then fallen into his arms. He'd scooped her up and whooped with joy, and she'd been all smiles. He remembered the ballet recital when she was five and not a single kid on the stage had a clue what to do. It had been a whirl of sparkles and spangles on tiny little bodies, all going in different directions. He remembered the breakfast she'd made for him on Father's Day when she was ten — overcooked eggs and burnt toast that he'd eaten as if it was five-star cuisine.

How could he have forgotten all that? How could the bad times have dominated his memories, shoving the good times aside until he barely remembered them?

Kari must have put this photo in his bag before he'd stormed out of the house yesterday. Kari, who was back in Rainbow Valley right now, most likely wondering where the father of her baby was and how he could have acted like such a colossal bastard.

Marc dropped the photo to his lap. God in heaven . . . what was he *doing* here?

He'd told himself that seeing the country would open him up to new opportunities he didn't even know existed. That after a few years, he wouldn't even remember what life was like in Rainbow Valley because there was a whole world out there for the taking. But being here now had given him a glimpse of that kind of life, and it seemed like a miserable proposition. A stark highway, a cold barstool, alcohol that had muddled his mind, and a nameless woman who was just looking for a good time. *That* was the life he thought he wanted?

Then he remembered his deal with Kari. No commitment. No strings. Just sex. Was that all she'd ever wanted from him, too? Just sex?

Then he thought about how they made love, about how she looked up at him afterward, her green eyes shining with satisfaction. Looking back now, he could see that their relationship had changed. In a matter of just a few weeks, she'd become a different woman, one he admired in a way he couldn't have imagined that rainy night she'd shown up on his doorstep. The more his respect for her grew, the more desperate he felt to be with her.

But how did she feel about him?

It was a scary question, because he wasn't sure of the answer. Then he remembered her words right before he stormed out of his bedroom.

I would never leave you.

She'd said it not once, but twice. He'd ignored her both times, telling her she didn't mean it, that she wouldn't be there when the going got tough. How could he have discounted her words as if they meant nothing when they meant everything to him? Would she ever forgive him for that?

He looked at the photo again. It was nothing but gray blobs and dark shadows, but he knew somewhere in it was his future, the kind of future he couldn't have imagined wanting but now he craved with everything he had in him. He thought about calling Kari, only to remember one more thing from last night — his phone was out of juice. He looked at the room phone and thought about picking it up, but what would he say when she came on the line? He always screwed up when it came to saying the right thing. Always. And he couldn't risk that now. Not when they were hundreds of miles apart, when he couldn't take her in his arms and *show* her how much he cared.

His head was pounding. His heart was aching. The only way to make it all stop was to go home. Tell her what an idiot he'd been. Beg her forgiveness. Then take her in his arms and plead with her to love him as much as he loved her.

After what he'd done, though, he was afraid she'd never want to speak to him again.

Kari headed down to the vineyard to find the men stacking empty bins near the first several rows of grapevines. Daniel gave her a crash course in picking grapes. She put on gloves, picked up shears, and started in. At first it seemed like an easy task, but after thirty minutes, her arms and back ached, and nausea churned away in her stomach. She wondered how long she'd be able to keep this up before fainting dead away.

Nina arrived with Rupert and Bonnie, but Kari could already see Daniel was right. They'd never be able to pull this off with so few people.

"It's hard work," Nina told her. "Keep go-

429

ing as long as you can, but don't kill yourself. It's not worth that. There are a few more people on the way."

Kari nodded and kept on picking, but as the minutes passed, she grew more hopeless. She had to stop every few minutes and stand perfectly still, squeezing her eyes closed, willing her nausea to subside. The whole time, Daniel's words circled around inside her head. *We'll never get it done in time.*

Then she heard the rumble of engines, and she turned to see the most amazing sight.

In the distance, several cars and trucks were pulling through onto the property and making their way down the road. They circled the house and came to a halt near the gate leading to the vineyard. People piled out — some Kari knew and some she didn't — and every one of them was dressed for dirty work.

Kari walked over to Nina. "What's happening?"

"I'm not sure. I told only a few people."

Gus got out of one of the cars. Nina called out to him, "Gus! What's going on?"

He walked over. "When you told me about the storm, I told a few other people. Pretty soon everybody was spreading the word.

There'll be more folks here soon."

"They're coming to pick grapes?" Nina asked.

"Yep. The moment people found out Marc was in trouble, you couldn't keep them away."

Within the next half hour, Kari watched in awe as at least thirty people grabbed bins and shears and headed out to the field. Then Rosie and Estelle brought ice chests with food and drinks and set up a spread in the barn. Kari stuck with the story that Marc had taken a motorcycle trip and was out of pocket and had no idea the storm was on its way. Not a solitary person questioned it, and Kari knew it was because they assumed if Marc wasn't there, there had to be a damned good reason why.

Then Angela arrived.

Kari automatically felt a rush of apprehension. Angela belonged there, and in the last twenty-four hours, Kari had begun to feel as if she didn't.

When Angela came through the gate into the vineyard, she stopped to stare at Kari. Kari shoved her hair out of her face, but she could only imagine what she looked like wearing grape-stained gloves, with sweat pouring down her temples, her arms already scraped up from the grapevines, and the red welt of a wasp sting on her neck.

"I talked to Uncle Daniel," she said, nodding over her shoulder toward the barn. "He said he can't get in touch with my dad."

"Yeah," Kari said. "He took a motorcycle trip, and we can't get hold of him. And he forgot the power cord for his phone, so if it's out of juice, that's why he's not answering."

"If he knew what was going on, he'd be here."

"Of course he would."

Kari clipped another bunch of grapes and tossed it into the nearly full bin at her feet.

"You're helping," Angela said.

"Yeah," Kari said, "I'm helping."

Angela kept looking at her, as if the sight of Kari picking grapes just didn't compute. "Why?" Angela asked.

Why? Oh, *God.* There were so many answers to that question. *Because I love your father. I love this vineyard, and so does he. I want to stay here forever and raise our baby together.* But those were things she couldn't say yet, so she finally settled on something that was just as heartfelt and the absolute truth.

"Because your dad helped me when I needed it the most. And now there's nothing I wouldn't do for him."

Angela regarded her for a moment more, then grabbed a cluster of grapes, clipped it, and tossed it into the bin that was nearly full. "Be sure not to lift that," she told Kari. "I'll do it. I'm used to it. And here. Let me show you something about the shears. If you'll hold them like this, you can cut through the vine a whole lot easier."

Kari worked side by side with Angela as the storm drew closer and dark clouds billowed on the horizon. Kari had to agree with Daniel. Picking grapes was the shittiest work imaginable.

Soon daylight faded to the point that Kari was having a hard time seeing the grapes to pick them. She was just wondering what they were going to do when it got completely dark, only to have Rick from Rick's Automotive show up with two of his employees, all of them driving trucks with spotlights on the roofs so everybody would be able to keep on picking. Kari stayed on the verge of tears the whole time because her muscles were screaming, she was nauseated, and she wasn't sure she could pick one more cluster of grapes even though she had to no matter what. But the biggest reason she felt like crying was because this place was so amazing and these people were so wonderful. And then something happened that finally pushed her over the edge.

Luke and Shannon showed up.

They said they were in San Antonio on their honeymoon, but they heard Marc was in trouble, so they came back right away to help. The very idea of them hurrying home from their honeymoon was just a little too much wonderful all in one place, and way more than Kari could handle.

"Kari?" Angela said. "What's wrong?"

She wiped her cheeks with her dirty glove. "Nothing," she said, because nothing was. It was right, so much more right than she ever could have imagined. She wished she could talk to Marc. She wished she could tell him how much all these people cared about him. Ask him how he could even think of leaving this town, turning his back on the very thing she'd been looking for all her life.

And then she'd tell him she loved him.

CHAPTER 19

Marc was an hour and a half away from Rainbow Valley when he saw the storm clouds.

At first it was nothing more than a graying of the sky to the west, but as the clouds bulged and swelled into dark thunderheads, his apprehension grew. These were the kinds of clouds vintners feared the most at harvest time. He'd seen a big storm system on the radar yesterday, but he was sure it was going to swing north of Rainbow Valley. This one looked to be heading right for it.

He cursed himself for forgetting his phone charger. He needed to see a weather report. Find out what was behind those dark clouds and how much rain they could conceivably dump. But did it really matter? Nothing could be done if Daniel couldn't get a crew in there, and chances were excellent he couldn't. But if that storm hit Rainbow Valley dead center, the crop could be ruined.

Damn it! Why hadn't Daniel brought the grapes in when he had the chance?

He had to know what was going on. He had to.

Fifteen minutes later, he came upon a gas station. No pay phone. Did those even exist anymore? He went inside and asked the guy behind the counter if he could use the phone. As he started to dial, all at once it dawned on him he didn't know Daniel's number. Hell, he didn't know anybody's number. They were programmed into his cell phone, which was currently dead in his pocket.

Then he realized he could call directory assistance and get the number of the wine store in town. But when he called the number and the phone rang, nobody picked up.

Get home. Just get home.

He got back on his motorcycle and hit the highway again. The stormy skies were bringing darkness much sooner than usual. He drove faster than he really should have, even though he had no idea what he'd be able to do when he got to the vineyard. An average harvest meant a couple days of effort, so even if the crew Daniel had scheduled could come early, it wouldn't be enough men to do the job.

By the time he neared the Rainbow Valley city limits, a few raindrops began to fall. Two minutes later, the heavens opened up. Marc ducked his head against the wind and the deluge of rain, which was forcing him to go slower so he didn't lay the bike down going around curves. And all he could think was, *I'm too late. The crop will be ruined.*

He felt the loss already, forming a hole in his heart so deep he was surprised it could still pump blood. If only he hadn't gotten it in his head that he wanted to leave Rainbow Valley in the first place, this wouldn't be happening. If he hadn't acted like a bastard to Kari and realized where his future really was, he would have been at the vineyard, finding some kind of solution.

But no. He'd screwed up things on both fronts, so when he got home, he'd find an entire crop on the verge of being destroyed and a sweet, beautiful woman he'd hurt so deeply she'd probably never forgive him.

As he came around the last curve, he saw the lights from the vineyard shining weakly through the falling rain. A few minutes later he drove through the gate and started down the long gravel drive.

Then he saw the most unbelievable sight.

The house was nearly dark, but cars and trucks were everywhere. The driveway was so full he had to plow across the rain-soaked lawn to circle the house, where he saw even more vehicles.

And then he saw them. People. In the vineyard. Everywhere there were people.

He leaped off his motorcycle and hurried to the vineyard gate, feeling as if he was moving through a dreamworld where things couldn't possibly be as they seemed. One by one, he started to recognize the people. Gus. Rick. Terri. Luke and Shannon. Bonnie. Rupert. Other friends and neighbors. They were dripping wet and filthy dirty with grape-stained gloves, still clipping one bunch after another and tossing them into bins as rain bombarded them. Three big trucks, each with a pair of spotlights, lit each row so they could go on picking in the dark.

Not a single one of these people were part of a paid harvest crew. Not one. Yet they were harvesting his grapes? From the look of things, they'd been at it for hours.

He turned to see Michael driving the tractor to the barn, and behind it was a trailer full of grapes. Daniel and Ramon were grabbing the bins off it, manhandling them into the destemmer/crusher to prepare them for the fermentation tanks.

Marc ran to the barn, shouting over the thundering rain, "Daniel!"

438

Daniel spun around. "Marc! Where the hell have you been?"

"Never mind. How much of the crop is in?"

"Maybe eighty or ninety percent."

Marc was dumbfounded. They'd gotten that many of the grapes in? How the hell had they done it?

"Is Kari in the house?" he shouted.

"No. She's in the vineyard!"

Marc felt a shot of apprehension. "She's picking grapes?"

"Yeah. She's about to drop. I tried to get her to stop, but she refused to quit!"

No. She had no business out in this weather exerting herself like that. Not when she was pregnant. If anything happened to her, he was never going to forgive himself.

All at once thunder crashed, and in the distance he saw a zigzag of lightning. "The storm's getting worse!" he shouted to Daniel. "I want everybody out of here! Help me spread the word!"

Daniel abandoned the machine and hurried after Marc. They ran into the vineyard, where they shouted at everybody to drop everything and head for home. As Marc's rain-drenched friends and neighbors headed for their cars and trucks, he knew he owed them a debt of gratitude he could never repay.

"Dad!"

Marc turned to see Angela running up behind him, rain soaked and grape stained.

"I think Kari's sick!" she shouted.

"Where is she?"

"This way. Hurry!"

Marc ran after Angela, row past muddy row, until he finally spotted Kari. He slogged through the mud to where she stood. She was clutching a grapevine in one hand and shears in the other, her head bowed.

"Kari!"

Her head jerked up.

"You shouldn't be out here!" he shouted. "Get inside!"

"Not finished! There are more grapes!"

"Leave them!"

Another bolt of lightning sizzled through the sky. He took her shears and tossed them down. Then he grabbed her arm and pulled her along. She stumbled a little and righted herself, but when she stumbled again, he could tell she was on the verge of collapsing. Finally he just swept her into his arms.

"Angela!" Marc shouted. "Find Aunt Nina! I want you both in the barn!"

He hurried through the vineyard gate, fear hammering him all the way to the house.

Please God, don't let anything happen to her. And please let our baby be okay.

The rain came down in torrents, but he ducked his head against it and carried her across the deck and into the house. When he got to his bedroom, he laid her carefully on the bed. She took a deep, shaky breath and let it out slowly, blinking open those beautiful green eyes. He waited for her to smile. She didn't. Instead, she looked wary and apprehensive, and he knew why. She didn't know what was in his head right then. The last time they talked, she told him she was pregnant, and what had he done? He'd gotten on his motorcycle and driven away. How much more of a bastard could he possibly have been?

He grabbed towels from the bathroom, wiped his own dripping hair, then sat down beside her. Her hair was wet and tangled, a shock of auburn against the pillowcase beneath her head. The pink streak in her hair had faded, but he could still see it, reminding him one more time of the joy she'd brought to his life. But lying in this bed right now, she looked small and weak and helpless, and he hated himself all over again for leaving her when she needed him the most.

He pulled off her dirty gloves and tossed

441

them on the floor. With a dry towel, he dabbed rainwater off her face. "Kari? Are you okay?"

"I'm fine."

"The baby?"

"We're both okay."

"Are you sure? You don't look okay."

"Just tired."

He wasn't sure about that. "You worked too hard out there. I want to make sure you're all right."

"It's okay. I'd know if something was wrong." She took a deep breath and let it out slowly. "I feel much better just lying here. But there's more to do. The rain is here, and we didn't get them all."

"Forget that for now. Just rest."

"But —"

"Most of the grapes are in. I'm here now, Kari. I'm going to go take care of the rest of it. I'm going to take care of everything." He took her hand, stroking it gently with his thumb, feeling like such a bastard for the grief he'd caused her.

"I'm so sorry for the things I said," he told her. "I never should have left. Can you ever forgive me for that?"

"Things get too hard for everybody sometimes. It's okay."

"No, it's not okay. I left when you needed

me the most."

"You're here now. That's all that matters."

No. He didn't deserve this. After what he'd done, what he'd said, she should be telling him to go to hell.

"You don't have to worry, Kari. I'm never leaving again."

In that moment, it was as if every bit of the tension she was holding on to melted out of her body. She blinked wearily, and he could tell she was on the edge of sleep.

"I need to get back out there," Marc said. "Just rest. Then later —"

"Wait. About Daniel."

"What about him?"

"He told me he wants to pay Angela's college tuition, but you won't let him."

"Kari. This isn't the time to talk about that."

"Just listen. Please listen. I know you think you don't need his money and that he's just showing off. But it's more than that. Whether you know it or not, Daniel is dying for your respect. He can't get it by running this place, because you'll always be better at that than he is. But if you take the money he earned by doing something *he's* good at and thank him for making your life easier, you're finally telling him you approve."

Marc had never once thought about it that way. All he'd ever seen was his brother's smart-ass behavior and assumed his success was some kind of accident because he couldn't possibly focus on anything worthwhile. But maybe it wasn't an accident. He'd worked hard. He'd given the market what it wanted, and he'd profited from it. Worse, Marc had always assumed that taking his younger brother's money meant Daniel was actually looking down on *him.*

Kari squeezed Marc's hand, looking at him earnestly. "He loves you, Marc. And so does everybody in this town. As soon as they knew you were in trouble, they dropped everything and came. It was amazing. There isn't anything they wouldn't do for you, and it's because you've done so much for them. Do you understand that?"

Yes. He did now. Right now his friends and family were driving home, soaked to the skin and feeling as if they'd been to hell and back, all because they'd come there to help him when his head was so screwed up he couldn't help himself.

"I understand," he said.

"And Luke and Shannon, too. They came home from their honeymoon. Can you believe it?"

"You're the one I can't believe. You're

pregnant. You shouldn't have been out there like that."

"I had to help. If I thought there was a problem with the baby, I'd have stopped. But at least I had to try. You love this place. I see you on the deck, looking out over the vineyard, and I know. *I know.* With everything going on, I think you lost sight of that, but if you never hear another word I say, please hear this. *You love this place.* And I couldn't let you lose even one tiny bit of something you love that much."

She was right. It was as if he'd been wearing blinders all these years, blinders created by all the pain and hard work and the misguided sense that he needed to leave in order to have a life. That wasn't true. This *was* his life.

Kari sighed wearily, as if the last words she'd spoken used up the final bit of energy she had. "Marc?"

"Yeah?"

Her voice fell to a sleepy whisper. "I love this place, too." She paused. "And I love you."

Those words hit Marc like an arrow straight to his heart. He bowed his head, feeling guilty and elated and ashamed and euphoric all at the same time. Even after everything he'd done, she *loved* him?

445

It was more than he ever could have hoped for.

Even with the gloves she'd been wearing, her hands were still rubbed raw. He brought her palm to his lips and kissed it, unable to believe he was getting another chance at this.

"I love you, too," he said.

The briefest of smiles crossed her lips, and she squeezed his hand. Then her eyes fell closed, and a few seconds later he realized she'd fallen asleep.

He knew now that her running away from her wedding hadn't been a cowardly thing for her to do. For the person she'd been at that moment, who was just learning how to be herself and was terrified of the consequences, it was the most courageous thing she could possibly have done. And he knew now that she wouldn't run from responsibility. She wouldn't leave him or their baby. She would stay and fight no matter how tough things got.

All these weeks he'd talked about his need to be free, to have no connections, no responsibility, nothing holding him back, telling her in essence that she'd better not be a woman who expected more because he didn't have it to give. But now he felt as if he'd give her everything he had in him, right up to his dying breath.

He had more to say to her. So much more. But right now she needed to rest, and he needed to help Daniel get as many grapes processed as he absolutely could. He was going back outside to finish what he should have started, because this place was his future. Nina and Daniel might be part owners, but Cordero Vineyards was his responsibility, now and forever.

And he never wanted it any other way.

CHAPTER 20

Three hours later, Marc and Daniel came back into the kitchen. Marc grabbed two dish towels out of a drawer and tossed one of them to Daniel. They rubbed the excess rainwater off themselves and collapsed at the table. Marc had sent Nina and Angela back to the house an hour ago. Nina wanted to drive home, but with the storm still raging, Marc insisted she stay the night. She and Angela were probably already asleep in Angela's room upstairs.

"You look like shit," Daniel said.

"That's because I feel like shit," Marc said. "You don't look so hot yourself."

"That's because harvest sucks. Particularly when you're doing part of it in the rain." Daniel sighed. "Okay. Let me have it."

"Let you have what?"

"Oh, come on. You're not letting this one go by. Just say it. If I'd harvested when I should have, this wouldn't have happened.

And you're right."

"Maybe you were right," Marc said. "Maybe the grapes needed another week on the vine."

"But the storm —"

"You couldn't have seen that coming. At least you got things moving when it looked as if rain was on its way."

"Yeah, well . . ."

"What?"

He rubbed his hand over his chin, staring at the tabletop. Then he looked up at Marc. "That wasn't me. I wasn't the one who decided we needed to try to harvest with or without a crew."

"Then who was?"

"Kari."

Marc blinked with surprise. "What?"

"I was ready to give up. She wasn't. I found out the rain was coming, and I just sat there like an idiot. She's the one who kicked everything into action. If not for her, the crop would have been ruined."

Marc would have liked to have said he was surprised, but was he really? That little piece of dandelion fluff was tougher than he ever gave her credit for.

"You've always made the hard decisions," Daniel said. "I've always depended on you for that, mostly because you're always right.

So I'm going to listen to you from now on. Do things your way. I'm going to run this place the way it should be run, the way it's always been run. We had a deal, and by God, I'm going to live up to my end of the bargain."

"No, you're not."

Daniel blinked. "What?"

"This isn't the place for you. It never was."

"What are you talking about?"

"You can leave Rainbow Valley anytime you're ready. Because I'm staying."

Daniel shook his head, as if Marc's words didn't compute. "Wait a minute. I don't get this. You spend years telling me you want out of here, and now suddenly you don't?"

Marc reached into the bag he'd taken on his trip. He pulled out the ultrasound photo and tossed it on the table in front of Daniel.

"What's this?" Daniel asked, and then his eyes grew wide. He flicked his gaze to Marc. "Dude. You gotta be kidding me."

"I'm going to be a father again."

Daniel's face fell. "Oh, crap."

"No. This is good."

"Good? How can it be good? I thought you were gung ho about getting off the daddy track."

"I was." He took the photo from Daniel

and looked at it again, and he couldn't stop the smile that crossed his lips. "Then I met Kari."

"So you're staying in Rainbow Valley?"

"Uh-huh."

"And Kari is, too?"

"Yep."

"That's what you want? To stay here and raise a baby?"

"That's what I want."

Daniel shook his head. "Holy *crap*. I sure didn't expect this. You must really be crazy about her."

"You have no idea."

"Well, thank God she's staying. You're not nearly as much of a stick-in-the-mud when she's around."

Marc shook his head. "I'm *so* glad to be getting rid of you."

Daniel grinned. "I'll be coming back just to irritate you. And to see my new . . . niece? Nephew?"

"Too soon to tell."

"This is crazy," Daniel said. "So have you told Angela?"

"Not yet."

"How do you suppose she's going to feel about this?"

"I don't know. We haven't had a chance to

talk yet. I'm sure she's upstairs asleep by now."

"So how's she feeling about college?"

"As far as I know, she's still there. And if I have anything to say about it, she'll stay there. So that means my finances are going to be pretty tight for some time to come."

"For God's sake, Marc! I told you I could fix that problem. Pay her tuition. But if you refuse to even consider —"

"Thanks for the offer. I accept."

Daniel looked at him with surprise. "Seriously?"

"Seriously."

A smile lit Daniel's face. "I'll transfer the money first thing in the morning. How much? Twenty grand? Fifty? I haven't kept up with college tuition, so I have no idea —"

"She'll likely end up in vet school. That alone will be at least one Porsche. Sorry you offered?"

"Nope. I'll make it a hundred."

"We can work it out later."

"And if that's not enough —"

"Will you shut up? I told you we can work it out later."

Daniel gave him a satisfied smile. "I'm going to hold you to that." He rose from his chair. "I'm heading to the cottage. Don't wake me for the next two days."

"Nope. We have some cleanup work to do tomorrow."

"I thought you said I could leave whenever I was ready."

"That's right. And you're not ready."

"That's funny. I swore I was." He sighed. "Fine. I'll be there."

He was halfway out the door when Marc called out to him, "Just so you'll know, the condoms in the dresser are expired. Don't use them unless you're ready to be a father."

Daniel winced. "Thanks for the heads-up. I'll be burning those in the morning."

As Daniel left the house, Marc headed for his bedroom to take a quick shower. Then he climbed into bed beside Kari and gave her a gentle kiss. She stirred a little, then was still again. She was a mess from head to toe, but he didn't care about that. All he cared about was that she was warm and safe and their baby was, too, and that all of them were home to stay.

The next morning, Marc left Kari sleeping and went to the kitchen, where he found Sasha on her refrigerator perch and Angela starting a pot of coffee. She wore a pair of cotton pajama pants with kittens all over them and a ragged Rainbow Valley Animal

Shelter T-shirt. With her dark hair tucked behind her ears, bare feet, and sleepy eyes, he could almost make himself believe she was still only ten years old.

"Is Aunt Nina still asleep?" Marc asked.

"Yeah. She's sleeping just fine. And if she didn't snore like a freight train, I probably would be, too."

Marc smiled. "When did you start drinking coffee?"

"Since I started pulling all-nighters to study for tests. UT is a little harder than Rainbow Valley High."

She grabbed another cup from the cabinet and set it on the counter, and they stood by, waiting for the coffee to brew.

"Speaking of college," Angela said, "I need to talk to you about that."

"Angela —"

"Dad —"

"No, listen to me," he said. "Your problems at UT will pass. You're too smart and too nice to be without friends for long. There are fifty thousand kids there. There are bound to be at least a few you fit in with."

"No. I don't want to stay there."

"You're just not thinking this through."

"No. I have thought about it. I don't like it there. It's just so *big.* It seems like there

454

are more kids in my freshman chemistry class than live in this whole town." She sighed. "Dad, I just can't do it."

Marc felt the most profound sense of disappointment. He'd always seen college as the pinnacle — the thing he was supposed to shoot for with his daughter. And now she was telling him she didn't want what he'd struggled so hard for her to have. But what was he going to do? Demand that she do something she hated?

He sighed. "Okay. If that's the way you feel about it. I don't want you to be miserable."

"But I've been checking into something else."

"What?"

"Now, don't freak out when I tell you this."

"I won't freak out," he said, knowing it was still a distinct possibility.

"I was thinking maybe I'd go to junior college for two years."

"Junior college?"

"Now, just listen, okay? There's one in Waymark. It's a lot smaller than UT. I can get a two-year degree as a vet tech. Then if I decide I want to transfer to UT and get my pre-vet classes, what better thing to have? But if I decide to stop, at least I'll have a degree with a skill that'll translate into getting a job in a field I already know I like."

Marc blinked with surprise. That actually made sense.

"I can either get an apartment in Waymark, or I can live here and commute." Angela took a deep breath and let it out. "So what do you think?"

"Are you sure you wouldn't rather transfer to another four-year college?"

"That would probably mean moving to Dallas or Houston, and they're even farther away from Rainbow Valley."

"Most kids your age can't wait to get away."

"I know. Maybe I'll feel that way some day. But for now," she said with a shrug, "I think I'd like to stick close to home."

As disappointed as Marc had felt before, that was how good he felt now. He couldn't say he hated the thought of having his daughter around a little longer. "I think that's a really good solution. How did you come up with that?"

"You taught me to take care of my own problems, didn't you?"

"So you were actually listening all that time?"

"Like I've ever been able to tune you out?"

Kari had been right. Things really did have a way of working themselves out.

"Where's Kari?" Angela asked.

"Still asleep."

"I don't doubt it. She worked really hard yesterday."

"You look a little tired yourself."

"Yeah, but I've done it before. She hasn't. Most people would quit after fifteen minutes, but she didn't." Angela sighed. "I'm sorry I treated her the way I did. It's just weird for me. You know. The two of you." She paused, staring at her hands. The coffeepot hissed and gurgled. Then she looked up. "Do you love her?"

The question hung in the air for several seconds while Marc made sure he could answer without his voice choking up. It was official. Kari had turned him into a total sap, and he didn't even care.

"Yeah," he said. "I do."

"Okay. If she makes you happy, she makes me happy."

Marc was ecstatic to hear those words. "I'm glad you've decided you like her."

"I never really didn't like her. I've just never had to share you with anybody. That takes a little getting used to, you know?"

"I know. So I hate to tell you that the sharing thing is getting ready to happen again."

457

Angela blinked. "What do you mean?"

"There's a reason Kari is so worn out. She hasn't been feeling too well lately."

"Is she sick?"

"Not exactly." Marc took a breath. "How do you feel about becoming a big sister?"

She looked at him dumbly. Then all at once a look of total disbelief came over her face. "A baby? That's the deal? You guys are having a *baby*?"

Marc nodded.

"Is that why she looked so sick out there? I thought she just wasn't used to picking grapes."

"Nope. Morning sickness. But that's supposed to get better with time."

"So you're good with it?" Angela said carefully. "It's okay?"

"Yeah," he said with a smile. "It's okay."

"Oh, my God. I don't believe it! Wait. So does this mean you're staying in Rainbow Valley?"

"That's right."

"Are you really good with that? That's okay, too?"

"That's okay, too."

Angela squealed and leaped into his arms. He caught her midair and spun her around. As he set her down, she whispered, "I love you, Dad," into his ear, and he whispered that he loved her, too.

Kari appeared at the doorway. Still in Marc's arms, Angela turned around and smiled. "Kari! You're up. Dad told me about the baby."

Kari's smile slipped away. She flicked a questioning gaze to Marc. But before he could say anything, Angela held out her hand to Kari.

Kari paused only a moment before hobbling over, and Marc enveloped both of them in a warm embrace. He figured Kari had never had a family hug, which probably explained why he could see her trying really hard not to cry. But sooner or later she'd have to get used to it, because this was the way it was going to be from now on. He never intended to stop closing his arms around the people he loved.

A few days later, Marc and Kari sat on the deck, watching as a stunning red-orange sunset gave way to a star-sprinkled sky. Sasha took up her perch on the windowsill, backlit by the kitchen light and sitting still as stone, looking like an Egyptian statue of a goddess in a cat's body. Brandy followed Boo around the yard, wearing a doggy smile of total delight. The moon cast a warm glow across the empty vines, and Marc could already imagine what they were going to look like next fall, heavy with grapes that were bursting with juice.

"It's beautiful even without the grapes," Kari said. "But I can't wait for spring."

Neither could Marc. Spring was the season of new life. By then Kari would be only weeks away from having their baby. He couldn't wait. He was already a father, and he was damned good at it. But having Kari to share things with this time was going to change everything.

He took a sip of wine, resisting the urge to pick up his phone and check the weather. Once harvest was over, it didn't matter so much. It wasn't until next season that he needed to be on alert again. Instead, he found his mind moving from one part of his life to another, one member of his family to another.

Angela was going to work at the animal shelter until she began junior college in the spring, which Shannon and Luke were thrilled about. Tomorrow Daniel was hopping into his little red Porsche to go wherever life took him, probably straight down the road to his next million. Then Marc thought about Nina and felt a twinge of uneasiness.

"I'm a little worried about Nina," he said.

"Don't be," Kari said. "She'll be fine."

"Maybe. But she still misses Curtis. I wish I could do something."

"You don't have to do anything. Just be there in case she needs you."

"I like to be a little more proactive than that."

"You don't need to be. When you make somebody yours, they know they never have to worry about facing anything alone ever again. Nina. Daniel. Angela. Even if they never need you again, they can live their lives with all the confidence in the world."

"Why?"

"Because you're their safety net. And mine, too." Kari slid her hand over his. "Gus told me the good Lord was watching out for me by bringing me to your doorstep. There are angels on this earth, Marc. You're one of them. You're a big, handsome, hard-headed angel, and anybody would be better off for having known you. You don't even know how important you are to the people you love."

He was finally figuring it out. But that wasn't the revelation that surprised him the most. What surprised him was how much he needed the feeling of being needed. It had worked its way inside him until it had become an inextricable part of who he was.

When he thought about how ready he'd been to walk away from all this, thinking he'd find something better out there, it scared the hell out of him.

"You have a safety net, too," Kari said.

"I do?"

Her eyes glistened with tears. "Yeah. Me."

Marc turned his hand over and grasped hers, loving her more with every moment that passed.

"I can be there for you every day of your life," she told him. "Pick up the slack when things get too hard for you. I'll never leave you, Marc. Never."

Marc was living a dream he didn't even know he had inside him, a dream he'd buried so deeply after Nicole left that it had taken until now for it to see the light of day. The dream of having a woman in his life, one who woke with him in the morning and went to bed with him at night, who brightened his life in ways he never could have imagined. Just seeing that mischievous look in her eyes when she dragged him to the bedroom, or watching her dance in the kitchen to that god-awful music, or seeing that goofy pink streak in her hair made him feel as if he was young again, as if everything he'd ever missed by becoming a father at age seventeen he was experiencing now.

Kari blinked, and a tear rolled down her cheek. "Am I yours?"

He leaned over and gave her a kiss, then brushed the tear from her face with his thumb. "You were mine the moment you showed up at my door that stormy night."

And because she was his, he figured it was about time the whole world knew it.

"You know I'm not good at this stuff," he told her, "so I'll get straight to the point." He reached into his pocket and pulled out a black velvet box. When he opened it and she saw the ring, her mouth fell open.

"I love you, Kari. I want you to live here with me from now on. Will you marry me?"

She opened her mouth to say something, but for some reason the words wouldn't come. Finally she just nodded, her lips tightening as if she really was going to cry. He slid the ring onto her finger. She turned her hand left and right, watching the ring glint in the moonlight. Then he took her hand, pulled her out of her chair, and settled her onto his lap. She circled her arms around his neck and kissed him, then laid her head on his shoulder.

"I hadn't felt it in so long," Kari said, her voice a near whisper. "Not until I met you."

"What?"

Tears gathered in her eyes again. "Loved."

Kari meant more to him than he ever could have imagined. She filled in all his blanks. Made him laugh when he was too serious. Listened to his problems. Acted as an emotional bridge to the rest of his family, connecting his heart to theirs at times when he loved them so much but he just didn't know what to say or do.

And now she was his forever.

THE DISH

FROM THE DESK OF JANE GRAVES

Dear Reader,

I like wine. Any kind of wine. I've learned a lot about it over the years, but only because if you use any product enough, you'll end up pretty educated about it. (If I ate 147 different kinds of Little Debbie snack cakes, I'd know a lot about them, too.) I can swirl, sniff, and sip with the best of them. But the fourth S: spit? Seriously? The theory is that one should merely taste the wine without getting tipsy, but come on. Who in his right mind tastes good wine and then spits it out?

My husband and I once went to a wine tasting/ competition where we took our glasses around to the various vintners' booths and received tiny tasting pours, which we were to sip, savor, and judge. By the time we sampled the offerings of about two dozen vineyards, those tiny pours added up. At first we discussed acidity, mouth feel, and finish, then thoughtfully marked our scorecards. By the end of the event, we'd lost our scorecards and were wondering if there was a frat party nearby we could crash. Okay, so maybe that spitting thing has some merit.

In BABY, IT'S YOU, the hero, Marc Cordero, runs an estate vineyard in the Texas Hill Country that has been in his family for generations. As I researched winemaking for the book, I discovered it's both a science and an art, requiring intelligence, intuition, willpower, and above all, heart. The heroine, Kari Worthington, feels Marc's pride as he looks out over the grapevine-covered hills, and she's in awe of his determination to protect his family legacy. For a flighty, free-spirited, runaway bride who's never had a place to truly call home, Cordero Vineyards and the passionate man who runs it are the things of which her dreams are made.

So next time I go to a wine tasting, I'm going to think about the myriad challenges that winemakers faced in order to present that bottle for me to enjoy. But I'm still not gonna spit.

I hope you enjoy BABY, IT'S YOU!

Jane Graves

JaneGraves.com
Twitter @JaneGraves
Facebook.com/AuthorJaneGraves

ABOUT THE AUTHOR

New York Times bestselling author **Jane Graves** is a nine-time finalist for Romance Writers of America's RITA Award, the industry's highest honor, and is the recipient of two National Readers' Choice Awards, the Booksellers' Best Award, and the Golden Quill, among others. Jane lives in the Dallas area with her husband and a very sweet kitty who kindly keeps her lap warm while she writes. You can write to her at jane@janegraves.com. She'd love to hear from you! You can learn more at:
JaneGraves.com
Twitter @JaneGraves
Facebook.com/JaneGravesAuthor

The employees of Thorndike Press hope you have enjoyed this Large Print book. All our Thorndike, Wheeler, and Kennebec Large Print titles are designed for easy reading, and all our books are made to last. Other Thorndike Press Large Print books are available at your library, through selected bookstores, or directly from us.

For information about titles, please call:
  (800) 223-1244

or visit our Web site at:
  http://gale.cengage.com/thorndike

To share your comments, please write:
Publisher
Thorndike Press
10 Water St., Suite 310
Waterville, ME 04901